The Occupation

Guy Walters

headline

First published in 2004
by HEADLINE BOOK PUBLISHING

First published in paperback in 2005
by HEADLINE BOOK PUBLISHING

10 9 8 7 6 5 4 3 2 1

ISBN 978 0 7553 2066 0

Typeset in Goudy by Avon DataSet Ltd,
Bidford-on-Avon, Warwickshire

Printed and bound in the UK by
CPI Mackays, Chatham ME5 8TD

HEADLINE BOOK PUBLISHING
A division of Hodder Headline
338 Euston Road
London NW1 3BH

www.headline.co.uk
www.hodderheadline.com

Guy Walters was a journalist on *The Times* for eight years, where he travelled around the world and reported on a wide variety of subjects. He is married with one son, and lives in Wiltshire. Guy's other novels, *The Traitor* and *The Leader* are also available from Headline.

This book is for
JONATHAN DYKES
1971–2003

Prologue

THEY DO NOT walk but stumble, shuffle. Their heads are bent into the solid wind, their bodies folded inwards with hunger and nausea. The lucky ones wear rough wooden clogs, the rest are barefoot, their soles long since hardened on the coarsely gritted footpaths and roads. Slung across their shoulders is a variety of tools – pickaxes and spades mainly – although some are too weak and carry nothing. The lamest are being supported by their comrades, dragged the two miles from the camp to 'the hill', a place where they know the weak will die either today, or perhaps tomorrow. Experience has told them that they will never see the day after that.

These are the ones who are badly infected with *la maladie*, *la malattia*, *la nauséa*, for there are many different names for 'the sickness'. Despite the prisoners' different tongues, the effects are the same: vomiting, diarrhoea, bleeding from the nose and the anus, utter listlessness. It is impossible to keep

1

clean if one has the sickness, and the prisoners can always tell who is about to leave them: they are the ones whose striped uniforms are the most bloodied, the most shit-stained. They do not even make the effort – their will has gone – but their comrades insist on dragging them to work. This is not just out of kindness, but also because their masters maintain that where there is breath there is productivity. If anybody remains in the camp, the guards will execute the same number of healthy prisoners as there are malingerers.

There are at least five hundred on the march today, of which at least five are not going to make it to the hill. They know that, their fellow prisoners know that, their guards know that, but all are stuck in a madness that insists work brings freedom, even if one is nearly a corpse.

The first death occurs within two hundred yards of the camp. His name is Francisco, a Spanish Communist captured during the Civil War. For the past two weeks, he has been working deep inside the hill, the place where *la nauséa* is worst. Francisco had started vomiting within a few hours, and by the end of that first day, he had lost so much blood that he nearly died. It is only through the ministrations of Oleg, a Russian, that Francisco has survived for this long, and it is Oleg who is now desperately trying to help him up.

'Come on, Franny, get up!' Oleg whispers in Russian. Oleg may be strong, but not even he can carry both his shovel and Francisco's pick, as well as Francisco himself.

The Spaniard does not answer. All that comes out of his

mouth is a delicate trail of blood. Oleg knows that his friend Franny is about to die, but he cannot just let him. He can see Franny's stomach convulsing, trying to retch, but there is nothing to leave his body, apart from blood and parts of his disintegrating organs. Franny's body is fighting itself, racked by a corporeal civil war waged by deformed and poisoned cells.

'Franny!' Oleg exhorts him once more, but this is a mistake. Running up towards them comes Rebs, SS Unterscharführer Georg Rebs, a deserter from the French Army who has thrown in his tawdry lot with his country's conquerors. Whether his brutality and fanaticism are those of the convert is hard for the prisoners to establish, but this is not the time to debate Rebs's motives.

'What is this man doing?' Rebs shouts in French.

Oleg looks back at him defiantly. There is no point in replying, not because there is a lack of common language but because there is a complete absence of pathos.

Rebs points his rifle at Francisco.

'Get up!'

Francisco does not get up. His body will not allow it.

Rebs pulls the bolt back on his rifle and slides a round into the chamber. The safety catch is disengaged. Oleg wants to do something, wants to help, but what can he do? Try to overpower Rebs? That will achieve nothing. Franny is a dead man – they are *all* dead men – so what is the point?

Oleg shuts his eyes as he sees Rebs squeezing the trigger. He will not watch yet another death. He will not watch his friend collapse flat on to the ground as the bullet punches the last traces of life out of his body. He has seen it too many times, and he will not watch it again.

The shot echoes briefly down the short valley that leads to the sea. Normally when guns are fired birds leave their roosts, but there are no birds here. It is said that the birds left when the Germans arrived, and it is a small piece of folklore that the prisoners find fitting to believe. All that stirs is the shuffling column, which briefly notes that it is now one short, its collective brain noting that there will be just a little more 'soup' per head tonight.

Oleg walks on, not looking at Franny's body.

'Where are you going, Russian scum?'

He turns to face Rebs. He knows enough French to understand. In fact, he knows the words for 'Russian scum' in six languages. Although Oleg is a calm man his overworked heart starts to pound.

'Why did you allow this man to collapse?'

Oleg has a good idea what he is being asked, as Rebs is pointing his rifle down at Franny. He shrugs his shoulders.

'Answer me!'

Oleg starts talking in Russian, knowing that whatever he says, in whatever language, is never going to excuse his 'crime'.

'What the hell are you saying?' shouts Rebs. 'What filthy language is that anyway?'

Oleg knows that phrase as well. He just stands there, looking down at the ground, down at this cursed earth. Oleg does not know much about the earth he is standing on, because he has very little idea where he is. For the past three years he has been shunted all over Europe, and now, as part of SS Construction Brigade I, he is presently residing in what his captors call *das Arschloch der Welt* – the arsehole of the world.

Rebs is still shouting at him, but Oleg does not care. He knows what is going to happen. It will happen to all of them, and now it is his turn. There is nothing he can do. He thinks of his dead wife, his dead son, his dead brother, and now he starts to think of his dead self, lying next to his dead friend in the cold dirt.

The *bolezna*, he thinks, at least he will not get the *bolezna* – the sickness.

July 1990

Although their presence has put the wind up his regulars, the publican of the Divers Inn on Braye Harbour is delighted. At six o'clock every evening, at least twenty to thirty of them drop in, their heavy workmen's boots leaving heavily defined imprints on the sand-sprinkled floor. They drink nearly as well as any Alderney man, he tells them, a deliberate encouragement to swell the contents of his old-fashioned cash register.

They come from all over Europe, these workmen, but mostly from England and Ireland: there are at least a couple of Frenchmen, the same number of Spaniards, a Greek who calls himself Harry, and even a chap who swears he's a Pole. The islanders are not accustomed to these foreigners: like islanders everywhere they are suspicious of strangers, even the English.

For the past fortnight, the men have been excavating the site for the foundations of a new hotel – Mannez Heights – which is to be a luxury affair, an attempt by the island to attract some badly needed big spenders. Perched on top of Mannez Hill on the far north-east of the three-mile-long island, the hoarding outside the worksite tells passers-by that the hotel will boast three restaurants, a swimming-pool with a wave machine, a gym and, most crucially, a casino. It is that, the hotel's owners hope, which will really draw them in.

The workmen are particularly ebullient tonight, not only because it is Friday but also because it is a fine evening. Even though Braye Harbour faces north, and the workmen will stay inside until midnight, the occasional glimpse through the pub's windows of anchored sailboats bobbing in the vestiges of warm sunlight makes them feel as though they are on holiday.

'Six pints, please, Dave.'

'Just for you, are they?'

'And after you've done, another six over 'ere.'

'You buying a round, Pete? Miracles will never cease!'

'So, then, Debs, which lucky man have you got your eye on tonight?'

The air is thick with such banter as well as cigarette smoke –

roll-ups being expertly fashioned every few seconds by thick, muddy fingers.

One of those ordering a large round is Mark, a South Londoner, who finds himself away from home for at least six months a year. He misses his family, but the money from jobs such as this is too good to turn down. As Dave pours the pints, Mark turns to his mate Ian, a man he's worked with for the best part of two decades.

'Tough that today, weren't it?'

Ian wipes his brow theatrically. 'I never known concrete like it. Them Jerries must have doubled the weight of the whole bleedin' island.'

'God knows what we're going through.'

'Probably some sort of fortress or something. The place is littered with them.'

Mark licks the gum on his cigarette paper and nods. 'I don't get it,' he says. 'The Germans must have spent their whole time here building, building, building. Why didn't they just enjoy it? It's not a bad spot, this.'

Ian laughs slightly.

'I expect they did. The Germans, I mean. They had slaves, didn't they, did all their work for them?'

'We could do with a few of them ourselves!' Mark exclaims.

Ian laughs again. 'They say they're all buried in the breakwater,' he says.

'Who?'

'The *slaves*,' says Ian. 'I was talking to some bloke the other

7

day, and he tells me that the Germans worked the poor buggers to death and dumped their bodies in the concrete in the breakwater. Hundreds of bodies, he says, maybe more.'

'Bit like the M25, then.'

'Come again?'

'That's meant to be full of bodies,' says Mark. 'Gangland killings and that.'

'No wonder it's falling to bits.'

The men both laugh.

'Here you go, gents,' says Dave. 'That'll be seven pounds fifty.'

'I'll get this,' says Mark, and picks off a ten-pound note from a large bundle he has stuffed in the back of his jeans.

'Ta,' says Ian. 'And then I suspect it'll be Roger's turn.'

'Speaking of which, where is he?'

'Roger?'

'Yeah.'

'He's here somewhere,' says Ian. 'He told me he was feeling a bit out of sorts, though.'

'Caught the sun?' asks Mark, taking a generous mouthful from his pint.

Ian shakes his head. 'No,' he says. 'He was right down that little shaft all day, the one with all that bleeding hardcore plugging it up.'

'Probably just knackered, then.'

'Yeah,' says Ian.

For the next minute or so, Ian and Mark stand in silence.

They, too, are a little tired – it has been a long week – but the pint is going down well, and it's good for them to think they've got an entire day's sunbathing ahead of them.

The remaining pints from the round are taken by their work-mates, one of whom is Colin.

' 'Ere, Col,' says Mark. 'You seen Roger?'

Colin sups his pint and gesticulates with his left thumb over his shoulder. 'Went to the gents. Said he 'ad a nosebleed,' he says, and then, glancing at his watch, 'although he's been there a while. Must be 'bout twenny minutes.'

'A nosebleed?' asks Ian.

' 'Sright. They can go on for ever them things. I 'ad one which lasted—'

'I think we should see if he's all right,' says Mark, putting down his pint, 'Twenty minutes is way too long.'

Ian nods and places his nearly empty pint on the wet counter. Together, the men make their way through the crowded bar, through the door marked 'Gentlemen' in battered Gothic script, and into the lavatory.

'Jesus Christ!'

'Rodge!'

There, sprawled on the floor, his mouth, chin, neck and chest covered with blood and vomit, is Roger. His head rests against the pedestal of a basin coated with yet more blood, and around him lie countless tissues dyed different shades of red.

Ian remains frozen while Mark bends down. 'Rodge!' says Mark. 'Can you hear me?'

Roger's chest is moving up and down rapidly, his breathing erratic. His eyes are glassy, and he is pale, terribly pale.

Mark turns to Ian. 'For fuck's sake, get some help! Go and get some fucking help!'

Chapter One

Berlin, February 1945

THE LIGHTS IN the bunker flickered in accompaniment to the muffled noise of the bombs. The occupants were too busy to notice, secure in the knowledge that above them lay eleven and a half feet of ferro-concrete and, above that, another four feet of sand. The bunker, it was claimed, was impenetrable to anything the Allies could drop on it. In fact, the greatest danger to the occupants came from within, for everybody seated around the large table in that cramped conference room late that night was equally wary of his neighbour. Ever since the previous July, when von Stauffenberg had nearly wiped them all out, nobody was above suspicion.

The remnants of the Third Reich's leadership were gathered for a 'situation conference' – a common enough event – but there was a curious atmosphere in the room, detected by many. Especially sensitive to the mood was Captain Gerhard Boldt, the aide to Colonel General Heinz Guderian, the army chief of staff.

11

He had felt a greater tension than usual up in the Reich
Chancellery, when he and the general had been searched
especially thoroughly for concealed weapons. He had felt it when
they entered the bunker, and had even seen it in the faces of
secretaries such as Fräulein Junge as they waited in the anteroom.

Although he dared not meet its gaze, it was the face of the
Führer that told Boldt all he needed to know about the state of
the Reich, its defeats and setbacks physically impressed on his
body. His spine twisted, his jowls heavy, his eyes red and
heavy-lidded, his pallor troglodytically grey, Hitler was like his
own ghost. His hands were so unsteady that it was sometimes
hard for him to sign documents, and after a row they shook
even more violently. Boldt had heard that Hitler's physician,
Dr Morell, had kept telling his patient that he should take
Luminal to calm himself down, but the Führer had replied that
he had no need of such medication. Instead, to reduce his
blood pressure, Hitler had apparently ordered Morell to drain
a few hundred cubic centimetres of blood on a regular basis.

Vampire, Boldt thinks, the man is vampire. Not only does he
suck our blood, but he also sucks out his own. He actually *wants*
to destroy us, destroy himself, wants us all to die rather than
accept defeat. For years, Boldt had accepted the 'last drop'
homilies, but had never, until that night, regarded them as
anything more than metaphorical.

'. . . and furthermore, I have been told that the latest reports
from Dresden suggest that the death toll could be as high as one
hundred thousand . . .'

The Occupation

The room gasped. Until that point, nobody had been listening that closely to Minister of the Interior Wilhelm Frick. He had been droning on in his soft, low, bureaucratic voice about tales of supposed production statistics, about how many trains were reaching their destinations, about food shortages and other equally stultifying topics.

Hitler coughed before speaking. 'One . . . one hundred thousand?' His voice was gruff and strained, so unlike the commanding bark heard at all those rallies held all those lifetimes ago.

'Apparently so, my Führer,' Frick replied, 'although I am informed that the numbers could be higher.'

Hitler smashed the table with a ferocity that made the room jump. 'This is a crime!'

'Quite so,' said Frick, his voice unemotional.

'They are slaughtering our women and children for their own sadistic purposes! It is monstrous!'

There was a loud murmur of agreement – an expression that Boldt couldn't help feel to be hypocritical. The Allied bombing of Dresden might well have been a crime, Boldt pondered, but we have committed quite a few ourselves. Was he really the only one thinking this? He looked at some of the men around him – Field Marshal Jodl, Admiral Dönitz, Guderian: what were they thinking? Did they really believe that the Allies are criminals in the same way as we are? Everybody knows what is happening to the Jews, but nobody talks about it. Surely the 'evacuations to the East' are worse than Dresden?

But their faces mimicked that of their beloved Führer, expressing indignation at this criminal act. Boldt noticed that the only man who looked impassive was Albert Speer, the Minister for Armaments. Handsome, elegant and patrician-looking, Speer's face stuck out among the rougher ones that surrounded him. It was to Speer that Hitler's next remark was addressed.

'Speer!' the Führer growled. 'What is happening to my vengeance weapons? Are they just sitting in the factories? What are you doing with them?'

Speer shrugged a little, as though someone had walked over his grave. 'It would seem that we can do very little, my Führer.'

'*Little?*'

'Things have been . . . difficult of late,' Speer replied, his tone bordering on the nonchalantly insolent. Boldt was impressed – there were very few who could talk to the Führer in that way.

Hitler's eyes widened so much that everybody around the table could see how bloodshot and yellow they were. 'It has been *difficult* for all of us,' Hitler shouted. '*Difficult* for our brave soldiers on both fronts, *difficult* for every citizen of the Reich, young or old. It has been *difficult* for everybody, Minister, and yet why are you the exception?'

Another shrug. Boldt found himself wincing at Speer's manner.

'I am in no way demanding for myself any exceptional or particular treatment,' Speer replied precisely, his top lip visibly moistening, 'although my Führer must appreciate that special-armaments production is almost impossible with such saturation bombing. If we were in a position to stop it, then of course things would be far less . . .'

Boldt realised that Speer was about to say 'difficult', but its repetition would clearly have been unwise.

'. . . I mean, we would achieve greater levels of efficiency.'

Hitler glared. He knew Speer was right – this was all Göring's damn fault. That drug-addled whale had managed the Luftwaffe so ineptly that it was now no more effective than a pre-war flying circus. It was just as well that the man was not present: he would have been swept away by the strongest torrent of savage abuse. 'So what is happening, Speer? Why exactly are your rockets not wreaking the havoc I had been led to expect?'

Speer swallowed. It was certainly not his fault that the V2 rocket had not been as effective as it was hoped, but he knew that if the Führer asked such questions, then one was obliged to reply as if it was one's responsibility. 'Once again, my Führer, there have been delays. Last month the factory in the Netherlands that produces the rockets' liquid oxygen was destroyed by the RAF. There has also been a question of launch sites. The Allied advance has been so rapid in some quarters that as soon as a launch pad is established it has to be moved again. We are . . . we are doing our best, my Führer.'

Hitler waved his right hand effeminately in the air, brushing away Speer's comments as if they were some mildly troublesome flies.

'And what about the V3, Herr Minister?'

The voice was not Hitler's. Boldt scarcely recognised it, as it was a voice that was seldom heard. The voice – thuggish, from the street, Boldt thought – was that of the Führer's *éminence grise*, some said his successor, Martin Bormann. As Party Minister in charge of Party Headquarters, the squat Bormann was said to control access to the Führer, and he had his stubby fingers in many pies. Like many army officers, Boldt did not care for Bormann, seeing him as the ultimate Party man. It was farcical that Hitler had made him commander of the 'People's Army', but even more bizarre appointments had recently been made.

'It is my understanding that the V3 is not yet ready to be implemented–' Speer began.

'Your *understanding*, Minister?' snapped Hitler. 'This does not sound particularly authoritative. All I need to know is *when*, Speer, *when*.'

Speer thumbed through his file once more, then pointedly gave up and shut it. 'My Führer, I feel that I must say something. As you know, the V3 is a highly technical weapon . . .'

Hitler snorted.

'. . . which requires much specialist knowledge and huge amounts of matériel. These are commodities which are in short supply . . .'

'Commodities!'

'. . . and there is a larger question of whether the V3, even if it works, will only cause the Allies to inflict yet more Dresdens on us–'

'I've had enough of this, Speer! I have three simple questions for you to answer.'

Speer wiped his top lip, then folded his arms.

'One,' said Hitler. 'Do you want Germany to win the war?'

There was a pause, a slight pause, but enough of one to ensure that Speer's reply was not taken at face value by anybody, least of all Hitler.

'Of course, my Führer.'

'Good,' said Hitler. 'Because if you didn't, I would have you shot, Albert.'

'Albert'. The use of Speer's first name reminded Boldt of how intimately the Führer and his architect had known each other. Speer did not speak, but he nodded.

'The second question is this: can you make the V3 operational?'

A longer pause.

'I can.'

'Good. Three. How long will it take?'

Speer smoothed the back of his well-groomed head with the flat of his hand. Boldt had never seen the man look so agitated, so clearly rattled. 'About a month, maybe six weeks. But I do need . . .'

'Excellent!' said Hitler, suddenly jubilant. 'You can have whatever is required.' He looked round the room. 'Each of you,' he said quietly, hoarsely, 'is to assist Minister Speer in any way you can. There is nothing more important than this project. If it works, the V3 will stop the Allies in their tracks. It might even do more than that, much more.'

The men around the table started to exhibit nervous smiles.

'May I ask something, my Führer?' said Guderian.

'Yes?'

'Where is the V3 and what exactly is it?'

'It's on one of the Channel Islands,' Hitler replied. 'Which one, Speer?'

'Abschnitt Adolf.'

'Adolf?' said Hitler, grinning. 'You are joking.'

'I'm not, my Führer.'

'And what did it used to be called?'

'Alderney.'

'And now why don't you tell the General here what exactly the V3 is?'

Speer took a deep breath and began.

*　*　*

It had been a long time since he was captured – only a few days after D-Day – and Captain Edmond Fellowes had had enough of Jersey. He bore no particular antipathy towards the island itself, but he certainly did towards the hovel of a POW camp in which he was detained. A veteran of No. 4 Commando since its first raid in March 1941, Fellowes hated being incarcerated more than most. The conditions in the camp were atrocious – the substance that passed for food was unpalatable, there was no wood for the tiny stove in the draughty hut, and it was almost impossible to get any proper exercise. Captain Fellowes was not one to gripe unnecessarily, but he certainly knew that he was malnourished. His complaints to his captors had been met with forced smiles and reminders that the Germans had even less food than their prisoners, who were fortunate to have their Red Cross parcels.

As there was no time difference between Berlin and Jersey, Fellowes was not to know that he swung his legs out of his bunk at exactly the same time as Albert Speer had been starting his nervous exposition – 1.35 a.m. precisely. He trod on the floorboards softly in his rubber-soled boots and bent down to the bottom bunk. 'Smith!' he hissed. 'Come on!'

Already awake, Pilot Officer Edward Smith threw off his meagre blanket and got up. For a few moments, both men checked themselves over. They were wearing battered farm labourers' clothes, bought for an usurious amount of chocolate from an islander who delivered small, irregular supplies of milk to the camp. It was disgraceful, thought Fellowes. The man should have given them the clothes for nothing. Instead, there had been a lot of moaning about how risky it was, how it might put him and his family in gaol or perhaps worse. Fellowes had been tempted to give the man an earful, but Smith had managed to calm him down, and had produced the six bars of chocolate that had bought the man's complicity, as well as the name and address of someone who could help them – a Mrs Campbell of Wellington Road in St Helier.

'Wirecutters?' asked Fellowes.

Smith patted his trouser pocket. 'Knife?'

Now it was Fellowes's turn to check. It was there, tucked into his right boot – six inches of Krupp steel pinched from a guard's tunic left in the washroom. Even when he was stealing it, Fellowes had known that the guard would never dare report its theft for fear of punishment.

Fellowes nodded back at Smith. 'Right,' he said. 'Let's go.'

The two men walked quietly between the bunks. The occasional 'Good luck, lads,' could be heard, causing Fellowes to smile appreciatively. The chance of getting out of the camp was minimal, the chance of making it off the island even slighter. Still, it wasn't going to stop him trying, as it had done others. There were some in this camp who seemed grateful to be out of the war, an attitude that earned no sympathy from Fellowes. Some had accused him of wanting to be a medal-winner and a hero, that all he was doing would get them into trouble. They had stopped short of telling him he was doing wrong, as each officer knew it was his duty to escape. Even if an attempt was unsuccessful, at least the officer should have derived some contentment that he had done his own little bit to disrupt the German war effort.

When they reached the hut's only window, the two men paused.

'Good luck, Smith,' said Fellowes.

'Same to you, Captain.'

The window was meant to be bolted, but the prisoners had undone it during the height of summer. Occasionally, a guard had given them some grief about it, but a packet of Red Cross cigarettes was the usual fee for keeping it open. Despite the failure of his earlier attempts, the regime was certainly slacker than Fellowes had expected – a combination of lack of morale and the German belief that the waters off Jersey were so treacherous that any prisoner trying to navigate them was likely to meet his doom. Fellowes thought the Germans were probably right, but it wasn't going to stop him. He had heard that some islanders had escaped during the early days of the occupation, and he saw no reason why he and Smith could not try to emulate them.

Gently, Fellowes pushed open the window, feeling the coolness of the night air caress his face. There were no searchlights in the camp, but there were haphazard patrols, which had been accompanied by dogs until the food shortages had become so bad. The prisoners couldn't believe that the Germans had eaten them until one of the guards had offered up a bowl of evidential stew that smelt suspiciously canine. None of them had dared try it, with the exception of a lieutenant from the Hampshire Regiment who said it tasted rather like his grandmother's cooking.

Fellowes stuck his head out of the window, looked left and right and, with some gymnastic polish despite his clothes and boots, launched himself out of the aperture in one movement. He landed more heavily than he would have liked, and remained crouched down, using his fingertips to keep his balance. For a moment, all he could hear was his breath, which was coming in short pants. Calm down, he told himself, for heaven's sake calm down. He forced himself to breathe more slowly, and as he did so, he tried to pick up any traces of noise.

Nothing. Perhaps some wind in the trees. Maybe the sea? He came up to a half-crouch, then stepped away from the window. He looked from side to side: his vision confirming his hearing – only a handful of sleeping huts and the constant backdrop of barbed wire gleaming dimly in the weak moonlight. He raised his right hand, then brought it down, signalling his partner to make his exit.

Smith's landing sounded like a trunk full of shoes falling from a loft. Fellowes cursed him silently, believing they might as well call it a night. Who would have thought Smith was a flaming Spitfire pilot? Surely fighter pilots were meant to be a graceful lot?

After fixing Smith with a glower, Fellowes turned to his right and, remaining crouched, walked ten brisk yards to the next hut. He did not run because that might have attracted attention, and made a noisy stumble more likely. Haste, not speed, Fellowes reminded himself. This is not D-Day, nobody is shooting at you – at least, not yet. He stopped at the hut and beckoned Smith over. This time the man had found a greater degree of nimbleness, and his passage was quieter than his landing. The two men edged their way along the side of the hut.

The barbed-wire perimeter was now only thirty yards away. They scampered towards the last hut before the fence. This next stage would be the most risky, as it would involve lying next to the fence, with no cover, and cutting through the barbed wire.

With Smith next to him, Fellowes edged his way along the side of the hut and waited. There was a noise, he was sure of it. It was the sound of a guard's footsteps.

They were getting louder now, more threatening.

Fellowes sensed Smith tensing next to him, a reaction caused not only by the looming guard, but also by Fellowes's smooth removal of the knife from his boot. He knew what Smith was thinking: It's madness, it will get us shot. Too bad. Fellowes had heard of too many commandoes being murdered by the Germans to have any sympathy for one of their number, even if this one was a mere dolt of a guard on Jersey.

Fellowes looked down at the knife. He did not relish violence, but he was good at it. When had he last killed? He remembered it clearly – it had been 8 June, two days after D-Day, in a firefight among the Normandy hedgerows. He had killed two SS NCOs, shot one, and bayoneted the other. It had been gruesome. No amount of training could have prepared him for the man's imploring look as he had driven the weapon into his heart. It had remained as the life quickly drained out of him, and although one of his men would later say the captain had been seeing things, Fellowes swore that the expression was still on the man's face two hours later.

The footsteps drew nearer. He would wait for the man to pass, and then he would dispatch him.

The guard appeared, his figure tall and thin. Fellowes steeled himself, his body tensed to go into action. He followed the deeply absorbed discipline of his training. Breathing calmly through his mouth, he stepped after the guard, his knife pointing towards him. In order to mask the sound of his footsteps, he walked in time with his intended victim, and stepped down on the balls of his feet rather than on his heels.

Fellowes leaped up, and smashed the hilt of the knife into the side of the guard's neck. As the man crumpled, Fellowes twisted his head to one side, simultaneously sliding the blade deeply into and across his neck. Just as he had been taught, the weight of the collapsing body provided much of the downward force needed for the knife to penetrate deeply. Fellowes could already feel the thick, warm liquid oozing over the back of his hand, and released the near-corpse gently, allowing it to crumple backwards to the ground. A low gargling sound was coming from the guard's exposed trachea. He could see the man's eyes – they, too, were imploring him.

Smith appeared at his side. Fellowes knew that the shock of what he had just done would come later. Without looking at Smith, he scuttled over to the barbed wire and lay down next to it. Smith was a second behind him, and started to cut the wire, far too slowly for Fellowes's liking. It was tough, but thankfully the cutters were strong enough for the task. In less than a minute, thought Fellowes, they would be free men.

* * *

Lieutenant Colonel Max von Luck took careful aim. His target was an elusive one, going first this way and then that, but von

Luck was an experienced shot and second-guessed his target's movements. He squeezed the trigger firmly and fired.

Damn! Missed! Still, he had another barrel. Just two seconds later, he fired again. Got it! As if thrown down by an unseen hand, the bird plummeted. Von Luck allowed himself a smile. The erratic flight of the pigeon always made it difficult to shoot, but that made it much better sport than some of the 'nobler' birds. The smile was also in appreciation of the fact that he was not going to eat just a plate of vegetables this evening. Now, if only he could get another, he would be delighted. However, there was little woodland left on Jersey, and the few pigeons that remained were extraordinarily wary. He would try, though – anything to complement those wretched potatoes.

'Good shot, sir.'

'Thank you,' said von Luck, addressing his deputy, Major Rudolf Hempel. 'Did you see where it went down?'

'Just over in those ferns, I think.'

Von Luck broke his shotgun and carried it draped over his right forearm. As he strode through the wet grass, he felt as though he was at home in Bavaria. The early fading February light, the fir trees, a late afternoon's shooting – all served to render a scene of pastoral tranquillity for which he was becoming increasingly wistful.

'Cigarette, Hempel?'

'Yes please, sir.' Hempel was indeed grateful – cigarettes were in short supply.

Von Luck took out a silver case and opened it.

'Ah! Your famous crested cigarettes, sir.'

'Left by my father when he died,' said von Luck. 'They're abominably stale, but they're the best I can do.'

'Tobacco is tobacco, stale or not. And with your family crest on, well, I'm sure it helps the taste.'

'I wouldn't know about that,' said von Luck, lighting Hempel's cigarette.

The two men smoked in silence. They didn't taste too bad, thought von Luck, better than the alternative, which was probably dried nettles or something.

'So, then, Hempel, what have you heard about our new arrival?'

'Admiral Huffmeier?'

'Indeed.'

Normally Hempel would have been wary of answering such a question, but he knew that here, in the large grounds of Rozel Manor, there was no chance of being overheard. He also knew that his lieutenant colonel was a fellow sceptic about not only the course of the war but Nazism in general. 'I'd heard he was a bad sort,' he replied. 'A real Nazi.'

'That's what I'd heard,' said von Luck, combing the ferns with a stick. 'Where is this damn bird?'

'I think it fell more over here.'

'You think so? All right.'

They looked in silence for a while, von Luck thrashing the ferns. This was bad news. The last thing he wanted was to have to deal with an intelligent maniac. In his position as head of civil affairs in the Field Command, it was von Luck's job to liaise between the Germans and the island authorities, a task to which he had set with much diplomacy and sensitivity. He had, he hoped, won the respect of the islanders as a fair and reasonable man, perhaps even reaching the status of a 'gentleman' in their eyes. But with Huffmeier two years' hard work would be ruined. God knew what would happen to the poor islanders now that he was in charge – they were half starved already. He swiped at the ferns again, more out of frustration with the situation than the non-appearance of a dead pigeon. 'So why is he here, Hempel? Why has our good general been replaced?'

Hempel shrugged his shoulders. 'Nobody really knows.'

'There must be a *reason*,' said von Luck, breaking the stick against a rotting branch. 'Shit. Where is this damn bird?'

'The only thing I can think of, sir, is that they're planning something.'

'Go on.'

'Well, one rumour puts it that we're going to make an attack on the mainland.'

'I don't think that's very likely, Hempel, do you? The troops are so hungry they're almost eating each other! They're not exactly fighting fit.'

'I agree, sir. But I'm afraid that's all I can think of.'

'Maybe you're right, maybe that's just what they're planning. No doubt someone in Berlin has looked at his maps and pieces of paper and decided that an attack in the enemy's rear is just what is required. But not even *he* would be so stupid. We do not have the landing craft, the equipment, nothing. We can barely feed ourselves and the islanders, let alone wage war. I tell you, Hempel, we are prisoners here.'

Von Luck picked up another stick and started thrashing again. After a minute, he was rewarded with his pigeon. 'I was beginning to think someone had taken it.'

'Not that unlikely,' Hempel replied.

'Now then, Hempel, all we need to do is to bag you one, and then we can go home happy.'

By half past four, it had grown too dark, and von Luck and Hempel called off their hunt for another bird. 'I'm sorry, Hempel, you shall share mine. He's not the fattest bird I'm afraid, but he will do.'

'Please, sir, you shot it, therefore it is yours.'

'Nonsense, Hempel! Besides, I can tell a hungry look in a man's eyes. You must join me at Linden Court for dinner. I insist.'

'That is very kind, sir.'

'Not at all.'

Even the horses they were mounting were thin. Von Luck had refused to shoot them, and had managed to wangle them some feed. The two men rode in silence, von Luck watching the slow, pale sun setting to his right. He sighed. It was Sunday evening, a time for reflection and writing up his diary, but he was glad of Hempel's company. This business with Huffmeier troubled him, and he wanted to chew it over further.

'Damn!'

'What is it, Hempel?'

'I had forgotten, sir. I'm sorry – I'm meant to be dining with Major Schwalm this evening. He's over from Alderney and wants to talk to me.'

'Talk to you about what?'

'Vegetables.'

'Vegetables?'

'Yes, sir. I do apologise.'

'That's quite all right, Hempel. It does, of course, mean that I shall have the pigeon all to myself.'

'I know,' Hempel replied, laughing. 'I have somewhat drawn the short straw.'

Vegetables, thought von Luck, it was always bloody vegetables. That was all they ever talked about, all they ever ate.

'Why does that bore Schwalm want to talk to you about vegetables anyway?' he asked. 'Hasn't he got enough of his own?'

'I don't know yet – maybe he was just looking for an excuse to get off Alderney.'

'I can't say I blame him,' said von Luck. 'Alderney is a real shit-hole. Jersey must feel positively cosmopolitan to him. What's he been doing there all this time?'

'No idea. I expect it involves digging and concrete.'

Von Luck laughed. That's all they had ever bloody done on these islands – dug into them, then poured concrete into the holes.

'Ask him, could you?'

'Ask him what, sir?'

'Ask him what exactly he's been doing. I'd like to know.'

Ten minutes later, accompanied by further apologies, Hempel wished von Luck a pleasant evening. Von Luck was gratified that Hempel eschewed the Nazi salute, always a sign that someone was on the side of the angels. The road down which he rode was deserted, and all he could hear was the sound of Satan's hoofs.

Without any warning, the horse halted.

'What is it, Satan?'

Satan merely shook his head, his tail whisking in agitation.

Von Luck looked around, mildly confused. It was unlike Satan to be so edgy: he must have seen something. He leaned forward and patted the top of the horse's head. 'What's the matter?' he whispered into his right ear. 'What have you seen?'

Satan flicked his head away in a gesture that reminded von Luck of a woman trying to break free of an unwanted suitor's grip. This was most out of character.

The sound of a branch breaking in a small copse fifty feet away revealed that Satan had indeed noticed something, and was not being tormented by a creature from another world. Instinctively Von Luck drew his pistol from its holster. Since the invasion in 1940 there had not been any significant acts of violence – or, indeed, of resistance – against the occupiers. Still, with the war going the way it was, there would doubtless be a few brave islanders who might fancy taking a pot-shot at an officer. There was also the small chance that it might be the two prisoners-of-war who had escaped the other night. They were obviously dangerous men – von Luck had been told they had even butchered a guard to escape.

'Come out of there!' von Luck shouted.

There was no further movement.

'If you do not, I shall shoot.'

Although it was not yet curfew time, von Luck knew there was another reason why an islander might be hiding among some trees. They would be searching for firewood, which von Luck himself had banned. The islanders were chopping down so many trees that he feared the island's eco-system would be threatened by the extent of their diminution.

More sounds came from the copse. In the dim light, von Luck could detect some movement, at which he pointed his pistol.

'Come on, out you come!'

Two figures stepped out from behind a beech tree, their arms high in the air. Far from being the ruffians or the POWs that von Luck had expected, they were two well-dressed women.

'Mrs Campbell! What in heaven's name are you doing?' Von Luck put away his pistol and grinned. 'Come, come, put your hands down.'

Gingerly, the two women did so. As he rode over to them, von Luck's eye fell on the woman standing next to Mrs Campbell – her daughter, Pippa. He had come across them on numerous occasions as they lived somewhere near Linden Court. Von Luck's housekeeper, Mrs May, a real old gossip, had told him that Mr Campbell was a professor of English at a university in Mexico, and his wife and daughter had been marooned on Jersey at the outbreak of war. Up to this afternoon, von Luck had done no more than exchange a few pleasantries with the two women, who had replied with the smallest modicum of politeness. In normal times, von Luck fancied that they would have established conventional neighbourly relations, and perhaps even gone so far as to invite each other round for dinner. There was no doubt that Mrs Campbell was an attractive woman, but it was on Pippa that von Luck's eye settled more often. He hazarded that she was in her early twenties, which made her – at most – ten years younger than him.

Von Luck dismounted. 'Now, what are you two ladies doing out at this hour?'

Neither replied.

'It's all right, Mrs Campbell, I'm not going to get you into trouble.'

She snatched a brief look at him. Her eyes were wet.

'Please, Mrs Campbell, don't worry. I did not mean to shock you.'

Still no reply.

'I assume that you're looking for firewood,' he said.

Pippa nodded, a gesture that earned her a rebuking glance from her mother.

'If you like, you can come back on Satan,' said von Luck. 'I'm sure he could carry you both.'

Mrs Campbell looked up at him. 'You— you mean it?'

'Of course,' said von Luck. 'It would be a comparative rest for him.'

'Honestly,' said Mrs Campbell, 'there's really no need. We're quite capable of—'

'I won't hear it! Come on – I'll help you up. You can sit one behind the other and I shall lead him.'

The women stayed still.

'Mrs Campbell – please. It would give me much pleasure. And if you're worried about your wood, then don't be – Satan and I can carry that as well.'

'But I thought that there was a ban . . .'

'A ban invented by me. So, you see, there's really no problem. Rules are made to be broken, even if they've been made up by me.'

Von Luck noticed Pippa smiling. 'That's better! Come on, then, Miss Campbell, let's get you on first.'

Even before he grasped Pippa by her thin waist to lift her on to Satan, von Luck told himself that he was being what the British called a 'cad'. When he did touch her, she looked straight into his eyes. Despite the presence of her mother, von Luck couldn't help but hold her gaze. Her eyes were pale green, unusually so. He knew full well what sort of look she was giving him, and it amazed him that she was being so bold, so indiscreet. On top of all his other problems, this was most unwelcome. He had been trying to avoid moments like this since he had got here, but here he was, rushing straight into one like a clumsy dog. It was too late now, he knew it.

*

The journey to the Campbells' house was far too short for von Luck's liking. For the most part, it was silent, and his attempts at conversation were once more met with that same cold politeness. Von Luck could hardly blame them – they were possibly still afraid of him, and would be extremely wary of being seen by their neighbours to accept German hospitality. Von Luck knew that the women who fraternised with them were called 'Jerrybags', a term that caused much amusement in the Field Command. There was an order that forbade Germans engaging in relationships with island women, but it was largely ignored. One only had to go down to St Ouen's beach on a summer evening to witness the order being breached *in flagrante*.

'This is our road,' said Mrs Campbell. 'We're just down on the left.'

Von Luck looked at the road sign – Wellington Road. He was amazed that someone in the Field Command hadn't renamed it 'Rommelstrasse' or something equally Germanic. But, then, not everything had changed. Although some of von Luck's fellow officers had opposed it, the islanders were still allowed to sing the British national anthem in church, albeit in a church bedecked with a swastika flag behind the altar.

The street was made up of a pleasant row of modern semi-detached houses, all of which had green window-frames and white walls. Their roofs were laid with corrugated tiles in the Spanish style, and the overall effect was one of middle-class decency and prosperity.

'This is us,' said Mrs Campbell. 'You can let us down now.'

'High Trees,' said von Luck. 'What a charming name. I'm always amazed at how inventive the English are with naming their houses. In Germany, the houses are just numbered.'

'That seems a shame,' said Pippa, 'but not surprising.'

'And what might you be suggesting, Fräulein?'

'Nothing,' Pippa replied, a half-smile on her lips. 'Nothing at all. You can help me down now.'

And still that same gaze, thought von Luck. Was he imagining it? Hoping for it? Certainly the latter, and he was sure it was there. Mrs Campbell gave him no such look as he helped her down, reinforcing von Luck's fancy that Pippa was indeed flirting with him. What the mother and daughter did share was nervousness, which von Luck disliked because the impression he was trying to create was intended to give rise to the opposite feeling in its recipients.

'So what number is your house, then?' asked Pippa.

'Well, it doesn't have one. It's just called Linden Court.'

'No, I mean your house in Germany.'

'That doesn't have a number either.'

'Really? What's it called?'

Von Luck felt slightly ill at ease. 'It's actually a castle.'

'A castle?'

Von Luck nodded.

'Does that make you a lord? Or a knight?'

'I'm afraid I'm just a mere count.'

'A count? That's hardly small fry.'

'Well, it is in Germany, you know. Nearly everybody is a count.'

Somewhat captivated by Pippa, von Luck did not notice that Mrs Campbell's attention had been deflected by the presence of her next-door neighbour, Mrs Miere, with whom the Campbells had never got on. Mrs Miere was always dropping hints that she knew they were up to no good, and the presence of von Luck would provide her with far too much ammunition for Mrs Campbell's liking.

'Come on, Philippa,' said Mrs Campbell. 'We must get inside. Please excuse us.'

'I'm sorry to delay you, Mrs Campbell,' von Luck replied, 'but please allow me to help you in with your wood.'

'No, no. That's quite all right. Just leave it here. Philippa will look after it.'

'You're quite sure?'

Pippa looked at von Luck and rolled her eyeballs.

'Yes,' said Mrs Campbell. 'I'm quite sure. You have done enough for us as it is.'

She was being brusque now, businesslike. It was clear that she wanted him no nearer the house than this. Well, he had to respect that: it was her house, and it was her daughter. Clearly she did not want either of them stained with his presence, no matter how decent he had been to them.

'In that case, Mrs Campbell – and you, Miss Campbell – I shall leave you to enjoy the rest of the evening. I hope our paths will cross again.'

'Many thanks,' said Mrs Campbell. The words were sincere, final. She was a tough one, thought von Luck.

'Thank you, Colonel,' said Pippa, looking straight at him.

'It was a pleasure,' he replied, raising an imaginary hat. 'One last thing. Allow me to give you this. He's not the fattest pigeon, I'm afraid, but I'm sure what there is of him will taste excellent.'

He could see the longing in their eyes, especially Mrs Campbell's.

'I'm afraid we cannot accept your very kind offer,' she said, after some quavering. 'We have taken far too much from you already.'

Von Luck knew what she meant. As far as he was concerned, they had taken very little, but in the opinion of their fellow islanders . . . 'I'm afraid I insist,' he said, and placed the pigeon on the ground. He mounted Satan and rode off. He resisted the temptation to turn round, at least until the end of the road, whereupon he glanced over his shoulder to see that the pigeon had gone. He smiled. Surely he had done a good thing. War criminal indeed.

Von Luck was not to know it yet, but the pigeon was not eaten by the Campbells, but by two other occupants of High Trees: two men who had recently escaped from a POW camp – Captain Fellowes and Pilot Officer Smith. They had to eat it in the attic, but it was no less delicious for that.

August 1990

'Not the fucking flowers again – I did them last year.'

'Come on, Bob, you know you love it. Think of all the beauty queens you can talk to.'

'Yeah, yeah. Why do you want to be this year's Miss Jersey? Ooh, it's because I work at the Bellevue Home for the Bewildered. Anything else? Yes, I've got a CSE in sunbathing. Wow. Which float do you think will win the Battle of the Flowers this year? Ooh, they're all so brilliant it's hard to tell. Come on, Brian, it's like Miss Bloody World, but slightly more crap.'

'I know, I know, but the readers love it, and it gives us a good excuse to put a bird on the front page.'

'Surely there must be someone else. Why can't you ask Tony? It's about time he did it.'

'I can't ask Tony – hay fever.'

'Hay fever? That's got to be bollocks.'

'I'm not kidding, Bob – there's even a note from his GP.'

'All right, all right. You win. But you owe me something decent after this. Something meaty. I'm sick of flower shows and "exciting new building projects".'

'That's a deal. But only if you do a good job on the flowers.'

'Done. But this is the last year, OK?'

'I don't make promises like that, Bob, you know that.'

With that, the editor of the *Jersey Record* turns on his heel and walks away. Arsehole, thinks Robert Lebonneur, the paper's chief reporter. He leans back on his battered swivel chair and lights a cigarette. Fucking flowers. Resentfully he breathes out a long grey jet of smoke at his screen. Still, at least it'll be a day out of the office. The Battle of the Flowers, indeed. Lebonneur hates it. He wishes he worked for a decent newspaper, like the *Evening Post*.

He looks at his watch. Quarter to twelve. Might as well have a pint – there's nothing else on today. He picks up his phone and dials an internal extension.

'Hello?' comes the voice at the end of the line.

'Pint?'

The owner of the voice looks across the office and smiles.

'Come on, Bob, it's not even twelve yet.'

'All right, Dave, you puritan, pint in fifteen minutes, then.'

'Make it quarter past?'

'Fine.'

Lebonneur puts down the phone. Half an hour, half a bloody hour. What can he do in half a bloody hour? To the left of his screen is a large and haphazard pile of paper, mostly consisting of press releases and yellowing scraps of fax paper. Perhaps he should go through it – bin most of it. Then he'll feel as though he's earned a pint. Good idea.

Within seconds, the metal bin is full. Ignoring it, Lebonneur keeps throwing piece after piece of A4 into it – or rather on to it – until each new scrap slides off and joins a new pile on the floor. What's this? *Jersey Girl, 15, nominated for finals of Young Musician of the Year 1988* . . . Oh, forget it, it can all go. Lebonneur picks up the rest of the pile and throws it on to the floor. Whoops, he thinks, as the papers scatter for several feet in every direction. Better get a bin-bag or something.

As he returns from the small kitchen with a large black bag, Lebonneur ignores the predictable comments concerning his sacking. Such jokes are a little close to the bone. Last year, he was nearly sacked for insulting – and almost punching – the managing editor and he is now on a final warning. He knows the newspaper would hate to lose him because he's just about the only reporter on the paper who gets any decent stories, but his fear of being out of work is even greater. He has three other mouths to feed and, at forty-four, Lebonneur knows there are very few jobs available to a man like him here on Jersey, never mind the mainland. He wouldn't move there, of course – being Jersey-born and bred he'd hate to – but if needs must . . . It didn't bear thinking about. He's realistic enough to know that being chief reporter of a Jersey paper counts for little over there. Besides, here the money is good, the taxes are low, the schools are great, the weather is better – in fact, everything is. It's not worth shooting his mouth off only to shoot himself in the foot.

It only takes a few seconds to stuff the papers into the bin-bag. A handful is still stuck in the bin so he pulls them out. One catches his eye: *Work starts on £20 million luxury hotel on Alderney.* This one doesn't look too pre-Cambrian, so Lebonneur keeps on reading.

1 July 1990

Today the Regius Hotels Group PLC announced that

construction work had started on their new flagship hotel Mannez Heights on the Channel Island of Alderney. The £20 million hotel will feature a casino, a state-of-the-art gym, a swimming-pool, three restaurants, as well as a glittering host of other facilities. Roger Bouverie, the managing director of Regius Hotels Group PLC, said, 'This is not only a great day for Regius Hotels but a great day for the Channel Islands and, in particular, Alderney. This will really put the island on the map, and will benefit the tourism industry of the Channel Islands as a whole. I am very grateful to all those members of the Islands' governing bodies, and especially Judge Ian Mollett on Alderney, who have made this development possible.' Mannez Heights is due to be completed in spring 1992, and it is hoped . . .

He stops. Yuk. There is only so much press-release English that he can read in a sitting. He loves the part about how this man Bouverie is so grateful to the politicians – all of whom have, doubtless, been given enormous bungs. Lebonneur has spent his professional life exposing such corruption, and in doing so has made many enemies. He suspects that his editor has been leaned on – 'Get this man Lebonneur off our backs' – which is probably why he is covering the fucking flowers.

He skims through the rest of the press release, and then it joins the black bag. For the time being he puts it down as yet another 'exciting new development'. Besides, it sounds naff, naff as hell.

*

Lebonneur takes a sip from his pint of lager. 'That feels good,' he says.

'Busy day?' asks Dave.

'Not really – but this is medicinal.'

'How come?'

'Been asked to do the sodding flowers again.'

Dave laughs, simultaneously flicking the ash from a Raffles on to the filthy pub carpet. Both men are in shirtsleeves, having left their jackets on the backs of their chairs. They know the gesture will fool no one, but they take a schoolboyish delight in the attempt at deception, no matter how feeble.

'How many times have you done them?'

'This must be my four-hundredth. And it's always the fucking same.'

'Still, it's a day out of the office,' says Dave.

'That's what I tell myself,' says Lebonneur.

The two men stand in companionable silence for a while.

'How's Rachel?' asks Dave.

'Not bad – been busy sorting out my mother's house. There's a shedload of crap in there.'

'I was sorry to hear about her. She was great fun, your mum.'

'Thanks. Good innings, et cetera, et cetera. It's the kids who'll really miss her. They used to love going over there for tea, listening to her stories of the war.'

The two men take a reflective swig of their pints.

'What are you going to do with her place?'

'We'll let it out. Should make us a few bob.'

'Nice. Very nice. You could give up this craphole.'

'I wish! It's not as big as you'd think, but it should give us something. Still, it'll certainly take the pressure off. Anyway, we've got to spend a mint doing it up – central heating needs putting in, rewiring, all that.'

'Who's going to do it for you?'

'God knows. Why? Do you know someone?'

'I do, actually. Bloke called John Mead. Nice chap. Drives a clean van, which I always think is a good sign.'

'Has he done anything for you?'

'Yeah – he converted our attic a while back. He did a good job. It still seems to be in one piece.'

'All right – I'll give him a ring.'

'Hello, is Mr Mead there?'

'I'm afraid not.'

'Do you know when he'll be back?'

'Well . . . er . . . I'm not too sure.'

'Oh?'

'Well, he's in hospital, you see . . .'

'Hospital?'

'That's right.'

'Oh dear, I'm sorry to hear it. Trust it's nothing serious?'

Silence.

'Hello?' says Lebonneur. 'Are you still there?'

Sniffing comes down the phone.

'Are you all right?'

'Yes, I'm sorry,' is the warbled reply.

'Don't be. I'm sorry to have disturbed you. I was calling to see whether John could do some work for me, but I'll leave it for the time being. I assume that's Mrs Mead?'

'It is, yes.'

Lebonneur can hear Mrs Mead blowing her nose. 'Is there anything I can do, Mrs Mead?'

Mrs Mead ignores the question. 'They won't tell me what's wrong with him.'

Lebonneur sits up at his desk. 'How do you mean?'

'They won't even let me see him. All they said was that he'd had an accident.'

'Where?'

'On Alderney, on that new hotel they're building. John was working over there for a few weeks . . .'

Even as Mrs Mead carries on speaking, Lebonneur clenches the phone between his neck and his shoulder and slips both his arms into his jacket sleeves. Fuck the flowers, he thinks. This is more like it.

Chapter Two

THERE WERE FEW who knew the treacherous six miles of water between Alderney and Les Casquets lighthouse, and George Pike was one of them. For the past five years, he had been acting as pilot for the Germans, guiding their vessels in and out of Braye Harbour, as well as navigating the two-hour trip over to the lighthouse.

The occupiers were not unappreciative: they had supplied Pike, his wife Daisy, and his six children with a large house in St Anne, and allowed him to come and go as he pleased. They knew they could trust him because Pike was an outcast, a former member of Mosley's British Union of Fascists who had sought refuge on Alderney, before the invasion in early 1940, to escape being interned under the new Defence Regulations. The islanders had found him a faintly sinister figure, but the Germans regarded him as one of their own.

Pike was presently sitting on the same craft he had used to

make his trip from the mainland – the *Wishbone*, a converted lifeboat. It had served him well and, what was more, the children loved coming on it. With only a handful of other civilians on the island, there were no other children for them to play with, so the *Wishbone* acted as a useful method of stifling boredom.

However, there were no children on board this evening because Pike was working. He looked at his watch – half past eleven. Whatever was coming, it was late. He lit a cigarette – a German one – and inhaled deeply. The cigarette burned down swiftly in the breeze, and in no time at all he had thrown the butt into the water. 'Oi, Heinz!'

'Yes?'

'What am I supposed to be taking into the harbour?'

'I'm sorry, George, I really don't know.'

Pike's companion was Sonderführer Heinz Herzog, a nice bloke, thought Pike. They had worked together many times, but tonight Pike found him a little more tense than usual. Perhaps it was not surprising – it was not often that they had to meet vessels so late at night. However, what might have been causing Heinz's edginess was the presence of around a hundred concentration-camp prisoners lined up in the harbour. Something important was being delivered, something large and unusual.

The prisoners looked freezing, thought Pike, but he kept his opinions to himself. Besides, he had seen far worse things over the years, far worse. If the Germans wanted to treat their prisoners like shit, that was their prerogative. Half of them were Jews anyway, so they pretty much deserved it. The rest were probably

Commies or Gypsies, so they deserved it as well. Still, some of what he had seen was gruesome enough even for him, especially the time when they had shot that Russian woman just after she had given birth on the side of the road. He hadn't wanted to look at what happened to the baby – he could guess.

Quarter to twelve. Their mysterious visitor was supposed to be here well over an hour ago. Pike yawned, longing for the warmth of his wife and his bed. How much longer would they be in that house, he wondered. The war was going badly for the Germans – everybody knew that, even the concentration-camp prisoners – so where were he and the family going to go? He doubted the islanders, if and when they returned, would appreciate his having served the enemy for the past five years. He certainly couldn't go back to the mainland, despite what Daisy wanted. Pike had brought the matter up only a few days ago with Major Schwalm, who had told him not to worry, that the Germans were certainly going to win the war, and in the unlikely event that they didn't, Pike could sail the *Wishbone* to Argentina with the rest of them. Ha-bloody-ha, Pike had thought, but once more he had kept his mouth shut.

Pike lit another cigarette. Come on, you sodding boat, get a bloody move on. The chances were it had been blown out of the water hours ago, and they were waiting here pointlessly. He pulled on the cigarette a few more times, then threw it overboard. Just as he did so, he heard a curious bubbling sound coming from about a hundred yards behind him.

'Heinz! To stern!'

Herzog raced to the back of the *Wishbone*. The bubbling grew into a full boiling, the water dancing crazily in the moonlight.

'What the fuck is that, Heinz? A whale?'

Heinz started laughing.

'No, you fool! It's a U-Boat! A damn U-Boat!'

'It's not funny, Heinz,' shouted Pike. 'If the bleeding thing was coming up any nearer we'd both be goners.'

'George! I'm sure he saw us through his periscope. Look! Here comes the bow.'

Pike and Herzog stood still, mesmerised by the appearance of the sleekly pointed bow breaking through the surface. Neither man had been this close to a submarine before, and both were overawed by the sinister majesty of the dark craft emerging from the black waters.

The conning tower was emerging now, larger than Pike had expected. Foaming white water was cascading down the tower, running back into the sea. Within a few more seconds, the rest of the submarine had come up, and the bow slowly crashed down into the water, sending out a wave that made *Wishbone* violently pitch and roll.

'Jesus wept!' cried Pike.

But Herzog was smiling. 'It's only when you see something like that you realise that we might not be defeated after all.'

Pike started his engines, the noise rendering any reply useless. He hoped Heinz was right, he really did. South America? No, thanks. It had taken him five years to learn German, and he was bad enough at that. But learn Spanish? Not a hope, Señor.

*

It took Pike half an hour to guide the U-Boat over to the breakwater. The only contact he had with her crew was the sound of 'Bitte, pilot!' being shouted from the conning tower. It had been quite a challenge to get her in, but as he moored the *Wishbone*, he felt proud of a good job done. He was more than ready for bed now, and certainly ready for a quick dram before that. He had only six bottles of whisky left so he rationed it carefully, but tonight called for an especially large measure.

However, what stopped Pike going home immediately was curiosity. As he walked up a set of steps on the side of the vast breakwater, he saw the line of prisoners shuffling towards him from the harbour. Behind them were three lorries, and what looked like Major Schwalm's car speeding ahead. He looked to his right, three hundred yards along the breakwater to the U-Boat, and dimly discerned some figures exiting from a hatch. They looked like top brass, he thought. No wonder Schwalm was here.

Pike stayed still and lit a cigarette. Schwalm's car roared by. It was going dangerously fast, Pike thought, especially when you considered that one slip could see the vehicle flying off the edge of the breakwater. Whoever was on that boat had to be bloody important. Pike watched the car squeal to a stop, then saw Schwalm leap out and run up to the figures from the U-Boat. Immaculate salutes all round, better than Pike had seen in a while.

His attention was distracted by the approach of the prisoners. They were like ghosts, he thought, grey-and-white-striped ghosts. They were nearly silent, barring the occasional cough. Pike felt no pity for them because to him the prisoners were like cattle. He thought it a little mad that the Germans treated their cattle so harshly, but there were plenty more.

For the next hour, Pike watched the U-Boat being unloaded. Thinking it wise to keep his distance, he dared not draw any nearer, but he could see that the prisoners were unloading a series of pipes. Pipes? What the devil did the Germans want pipes for? There were hundreds of the bloody things! He also saw some wooden crates, whose weight caused the prisoners to struggle.

Pike decided to go home when he saw a prisoner shot for dropping a pipe. The evening wouldn't have been complete without that, he thought. Another for the crabs to eat.

*   *   *

Dr Martin Aubin peered at the two men over his half-moon spectacles. They still looked undernourished, but otherwise they were in good shape. 'You've been looking after them well, Violet.'

'It's been a struggle,' Violet Campbell replied, 'but we're managing.'

'You're more than managing, Mrs Campbell,' said Pilot Officer Smith. 'D'you know she even gave us pigeon? It was gourmet night in the attic.'

Dr Aubin removed his spectacles and turned to face Violet. 'A pigeon, eh? Fell out of the sky, did it?'

Pippa replied before her mother could get a word in: 'Actually, it fell off the back of a German's horse.'

'Pippa!' hissed Violet.

'Well, what's the harm in that?' Pippa shrugged.

'I'm sorry, Dr Aubin, the officer who lives up at Linden Court seems to have taken rather a shine to my daughter.'

'I see,' said Dr Aubin, giving Pippa a paternally disapproving stare. It was easy to see why any man might take a shine to Pippa. There was something coquettishly mischievous in her manner, something that suggested she flirted with danger, and if that danger came in the form of a man, so much the better. There were many girls like her on the island, thought Dr Aubin, girls who had been unable to resist the allure of the handsome German officers, girls who found the idea of sleeping with them exciting and, moreover, rebellious. It was girls like that, thought Aubin, who came to him when they were 'in trouble'. He refused to help them, telling them that he was not that sort of doctor, but more often than not they did find help. The latest rumour was that a farmer's wife up in St John performed the abortions. As the island's chief medical officer, he had done his best to put a stop to such activity, but there were more pressing problems, such as malnutrition, to deal with.

'I take it this is Lieutenant Colonel von Luck,' said Aubin.

'The very same,' Violet replied.

Aubin nodded and let out a small sigh. He was quite a

heartbreaker, was von Luck. Pippa would not be the first to fall for him. Not that von Luck wasn't a gentleman – it would be hard to find someone on the island who could fault him – but he was still the enemy, handsome and decent or not.

'Oh, for heaven's sake,' said Pippa. 'There's nothing wrong with accepting a pigeon from a Jerry. We needed it, didn't we? Otherwise what would we have fed these two? Tomato paper?'

The thin tissue paper that wrapped tomatoes was one of the few commodities that Jersey had not run short of. It was used for sanitary purposes by the islanders and the Germans. Fellowes and Smith looked uneasily at the ground. It seemed as though they were about to witness a family argument.

'Pippa!' hissed her mother once more. 'This is neither the time nor the place.'

'Violet, may I give your daughter some advice?'

'By all means, Doctor.'

'Young lady, I would advise you very strongly against becoming friendly with Lieutenant Colonel von Luck. He may not be a bad man, but he is, after all, ah, a man, if you, ah, take my meaning. And he is the enemy too. Think of your reputation, Miss Campbell. And think what will happen when the war is over. We've heard on the BBC that Jerrybags in France are being tarred and feathered – some of them even stripped naked and shaven in public. I would, of course, hope that we were more civilised than the French, but you can never tell.'

Pippa merely glowered. She was sick of this. 'I can look after myself, thank you, Dr Aubin.'

'I dare say you can, but not in every way. I have seen lots of young women such as yourself at my surgery, and I am afraid I am not in a position to help them in the way they would, ah, like – do you understand?'

'I'm not a child, Dr Aubin. Look – all I've done is accept a bloody pigeon! Anyone would have thought I'd already made love to him.'

The room went silent. They were not shocked by the expression, but the use of 'already'. It suggested that the act was imminent, and that it was simply a matter of time.

'Go upstairs,' said Violet.

Pippa shook her head. She felt ashamed, but she was damned if she was going to show it. Instead of going to her room, she picked up her coat from the stand and made for the front door.

'Where do you think you're going?' asked Violet. 'I told you to go upstairs.'

'I – am – going – out. What does it look like?' With that, Pippa opened the front door, strode out, and slammed it behind her.

'I'm deeply sorry for this,' said Violet. 'It has not been easy for my daughter. In normal circumstances she would probably be married rather than living at home with her mother. It has perhaps somewhat arrested her.'

Dr Aubin held up his hands. 'She is merely a young woman – an intelligent and beautiful one at that – and she is at that time of her life. If you would like, I'll have a word with von Luck.'

'Do you think you could?'

'Well, I've dealt with him on a number of occasions – he has always seemed most reasonable. I don't know how he would react in a matter of this sort, but it's worth a try. I'm sure he would not wish to put your daughter's dignity at risk.'

'I would very much appreciate that, Dr Aubin.'

'Think of it as what we doctors call preventive medicine.'

Violet smiled weakly.

'Right, then! I'm sorry, gentlemen – I was here to give you these, of course.' Dr Aubin reached inside his battered brown leather Gladstone bag and brought out two small grey documents. He passed them to Fellowes and Smith. 'These are your identity cards, expertly forged by my own fair hand. You'll see that the photographs I took yesterday just about do you justice. As far as I know, no Jerry has yet rumbled one of my creations. You're both down as farm-workers, but obviously I've kept your physical characteristics the same. There's little you have to do now apart from remember your new place of birth, and sign them in your new names.'

The two men fingered the cards with unrestrained glee. Although he knew that what they were doing was desperately serious, Fellowes found himself responding to the boy within. He had made false papers when he was at prep school but here he was, twenty years later, having to use them for real.

'I think we'll need to practise our new signatures first, if that's all right,' said Fellowes. 'I don't fancy I'll be able to make "Edmond Le Quesne" look convincing at the first attempt.'

'Nor me with Edward Lainé,' said Smith. 'You've chosen colourful-sounding surnames.'

'They're typical Jersey ones – old Norman.'

Violet extracted two small sheets of paper and a couple of pencils from her desk. Within a minute the men had filled both sides of their sheets with their new names.

'They look fine,' said Aubin, 'but don't make your handwriting look too sophisticated – remember, you're meant to be a pair of labourers.'

Aubin handed the papers back to Violet. 'You'd better burn these,' he said.

Violet placed them on her desk. She would burn them later, when they had the fire going.

* * *

'So how was your friend Major Schwalm?'

'Well, for the most part, he was boring,' Hempel replied, 'just as you said.'

'And what did he say about the vegetables?'

'It seems he wants a lot more.'

Von Luck sat up. He was behind his desk at the Field Command, its surface almost entirely covered with methodically arranged piles of paper. They represented an enormous amount of work for which he was in no mood. Hempel's interruption was therefore most welcome. 'More? Why?'

'He wouldn't say,' said Hempel.

'I don't like it,' von Luck continued. 'If Schwalm wants more vegetables, that means he has more prisoners. If he has more prisoners, he must be building something new, something big. By the way, how many vegetables does he want?'

'Three tons of potatoes, the same amount of turnips . . .'

'He's got to be joking!'

'That's what he said. I told him it was out of the question, but he said that the order came from the top.'

'The top? Huffmeier?'

'No. From Berlin.'

'*Berlin?*'

Hempel nodded.

'Did he show you any proof of this?'

'No. He told me I had to take his word for it.'

'A likely story. I assume you told him it was impossible to supply him?'

'I did, but he threatened me, saying he would report my disobedience to Berlin, and that I would be answerable to the Führer himself if I did not deliver.'

Von Luck puffed his cheeks and blew out a resigned stream of air. He felt deflated, empty. If Schwalm wasn't calling Hempel's bluff – and there was every chance that he was, for the Führer's name was invoked at the slightest opportunity these days – something ominous was taking place on Alderney. 'How did you leave it?' he asked.

'I told him I would have to report back to you,' said Hempel. 'I hope you don't feel I'm passing the buck . . .'

Von Luck held up his hand. 'Of course not, Hempel,' he replied. 'You had to tell me, in the same way that I will have to tell our new commander-in-chief about this.'

'You're going to tell Huffmeier?'

'Quite so,' said von Luck, standing. 'If anyone's going to pass the buck around here, it's going to be me.' He walked over to the door and removed his cap from a school desk. Such items of furniture were strewn all over the Field Command, for the building in which they were housed was that of Victoria College. 'The last thing I'm going to do, Hempel, is take food out of the mouths of the people here on Jersey. They're on about half the amount of calories they need as it is. I see no reason why they should suffer because someone in Berlin has decided that he wants to turn Alderney into some concrete shithole.'

'Good luck, then, sir.'

'Thank you, Hempel,' said von Luck, holding the door handle. 'I suspect that I'll need it.' He pulled open the door.

'Another thing, sir,' said Hempel.

'Yes?'

'There was something else Schwalm mentioned.'

'Go on.'

'He only alluded to it, but he said they were losing a lot of prisoners at the moment through sickness.'

'Sickness? What sort of sickness?'

'He didn't say.'

'How many prisoners?'

Hempel shook his head. 'He wouldn't tell me. Once again, he clammed up. I got the impression it was a lot, though.'

Von Luck paused. There had been epidemics in the camps before – typhus was the biggest killer. 'It could be a lot of things,' he said. 'Look into it, though, would you? I'm surprised he hasn't asked for any medical supplies.'

'Yes, sir.'

Von Luck turned to leave.

'Oh, by the way, sir,' said Hempel. 'I'm sorry to have missed out on that pigeon the other night. How was it?'

'It was, er, very nice, thank you, Hempel. Yes! Very good indeed.'

With that, von Luck stepped out of his office. Hempel could have sworn that he had not told him the truth, but he put it down to an uncharacteristic display of nerves.

Von Luck paced down the wooden corridors angrily, barely acknowledging the greetings of those he passed. At six foot four, he found it easy to avoid eye-contact when he felt the need. Six bloody tons indeed. Answerable to the Führer. It was nonsense, it had to be. What in God's name were they doing over there?

Von Luck pushed open the door to the admiral's suite of offices, noticing that it was still painted with the name 'General von Schmettow'. Although it had only been a week since the admiral had taken over, von Luck had expected the man's first act in charge would be to ensure the door was corrected. Perhaps it was simply an oversight, or – and von Luck acknowledged to himself that this was fanciful – the man was being disobeyed. That was unlikely, but possible. Having met Huffmeier, albeit briefly at a reception to mark his installation, it had struck von Luck that the man possessed everything hateful that could be found in some of his fellow Germans. He was certainly without humour, and there was something of the machine about him, thought von Luck, something soulless: he was a man fabricated entirely of metal and wire.

Two uniformed secretaries turned up their heads to greet him.

'Lieutenant Colonel,' said one, a blonde Bavarian by the name of Heidi von Aufsess, 'this is a pleasant surprise.'

Normally von Luck would have indulged in some mild flirtation – commenting on how she managed to keep herself looking so wonderful when their diet was so bad, which she would have complemented by saying it must have something to do with their noble Bavarian blood, because the Lieutenant Colonel was looking very healthy himself, *very* healthy – but today von Luck was having none of it. Heidi could see it in his eyes immediately, and her tone changed to one more decorous. 'I assume you wish to see the admiral, Lieutenant Colonel?'

Von Luck nodded. 'Please tell him it's urgent.'

'He's on the telephone at the moment, but he won't be long.'

'Good. Thank you, Fräulein.'

'Or, at least, that's what he *said*,' said Heidi, looking at her watch.

'Oh?'

'He's got Major Schwalm on the phone. You know what a bore he is.'

Von Luck tried not to appear as interested as he felt. 'Yes, he is, isn't he? The poor admiral, having to deal with that windbag! I expect he gives him pretty short shrift, though.'

'Well, you would think so,' said Heidi, 'but Schwalm has been on the phone nearly all the time for the past two d–'

Heidi was interrupted by the door to the admiral's office being suddenly thrust open. 'Heidi!' a gruff voice said.

Its owner followed immediately after. Dressed immaculately in his navy blue uniform, Admiral Huffmeier initially cut an impressive figure, thought von Luck. But, then, who wouldn't in such a uniform? After a few seconds' inspection, Huffmeier's physical shortcomings became apparent: the round, sloping shoulders, the diminutive stature, the walk in which his short legs were kicked out from below the knees. His face was certainly not unpleasant, although there was something of the pugilist about it, with its flattened nose and crooked mouth.

'Heidi, I want you to get hold of the Bailiff– Von Luck! What are you doing here?'

Von Luck snapped to attention. 'I was coming to see you, Herr Admiral.'

Huffmeier squinted at him. 'Where is your salute, Lieutenant Colonel?'

Arsehole, thought von Luck. He was tempted to give the man the normal Wehrmacht salute, but decided against it. There was no point in riling him, at least, not yet – not when he needed something from him. It was, therefore, with some reluctance that von Luck performed his most perfunctory 'Heil Hitler'.

'That's better, Lieutenant Colonel. Now, what did you want to see me about?'

'Alderney, Herr Admiral.'

The squint continued. If its effect was intended to unnerve, it had only limited success. Von Luck supposed that it was doing more to mask Huffmeier's reactions than to unsettle its recipient.

'What about Alderney, Lieutenant Colonel?' The voice was slow, deliberately calm.

'I understand that Major Schwalm has requested a large – very large – consignment of vegetables from us.'

Still that squint. Then Huffmeier turned his head pointedly back to Heidi. 'Heidi. Get the Bailiff here. Immediately. And tell him to bring Jurat Mollett as well.'

'Certainly, Herr Admiral.'

'And you, Lieutenant Colonel,' said Huffmeier, 'can step into my office. I'd also like to talk to you about Alderney, but I want to do so before Marais and Mollett arrive.'

As Bailiff of Jersey, Richard Marais presided over the island's governing body, the States. Assisting him were two law officers, the attorney-general and the solicitor-general; the former was Peter Mollett, who also held the office of jurat – one of twelve legislators elected for life. After their occupiers, Marais and Mollett were the two most powerful men on the island, and

Marais regarded it as their job to make the States act as a buffer between the Germans and the islanders.

It being a Saturday afternoon, Marais had been gardening when Heidi called, so he found himself driving over to the Field Command in a battered pair of heavy woollen trousers and a spectacularly holey jersey. As he negotiated the potholed roads, he reflected that there had been a time during the occupation when he would have changed into a suit, no matter how urgently his presence was required by the Germans. However, with the way the war was going, he could afford to show how lowly he regarded the invaders by not deigning to dress up. It gave him some delight that he was especially scruffy, his hands still caked with mud, his hair slightly wild when compared with its quotidian smartness, slicked back into a dark widow's peak.

He reached Mollett's house after a quarter of an hour and tooted his horn. Although Mollett had a car, the fuel shortages were now so acute that Marais was the only islander, other than the doctors, who was permitted to drive. Everybody else made do with bicycles – many of which had long since lost their tyres – or went about on foot. This had had the effect of making some of the more rural parts of the island even more cut off than they had been before the war, and Marais had found that the isolation had bred a resurgence in superstition. Shortages and hardships were no longer blamed on the Germans, but on 'bad spirits' and occasionally 'witches'. It was as if some had returned to the Middle Ages, Marais told the States, and he had insisted that it was essential, no matter how difficult, to ensure that no member of the island's community was allowed to become too isolated.

Peter Mollett was dressed similarly to Marais, although he was not quite so scruffy. Many islanders had worn the same clothes for almost five years, and the sight of threadbare and repeatedly patched-up garments was a ubiquitous feature in the streets of St Helier.

'What's all this about, then, Dick?' said Mollett, as he contorted his huge frame into Marais's car.

'I've got no bloody idea,' said Marais. 'All I know is that it's urgent, and that it couldn't wait until Monday morning.'

'I expect it's nothing – just Huffmeier flexing his muscles, wanting to let us know that he's still in charge.'

'I hope that's it,' said Marais, willing the car up a steep hill. 'My only worry is that this is going to be something to do with food.'

'More cuts, eh?'

'I expect so – if he tries I'll tell him I'll have him hanged as a war criminal after the war. It's been hard enough keeping his hands off our Red Cross parcels.'

'Well, at least von Luck should be on our side,' said Mollett. 'Surely he would have told Huffmeier that the population can't exist on anything less.'

'I fear that von Luck's position has been somewhat undermined by Huffmeier. The admiral is a nasty piece of work, and I doubt that von Luck can do much to sway him as he could with Schmettow.'

The two men fell silent.

'Do you think we'll make it?' asked Mollett.

'What? To the end of the war?'

'No.' Mollett laughed. 'Up the bloody hill.'

'Touch and go,' said Marais. 'You're pushing if we don't.'

Von Luck stood as the two Jerseymen were ushered into Huffmeier's office by an orderly, who was obviously startled by the nature of the men's attire. It came as no surprise to him that Huffmeier remained seated – not for him the common courtesies that the general always displayed, no matter how bad relations had got. Von Luck knew that his expression would doubtless reveal that the business in hand was grave, but he was not going to alter it to suit Huffmeier. What he had been told was disgusting, despicable, monstrous, criminal – a combination of all these things and yet worse still.

'Good afternoon, gentlemen,' said Huffmeier, his voice absent of any meaning that the salutation might hold.

Marais and Mollett did not reply.

'Would you like to sit down?' asked Huffmeier.

Mollett made for a chair but Marais interrupted him. 'I shall prefer to remain standing, Admiral.'

Huffmeier shrugged. 'As you wish.'

Silence. Von Luck wanted to draw out his pistol and threaten Huffmeier, tell him that there was no way he was going to issue the order. He stopped himself, knowing that such an action would prove little more than a gesture and would certainly see himself in front of a firing squad.

'Gentlemen,' Huffmeier began, 'I have an order here from Berlin. You will not like it, but that is not my concern.'

Marais and Mollett shifted on their feet, the latter clearing his throat.

'It is really very straightforward,' said Huffmeier. 'I require one thousand islanders to volunteer to work on the fortifications on Alderney. They should be fit, under the age of fifty-five and above the age of fifteen. They can be either male or female – although no fewer than seventy-five per cent male. They should assemble at Albert Pier on, let me see, I shall be generous here, Wednesday morning at six a.m. If you require any military assistance in enforcing this order, I shall put my men at your disposal. Are there any questions?'

Von Luck had never seen Marais look so flabbergasted. Normally so urbane, so calm in a crisis, so eloquent, here he was, his mouth open, unable to find any words. Mollett's reaction was simply a murmured 'Christ alive.' Von Luck wanted to speak, to reassure them that he would do everything in his power to frustrate the order but, once again, he opted for silence. He could see what the men were thinking: putting already weak men, women and children to work – and heavy physical work at that – would destroy many of them. This was as good as selecting a thousand people for an early grave. In the eyes of Marais and Mollett, and indeed in von Luck's, the order was for nothing less than murder.

Marais was the first to speak. He struggled to keep his voice at an even pitch. 'You said . . . you said "volunteers".'

Huffmeier nodded. 'I did.'

'And what if no one volunteers?'

'Then I shall simply round up the necessary number by force. You will make life so much easier for yourselves if we do not have to go down that route.'

'You must realise, Admiral,' said Marais, 'that you will be sending these people to their deaths.'

'I don't see you complaining about all the other labourers on the island, Herr Bailiff. You've had Poles, Russians, Gypsies, French, Spanish – all sorts of mongrels – here for the past five years and the States have done nothing about them. Now it's your own people you get all indignant! Forgive me, but you are displaying a double standard, a certain hypocrisy.'

'You know as well as I do that there is nothing I can do about the Todt workers,' said Marais, barely maintaining his composure, 'but when it comes to the people under my jurisdiction, then yes, I will do as much as I can to save them. I should also remind you that you are committing a crime, Admiral, and after the war, I shall see that you are tried in any international tribunal there may be.'

Huffmeier smiled. 'The only tribunals held after the war will be those held under the flag behind me. I have little to fear from my own people, Herr Bailiff.'

Marais looked up at the swastika with undisguised venom. 'You are oddly sure of yourself, Admiral. I'm afraid I do not believe you to be very wise, and neither do I believe you to be much of a soothsayer.'

'We shall see,' said Huffmeier. 'We shall see. All that matters to me at the moment is that you do as I say.'

'I will not,' said Marais. 'The States of Jersey will never accede to such an order. You will have to use force.'

'Be very careful,' said Huffmeier. 'Are you sure you meant that? Would you not like to take back those words?'

'No, I would not.'

Huffmeier placed his fingertips together. 'In that case, you can count yourself among the one thousand.'

'I had already,' said Marais.

'Von Luck.'

'Yes, sir?'

'Take these two gardeners out of here and explain to them the gravity of their situation. If I cannot persuade them, perhaps you can.'

'Yes, sir.' Von Luck turned to Marais and Mollett. 'Gentlemen, would you like to follow me?'

Marais's expression suggested that that was the last thing he wished to do, but von Luck stared back at him fiercely. 'Come on,' his eyes were saying. 'I need to talk to you.' It worked. Marais nodded.

'You know that I am on your side,' said von Luck, as soon as he had shut his office door.

'But this is monstrous, von Luck!' shouted Marais. 'What in God's name is it all about?'

'I really don't know, Herr Marais, and that's the truth.

I for one don't understand why they need so many workers over there. I know that a few hundred Todt workers are going there over the weekend as it is. I'm told there is some sort of illness going around on the island, but I can't believe it's so virulent that it's killed as many as we're sending over. We've got pretty good at dealing with things like typhus over the years.'

'Will Huffmeier really force us at gunpoint?' asked Mollett.

'Oh, yes,' said von Luck. 'He's an out-and-out Nazi. Anyway, this news calls for a drink. I'm afraid all I can offer you is some rather old schnapps.'

'Anything,' said Marais, 'Anything at all. I'd drink the little petrol left in my car if it wasn't so valuable.'

Von Luck laughed hollowly as he poured three shots. 'Here you are, gentlemen.'

'There's not much to celebrate,' said Mollett.

'No, you're right there,' said von Luck, then knocked back the burning liquid in one gulp, 'but there is much to anaesthetise.'

The two Jerseymen took rather more frugal sips from their glasses.

'Although perhaps there is something to celebrate,' said von Luck.

'Oh, yes?' asked Marais.

Von Luck poured himself another glass. 'Our common endeavour, gentlemen,' he said. 'To stop the deportation.'

'You mean . . . you mean, you will help us?'

'Absolutely. I've spent the past few years doing as much as I can to keep you all alive, and I'm not going to undo my hard work now.'

'I'll drink to that,' said Mollett.

'So will I,' said Marais.

The two men knocked back their drinks.

'One question, von Luck,' said Marais. 'How?'

'I'm not entirely sure,' he replied, 'but I suspect the first thing we'll need to do is to pretend that I've persuaded you to go along with the order. That will buy us some goodwill, under which I can perhaps manage to foul things up at this end.'

'This is a very brave thing you're doing, von Luck,' said Marais.

'Well, let's just say that I don't fancy appearing in front of a tribunal held under a Union Jack.'

'I think you're being too modest.'

Before von Luck could reply, there was a knock on the door. 'Yes!' he shouted.

An orderly walked in and saluted. 'Sir! Dr Aubin is here to see you.'

'Aubin? What does he want?'

'He said it was confidential, sir.'

'Did he, now? All right – show him in.'

*　　*　　*

Lebonneur knocks hard on Mrs Mead's door. While he waits, he looks up and down the house. Not a bad place, he thinks, must be at least four bedrooms. Builders don't do too badly on Jersey, and clearly Mead is no exception. It's even got a view of St Aubin's Bay, which must make the house worth a bit.

Come on, he thinks. He peers through the frosted-glass window, hoping to detect movement. Nothing. He knocks again, harder this time. This is like doorstepping someone.

Just as he is about to shout through the letterbox, Lebonneur is rewarded with the sight of a white apparition approaching the door. At last.

'Hello?' The voice is frail.

'Mrs Mead? It's Robert Lebonneur here, from the *Record*. We spoke about fifteen minutes ago.'

Mrs Mead lifts the latch and opens the door until it is checked by the chain. The first thing Lebonneur notices is that her eyes are very red. She is clutching a white tissue to her chest. Late fifties, Lebonneur reckons, not bad looking either.

'You said that it was all right if I came and spoke to you about your husband, Mrs Mead. Would that still be OK?'

Mrs Mead nods almost imperceptibly and remains still.

'Er, may I come in?'

'Yes, of course, I'm sorry.'

She unhooks the chain and Lebonneur steps inside. 'Lovely house you have, Mrs Mead.'

'Thank you.'

Lebonneur follows her down the corridor to the kitchen. Along the wall are photographs of the Meads' children, culminating in their graduation portraits. There is also a

70

photograph of Mead himself – slightly tubby, big smile, bald. Looks like a nice enough chap.

'It's very good of you to talk to me,' says Lebonneur, as he walks into the kitchen.

Mrs Mead sniffs. 'Well, I thought you might be able to help me,' she says. 'Find out what's the matter with him. After all, you journalists are a nosy lot.'

'We are that, Mrs Mead. So, tell me, when did Mr Mead have his accident?'

'The company said it was two days ago.'

'What happened?'

'Well, this is it, you see – I don't know. They won't tell me how bad it is or anything. What makes it worse is that I'm not allowed to see him.'

Lebonneur watches Mrs Mead's lower lip start to tremble, but she composes herself, tilts her head up a little and sniffs in a noseful of air. 'This must be very difficult . . .'

'No, it's fine,' says Mrs Mead. 'It's good to have someone to talk to. My children are overseas at the moment.'

'And have the company told you whether it's serious?'

Mrs Mead shakes her head.

'I assume you've complained,' says Lebonneur. 'I mean, this is obviously highly irregular.'

'I have – until I'm blue in the face – but the hospital says I can't come as John needs complete rest and they're worried that my presence will disturb him.'

'Have you spoken to the company?'

'Regius? Oh, yes – but they treat me like Pass the Parcel. Someone always refers me to someone else. I tried calling the head man there—'

'Bouverie?'

'That's the one, but he's forever away.'

Bollocks, thinks Lebonneur, an expression he keeps unspoken. 'A likely story,' he says. 'Have you tried the police?'

'Just once – they told me that what goes on at the hospital is none of their business.'

'I suppose, technically, they're right.'

'So can you find out for me, Mr Lebonneur?'

'I shall certainly do my best. It's amazing how the *Record* still manages to open a few doors. I also know a couple of people at the hospital who might be able to shed some light.'

'I would be very grateful.'

'Not at all. One thing, though.'

'Yes?'

'Would you be willing to be interviewed about it?'

Mrs Mead pauses.

'The article would obviously be very sympathetic,' says Lebonneur.

Mrs Mead bites her bottom lip. 'Well, I don't see why not.'

Great, thinks Lebonneur. This should be a cracker. *Jersey builder in mystery accident*. 'That's very good of you, Mrs Mead – besides, I'm sure the publicity will help your case . . .'

A knocking on the front door. Mrs Mead frowns. 'I wonder who that is. Will you excuse me?'

'Of course.'

Lebonneur watches her walk down the corridor to the front door. 'Hello?'

He can hear the muffled response.

'Mrs Mead?'

'Yes?'

'My name is PC David Bonnard. I was wondering if my colleague and I could come in.'

The policeman is accompanied by a woman constable. Their faces are deeply serious. As they remove their hats, Lebonneur knows exactly why they have come – *Jersey builder in mystery death* – but then he curses himself for being too cynical and thinking in headlines.

* * *

The weather was beautiful that Saturday afternoon, although it did little to lift Pippa's spirits. Even the thought of a swim and some sunbathing over at St Brelade's held little appeal.

'Come on, darling, there's no need to be like this,' said her mother. 'You're worse than a teenager.'

Violet's temper had improved significantly since Dr Aubin had been round a couple of days ago. Fellowes and Smith, issued with their identity cards, were out of the house for the afternoon in an attempt to find a boat.

'I'm sorry,' said Pippa. 'I'm just feeling a little blue.'

'You'll get over him, you'll see.'

Pippa shut her eyes. Oh, God. Here we go again. The old bat hadn't stopped banging on about von Luck since he had taken them home on his horse. '*Mother*! Would you *please* stop this?'

'I only want what's best for you, that's all.'

Pippa did her best to keep cool. If there was anything guaranteed to make her want to see von Luck even more, it was her mother forbidding it. 'I'm sure you do, Mummy, I don't doubt it,' she said, grasping her mother's hands. 'It's sweet of you to look out for me, but you must remember that I'm no longer a little girl. I know you don't believe it but I'm capable of making my own decisions, and I promise you I'd never do anything to shame you. Yes, of course I find von Luck attractive – what woman wouldn't? – but does that mean I'm going to share his bed? No, not at all. Anyway, I'd have thought it was useful for us to have a German on our side.'

Violet looked at her. 'Will you promise me you won't?'

Pippa widened her eyes in an attempt to convey sincerity. 'Yes, mother. I promise.' It was a lie – of course it was. She saw no reason why she should curtail her behaviour just to suit her mother's and the islanders' mores. Pippa let go of Violet's hands. 'I think I will go out after all,' she said, 'I could do with some sun.'

'Where will you go?'

'Now, Mummy, I've made you a promise . . .'

'Sorry, I was just asking – I wasn't accusing you of anything.'

'I think I'll cycle over to St Brelade. I could do with the exercise.'

'All right, but be careful down the hill – your brakes are hardly–'

'Mummy!'

'Sorry, dear, but please be careful – you remember what happened to Eleanor's little girl.'

Pippa was about to explode, but she let it pass. It wasn't worth it: her mother would always be like this – well meaning but interfering. Would she be like this one day, when she was a mother? *When she was a mother*. It seemed the least likely thing in the world. She pecked her mother's forehead and whispered, 'See you later,' in the most reassuring tone she could adopt.

As she cycled away, feeling the breeze on her face, Pippa felt instantly relieved, unburdened. She even managed to wave hello to Mrs Miere – now she really was an old bat.

Violet watched Pippa walk her bicycle down the short drive to the road. It had been hard looking after her. Pippa was like her father – so sure of herself and so headstrong. They were qualities she had always found attractive in John, but not so in Pippa. Was she just being old fashioned? Perhaps. Pippa's generation would have to be tougher than hers, a little more pushy. Or maybe it was the occupation that had done it, depriving Pippa of a normal young adulthood.

She walked through into the sitting room, its furniture tired and tatty after years of enforced neglect. Above the mantelpiece was the photograph of John, which she took down. She missed him so very much. At least he would have known how to deal with their daughter. She smiled at the thought of the fireworks that would have erupted between them. But, then, so sad for John to have missed out on watching his daughter turn from a girl into a woman. Had she done a good job without him? She wasn't sure, because at the back of her mind ran the name 'Von Luck'. If he had been British she would have been delighted, but he was the enemy. Why was Pippa being so obstinate about that? Did she not know that it was tantamount to treachery to entertain the attentions of a German?

Mrs Campbell's moralising was rudely swept aside by a tremendous noise coming from the hall. What was that? It sounded like the door being broken. She dropped the photograph; the glass in the frame smashed into myriad pieces. No – it couldn't be this – it couldn't be what she had always feared, a fear that was confirmed by a German soldier bursting into the room, his submachine gun pointing directly at her. He was so enormous he seemed to fill the entire space. 'Hands up!'

She froze.

'I said, "Get your hands up!"'

Violet lifted her hands above her head. She could feel an almighty rush of adrenaline surging through her – her legs started to shake violently, but she did her best to control them.

Another soldier came into the room, followed by two men in plain blue suits. Gestapo. She shut her eyes briefly, willing them away. Thank God Pippa had gone out, and thank God again that Fellowes and Smith were not here.

'Mrs Campbell?' The voice was stentorian.

'Y-yes?'

'We are here to search your house for two escaped prisoners-of-war – Captain Edmond Fellowes and Pilot Officer Edward Smith. We understand that you are hiding them here.'

'I don't know what you're talking about!'

How did they know? Someone must have told them. Who? A neighbour? Mrs Miere? No – surely not. Not even she could be that treacherous.

'I think you do, Mrs Campbell,' said the agent, who indicated to the soldiers that they should search the house.

For the next minute, Violet trembled in silence, watched over by the two Gestapo men. She could hear the heavy clumping of boots, furniture being moved, furniture being destroyed, and even a window being broken. Savages. They would find nothing, she thought, for she had been meticulous.

The soldiers came back into the room.

'Nothing, sir,' said one, in German.

'*Nothing?*'

'Yes, sir.'

The agent approached Violet, his face so close to hers that she could detect stale tobacco on his breath. Coupled with her nerves, the smell almost made her retch.

'Where are they?'

The question was delivered slowly and simply.

'I'm – I'm sorry, Herr . . . Herr . . .'

'Bouhler.'

'. . . Herr Bouhler, but you must have been misinformed. It's

77

only me and my daughter who live here.' As she spoke, Violet became aware of the other agent walking round the room.

'You are lying, Mrs Campbell. You do realise what the penalty is for sheltering escaped prisoners?'

'Of course I do.'

'If you co-operate with us, I shall recommend that you receive a lesser sentence. Of course, if you do not the full force of law will have to be applied.'

Law, thought Violet. This was not law – not in the sense that she knew it. 'There is very little I can tell you,' she said, 'except I am not guilty of what you accuse me.'

The other agent was going through the desk now – she could hear him rifling through her papers.

'If you were a man,' said Bouhler, 'I would have hit you by now. But, as you know, we have a good reputation on these islands to maintain, so I am not going to touch you. At least, not yet.'

Violet thought that her heart was pounding so hard and so fast that it must be visible through her blouse. She had thought about torture – often in the small hours when she awoke – and whether she would be able to sustain it. Probably not, but she would damn well try. And even if she died, well, at least she would have done what was right. Better to die now with a clear conscience than live to a hundred with a guilty one. But don't be so defeatist – you're not caught yet.

The second agent came back into her line of vision. He was smiling. What had he found? He passed two sheets of paper to

Bouhler, who looked at them quizzically at first, before his face, too, broke into a smile. He held the pieces of paper up to her face. 'So, who are Edmond Le Quesne and Edward Lainé? Their Christian names seem familiar, Mrs Campbell.'

It took enormous strength of will to stop herself fainting, and Violet succeeded, at least until she was smacked violently across her right cheek.

Chapter Three

'I'M TELLING YOU, Bob, builders and workmen die the whole bloody time.'

'Not like this they don't.'

'What do you mean, "not like this"? You don't even know how this man Mead died, so how can you say, "not like this"?'

Lebonneur lights a cigarette. Christ, the man is being even more of an arsehole than usual. What is it about newspaper editors? Are they lobotomised as soon as they've accepted the job? Take one perfectly good journalist, make him an editor, *et voilà*! One brainless suit.

'*Look*,' says Lebonneur, stabbing his cigarette in the air, 'don't you think it just a little strange that his wife was not even allowed to see him? Isn't it a bit odd that they won't tell her how he died? I mean, for fuck's sake, that's just plain weird, Brian, plain bloody weird.'

'Perhaps he was so badly hurt that the hospital didn't want to upset her – come on, that's not so unusual.'

'You'd be right if that was what they told her, but they've told her fucking *nothing*!' On the last word, Lebonneur slams his right hand hard down on his desk. A whirlwind of ash rises from the overflowing ashtray, sending fragments of grey all over the keyboard.

'I'm not having this, Bob – I'm not having you talking to me like this. This isn't some Yank TV show in which the idiot editor is forever stifling the genius reporter.'

'Really?'

'Yes – *really*. I'm not an idiot and you're certainly no genius. You're just looking for something that means you won't have to do the flowers – well, it's not going to work.'

Lebonneur slumps back in his chair. A small voice tells him to think of Rachel and the kids, but he is too wound up, too spoiling for a fight. Besides, it's clear that his editor is fundamentally wrong. Lebonneur does his best to sound calm. 'I'm not saying I'm a genius, and I'm certainly not saying you're an idiot, Brian. When did I say that? Never. But you must listen to me – I'm the chief reporter on this paper for good reason. You employ me to know when something stinks, and this smells really bad, Brian, really very bad indeed. All I'm asking is that you give me a couple of days to ferret around. I'll *do* the flowers, of course I will, I can do them in my sleep, but please just let me have a look at this in the meantime. If I'm wrong and you're right, I'll do the flowers every bloody year until I retire. Come on, Brian, that's fair.'

Not a smile, not even the trace of one. 'I'm sorry, Bob, but it's still a no. Like I said, builders die every day on big projects like this – it's nothing more than a nib.'

'A *nib?*'

'That's right, Bob – a nib.'

This is ridiculous, thinks Lebonneur, bizarre. How can Mead's death be consigned to the 'News in Brief' section on page two? Why can't he see that it's so much more than that?

'I also don't think that it's going to help the hotel if we start running stories about dead workmen.'

Lebonneur sits up. '*Help the hotel?*'

'That's right. Mannez Heights is a big development – and it's more than good for Alderney, it's good for all the islands. Come on, you know how much we need tourists – what's the point in writing negative stories about things like this? Your man Mead was probably half cut and fell off some scaffolding. No doubt he looked a mess, and the doctors decided they didn't want to hurt his old dear's feelings. I admit they could have done a better job, but surely you can see that even if it was a story it's not going to do the islands a whole world of good if we bite the hand that feeds us.'

Lebonneur takes a long, pensive drag on his cigarette. So this was what it had come to – the interests of business rather than the interests of the public, all wrapped up in a bundle of clichés. He picks up the press release. 'So, are Regius Hotels PLC a big advertiser, then, Brian? Is that what this is about?'

'As a matter of fact they're not, *Bob*, and even if they were, my decision would be the same. And while we're at it, I don't particularly want to hear any bullshit about newspapers crusading for the truth and being the first draft of history – that's all crap, and you should know that by now. You've got to think of the bigger picture, think of what's good for the islands, what's good for their economies, what's good for all of us in the end.'

'What's good for the States, more like.'

'Oh, yes? What do you mean by that?'

'Stop being so naïve, Brian.'

'I'm sorry, Robert, I'm really not following you.'

Clumsily Lebonneur extinguishes his cigarette, sending more ash over his desk. The butt continues to smoke, its trail curling up satisfyingly towards his editor's face. 'You know as well as I do,' says Lebonneur, 'that those old farts on the States are as bent as a three-bob note. Hotels like Mannez Heights only go up if the backhanders are large enough – I'm sure it happens in poor little Alderney as much as it happens here.'

A sigh from his editor. 'Not this again. You've been banging on about this for—'

'For *years*,' says Lebonneur, 'and for years you've never let me write it. All right, occasionally I'm allowed to expose some small fry, but so what? Councillors are on the fiddle all over Britain, and the same goes for us here. But it's not just about some bloke taking his mistress on a free trip to St Malo with lunch at the Duchesse Anne, but about systemic corruption. The whole States needs to be pulled down and started again—'

'Robert—'

'—and finally replaced by some decent, honest people, and not just a pack of venal lawyers desperate to line their already luxurious nests with, I don't know, fucking finest angora—'

'Robert!'

'What?'

'Just do the flowers, OK?'

He regrets the word before he even utters it: 'No.'

'No?'

'That's right. *No.*'

'So you're refusing to do as I say? You know what this means?'

'It doesn't mean anything, Brian, because as of this second I am no longer your employee.'

'You're back early, darling.'

'Am I?'

Rachel looks at him quizzically. 'Bob? Whatever's the matter?'

Lebonneur lifts his hands in the air as if to indicate nothing, but his face is too loaded with meaning to fool his wife of fifteen years.

'Are you drunk?'

'No - although I've been trying to get drunk for the past three hours.'

Rachel's head sinks forward, her chin briefly resting on her chest. 'Oh, no, not this again. Why, Bob? What now?'

'I've . . . I've . . . Well, I might as well tell you straight . . . Where are the children by the way?'

'Over at Katherine and Ian's. Tell me what?'

'I've resigned.'

A pause. Lebonneur watches his wife take a deep breath and let it out. She opens her mouth, as if she is about to speak, then closes it. She does so again before she finally manages to get something out. 'Why? Why, Bob? *Why?*'

What to tell her? Brian was right in a way – to give her the crusading-journalist bit would sound crap. He was only the bloody reporter on a newspaper in Jersey, for Christ's sake, not Woodward and Bernstein. 'Well,' he says eventually, 'I didn't want to cover the flowers.'

It sounds pathetic, childish.

'*What?*'

'I didn't want to cover the flowers. I wanted to do something else, but that shit of an editor wouldn't let me so I resigned.'

'You resigned over *that?* For heaven's sake, Bob, what on earth are we going to *do?*' Her voice is high-pitched now, not hysterical, because Rachel is not that sort of woman. Her calmness is one of the reasons Lebonneur married her.

'I'm sorry, Rachel, I really am. I'll find something, I'm sure of it. May I at least have a hug before you slap me or whatever it is you want to do?'

He walks over to Rachel, a little unsteady on his feet. She embraces him as though he were a dustbin.

'You could hug me a bit tighter than that,' he says.

She doesn't hug him any tighter. Instead she releases him. She holds him by the hands and looks him straight in the eye. 'Listen to me, Bob. I know you're pissed, but just listen.'

86

Lebonneur nods. He doesn't believe himself to be drunk, which, the back of his mind tells him, means he probably is.

'Have you really resigned? Or have you just said you have?'

'No, I've definitely resigned.'

'In writing?'

'No.'

'So you could ring Brian tomorrow morning and say you've made a mistake?'

'Not a chance.'

'Why not?'

'Because I'm not going back there. I've left, do you see? Gone. Kaput. *Finito*. Black bin-bag gone. Vamoosed.'

'All right! All right!'

'That cunt wanted me to do the flowers—'

'So you've told me. What I'd like to know is, how are we going to pay the mortgage?'

'We'll manage,' says Lebonneur, walking into the sitting room. 'We can always sell my mother's house.'

'And then what?' says Rachel, following him. 'It's not enough to live on for ever.'

'I know, I know, but it'll buy me some time. Perhaps I'll just do something completely different. I don't know. Sell cheese or something. Make black butter. Maybe even wine. *Wine*. Now, there's an idea . . .'

'What are you doing?'

'What does it look like? Pouring myself a – what is this?

Pouring myself a J&B blended something or other. Nothing special, cooking whisky, but it'll do.'

'I wish you wouldn't.'

'Sorry, darling, but it's not every day you resign.' Lebonneur takes a small sip from the glass, as if out of respect for her. 'There,' he says. 'I'm not drinking to get drunk, just going to enjoy the taste.'

Rachel folds her arms. 'I can see there's no point in talking to you now.'

'You're probably right.'

Lebonneur sits – or, rather, collapses – on to a large armchair. 'Aaah,' he sighs, 'do you know what, darling? For the first time in twenty – no, *twenty-five* years, I feel like a free man.'

'Congratulations, Robert. Very well done.'

' "Robert". I must be in the doghouse.'

Rachel doesn't reply, but instead looks at him with an expression distilled from pity and scorn.

'By the way, darling,' says Lebonneur, 'what are all these cardboard boxes doing in here?'

'They're from your mother's house – they're full of letters, scrapbooks, photographs, diaries. I've been going through them.'

'Wow. There's quite a lot of stuff.'

'Yes, Robert. There is a lot of stuff.'

Her tone, unnoticed by Lebonneur, is that used by tired adults when talking to a small child. He stands up.

'Now what are you doing?'

'I think I'm going to have a look through some of that stuff.'

'Please – not now.'

'It's *my* mother's stuff.'

'Yes, but I'm the one who's been working through it. I'm not having you – oh, God, all right, do what you like. I'm going out. I'll see you later – much later, probably.'

'You're not leaving me, are you?'

Rachel stares back.

'Come on,' he says, 'surely there's nothing more irresistible than a jobless drunk.'

Just before she turns on her heel, Lebonneur swears that he sees the trace of a smile. Too good for me, he thinks, then opens a cardboard box, from which an invisible cloud of dust wafts out, causing him to sneeze. 'What a lot of stuff.'

He finds the diary after an hour.

There are at least two dozen boxes in all, and the first three Lebonneur sifts through are full of small black-and-white photographs, some of which have been stuck into large burgundy albums that smell faintly of damp. The next few contain letters, mostly written in immaculate copperplate. For the most part they are mundane – bread-and-butter stuff – but Lebonneur finds himself grinning at the occasional reference to an argument or someone's misbehaviour.

Some of the boxes contain shoes and hats – why are these being kept? – and then there at least seven or eight full of books. All this lot can go down to the library, thinks Lebonneur. They're mostly a dull lot. He can't understand why Rachel hasn't taken them there already. Perhaps, he thinks charitably, she wanted him to go through them first. Treherne. Etherege. *The Theme of Wonder in the Eighteenth Century*. No thanks.

Just as Lebonneur is closing the box, his eye is caught by the spine of a small brown book. He doesn't know why he notices it because there is nothing remarkable about it. Perhaps it is that – its very lack of remarkability. Lebonneur puts it down to his bloody-mindedness and pulls it out.

There is a small piece of brown string threaded through the covers, which Lebonneur eventually breaks, rather than unties, with drunken difficulty. He opens the book, the spine cracking. He leafs through its handwritten contents, absentmindedly at first, then with increasing curiosity.

'Hello,' he says, 'it's in German.'

He takes a swig from his glass and, without looking, tries to place it back on the side table. The attempt is unsuccessful, as the glass and its contents fall on to the floor.

'Oh, fuck!'

Lebonneur gets up in a vague quest to find something in the kitchen to mop up the whisky, but he is pulled down again by the book. He glances briefly at the carpet – it'll be fine, he thinks. Anyway, he can't get any deeper into the doghouse.

It does not take Lebonneur long to realise that he is holding a diary. The dates and his O-level German tell him that it was written between 2 February 1944 and 4 April 1945, although there are plenty of blank pages after the final entry. Why? Did the writer just get bored with writing it? Had he lost it? Whose diary was it anyway?

Lebonneur flicks the pages back to the beginning. There is no name to be found. Come on, give me a clue, give me a clue. Nothing – not even a set of initials. He sits back, and starts leafing through the entries to see if he can find any familiar words among the German. St Helier . . . St Ouen . . . St Brelade . . . Linden Court . . . Rozel Manor . . . St Helier . . . Linden Court . . . Linden Court.

He notices that 'Linden Court' appears particularly frequently, most regularly near the beginning of entries. This has to be where the diarist lived, he thinks. Linden Court. It sounds grand, although Lebonneur has never heard of it.

Clumsily, he reaches for the telephone and dials a five-digit number.

'Société Jersiaise,' comes a polite-sounding woman's voice.

'Ah, hello,' says Lebonneur, collecting himself. 'Is Terry there?'

'Just hold on – who is it, please?'

'Tell him it's Bob.'

'Hold on.'

Lebonneur holds on for an age, although he does not notice the time passing, as he is trying to translate the diary.

'Hello?'

'Terry?'

'Speaking.'

'Terry, hi, it's Bob here.'

'Hello! How the devil are you?'

'Fine, just fine. Listen, I wanted to ask you a quick question. You know all about the occupation, don't you?'

'Pretty much. It is sort of my job.'

'Do you know which German lived at a place called Linden Court?'

'Up on St Saviour's?'

'If you say so.'

'That'd be Max von Luck, Lieutenant Colonel Max von Luck to be precise.'

'Who the hell was he?'

'He was the head of civilian affairs for the Germans. Liaised between us and them. He was well liked by all accounts. Quite the gent, and a bit of a ladies' man into the bargain.'

'What happened to him?'

'Well, no one's quite sure. Some say he became a POW after the war, but no records confirm that. I think I'm right in saying that my predecessor tried to track him down in Germany some time in the early seventies, but he drew a blank.'

'He can't have just disappeared.'

'People did, Bob. A lot of people. Some used the confusion at the end of the war to start a new life, clean slate and all that.'

'How about South America? I thought all the Nazis ended up there.'

'Many did, but I doubt von Luck was among them. He was no Nazi. Not for him cocktails with Mengele.'

Lebonneur laughs. 'Sounds like a crap play,' he says.

'What? *Cocktails with Mengele*? Ha!'

'Well, Terry, thanks very much for that.'

'Why do you ask anyhow?'

'Well, I think I've just found his diary.'

'*Really?*'

'Yes – it's just turned up in my mother's stuff.'

'You know, I'd love to have a look at it.'

'Well, why not come round now?'

A pause.

'All right – I'll see you in half an hour.'

'I must warn you – I'm a bit smashed.'

'Oh?'

'I'll tell you when you get here.'

Lebonneur puts down the phone and carries on looking through the diary. Soon another word leaps out at him. As he rifles through the pages, he notices that it becomes increasingly frequent. The word, which because of recent events resonates deeply with Lebonneur, is 'Alderney'.

* * *

The hill up from the beach at St Brelade was steep, and even though Pippa swore to herself she would stay on the saddle, she had to walk the bicycle up the last two hundred yards. It had been a pleasant couple of hours on the beach, she thought, barring the unsolicited attention of a persistent German soldier, who had strutted and preened his somewhat emaciated form past her every ten minutes. She was accustomed to such attention, although that did not make it any more welcome. There had been a desperation in the man's eyes that she had found almost comic, and she had done her best not to laugh. More often than not, their mighty conquerors had precious little ego when it came to such matters, and Pippa had been told that some Germans had turned deeply unpleasant when their crude wooings had been rebuffed. There had been rapes, of course, but those who had been violated had never reported it, for fear of earning the unwanted 'Jerrybag' sobriquet. It was unfair, but there were many – especially the older women – who maintained that even to have been raped suggested that the girl must have given the Jerry some sort of signal.

Breathless, Pippa reached the top of the hill, and started freewheeling her bone-shattering bicycle down towards St Aubin's Bay, at the other end of which was St Helier. High Trees was on the outskirts of town, and Pippa estimated that she would be home in time for tea – albeit far from the type of tea they would have enjoyed before the war. They had no bread, no butter, no jam, no biscuits, not even tea itself. Instead, bramble leaves provided an ersatz version of the beverage, a drink many islanders had been doing their best to enjoy for almost two years. You could still buy tea, but only if you were willing to part with thirty pounds for a mere pound. Tobacco was even more expensive – Pippa had heard that the going rate was now a hundred and twelve pounds per pound. Islanders knew that anybody who smoked proper cigarettes and drank real tea had either struck it rich on the black market or was sharing their bed with a German.

The image immediately brought von Luck's face to her mind. She smiled when she thought of him, a reaction that she became aware of as she neared the bottom of the hill. She must look like an idiot, her tatty skirt billowing behind her, a huge grin on her face. Or perhaps she did not look like an idiot, but rather as though she was in love. *Love?* No, that was impossible – she was not in love with the man, she hardly knew him. He was certainly handsome, tall, well built, but those qualities alone were not enough for love.

Pippa pedalled hard along the path that curved in unison with the sweep of the bay. Other cyclists and those on foot either wobbled or jumped as she approached them, her left thumb frantically pinging the bicycle's rusty bell. *Love?* Yes to lust, certainly, no question about that, but love was something else. She was far too old to fall in love just like that – she was no longer a girl, for Pete's sake. And yet was it possible? There was indeed something in von Luck's manner that touched her deeply, made her lose her breath whenever she saw him.

She reached the bottom of Le Mont Marais five minutes later. Although it was not a steep climb it was a long one, and she knew that she would be cycling especially slowly around the entrance to the German Field Command. That would mean more lascivious attention from the Jerries, but that was unavoidable. Eyes firmly ahead, ignore the guttural catcalls, and that would be the end of it.

However, Pippa was surprised to find that the guards paid her little attention. Normally there would have been a wave, some sort of lustful acknowledgement, but today there was nothing. The four men on duty were looking straight ahead, their expressions rigid. Perhaps it was the presence of this new admiral, thought Pippa; apparently he was a stickler for discipline.

It was not until she saw the face of Mrs Miere that Pippa started to feel uneasy. For the first time in ages, the old bat was actually smiling. There she was, walking along the pavement towards her, no doubt on her way to bridge with Mrs Cohu, with a large yellow smile tightly stretched across her leathery features. Why was she so happy? As long as Pippa had known her, Mrs Miere had never smiled, had never allowed her lips to form anything apart from a downwards movement.

'Good afternoon, Miss Campbell,' said Mrs Miere, as Pippa cycled past her.

The shock of the greeting almost dismounted her. Pippa braked hard and turned round.

'Good after—' Pippa began, her sentence interrupted by the fact that Mrs Miere continued to walk down the hill, her head wobbling in a way that Pippa had always found infuriating and a mark of her meddlesome nature.

Pippa stood and stared. Why was the old bat so happy? There was surely nothing that could make her so, apart from . . . No, it was inconceivable. There had been rumours about informers since the day after the invasion, but nobody knew for sure. Pippa remembered Dr Aubin once telling her how the Gestapo headquarters down on the Havre des Pas in St Helier often received anonymous letters inviting the police to search the house of Mr and Mrs So-and-So for their illegal supply of coal or, worse than that, a radio. Rumour, thought Pippa, as she watched the figure of Mrs Miere walking away from her, it was just rumour.

Pippa started pedalling once more, her heart rate increased not only by the physical exertion. Something was wrong, she knew it. The faces of the guards, Mrs Miere's sly greeting – both created in her a feeling of panic. Her legs started to tremble as she pushed down on the pedals. She might be cycling to her death – a death that lay just round the corner. All she had to do was turn down Wellington Road, and there would be a squad of Germans, rifles at the ready, poised to release a volley of shots that would tear her to pieces. Was she being melodramatic? Perhaps Mrs Miere was simply in a rare good mood. And it was also possible that the guards had been recently disciplined.

The entrance to Wellington Road approached on the left. The walls, the pavement, the occasional daffodils – all looked so ordinary, so peaceful. Pippa looked for a sign, a clue that might reveal something was amiss, but there was nothing. That was the problem – *nothing*. Or, more specifically, *no one*. It was a pleasant Saturday afternoon – she would have expected at least to see Mr Falla tending his flowerbeds. But there was no Mr Falla, an absence that was as strange to Pippa as the smile on Mrs Miere's face.

Pippa turned left, reckoning that if she was entering a trap, she was probably already in it. She prayed hard that nothing was wrong, that her mother was simply waiting for the kettle to boil, and that Fellowes and Smith were still out on their reconnaissance.

She pressed down on the pedals. She would cycle past the house, look to see if everything was all right. It was a good compromise, Pippa thought, the only option now that she had come this close.

She looked to her left as she rode past. For the fraction of a second, everything looked normal – the wrought-iron gates, the flowerbeds up the short drive, the peeling green paint of the window-frames . . . The window! There was a face, she was sure of it. It was only a glimpse, but there was a face, a pale face, a man's face. It had moved as she cycled past, darted back into the darkness of the upstairs bedroom. One of the officers? No, definitely not. It was cruel face, almost like the one Pippa remembered from the cover of a book of ghost stories she had once owned.

She cycled hard now. She wanted to cry, scream, but part of her insisted that she must not break down, that she must keep going. Mummy, – oh, no, oh, God no. Where could she go? Whom could she trust? Nobody. These bloody islanders, these fucking people. They were cowards, traitors, even. Why weren't they all doing their bit? Why was it only the few of them that helped the escaped POWs, the escaped Todt workers? Oh, God, Mummy, what have they done to you? I'm so sorry, so sorry.

'Halt!'

The shout came from behind her.

'*Halt!*'

Halt? Should she? What if she didn't? They would shoot her. But if they captured her they would shoot her anyway. Keep pedalling, don't give up. There was an alleyway just up to the right – if she could make that she would be safe, at least for the time being.

A dull crack. What was that? A gunshot? Oh, please let me live, let me live. But don't just plead – *act*. You'll only live if you do something. Swerve, that's it, swerve, make it harder for them to hit you.

Pippa's swerve was more of a wobble, but it was no less effective for that. Although she didn't know it, the second shot missed her right shoulder by less than a foot. If she hadn't swerved it would certainly have hit her. Here's the alleyway, Pippa thought, make sure you don't fall off as you turn into it.

It was too late for Pippa to curse herself for not looking after her bicycle properly, but curse herself she did as she found herself losing her balance. A deep sudden pain on her right hip, then at the top of her right arm as dirt and grit dug and scraped into her bare flesh. All she could see was what was ahead of her. The alleyway, run down that alleyway. Ignore the pain, because what you have to do today is to live. That is all you have to do – stay alive. Stay alive for Mummy, for Daddy. Stay alive for the POWs – oh, God! Smith and Fellowes! What would happen to them?

The alleyway was formed by the back fences of gardens, fences too high for her to scale. She was half running, half limping, looking desperately for a gap, a hole, a hiding-place. She knew that any second now she would feel the brutal blow of a bullet smashing into her back and knocking her to the ground with the force of ten fists.

She was living for each second, her brain trying frantically to work out how to ensure that her body would stay alive until the next second. She could think no further ahead than that, her life compressed into a series of insignificant portions of time.

There was a gap! Thank you, God, thank you. Pippa didn't turn round. If she had, she would have been petrified by the sight of four soldiers entering the alleyway, the leader of whom had just spotted where she was going. Instead she found herself running into a small garden, at the end of which was a house similar to High Trees. A vague sense of propriety told her that she was trespassing, that this was wrong, but she dismissed the absurdity of it.

She ran up to a wooden-and-glass door and wrenched it open. Unlocked!

'Who the hell are you?'

A man with a moustache. A cardigan with holes at the elbows. The smell of old pipesmoke. She recognised him – it was that old colonel, whatshisname. Does it matter? No. Just barge past him, knock him over, he'll be all right. Pippa did so, sending the old man colliding with a coat stand.

'I'm sorry!' she shouted. 'Sorry.'

The apology felt ridiculous, but the necessity to utter it was deeply engrained. Never mind that she was running for her life, manners were manners. How very English, how very stupid. Pippa knew where the house was – it was on the main road. If she ran out of here, she might be seen, but she knew that running back was out of the question.

She opened the front door, and darted across the lawn, through some rose bushes – more pain! – and on to the pavement. There was nobody – at least, nobody to be seen. Which way? Right? No – that would take her back to the entrance of her road. Straight across? One large, open field – no cover. So it had to be left then, up towards St Saviour's school. There were lots of big houses up that way and big gardens, with shrubs and trees.

Big houses. Perhaps there was someone she could trust.

*　　*　　*

Von Luck had reached Linden Court that Saturday afternoon at just after five o'clock. After seeing Marais and Mollett to their car, he had decided that there was nothing he could achieve by staying at his desk. He usually found that his head cleared as soon as he stepped out of the building, instantly ridding itself of the bureaucratic clutter of quotas, permits, orders, questions, requests, demands, statistics and God knew what. He needed to think, to work out how to stop the deportation, something he found more hateful with every passing minute.

Although von Luck did not find the exterior of Linden Court particularly agreeable – far too 1920s boxy and modern – the interior was spacious and comfortable. The furniture was almost agreeable, von Luck thought, although much of it was new, barring a shabby old armchair that was by far the most comfortable in the house, an armchair in which he was presently sitting before an unlit fire.

He was tempted to pour himself a drink – perhaps a glass of Alsace Sylvaner he had found in the cellar – but he decided against it. No, he must clear his head after that schnapps. What he did need was tobacco, a craving that forced him over to a low oak table, on top of which was a silver case that contained some unmentionably stale cigarettes, which bore his family's crest.

After the first drag von Luck coughed – did these things really help clear your lungs? – walked over to the mantelpiece and leaned against it. How? How? Sabotage the boat? Pointless – there were plenty more boats. Convince Huffmeier that it was a bad idea, and that it might well get them all imprisoned – or worse – after the war? Impossible. Huffmeier would only listen to those above him, and on these islands there was no one above him. He reported only to Berlin. *Berlin*. Perhaps there was something in that. A forged order, telling Huffmeier to put the deportation on hold? It was risky, but it was bound to be. Besides, thought von Luck, it would be unspeakable to sit there and let a thousand innocent people go to their deaths.

Huffmeier had never told von Luck which department in Berlin had issued the order, and he knew better than to ask: nosiness only got you into trouble with Nazis such as the admiral. Such men had dwelt for well over a decade in an atmosphere of suspicion and distrust, which had made them extremely wary of anyone who asked for information, no matter how innocuous the request.

However, there would be others who knew. Heidi von Aufsess for certain – she had handled all of the general's correspondence, and was presumably doing the same for the admiral. There was also Oberleutnant Petersen at the Naval Communications Centre, with whom von Luck was on good terms. He saw nearly every signal that came to and from the islands, and would definitely have dealt with an important order from Berlin. There would be others, but those were the two von Luck knew well enough to be able to trust – or, rather, to hope he could trust. If they failed, he would ask Hempel to ask Major Schwalm – it was a last resort, but Schwalm was the type of puffed-up little prick who took much delight in showing off that he was directly connected to Berlin.

Whom should he ask first? He would certainly get a response from Heidi, but von Luck had no wish to be in her debt. She was no blackmailer, but it made him feel uncomfortable to think she might gain some sort of hold on him. Although intelligent, she might not understand his motive and would ask too many questions, too many awkward questions. No, he would try Petersen first. He was no Nazi, and neither would he be the type to raise his eyebrows.

Von Luck flicked his cigarette into the fireplace. He coughed again, hackingly. Blasted things. So this was it – phone Petersen, find out who had sent the telegram, then do his best to forge another incoming signal. He would need Petersen's help for that,

too, but von Luck could not count on it until he had performed
the first favour. And what if Petersen should refuse? Well, he
would have to appeal to his better nature. There was no other
way – at least, no other way that didn't involve threats and
violence.

Von Luck walked over to the telephone. He paused before he
picked it up. After this phone call there was no going back.
Effectively, he was becoming a traitor, but von Luck brushed that
off as a legal nicety. How could one betray a country that had
been taken over by a bunch of gangsters? They were just
hoodlums, he thought, common criminals. Von Luck had heard
that Schellenberg, the head of the SS intelligence service, even
had a machine gun built into his desk in Berlin. Very Al Capone,
very Chicago, typical picture-book gangster stuff. There was no
way that von Luck was going to be loyal to people like that, to
people who murdered and called it lawful.

He swallowed, then lifted the phone to his ear. Being so close
to the Field Command, he normally had a good connection, but
it was a tense half-minute before an operator was on the line.

'Good afternoon,' came a female voice in German.

'Could you connect me to Oberleutnant Petersen at Naval
Communications?'

'Hold on, please, sir.'

Von Luck did so. He gave it a fifty per cent chance that
Petersen would be there. He looked out of the window – the
light was fading, but it was going to be a fine evening, almost
spring-like. It had hardly been the best afternoon to spend

104

indoors, but such thoughts were merely wistful compared to the vexed question of the deportation.

The other thought that ran through von Luck's mind as he waited was the conversation he had had with Dr Aubin, which could not have been worse timed. With Marais and Mollett waiting awkwardly in the corridor, Von Luck had told Aubin that he would only start obeying the British when the British had won the war. He appreciated that he had some reputation as a ladies' man, but his affairs – and they were not as numerous as people suggested – were always discreet. It was a matter for him and Miss Campbell if any relationship was to occur, and not for a medical man. Naturally von Luck did not tell Aubin that he found Pippa attractive, and had merely dismissed her as 'presentable and very English'. Von Luck knew that Aubin was too sly to take such a comment at face value, but there was little time in which to convince him otherwise.

'Oberleutnant zur Zee Petersen speaking.'

At first, von Luck didn't notice the voice in his ear.

'Hello?' said Petersen. 'Who is this?'

'Petersen! I am sorry – Lieutenant Colonel von Luck here.'

'Good afternoon, von Luck. How can I help you?'

'I'm afraid that this is a very delicate matter, Petersen,' said von Luck, the phrase reminding him of the type of language Aubin had employed.

'Carry on.'

'I need you to track down a cable for me. It was sent to the admiral from Berlin.'

There was a pause.

'On whose authority is this request being made?'

'No authority apart from that of one decent man to another.'

He hoped Petersen understood. 'Decent men' – that was what they called each other, those who were against the Nazis. A few of them had drunk a clandestine toast last July in Linden Court, after the failed bomb plot that had so nearly killed Hitler, to the 'decent men' among them. Petersen had been there, and he had raised his glass.

'I see,' said Petersen, a note of apprehension in his voice.

'I wouldn't ask unless I thought it important,' said von Luck.

A sigh.

'All right, then, maybe.'

'Thank you, Petersen – I mean it.'

'What's the cable?'

'It would have come in earlier this week, straight from Berlin, top secret, for the admiral only, and it would be concerning a request for civilian labour from Jersey to go to Alderney.'

'I can't tell you about them,' said Petersen.

'*Them?*'

'Well, there were two cables. But that's all I can tell you.'

'Come on, Petersen, you could at least tell me who they were from.'

There is a pause.

'Petersen?'

'All right, one was from Speer, and one from . . . I shouldn't say.'

'Petersen! Please! I beg you!'

Petersen sighed. 'And one from Bormann, of all people.'

'What did it say?'

'That all work on Alderney was of the utmost importance, and anybody who interfered with it would be summarily shot.'

Von Luck breathed out. 'Did it say what sort of work was going on?'

'No. But I can tell you there have been several cables about Alderney recently. I've had to route quite a few to that idiot Schwalm.'

'And none of them gave any clue as to what's happening?'

'Nothing. Although whatever it is must be dangerous, because Schwalm says he's losing labourers faster than he can replace them.'

'Losing them? How? Sickness?'

'I'm not a fucking oracle! I've told you far too much as it is. For heaven's sake, von Luck, what are you trying to do?'

Von Luck paused. It looked as though he had pushed Petersen as far as he would go. Was it wise to ask the man to help him? If Petersen was caught concocting a cable, he would be executed. Well, too bad, there was no other option. Maybe Petersen had a little more to give.

'I need something else,' von Luck said, 'something that might get you into trouble, a lot of trouble.'

'Come on, von Luck, the war is nearly over. I've got a family to get back to. Please don't ask me to do anything dangerous.'

'It's essential, Petersen. I really must insist that you help me.'

'Whatever it is, I won't do it.'

'Will you at least listen to what it is?'

Another sigh. 'No. Or, at least, not over the telephone.'

'So you'll come and see me? Talk it over here at Linden Court?'

'All right – I will. When?'

'As soon as you can.'

'What? Tonight?'

'Yes,' said von Luck. 'Any time. As soon as you come off duty.'

'It'll be about eight o'clock.'

'Thank you, Petersen, thank you.'

'But I won't guarantee anything.'

'Fine.'

Just as von Luck replaced the telephone, he heard an almighty smash coming from the rear of the house. It sounded like the kitchen door. Who the hell was it? The Gestapo? It had to be! But how did they know? What could they know?

Von Luck rapidly unbuttoned his holster and withdrew his Luger. There was no way he was going to die a criminal's death, beaten up by these bastards in some tawdry cell. He would kill some of them at the very least, and no doubt he would be shot, but at least it would be a soldier's death. His late father would have been proud of him, he thought. He had hated the Nazis, hated what they had done to what he proudly called 'the most civilised nation in the world'.

He pointed the pistol at the door, but far from the clumping of boots and the shouts that he expected, all he could hear was the sound of a single person running down the corridor. Who, in God's name, was this? Mrs May, the housekeeper? No – it was her night off. A thief, then?

Von Luck took the slack off the Luger's trigger as the drawing-room door was slammed open. He almost fired it at the intruder, not out of self-defence but from shock at her identity. 'Miss Campbell! What's the matter?'

He put the Luger on an oak table and rushed to greet her. She looked a mess – her skirt was torn, her right arm bleeding, her face almost blue with exertion. Raped, thought von Luck, she must have been raped. 'Sit down. Here – you must sit down.' Von Luck led her to a sofa, on to which Pippa collapsed.

'My mother . . . they've got my mother . . .'

'Who, Miss Campbell? Who?'

'The Germans . . .'

'The Germans? Which Germans?'

It would have been some soldiers down on the beach – it had happened before and the rapists had been shot. Von Luck swore to himself that whoever had done this would meet a similar fate.

'The Gest– the Gestapo,' Pippa blurted out.

'*The Gestapo*? Are you sure?'

'Yes – I saw one of them. He was in the upstairs window. They chased after me – nowhere else to go but here. Will you promise me I'll be safe? Please? And my mother? Promise me she'll be safe too?'

'Where are they?'

'I don't know – I think I must have – must have got away from them.'

Von Luck looked out of the window – nobody was coming up the drive. 'Why the Gestapo, Miss Campbell? Why would they want you and your mother?'

Pippa looked straight into von Luck's eyes. Once again, he couldn't help but be struck by the intensity of their expression, the brilliance of their pale green. Even though she was scared, deeply scared, von Luck still found himself attracted to her. She was breathing less heavily now, although the pants were giving way to sobs. 'They've got her,' she began, her eyes still holding his, 'because we are . . . we are sheltering those two prisoners-of-war.'

Von Luck shut his eyes and gripped Pippa's arms. '*Mein Gott*,' he murmured. '*Mein Gott*.' He looked at her. 'You're being serious?'

She nodded, which caused von Luck to shake his head. He released his hands from her arms.

'They even ate your pigeon,' she said, laughing nervously.

Von Luck reciprocated with a laugh that was little more than a defined breathing out through his nostrils. He then breathed in deeply. 'I am sorry, but there is little I can do, Miss Campbell.'

'What? There must be *something*.'

'This uniform is not a British uniform,' he said, 'and, on paper, you and I are enemies.' He felt wretched, but what else could he say?

'I know that,' said Pippa, forcefully, 'but I am appealing to you as a decent human being. You're not like the rest of them.'

'Decent.' The word struck a chord with von Luck. She was right, of course, but it would not be enough to stop him doing his duty. 'All I might be able to do, Miss Campbell,' he began, measuring his words, 'is make sure that you and your mother are not . . . are not . . . dealt with as harshly as military law allows.'

Pippa stood up. Her eyes were furious now, glowering at von Luck as though he was something less than scum. 'You *are* like the rest of them!' she shouted. 'All your kindnesses were simply a means of getting into my – my knickers!'

'Please, Miss Campbell, it would be best if you did not shout.'

'I might as well have let myself be captured! You're going to hand me to them anyway!'

Pippa turned and made for the door. She really was about to leave, thought von Luck, to throw herself to those dogs. His mind raced. The easiest thing would be to let her go, but it would be the hardest thing to live with. And if she stayed? Well, that would create enormous difficulties, but at least he would be able to look at himself in the mirror. 'Where are you going, Miss Campbell?'

'What does it look like?'

'Please, Miss Campbell, it would be better if you stayed here for a little longer, yes? Perhaps we can work something out.'

Pippa paused. 'I think I know what you mean.'

It took von Luck a few seconds to realise what she was implying. 'No!' he said. 'In the name of God, no! This is not a way of taking advantage of you – despite what you think. I am

111

really not that type of man. It would simply be wrong of me to let you leave. The Gestapo are still prowling around for you, no doubt – I couldn't have it on my conscience that I just let you fall into their hands.'

Pippa shook her head. 'But what difference does it make? You're still going to hand me in eventually.'

She walked briskly towards the door.

'Miss Campbell! Come back here – I mean it.'

Pippa looked round to see that von Luck was aiming his Luger at her. He was smiling.

'Does this help to make up your mind?' he asked.

Pippa summoned up the trace of a smile. 'Yes,' she said. 'I suppose it does.'

'Now – come back here and sit down.'

Pippa did so, her eyes warily studying the gun.

'Good,' said von Luck. 'Now, you stay there while I shut the curtains and go and check out at the back.'

'Colonel,' she said, 'I'm very grateful.'

'There's no need. You're right, I'm not like the rest of them.'

After closing the curtains, von Luck left the drawing room, his Luger still in his hand. He walked down to the kitchen and looked out into the back garden. No one. She had done well, he thought. God knows how she had given them the slip. She must have run like the wind. He poured himself some water, drank it, then refilled the glass for Pippa. What in God's name was he going to do with her?

* * *

Corporal Roland Giesing was dying for a cigarette. He was hungry, too, almost famished, but given the choice between a plate of *bratwurst* and a cigarette, he would still have plumped for the tobacco. It was just like Heinrich had said the other night: food makes you want a cigarette, but cigarettes do not make you want food. Better, then, to smoke and kill the hunger. But sentry duty was always the worst – hour upon hour of standing around, a time that cried out for a healthy supply of cigarettes.

'Come on, Franz – you must have a cigarette somewhere in that shabby tunic of yours.'

Giesing's fellow sentry, Lance Corporal Franz Heim, was unable to oblige.

'I'm sorry, Roland, I've already told you, I've run out.'

'Rubbish,' said Giesing. 'I saw you having one earlier on.'

'My last.'

'I don't believe you.'

'That's too bad – it's the truth.'

The two men remained in silence for a while. They were guarding the resistance nest at Bel Royal, which was in the middle of the bay. Their duties included controlling the traffic, such as it was, that passed along the road. Already six o'clock, it would be curfew in an hour, so Giesing was expecting an easy six hours until midnight.

The sergeant had told them to be on the lookout for two

escaped prisoners-of-war, who were disguised as labourers called Le Quesne and Lainé, but both Giesing and Heim had been rather wary about the prospect of catching them. Hadn't they killed a guard at the camp? They had, the sergeant said, so be careful. There was a manhunt going on all over the island, he added, and all sentries were required to be especially vigilant. Both Heim and Giesing had looked at each other, their eyes registering mutual cowardice. There was no way, thought Giesing, that he was going to risk his neck to capture some POWs. Not now, not when the Allies were doing so well.

The noise of a car disturbed Giesing's thoughts. It was approaching from the direction of St Helier and it was driving rapidly. Giesing squinted in the dim light, and made out that it was a small Opel. He knew who that was – the Gestapo. Better to wave them through, rather than endure their scowls. 'Here come our friends from the old boarding-house,' he said.

Heim laughed. The fact that the Gestapo occupied such an unsinister building still caused amusement among the rank-and-file, even those who had been on the island for five years. 'They look as though they're in a hurry,' he said.

'They always are. I suppose we should let them through.'

However, the car began to slow down, and it soon pulled to a halt in front of the two men. A thin, pallid face leaned out from the passenger window and shouted at them: 'Corporal! A young woman! Have you seen a young woman?'

If the man's face hadn't been so disquieting, Giesing would have cracked a ribald joke. 'No,' he replied.

'We're looking for a Miss Philippa Campbell. She is wanted for sheltering the two prisoners-of-war. Got that? Philippa Campbell! Let no one go past without checking their papers, no matter how innocent they look.'

Giesing nodded, at which point the driver of the Opel gunned its engine and sped off.

'She must be a bad girl, this Miss Campbell,' said Giesing.

Heim let out a lecherous chuckle. 'In that case, let's hope we find her. I could do with a bad girl.'

'Well, if we find her I'm having her first.'

'Pulling rank again, Corporal?'

'Yes, of course. Unless you have a cigarette. Then I will gladly surrender my position at the front of the queue.'

'You mean it?'

'Yes. Why? Have you got a cigarette?'

'It's possible,' said Heim, with a grin.

Giesing ran over and pretended to beat up his friend. 'You lying shit! I really will have you shot. Hand them over.'

Had the two men not been engaging in such horseplay, they might have noticed the figures of two men who had been listening to their entire conversation as well as the exchange with the occupants of the car. Smith and Fellowes had been on their way back to Wellington Road, confident that they would reach its safety in time for the curfew. It was a confidence that had just been shattered.

* * *

115

Although by no means obese, Major Ernst Schwalm was by far the best-fed creature on Alderney. He even had the suggestion of a belly, a feature of which he was somewhat fond. In his eyes, its presence showed both the prisoners and his own men that he was the superior male. Neither was diet the only sphere in which Schwalm sought to excel. When they had shipped over half a dozen Algerian whores from France, it was Schwalm who insisted on sleeping with each of them first, a process that took nearly a week, much to his men's chagrin and, indeed, their private mirth at his apparent lack of priapism.

It was this belly that Schwalm was rubbing that Saturday evening. He had just enjoyed a passable supper, and he was now ready for some Cognac. Normally he would have been content, but the arrival of the submarine the other night had created a vast number of problems for him.

The largest problem was sitting opposite him, in the form of SS Captain Maximillian List. Until a week ago, List had been merely the commandant of the thousand-strong Sylt concentration camp in the south-west of the island, which came under the auspices of SS Construction Brigade I out of Neuengamme back in the Reich. But now List had subsumed the inmates of the remaining three labour camps – Norderney, Borkum and Helgoland – under SS control, making him the *de facto* commandant of the whole island. On paper, certainly, Major Schwalm was still the commanding officer of Abschnitt Adolf, but it was List who was really in charge of what Schwalm had hitherto regarded as his personal fiefdom.

However, Schwalm still had the responsibility of keeping the island supplied, and it was his job to provide the SS and their scientists with everything they required. His other problems were therefore bureaucratic and administrative, and only seemed worth overcoming because the project was so important. It was hard, especially with that bleating upstart Hempel, to persuade them in Jersey to give him what he wanted, but he felt he had managed it. Did the man not want to win the war?

Schwalm picked a small piece of chicken out of his mouth. He looked across the table at his dining companion, idly scrutinising the man's wiry hair and his somewhat femininely pouting lips. There was indeed something perverse about his features, something that matched his reputation. It was said that List liked personally to strangle a prisoner from time to time – apparently he got some sort of sexual kick out of it. Schwalm found the notion distasteful rather than immoral, although what he found more offensive was that it was a waste of the workforce. By all means work them hard and, yes, even to death, but there was no point in *murdering* them. 'So, then, Captain,' he said, breaking a silence that had been holding court for at least a couple of minutes, 'how is it proceeding up on Mannez?'

'Too slowly,' said List, his voice hoarse from barking orders, 'which is why we urgently need that extra labour from Jersey.'

'It is coming on Wednesday – I have the admiral's word for that.'

'There is also the problem of this wretched sickness,' said List, 'which I am told by the scientists is unavoidable in work of this sort. They, of course, take precautions, but it is impossible to give the prisoners any form of protection.'

'Do you think a thousand should do it?'

List shrugged. 'It might. Anyway, if we get through that lot, there are presumably plenty more on Jersey.'

'Thousands. And don't forget Guernsey as well – there are several thousand there.'

'Good. We might just need them.'

'Is it really that bad?'

'Only in the centre of the hill. It would appear that the average prisoner lasts a little less than a week when he or she is down there. Some only go on for a couple of days before it becomes necessary to dispose of them.'

'How many have you had to deal with?'

'What? Disposals?'

'Yes.'

'I would say around three to four hundred at present, although one has to take into account the natural wastage that occurs in other parts of the complex. In total, we are probably losing around a hundred prisoners per day.'

Schwalm's eyes bulged with incredulity. 'One hundred *per day*? What are you doing to these people?'

'They're not people, Herr Major.'

Schwalm brushed it aside. 'All right, all right, that's a marginal point, but it still seems rather too many.'

'Unlike the army, Herr Major, the SS prides itself on working its prisoners hard. You do know that work creates freedom, don't you? *Ergo*, the harder you work, the more free you become.'

List was smiling now, carried away by his own rationale.

'I can appreciate that, *Captain*,' said Schwalm, vainly reminding List that he was superior in rank, 'but surely there comes a point when you can work prisoners too hard, and their deterioration only leads to inefficiency.'

'I disagree. When one has an almost limitless pool of labour to draw on, it makes sense to work prisoners to extinction, as one is getting the most out of them. In this way, one is always getting a supply of fresh, eager labour that replaces the defunct. Besides, working them to death brings them the ultimate freedom.'

Schwalm pursed his lips, as if savouring List's argument. He couldn't deny that it made some sort of sense. 'I think a Cognac,' he said, 'don't you?'

'Thank you, Major,' said List. 'I could murder one.'

Chapter Four

'FOR A WOMAN of your age, Mrs Campbell, you are surprisingly attractive.'

Violet did her best to ignore Bouhler's words. Instead she concentrated on the green-and-white-striped wallpaper behind him. It bore a patchwork of brown stains that revealed the Gestapo headquarters in St Helier was suffering badly from damp. This was not the dungeon she had expected, just a typical boarding-house bedroom in a typical Victorian terrace. Filing cabinets lined the walls and, incongruously, just to the right of a damp-crinkled poster of Hitler, there was a rather lurid water-colour of a litter of kittens. Why had no one got rid of that ghastly picture? she found herself wondering. Did this man Bouhler, sitting opposite her, really like it? Or had he simply not bothered to take it down over the past five years?

'Mrs Campbell? I hope you are listening to me.'

'I am,' she said quietly. It still hurt to speak, as the right side of her face was considerably swollen from the blow Bouhler had dealt her back at the house.

'I was just telling you that you are surprisingly attractive, Mrs Campbell. It is a compliment. You should have said thank you, or words to that effect.'

Ignore him, she told herself, he's playing with you. Just do as he says, play along with him. Anything to save Pippa, anything to save the officers. Of course she didn't want to die, it terrified her, but she was willing to sacrifice herself if it gave them a chance. John. Poor John. Would he understand? He would, she was sure of it. He would be proud to have a wife who had died defending her country. How would he cope, though? Would he marry someone else? Too many woulds! Just keep your head, stop thinking. Go blank.

'Thank you,' she said.

Bouhler flicked through a file. 'Your daughter appears to have inherited your good looks.'

'You're too kind.'

'I would very much like to meet her,' said Bouhler, a tight grin creasing his face.

Don't let him get to you. You know what he's preying on. Violet nodded, maintaining her gaze on the watercolour. It really was truly awful.

'Although unfortunately your daughter did not want to meet us,' Bouhler continued.

Violet sat up and looked directly at Bouhler. 'Where is she?' she asked.

'Now, fancy that! That is exactly what I was about to ask you.'

'You must know!'

'No, Mrs Campbell, I am afraid I don't. Although I suspect you do.'

Bouhler sat back in his chair, and clasped his hands together before allowing them to rest just above his groin.

'What happened to her?' asked Violet. 'Please tell me!'

'Well, the last we saw of her was when she was running away from us, heading in the direction of St Saviour's. You should be grateful that some of our soldiers are spectacularly bad shots.'

Violet closed her eyes. What had she done? They were all going to die, be executed, because she, Violet, had some self-important sense of patriotism and duty. Perhaps it would have been better just to be like the rest of them and stay quiet, sit out the occupation. Instead of being here, they could have been safely at home, cooking whatever meagre remains they had from the Red Cross parcels, and looking forward to seeing their husband and father again.

'All I need to know, Mrs Campbell, is where you think she might have gone.'

This was too much. 'For heaven's sake, man! Do you think I would tell *you*? Do you really think that I would tell the Gestapo where I thought my daughter was hiding? Is that how it is in Germany? Mothers informing on their daughters? Really? Even if I did know where Pippa was, I would never, repeat *never*, tell you.'

Bouhler did his best to maintain a phlegmatic air. 'Of course I would not expect you to inform on your daughter, but I would certainly expect you to attempt to save her life. You see, Mrs

Campbell, as I am tired of telling you, you are in a very serious situation indeed. If you and your daughter co-operate, it is far more likely that your lives will be spared by the authorities. Naturally, if you prove difficult, and your daughter is captured rather than gives herself up, your chances of survival are non-existent. I do not see it as a difficult choice. Remember, those officers are not simply escaped prisoners, they are also murderers. You would not shelter a murderer in peacetime, so why do it now? Hmm? Come on, Mrs Campbell, please be reasonable and see a little sense.'

Violet thanked God she didn't know where Pippa had gone. Something in Bouhler's words and manner was seductively reassuring. There was a logic to what he was saying, but Violet had to remind herself that the logic was skewed. It was the logic of the criminal, the rationale of the powerful and corrupted.

'Even if what you say is true, Herr Bouhler . . .'

Now it was Bouhler's turn to sit up. 'It is, Mrs Campbell – most certainly.'

'. . . it is of no consequence to me. I have not the first idea where my daughter may be hiding.'

Bouhler slammed his hand down hard on the table. 'You are being a fool!'

'I'm telling you the truth!' Violet shouted. 'You will simply have to find Philippa on your own. No matter what you say, I cannot help you.'

Bouhler sat back again. 'I see,' he said. 'I see. All right, then, let's change tack. If you don't know where your daughter is, how about the prisoners? Surely you must have some idea where they are. It would be impossible for you not to know.'

So they were still safe. Thank God for that. What had happened? Had Pippa managed to warn them? 'I'm sorry, Herr Bouhler, but I cannot help you.'

Although Violet had not admitted that she had been sheltering Fellowes and Smith, she knew she couldn't explain away the pieces of paper with their practice signatures. Instead, she had decided to act dumb.

'Of course you can't,' said Bouhler. 'You are a woman of high principle who will not betray her fellow countrymen. No doubt you think that the murder of one of our soldiers was simply an act of war – an action that should be congratulated perhaps. Yes?'

Violet allowed herself to nod. Where was this going?

'Well, if you regard killing guards as a legitimate act of war, then presumably you will find my detaining and questioning you equally legitimate. You are, Mrs Campbell, an enemy to my country, and therefore an enemy to me. I shall do whatever is in my power to track down Fellowes and Smith, because they, too, are my enemies. If you are all that stands in my way, I see it as perfectly legitimate – especially in wartime – to commit the same sorts of legitimate acts on you as the prisoners did on Private Gerhard Klein from Hamburg, who happens to leave a wife and three children.'

This meant torture, that much was obvious. She could feel herself start to tremble, her heart thumping furiously, willing her muscles to pick her up and run out of the room. She tried to make her next sentence sound calm: 'So, you mean to torture me, do you, Herr Bouhler?'

'Indeed I do. In fact, the law even allows me to, so do not get any ideas that what I will do to you is illegitimate, because it will be quite the opposite.'

'According to your laws, not mine.'

'It is we who are in charge, Mrs Campbell, despite your valiant efforts.'

'Being in power does not necessarily confer morality on your laws, Herr Bouhler.'

Bouhler smirked and tilted his head to one side. 'An interesting notion, Mrs Campbell – charming, in fact – but a naïve one. Anyway, I have neither the time nor the energy to indulge in such a childish philosophical debate. What I'd really like to do is show you this.'

Bouhler opened a drawer underneath the table and produced a manila file. No doubt this was going to be some form of contract, thought Violet, some scrap of bureaucratic nonsense that in some way would give Bouhler 'permission' to torture her. The file only contained one piece of foolscap, which Bouhler looked at briefly before handing it to Violet. 'This,' he said, the sheet still in his hand, 'is something I've been working on for the past few days. So far, I have not yet had an opportunity to use it, as it were, but it looks as though you are going to give me one. I am very grateful to you, Mrs Campbell, very grateful indeed.'

The Occupation

Violet stretched out her shaking hand and took the paper. She felt so weak, she could barely grip it. The top of the sheet contained one word – 'Menu'. What followed made Violet almost physically sick.

<u>Starters</u>
Thumbnail extraction
Little finger breaking
Branding (on inside of thigh)
Water retention
Flogging (50 strokes on back)

<u>Main Courses</u>
Branding (on face)
Eyelid sewing
Ear removal
Kneecap shattering
Rape (women)
Genital electrocution (men)

<u>Puddings</u>
Branding (on nipples)
Removal of little toe
Flogging (50 strokes on soles of feet)
The iron
Scalding (hands)

Violet was speechless. This represented a barbarism she could not begin to comprehend. Her eyes scanned up and down the list, trying to establish what might be the least painful of the tortures.

'I'm very proud of my little menu,' said Bouhler. 'As you can see, I have put a lot of effort into it.'

Violet tried to reply but her throat was too dry, her mind too confused, her whole being too terrified.

'So what I want you to do, Mrs Campbell, is to select your starter, main course and pudding. You do not have to tell me all of them now, but I'd appreciate it if you could tell me your starter as soon as possible. Your other option, of course, is to tell me where the prisoners and your daughter are, and then I'm afraid I shall have to put away my menu for another day. Understand?'

Violet began to weep. She tried not to, but the force of the tears was irresistible.

'There, there, Mrs Campbell, the starters are not *so* bad. I'm sure you'll be able to cope. I admit, it does get a little nasty after that, but don't worry about those for the time being. Now, then, what's it to be? I particularly recommend the first item on the menu, the thumbnail extraction, *une spécialité de la maison*, as it were.'

This had to be a bluff, Violet thought. It was too despicable. Things like this didn't happen, not any more. She looked up at Bouhler through her tears, and immediately realised that they did.

The Occupation

*   *   *

Cliché funeral weather, thinks Lebonneur. It's not raining as such, but there's a sea mist combined with the lightest of drizzles that succeeds in covering the mourners with a fine sheen of water on their coats. Mrs Mead is protected by a black umbrella held up by her son, and just under its dripping rim Lebonneur can see that she is not crying. Tranquillisers, he thinks. They've probably doped the poor dear up to the eyeballs. The Meads' daughter most certainly is crying, comforted by a young man with long hair whom Lebonneur assumes to be the boyfriend.

The coffin is lowered shakily into the ground, an act that redoubles the expression of the daughter's grief. Lebonneur looks away. For the first time in his life, he feels like a voyeur. He is no longer a journalist, so why is he here? What good is this doing? He's not writing about it – unlike Henderson, the fat worm of a graduate who is currently sheltering beneath a Scots pine. Smarmy little shit. All one can ever see coming out of the editor's arse are Henderson's shoes, so massive is his toadying. No doubt he'll write this up as a terrible accident, and it'll be chopped down to a nib, and that will be that. So fucking unfair.

Perhaps that's why I'm here, Lebonneur reflects. Because what's happened to the Mead family is unfair. Why should Mrs Mead have to be throwing earth on to her husband's coffin? And why, for heaven's sake, couldn't she have seen his body? We don't think you should, Mrs Mead, a bad idea, Mrs Mead, he's not the same man, Mrs Mead, it's not how you'd want to

129

remember him, Mrs Mead. And the coroner's report! A fucking disgrace if ever there was one. 'Massive internal haemorrhaging brought on by a fall. Verdict: Accidental death.' That was it. No inquiry, nothing. For *them*, he was just another bloke on a building site who was probably pissed. Anyone would have thought he was a navvy on the Panama Canal.

Lebonneur glances at the other mourners. There are about twenty in all – family members, by the look of things, and a couple of men with leathery, sun-beaten skin. Workmen? They look wrong in their suits – they must be workmen. He'll talk to them afterwards, collar them in the pub. For the time being, all he can do is to stand, watch and reflect.

'I was wondering if I could have a quick word with you.'

'Who's asking?'

What to say? He instinctively wants to tell the two men that he's a journalist, but that wouldn't help.

'I'm Robert Lebonneur, a friend of Mrs Mead's. I've, er, just been taking care of a few things for her.'

'Funeral and that?'

Lebonneur nods.

'They say that organising a funeral and all the other things is actually a help when someone dies,' says one of the workmen. 'Stops you sitting around doing nothing. Gives you a sense of purpose.'

'You're not wrong, Mr . . . Mr . . . ?'

'Mark Fowler, and this is Ian, Ian Andrews.'

'Hi,' says Lebonneur. 'It's good of you both to come.'

'Not at all,' says Mark. 'Didn't know him very well, but John was a nice bloke. We owe it to him to be here. Besides, it's nice to get away from the site.'

'Oh, so you're working over on Alderney? On the new hotel?'

'That's right.'

'How's it going?'

'Oh, you know, a bit behind,' says Mark, 'but then these things always are.'

'So did you see John's accident?' asks Lebonneur.

'No,' says Mark. 'No one did. It was Ian here who found him. Lying at the bottom of that Jerry gun tower, weren't it?'

' 'Sright,' says Ian, taking a mouthful of lager. 'Poor bugger. He was still breathing – although only just. He must have lain there all night.'

'Really?'

'Yup – he'd been doing some overtime on his own the afternoon before, wanted to make up for the couple of days he'd had off sick.'

'Sick?'

' 'Sright. He'd been a bit under the weather, said he'd been overdoing it in the pub in the evenings.'

'What was wrong with him?'

Ian shrugs and looks at Mark.

'Just seemed a bit off colour,' Mark says. 'Me, I'd say it was that bleeding scampi in the pub. Enough to make anyone take to their bed.'

'So did he get better?' Lebonneur asks.

'A bit, you know. He wasn't a hundred per cent, but he seemed all right. He wasn't the youngest chap on the site, if you get my meaning.'

Lebonneur nods. 'I understand.'

'To be fair to him, mate,' says Ian, 'he hasn't been the only one. Rodge was so bad he had to go back to England.'

Lebonneur feels his pulse quicken. 'What was wrong with him?'

'Not sure,' says Mark. 'We found him in the toilet one night puking his guts out. They flew him straight off the island the next morning and took him to Southampton hospital.'

'What happened to him?'

'No idea. We're still waiting to find out. The company said it was probably food poisoning or an allergy, something like that. Poor bloke, though, he was in a bad way.'

'He was indeed,' says Ian.

The three men stand in silence.

'Listen, can I get you gents a drink?' says Lebonneur.

'Now, you're a gentleman,' says Mark. 'I'll have a pint of wife-beater.'

Lebonneur laughs. 'You?'

'Same here,' says Ian.

Lebonneur orders three pints of Stella Artois, which arrive after a couple of minutes.

'To John,' says Mark.

'To John,' Lebonneur and Ian say in unison and raise their glasses.

'That's good,' says Mark, wiping his mouth with the back of his hand.

'Too right,' says Ian.

'One thing, though,' says Mark, his eyebrows knitted together.

'Oh, yes?'

'I remember both John and Rodge complaining about something – their boots. Said they'd got too small.'

'Too small?'

'That's right. Said their feet and ankles had swelled up.'

'Do you know why?'

'Not a clue, mate.'

'Has this happened to anyone else?'

'No,' says Mark. 'I don't think so.'

'So just them, then?' asks Lebonneur.

'I think so,' says Mark. 'Ian?'

Ian shakes his head. 'No. Anyway, why're you so interested?'

Lebonneur is momentarily thrown off balance. 'Well, Mrs Mead just wants to know a bit more about her husband's last days,' he replies. 'Just wants to put a few pieces together.'

Ian nods. 'I see. Company not told her much, then, is that it?'

'That's right,' says Lebonneur. 'They're an uncommunicative lot, aren't they?'

'Companies like that always are when something like this happens,' says Mark. '*Plus ça* fucking *change*, mate, I'm telling you.'

*

133

Lebonneur gets back home at around half past five. The house is empty, so he takes the opportunity to pour himself a sly whisky. How unemployed is this – drinking spirits at teatime? Sod it, he thinks, he's a free man, a *free* man. Irony, of course, plenty of irony. There's something big going on over on Alderney, he can feel it, yet he's not even working for anyone. Perhaps he should try to get a freelance commission from one of the nationals. Maybe – although not yet, they'd want more first. Besides, there was always the chance they'd nick it and invade the islands with their own men. No, better to keep it quiet, wait until you know *everything*. There's no way he's going to hand something like this over to some wanker in Fleet Street.

He looks over at the other end of the sitting room. All those bloody boxes still. Perhaps he should take them into the garage or something. Tomorrow, he'd do it tomorrow. Not now, he had too much to think about. He'd get an earful from Rachel about it, but too bad. There were people he needed to call. He'd try Pete again down at the hospital. He couldn't help him last time, but he'd work on him again. The same with Andrew at the coroner's office – those buggers had to know something about how Mead had died. Alderney, he needed to talk to someone in Alderney, but who? Lebonneur had only been to the island once – a weekend a few years back with Rachel – and the only person he knew there was the owner of their bed-and-breakfast. And he also needed to track down this builder, Roger Harris, the poor bloke who'd been flown over to Southampton. He'd do that first. It was going to be a tough one, as neither Mark nor Ian had known his number, and the last place Lebonneur was going to ask was sodding Regius Hotels.

He picks up the phone and dials Directory Enquiries, which gives him the number for Southampton General Hospital.

'Hello. This is Southampton General Hospital . . .'

'Hello, I was trying to get hold—'

'. . . You are currently in a queue and will be answered shortly.'

Fuck. A bloody machine. What is it with these places? Did they not know that people wanted to talk to people? That was kind of the point of having mouths and ears. Here we go, Vivaldi's *Four* Fucking *Seasons*. How long was this going to go on for? Spring, Summer, Autumn and Winter?

Lebonneur waits for an impatient two minutes, then nearly gives up until he hears, 'Sorry to keep you waiting.' Yeah, right.

'Hello there,' he says. 'I was trying to track down one of your patients – a Roger Harris.'

'When was he admitted?'

'It would have been a couple of weeks ago.'

'Hold on, please.'

The line goes dead. Lebonneur hates that – he has no idea whether or not he's still connected. How long will it be this time? Ah, here we go.

'Hello,' comes a tired female voice. 'Renal unit.'

Renal unit? Could this be right?

'Er, yes,' says Lebonneur. 'I'm trying to speak to Roger Harris, one of your patients.'

'I'm sorry, sir, I'm afraid that won't be possible.'

'Oh?'

'Are you a family member, sir?'

'Yes, I'm his brother.'

A sharp intake of breath down the line. Lebonneur knows what this means.

'It's best if you speak to your mother, Mr Harris. I understand she will be here shortly – I'll ask her to call you.'

'I . . . see. Um . . . no, tell her not to bother, that'll be fine. I'll, um, ring her later.'

Lebonneur puts the phone down. Two deaths. One of kidney failure presumably, another in a fall, yet both had swollen ankles. Was it a symptom of some kidney disease?

'Bob!'

Lebonneur is too engrossed to hear Terry banging on the window behind him.

'Bob!'

He turns round with a start. Terry? What the hell is he doing here? He looks excited. 'Hello, Terry. What's up with you?'

'Does your bloody doorbell not work?'

Lebonneur shakes his head. 'Sorry – must get it fixed some time.'

'Anyway, can I come in? I want to talk to you about this diary.' He holds up the small brown book that Lebonneur had lent him a couple of days ago.

'Of course. Hold on.' Lebonneur walks to the front door and slips it off the latch. 'Come in,' he says. 'Blimey! You look as though you've just won a massive bet or something.'

'Better than that,' says Terry, rushing straight in, 'and at the same time much, much worse.'

* * *

Von Luck cleared his throat. 'Miss Campbell?'

Pippa was sitting in his old armchair, staring at the still unlit logs in the fireplace.

'Miss Campbell?'

Slowly, Pippa turned her head. She looked exhausted, as well as worried, deeply worried. The effects did not diminish her beauty, although von Luck put such thoughts to the back of his mind.

'Yes?' she asked croakily.

'I have a plan,' he said, squatting down so his head was level with hers.

'You have?' Her eyes brightened a little.

'You are going to hide here,' he said, 'in the attic. I shall tell Mrs May, the housekeeper, that you—'

'But—'

'Don't worry. Mrs May is perfectly trustworthy.'

'But I know her – she's an old gossip!'

'Yes,' said von Luck, 'which is why I knew all about you and your mother. However, we have little choice in the matter. I am not around most of the day, and she is, and it would be impossible for her not to discover that you are here. She will also be able to feed you, which I shall not have time to do, as well as attend to any more personal requirements you may have. Please, Miss Campbell, it is the only way.'

Pippa nodded. 'All right.'

'Good. Now, your mother. This evening I shall go down to the Gestapo headquarters and speak to Inspector Bouhler. I shall do my best to establish what he knows and, furthermore, will attempt to see whether any leniency can be applied.'

'Colonel, that is so . . .'

Von Luck held up his hands. 'Please. Think nothing of it. It is the least I can do. However, I should warn you that the harbouring of escaped POWs is considered a serious offence, and I cannot guarantee that my visit will achieve anything.'

'I am very grateful to you, Colonel.'

Von Luck could tell that she was. She was smiling and her eyes, although wet, held a little more hope than they had when he had walked into the room. 'One other thing,' he said.

'Yes?'

'I have an important visitor coming here this evening, and I shall need you to be out of the way. I shall only be able to go down the Havre des Pas after he has gone. I am sorry that I cannot act any sooner, but the matter I have to deal with is extremely important, more so than any of us.'

'What is it about? Can you tell me?'

'I'm afraid not,' said von Luck, 'although I hope, if I survive the war, that I will be able to tell you.'

'*Survive the war?* I don't think you're very likely to die. Not at this stage.'

'I wish I had your confidence, Miss Campbell, I really do, but I am afraid anything can happen, perhaps even in the next twenty-four hours.'

Pippa's brow furrowed. 'Whatever it is, Colonel, I hope you do survive. You are . . . you are a good man.' She tilted her head down. 'Sorry,' she said. 'That sounded crass.'

'Not at all. It sounded sincere. It is kind of you, Miss Campbell.'

'Pippa. Please call me Pippa. If I'm to be your ghost in the attic, I think it only appropriate that you should call me by my Christian name.'

Von Luck laughed. 'Certainly, *Pippa*. And you shall have to call me Max. I don't like this Colonel business. I am not, after all, your captor, but your host.'

'Max,' she said, then repeated it, as if trying the name for size: 'Max.'

Their eyes met. Von Luck knew what that meant, but he could not act on it now. If there was ever going to be a right time, now was certainly not it. He stood up, and as he did so, he switched her knee playfully with his right hand, as if to acknowledge that he was aware of what was happening. 'All right,' he said, with a smile. 'It's time I showed you to your attic. Pet— my guest will be here soon.'

'What were you about to say?' she asked.

'I was about to mention the name of one of my fellow officers, but I thought it best not to.'

'I see,' said Pippa.

She did not look convinced. No doubt she thought he was about to say a woman's name. Well, let her think that. Perhaps a little jealousy would not go amiss.

'Petersen! Many thanks for coming.'

Petersen looked dubious. Von Luck could see that he was going to take a lot of convincing. 'I'm afraid my housekeeper has the night off,' he said, 'so we will have to make do with what I can find in the kitchen. I take it you're hungry?'

'Famished,' said Petersen, unbuttoning his coat.

'Here, let me take that.'

Von Luck slung Petersen's coat over his arm and led him to the kitchen, hanging the coat up on a rack in the downstairs corridor as they passed it.

'So how are you keeping?' asked von Luck, as he searched through the kitchen cupboards. 'Bearing up?'

'More or less,' said Petersen, who was leaning uneasily against a Welsh dresser.

'I think Mrs May keeps a few bottles of beer somewhere in there,' said von Luck. 'Why not have a look?'

'Thanks,' said Petersen.

Von Luck studied him as he opened the dresser. A former U-Boat man, Petersen wore a large beard, inside which nestled his rather delicate features and deep brown eyes. He had left the U-Boats after four patrols, suffering from severe battle stress. A family connection within the higher echelons of the Kriegsmarine had enabled a transfer to the islands. Petersen deserved it – von Luck would not have spent five minutes on a U-Boat, let alone five months. Petersen had lasted the war for this long, and it was clear that he was not minded to risk his life for a cause he might regard as unnecessary. Von Luck's problem, therefore, was to convince him that the fate of a thousand islanders was a worthwhile cause.

'I think I've found it,' said Petersen. 'Oh, look, it's Stella Artois.'

He turned to give von Luck a nervous, almost boyish, smile. 'I haven't had such good beer in many months.'

'Open it, open it!'

Petersen passed a bottle to von Luck and unscrewed the cap of his own. He took a long swig. 'Yuk!'

'What's wrong?'

'I think it's gone bad.'

Von Luck opened the cap of his bottle and took a tentative sip. Petersen was right – it was a little old. 'It's drinkable, though,' said von Luck. 'At least it won't kill us.' He cursed himself. The joke was perhaps in bad taste.

'I suppose you're right,' said Petersen, warily. 'Well, anyway, cheers, von Luck.'

Von Luck lifted his bottle. 'Cheers, Petersen. Here's to decent men.'

'Decent men,' said Petersen, and took another swig. 'Yuk!'

Von Luck laughed. 'I'm sorry – I've got some wine. We'll have that in a moment.'

There was a brief silence as von Luck continued on his quest for anything edible.

'So what is it you want me to do?' Petersen asked.

Von Luck had been debating how he would broach the subject. He had decided that the direct approach would be more respectful. An intelligent man like Petersen would not require a long preamble.

'It's quite simple,' said von Luck, his head deep inside a cupboard. 'I want you to forge a telegram from Berlin that orders Huffmeier to stop the deportation.' He waited to hear a splutter, but instead there was silence. That was to be expected. He reached into the back of the cupboard where, in the musty gloom, he found a tin of ham. 'Here we go.'

He turned round, and found Petersen still leaning against the dresser, but now he was pointing a pistol straight at von Luck's heart. Von Luck momentarily shut his eyes, as if he was trying to close himself off from the reality of the situation. Shit, he thought. Shit. Petersen was not a decent man. Far from it. You are a fool to have trusted him, a fucking fool. 'If you're going to shoot me, I'd rather you did it now.'

Petersen's eyes glared out above the wiry thickness of his beard. 'I don't know if I am,' he said. 'It all depends on whether you do anything stupid.'

'I assume from this that you don't want to help me.'

'Stop being so bloody flippant!' Petersen shouted. 'You always were just like the British. So sarcastic the whole time! So self-confident. It's no wonder you've screwed so many of their women.

142

They must love you, those girls, with your manners and your title.'

'I'm sorry, Petersen, I'm not, uh, following you.'

'There's nothing to "follow". All you need to know is that your days of wooing are over.'

'Oh? So you *are* going to shoot me?'

Petersen stayed silent and took a swig of beer. 'Yuk.'

Von Luck weighed up his options. Petersen was not quite the out-of-control pistol-wielding lunatic – he was a lot calmer than that. The weapon was rock steady in his hand. Should he make a move on him? Or try to talk him out of the situation? It was clear that Petersen was only doing this because he didn't want to help von Luck with his scheme. 'Look, Petersen, if you do not want to help me, you don't have to. We can just pretend that this never happened. You go your way, I'll go mine. I know that you've got a family, and that you don't want to take any risks. I understand that. Please, put the gun down, we'll finish our beers, and then call it an evening. How does that sound? Eh?'

Petersen shook his head. 'You don't understand, von Luck,' he said. 'You haven't a clue. I'm not doing this because I want to save my skin, but rather, because I'm still a patriot. I'm not one of your "decent men", but I am a German! I would do *nothing* to betray my country, even at a time like this. If Berlin wants to deport a load of islanders, let them! That's their business. What's it to you? Millions of people have died in this war, and it's about time *these* bloody people knew what war was like! Do you know what it's like to be depth-charged, von Luck? No, I don't suppose you do. When the ping of the Asdic bounces off your hull, and you know you're already so deep that the rivets are firing out of the bulkheads, and the knowledge that they're about to drop several tons of explosive on you – do you *know* what that feels like?'

Von Luck shrugged.

'Of course you don't! Because you're just a fucking desk soldier, a lawyer, full of supposedly noble ideals, ideals that are in fact treacherous and undermine everything men like me have fought for.'

'What do you want?'

'What do I want? I want to hand you in! That's what I want! I'm going to telephone the Gestapo and tell them to come over here and arrest you. You're a traitor, von Luck, fucking vermin. What's going on over on Alderney could make us win this bloody war, and you run the risk of stopping it. Is that really what you want? For Germany to lose the war?'

'What *is* going on over there, Petersen?'

'I'm not going to tell you that, von Luck.'

Pippa heard the shot up in the attic. At first she did not realise what it was, but as soon as she did, she gasped, instinctively putting her hand to her mouth. 'Oh, God,' she whispered. 'Oh, God.'

Who had shot whom? Was it Max? Was that what he had meant when he talked about not surviving the war? Yes! Of course it was! No wonder he was so insistent that he would tell

Mrs May about her, because he knew he was going to die. Rescuing her had been his last act, an act of decency.

Think positively. It might not have been Max being shot but him shooting someone else. If he has shot someone, then he might need help with the body. *Help with the body.* What was happening to her? The idea of such a gruesome task would have repelled her just a few hours ago, and yet, even within that short space of time, she had already become brutalised.

Pippa flung off the blanket and got up, making sure that she didn't hit her head on the low ceiling. She made her way forward hesitantly in the near-darkness. A very dim light was coming in through the rafters, which enabled her to avoid cracking her skull or tripping over the assortment of clutter strewn over the floor.

She crouched by the trapdoor and listened once again. Not a sound. Slowly, she lifted the handle and held the door ajar. Silence. What now? Lower herself down? Or wait? Give it a few more minutes?

She could not wait. She opened the trapdoor completely and looked down to the landing nine feet below her. Gingerly, she crouched, leaned forward over the opening and placed her hands on either side of the frame. She eased herself forward, then sat on the edge of the opening, her legs now dangling free. Taking a deep breath, she wriggled herself so she was about to fall out. This was it, the point of no return.

Her arms taking the strain, Pippa pushed herself out through the trapdoor. For a couple of seconds she stayed there, her arms straightened, half of her body in the attic, the other half out of it.

Another breath, and she let herself drop down until she was hanging by her hands, the contortion causing a bolt of pain to shoot through her right arm. She stopped herself making a sound, and then, with a silent prayer, she dropped the remaining couple of feet to the ground.

Pippa thought her landing must have shaken the entire house. She stood in the corridor, panting. Her right leg and right arm hurt, but she barely noticed. All her senses were concentrating on her ears, trying to establish whether she could hear anything. Perhaps there was something, a slight shuffling sound coming from downstairs. Was a body being dragged? Please, God, let it not be his, anybody's body but his.

After what seemed like an hour of creeping Pippa reached the staircase. She peered round the corner and looked down to the hall, half expecting to see a torrent of blood. Instead she saw a man walking backwards, clutching a body under its arms and around its chest. Pippa recognised at once that the man was Max, and that the body was that of his mysterious visitor. The strength of the relief made her feel faint. 'Max!' she whispered. 'You're alive!'

Von Luck's head darted round to look up the stairs.

'Pippa! What are you doing there?'

'I heard a shot,' she replied, walking warily down the stairs, 'and I came to see if you wanted some help.'

'I think I can manage,' said von Luck, grunting as he heaved Petersen's body another few feet along the hall. The action caused the dead man's head to roll clumsily round to face Pippa.

'Who . . . who is he?' she asked.

'He is – or was – Oberleutnant zur See Petersen,' said von Luck, 'and I killed him because he was going to kill me.'

'What . . . what happened?'

'He was going to shoot me, but I managed to shoot him instead.'

It wasn't until she reached the bottom of the stairs that she realised von Luck's lip and right eyebrow were bleeding. She looked at him with concern. 'You're hurt! Are you all right?'

'I'm fine,' said von Luck. 'Don't worry about me. We had a fight, so if you can see any blood it's because of that. I'll live.'

'It looks like it might be my turn to nurse you,' said Pippa, mildly castigating herself for making such a coquettish remark over a corpse.

'Perhaps later,' said von Luck. 'But first I need to hide Petersen.'

'Where?'

'He can go in the cellar for the time being. From memory there are a couple of trunks in there we can use.'

'But why hide him at all? Surely you can just ring—'

'That is out the question!'

Pippa was taken aback by von Luck's sudden snapping at her. 'I'm sorry,' she began.

Von Luck sighed. 'No, forgive me,' he said. 'It's just that I cannot talk to anybody about why Petersen came to see me.'

'Which was?'

Pippa found herself being scrutinised by von Luck. It was a different look from the one she was used to. This was not a physical evaluation, but something much deeper than that.

'I shall tell you after I've come back from seeing the Gestapo about your mother. In the meantime, I'd appreciate you helping me with Petersen.'

Pippa looked down at the body. Blood oozed out of the small wound on the left of his chest; a few drops had already made it to the hall's wooden floor. Pippa bent down, lifted Petersen's legs by the ankles and signalled with a nod that she was ready.

* * *

The location, the time of the day, the fact that the thirteen men were all dressed in their weekend clothes – all would have made a casual observer feel that this meeting was an informal one. But the atmosphere in Richard Marais's drawing room that Saturday evening was anything but. He had summoned the members of the States as soon as he and Mollett had returned from their meetings at the Field Command. They had arrived within half an hour, and so far the meeting had been going on for well over two hours. Now that it was after curfew, Marais was a little anxious about his wife's ability to cope with such a large number of unexpected guests, but he had the feeling that trivial matters such as bedding and food would hardly arise over what was bound to be an all-night meeting.

Marais had the princely total of two bottles of Armagnac to share with his fellow legislators. He had kept them for the past five years, promising himself that he would open them upon liberation, but tonight seemed like a good occasion on which to enjoy them. Anything, he had said to the jurats, to lighten the mood. The men had needed no encouragement, and were sitting around savouring the brandy in an assortment of teacups, mugs and tumblers – the Marais brandy balloons having long since been 'borrowed' by a German colonel.

'So, do you really think we can trust von Luck?' asked David Portelet, an elderly member of the States who had been a jurat for nearly forty years.

'I think so,' said Marais, his tone more confident than his words.

'But what if he fails to stop it?'

'Then we go with the second option, which is to oppose the deportation by not obeying the Germans.'

Portelet sat back. 'I don't know, Richard, I really don't . . .' He left the words hanging in the air.

'Please carry on, David,' said Marais. 'The floor is yours, as it were.'

Portelet's chin rested on his chest. His body was clearly tired, but his brain was still as sharp as it always was. 'As I see it,' he began, 'we have acted as a pretty good buffer between the population and the Germans for the past five years. We have managed to curb some of the Germans' more brutal demands, as well as ensuring that the population is, more or less, cared for in a benevolent fashion by us and them. It has not been an easy role to play, but you, Richard, as Bailiff, have handled it adroitly. To the population, it looks as though you have given away far too much to our invaders, but those of us in the room know that you have simply understood that by giving way in some areas you have gained in others – your securing of the *Vega* to come here with its Red Cross parcels being a case in point. We are all very grateful to you, and I trust that after the war, when the dust has settled, the recriminations been met, your reputation shall emerge intact and, moreover, enhanced, as a man who did his best to guide the States through this, our most difficult time.'

'Thank you, David,' said Marais. There was a sting in the tail, he thought, there always was with Portelet. 'Although I have the feeling that that was merely a prelude.'

'Quite so, quite so,' said Portelet. 'And it is this. Let us assume, for the purposes of argument, that Colonel von Luck will fail in his humanitarian quest. We are then left with the choice of an opposed deportation, or an unopposed deportation. The consequences of both are the same. One thousand of us will, no matter what, be sent to work on Alderney. However, the problem in opposing the deportation is that the violence that will erupt will endanger many more lives. We are defenceless, Richard, and even though, thanks to the Red Cross, the Germans have less food than us, they are still armed to the teeth. What can we do to stop them? I see fights on quaysides, resulting in people being thrown into the water. I see summary executions against the walls of barns. I see mothers being snatched from children. I see men being beaten, some to their deaths. That, gentlemen, would be the price of resisting this deportation. Another – what? – say, one hundred deaths? Fewer perhaps, but who's to say?' He went quiet, perhaps hoping that the effects of his words would resonate around the room.

Despite his frailty, he could be quite the orator when he wanted to be, thought Marais. 'So what you're saying, David,' said Marais, 'is basically that we should do as we're told, play along with it, because it's going to happen anyway?'

'In a word – yes.'

Marais thought Portelet's argument was despicable, but he kept his opinion to himself – at least for the time being. The room felt distinctly uneasy as the twelve jurats changed position, took sips of Armagnac, coughed. 'Peter?' he asked, looking at Mollett.

'It's a tough one,' said Mollett. 'Very tough.'

Damn, thought Marais. He's wavering. 'We know it's tough, Peter, but what do you think?'

'Well, David's got a point. After all, we didn't oppose the deportations in 'forty-two and 'forty-three.'

'You're right,' said Marais. 'We didn't, but this is very different. Then, islanders were being sent to internment camps on the Continent, not to concentration camps where they would be worked to their deaths. As we know from their letters, all two thousand of them are alive and being treated relatively well. If they were being sent to concentration camps in 'forty-two and 'forty-three, I like to think that we would have resisted.'

'But what good would that have done?' asked Mollett.

'It would have given us some pride,' said Marais, 'something that we could have held up to the world and said, "Look. We were unarmed and overwhelmed, yet we still refused to let our people go." '

'But how many lives is that pride worth?'

'Well, it's certainly worth *my* life,' said Marais.

The room went quiet as each man pondered the implication of Marais's words.

'So if we resist this deportation,' asked Mollett, breaking the silence, 'what would you say to the mother of, let me think, a teenaged boy who was shot while trying to escape the round-up?'

'I would tell her, although not in so few words, that she should be proud of her son. In his own way, he had fought against the evil of Fascism. Look, when the war is over, people are going to ask questions about how we behaved, and I want our reputation to remain intact. I want us to be able to hold our heads high. I know resisting the deportation will be dangerous, but perhaps it's finally our turn to do our bit, turn round and tell the Germans that we're not cattle, ready to be pushed around.'

A jurat sitting on the piano stool cleared his throat.

'Yes, George?' said Marais.

Marais had never liked George Le Fanu. He was a small man who thought himself infinitely wise, an effect he liked to engender by sucking at an empty pipe and speaking slowly. 'It is my belief,' he began, 'that resisting the deportation may also result in a wave of German violence and brutality. It might give the Nazis an opportunity to murder us all – who knows what terrible acts our new Admiral Huffmeier is capable of?'

'I hardly think that Huffmeier is going to shoot everybody,' said Marais.

'You can never tell,' said Le Fanu.

Marais looked round the room. 'Does anyone else think that?'

Only a few heads shook. The others looked anywhere but at Marais. He was losing them, thought Marais, they were going the way of Portelet and Mollett. 'Peter,' he said, 'you asked me how I would feel if I had to tell a mother why her son had died. Let me turn the question round. What would you say to a woman whose son died working on Alderney, a place he was sent to without any resistance from us? Do you not think that it would make her feel a little better that we had done everything we could to stop this crime being committed?'

Mollett cleared his throat. 'I would tell her that if we had opposed the deportation, many more sons like hers would have died. Come on, Richard, you know as well as we all do that there are no correct answers any more – just ones that are a little less wrong.'

'The less wrong answers are those that reflect our values,' said Marais. 'Values that are not based on cowardice or convenience . . .'

At his use of the word 'cowardice', several jurats started protesting. The loudest among them was William Brocq, a middle-aged solicitor whom Marais secretly felt to be venal, a suspicion confirmed by the fact that Brocq still carried a pre-war belly. 'This is not cowardice, Bailiff, merely self-preservation.

Surely it is only pragmatic to sacrifice some of our number in order for the rest of us to survive.'

'Perhaps you're right, William,' said Marais. 'In which case I'm sure you'll be the first to volunteer for work on Alderney on Wednesday morning.'

'This is most unfair,' said Brocq. 'You know as well as I do that I have important duties to attend to that would make it impossible for me to volunteer.'

'Of course, William,' Marais replied, smiling, 'although if you did volunteer I'm sure I could find someone to look after your duties while you're away.'

Brocq started to speak, then clearly thought better of it.

Marais looked around the room, barely able to mask his disappointment. These men were not bad, but they were weak. He knew that some would be on his side, but they were keeping quiet. He was most disappointed with Peter, whom he had felt he could rely on to take an honourable line. Such was the nature of wartime, he thought – it revealed the worst in men's characters.

'It is clear that we could talk without resolution for the rest of the evening,' said Marais, 'so I propose we put the matter to a vote.' His suggestion was met with a series of nods. 'Good. It shall be a straight majority vote. I shall not vote, but in the event of a tie I shall make the casting vote. Is everybody happy with that?'

More nods.

'Good. In that case, could those who wish to let the deportation take place unopposed please raise their hands?'

There was a pause as the jurats looked at each other. Portelet raised his hand – somewhat feebly – followed by Brocq, Le Fanu and Mollett. Marais had held out some small hope that he would not see Mollett's hand, but there it was. Up went another – that made five. Great, thought Marais, just leave it at that. Please, no more. Marais drew his breath, readying himself to declare the outcome, which was historic for Jersey and, indeed, for Britain. 'I see five hands,' he said, 'which means . . .'

'Hold on, Richard,' said Mollett. 'Andrew's hand is up.'

Marais could not help but glower at Jurat Andrew Foley. He wanted to tell him to put his bloody hand down, but in his role as Bailiff it was not his place to attempt to manipulate the vote as it was cast. 'Is that all?' he asked.

The remaining six men looked at him in turn and shook their heads, with one, James Jourdache, even giving him the suggestion of a wink.

'In that case,' said Marais, 'I declare the vote a tie. As we have agreed, I, as Bailiff, have the casting vote. It should come as no surprise to you that I cast my vote for an *opposed* deportation. The motion is therefore defeated by seven votes to six.'

Marais took a large slug of brandy. He wished he could have drawn some succour from the result, but he was far too enraged with the six jurats who had voted to acquiesce with the Germans. As he put down his glass, he noticed Mollett exchange a furtive glance with Brocq, which made him feel even more uneasy.

* * *

Miraculously, von Luck's car started immediately. It had been unreliable as of late, which he suspected was to do with a deterioration in the quality of the fuel. He had tried to discover who had been watering it down, but his enquiries had drawn a blank. With the shortage of vehicles on the island, who could possibly need it? Still, like any commodity that was in short supply, its scarcity alone increased its value, even if there was no corresponding demand for it.

Von Luck's driving was a little erratic. Preoccupied not by thoughts of petrol but by Petersen, he found himself clipping a kerbstone as he drove down Bagatelle Road towards St Helier. Petersen had been the first man von Luck had killed, and he was finding the fact that he was now a killer – no matter how justified – somewhat unpalatable. Had Petersen deserved his death? On a pragmatic basis, yes, he had – most certainly – as it was clearly a case of him or me. But on a deeper, moral basis, von Luck had his misgivings. Petersen was simply a man who had wanted to go home, to be reunited with his family. Yet even though he had suffered on his submarines, von Luck still felt that Petersen should have helped him – after all, they all wanted to go home. But did Petersen's weakness justify his death? Perhaps not, but it had been Petersen who had introduced the weapon to the situation and, worst of all, had threatened to take von Luck to the Gestapo.

The Gestapo. How ironic that he was going to see them anyway. Throughout his time on Jersey, von Luck had kept well away from them, especially from that monster Bouhler, whom even the general had found sinister. No doubt it was Bouhler who was 'questioning' Mrs Campbell, a thought that sent a shudder down von Luck's spine. Now *there* was someone he would have no compunction about killing. Von Luck felt the reassuring weight of his holster against his left hip. There was every chance that he would kill again this evening.

He arrived outside the Gestapo headquarters a little after nine o'clock. Such a nondescript building, he thought. How typical of the Gestapo to have chosen it. It looked banal, like the faces of so many of its agents. They were the little men, the third type in von Luck's classification of Nazis – the bureaucrat, the man obsessed by rules. They were the type of men who would stay in boarding-houses like this when they came on holiday, he thought. No doubt Bouhler had chosen the building because it made him feel at home, perhaps even reminded him of happy times with his family, if indeed he had one.

Von Luck opened his car door and stepped out into the night. He could hear the waves break just a couple of hundred yards away. They were loud, but not loud enough to muffle the sound of a woman screaming.

Chapter Five

'BY THE TIME the shell leaves the barrel, it will have reached a speed of over eleven hundred metres per second.'

Although SS Captain List was by no means a scientific man, even he was impressed by the figure. 'That is astonishing, Professor! How long will it take to get to London?'

Professor Karl Fellner smiled. 'We estimate around four minutes. Perhaps a little less.'

'And what is the rate of fire?'

'Each battery of five guns should be able to deliver one shell every minute,' said Fellner. 'As the V3 has five batteries in total, that means five shells per minute, or around three hundred per hour.'

'The city will be flattened in no time!'

Fellner took off his spectacles. 'Yes,' he said. 'Yes, it will. And with the nature of our warheads, the land will be poisoned for generations to come.'

'Once the Allies have seen this, they will think again before advancing on Berlin. The Führer promised us such a weapon, and here it is – just in time to change the course of the war! We were right to place our faith in him, Fellner. And think of the irony! Launched from right here, one of their own islands!'

Fellner could see the gleam in List's eyes. He would do well to curb his enthusiasm. 'Er, Hauptsturmführer, I must tell you that I do anticipate a few technical problems, which might reduce that rate of fire, but not significantly.'

List frowned. 'I do not like to hear talk of technical problems, Professor. We have no room for error.'

Fellner pulled nervously at his collar. He had worked with the SS for many years, but this man List frightened him more than any other SS officer he had ever met. There were plenty of rumours going round the island about him, none of which had been proved but, thought Fellner, there was no smoke without fire. The strangulations, the beatings, the shootings – one of Fellner's colleagues, Dr Heinz Pleiger, had told him he had heard from a prisoner that List found sexual gratification in watching a man die. Imagine, said Pleiger, the last thing you saw was List masturbating over your dying body. Fellner had almost been sick at the thought, and had implored Pleiger to get back to his work. 'I quite understand,' he said. 'There will be no technical problems. The best men left in the Reich are working on this project, so everything should run smoothly.'

'That's more like it,' said List, his smile returning. 'And how about the warheads? I assume they are coming along well.'

'Professor Kramer assures me that the warheads are being produced at the required rate.'

'Which is?'

Fellner cleared his throat. He knew that List was not going to like his response. 'Around thirty per day.'

'*Thirty?*'

'Yes, Captain.'

'At that rate we will use them all up in a few minutes. That is a disgraceful amount, Professor, almost criminal!'

Criminal. Fellner did not like List's use of the word. It suggested there should be some form of punishment, and the idea of being punished by List made Fellner tug even harder at his collar.

'I see your, ah, point, Captain,' he said, 'but it's . . . um . . . a slow and complicated process. Not to mention dangerous. Many of the labourers are falling sick in the manufacture, and we are finding it harder and harder just to keep up with thirty a day. You will need to talk to Kramer, of course, as all this is what he tells me.'

'I do not wish to talk to Kramer,' said List, ice-cold. 'I wish to talk to you, Professor Fellner, as you are the scientist in charge of the project. I do not like your attempt to abnegate responsibility.'

'But the – but the warheads are outside my professional expertise,' Fellner protested. 'My speciality is ballistics and—'

'I have no interest in whether your speciality is in ballistics or in making sauerkraut. All I need to know is whether you can double the production of the warheads.'

'Double it? But, Captain, that would be impossible, we do not have enough labour.'

'Then you should ask for more. Listen, Professor, I am here to ensure that this project runs quickly and efficiently. I am here to help you, do you see? Whatever you require, I will get it for you. In a way, I am your slave.'

Fellner smiled uneasily.

'So, then,' List continued, 'would you like some more labour?'

Fellner nodded.

'Fine,' said List. 'We have another thousand workers arriving on Wednesday, of whom you can have at least a hundred. The rest are needed for construction purposes. Would that suit you, Professor?'

'It would, Captain, very much so.'

'And with this extra hundred, you would be able to produce sixty warheads per day?'

'Yes, yes. I'm sure we could. Yes. Of course . . .'

'Of course what?'

'Of course, uh, it depends on how long – how shall I put this? – the workers remain, uh, fit enough to work.'

List smiled. 'You mean it depends on how quickly they die? Stop being so coy, Professor! These workers are not people, not like you and me. They are merely the troglodytes who inhabit these godforsaken islands. The more we work to death, the better. Besides, there are plenty more of them on Jersey and Guernsey to keep us going for months. I'll say it again, Professor, all you have to do is to ask.'

Fellner nodded. The man was insane, a barbarian. What was he, Fellner, doing here? All his learning, all his erudition – it was being wasted on these people. No, not wasted, but corrupted, abused, raped, even. Science was meant to be pure: that was what old Professor Friedrich had taught him, but Professor Friedrich had lived in different times. Science had become evil, thought Fellner, merely another tool in the hands of madmen. It was monstrous, and what made it worse was that he was too cowardly to do anything about it. He knew that the only escape was death, but he had not even come close, had not even got himself a pistol.

He looked at List. 'Many thanks, Captain,' he said quietly. 'I appreciate the efforts you have been making for me.'

'I am not making them for you, my dear Professor, but for the Führer!'

Of course you are, thought Fellner. Of course you damn well are. And it is cowards like me who let men like Hitler and you take control. And it is the work of cowards like me and Kramer that will shortly kill hundreds of thousands of people. Fellner wanted to weep, but all he could do was force a grin and return List's Nazi salute. He hated himself, a feeling made greater by the fact that he was too spineless to do anything about it. How could he look his family in the face when he got home, if indeed he still had a family?

There was a solution, an honourable way out that would not involve having to kill himself. He would tell the Allies, then fate could take its course. The more Fellner thought about it, the more appealing the idea became.

* * *

It was unusually cold that Saturday night, and Captain Fellowes and Pilot Officer Smith bore the brunt of the unseasonable weather. After hearing the exchange between the German guards and the occupants of the car, they had fled inland, running alongside a small, winding river. After a few minutes they had come across a wood, whose trees were largely unscathed by foragers. Fellowes had decided they should hide there for the night, and it was in a small hollow they had scraped out of the damp mud that they were now lying, hugging each other to maintain some semblance of warmth.

'I don't see any way out of this,' said Smith.

'We need to be more positive than that,' said Fellowes. 'We're not caught yet.'

'Not yet,' said Smith, 'but I'm only being realistic. Look, our identity papers are as good as useless. We've got no food and I hardly call this shelter. And what do you think the chances are of the Campbell women keeping their mouths shut if they're captured? I'd say pretty slim.'

'All right,' said Fellowes. 'So what do you suggest? That we hand ourselves in?'

Smith stayed quiet. The two men had broken apart during the discussion and were lying side by side, looking up at the moonlit branches. They were both tired, wet and hungry, and it was only natural that Smith should be complaining. Fellowes's morale was not exactly high either, but he had more resources to draw on than Smith. He was a good seven years older and had seen plenty of action. He had had to chivvy lads like Smith many times, and it never got any easier, especially when part of you agreed with what they were saying.

'All right,' said Fellowes. 'I admit, we're not in an ideal situation. However, situations are rendered far worse if you believe them to be hopeless. As soon as you start to think positively, you act positively, and when you do that, your chances increase. Understood?'

Smith sighed. 'Yes. Yes. Perhaps you're right. I apologise.'

'There's no need,' said Fellowes. 'It's perfectly understandable. If we're caught they'll kill us, not just because we killed that guard but because they'll think we're spies. We *have* to escape, Smith – don't you see? We have no choice in the matter.'

'Understood.'

'Good. Now, as far as I see it, we have two options. One, we still attempt to steal a boat. Or, two, we live off the land for as long as we can. With this weather, I don't fancy number one for the time being – we might as well kill ourselves here and now rather than try to get to France. Which leaves number two. To do that, we need a friend, and the only person we can trust on this bloody island is that doctor, Aubin. So, tomorrow, I suggest we try to track him down.'

'How?'

'Well, if he's a doctor, he should still have a telephone. If he has a telephone, we can contact him. So, all we have to do is find a telephone. That might be risky, but it's our only chance.'

'It sounds like a long shot.'

'Perhaps,' said Fellowes, 'but with the Campbells captured,

Aubin is our best bet. If we don't get hold of him, we're eating grass or trying to pinch food from farmyards, neither of which I much fancy. Mrs Campbell said the farmers around here will shoot at any noise they hear in the night, and I can well believe her.'

'We could just *ask* a farmer.'

'No chance,' said Fellowes. 'How could we trust him?'

* * *

'This is unbelievable.'

'I know,' says Terry, 'but it's all there.'

'Are you sure your German's all right?'

'*Einwandfrei.*'

'Come again?'

'Faultless.'

Lebonneur takes another mouthful of whisky. He looks at Terry, studying the man's pebble glasses and combed-over strands of hair. At school, he would have been the type to whom Lebonneur would have given a hard time for being a square. But he likes Terry, because Terry is a genuine enthusiast. There is no one on the island who knows more about the occupation than him – he even produced a map of Jersey that showed every gun emplacement, every resistance nest, every – what was it again? – 'light howitzer in a semi-permanent position'.

'You know, Bob, this is quite a find.'

'The understatement of the century, Terry. This changes *everything*. There's a lot now that makes sense, a *lot*.'

'What are you going to do?'

'Keep it quiet for a start. No one must know about this diary and what it contains – at least, not yet.'

Terry looks nervously at the floor.

'What is it, Terry? Have you told someone?'

'No, not really.'

Shit, thinks Lebonneur, *shit*.

' "Not really"?' he asks.

'Well, I may, um, have told Sarah at the Société about it.'

'Oh, Terry,' Lebonneur sighs, 'why did you have to do that? What exactly did you tell her?'

'I'm sorry. I suppose I was just a little excited – couldn't help myself.'

'What did you tell her?'

'Um, not much, really. I told her that you'd found the diary in your mother's stuff, and that it was quite a gem.'

'That was all?'

Terry didn't reply.

'Please, Terry, I *must* know.'

'I may have told her about Alderney.'

'What *specifically* about Alderney?'

'That the Germans had built some sort of weapon inside a hill. That was it, I promise you.'

'You swear?'

'Honest to God. I also read her the bits about women, you

know, the romantic bits, but that was it, I promise.'

Lebonneur slumps back in his armchair, then suddenly starts forward. 'Oh, fuck!'

'What? *What?*'

'Sarah's husband, whatshisface, he's on the States, isn't he?'

'Who, Mark? Yes, that's right, he's been a jurat for years.'

Lebonneur cups his hands and buries his face in them. This is the worst possible news. Terry and his big sodding mouth could ruin everything, the whole fucking thing. 'Sarah is bound to tell Mark,' says Lebonneur, his voice muffled by his hands, 'who is then bound to tell the rest of the bloody States. Once they know, we're buggered.'

'It can't be as bad as—'

Lebonneur lifts his head up violently. 'Yes, it bloody well can! These people will stop at nothing, don't you see? This isn't just about fiddling the books, Terry, this is huge – fucking huge! People have already died because of this and I see no reason why more won't.'

'I think you're being a little melodramatic, Bob—'

'Really? Try telling that to Mrs Mead. Or the poor bloody Harris family who are presently sitting in Southampton General bloody Hospital weeping over their dead father. And you only have to look at the diary to see what they're capable of! Can't you see, Terry? History's starting to repeat itself. People are being murdered—'

'Murdered?'

168

'Yes, *murdered*. Probably not Harris, although he was as good as murdered, but certainly Mead, I've no doubt about that.'

'Are you sure? I mean this is a very serious—'

Lebonneur slaps the diary with the back of his hand. 'You've read this, Terry. You've *seen* what happened. You know what they're hiding – isn't it obvious that they'd kill to protect it?'

Terry shrugs.

'John Mead didn't fall to his death,' Lebonneur says. 'I'm sure he was pushed.'

'Why, though? Why him?'

'Because he was ill, that's why. He was ill in the same way as Harris was ill, and in the same way as those von Luck writes about were ill. The illness is the key, Terry, I've no doubt about that.'

'What is this illness, then?'

'Haven't a clue. All I know is that it involves vomiting, swollen ankles and kidneys. I'd bet my bottom dollar that Mead was killed because he was starting to show signs of this illness, an illness that would reveal what lies in Mannez Hill. They whisked Harris off quickly, but they knew they couldn't do that again, so Mead "accidentally" falls off a gun tower. Unfortunately for them, he doesn't die immediately, so they have to keep him under wraps so no one can see any signs of the illness. Then they stall, waiting for him to die, leaving poor Mrs Mead in the dark.'

'That's quite a theory.'

'It's more than that – it's the truth. Unless we do something, more of those builders are going to die, you mark my words.'

' "We", Bob, "we"?'

'That's right – "we". You're in this too now, Terry.'

'But I've got to work, got things to do.'

'I know that, but I insist you help me. Look, I'm not asking much. It would be great if you could go through your records and see if you can find anything that backs up von Luck's diary. Could you at least do that for me?'

'Sure.'

'And Marais. Find out all you can about him.'

'OK.'

'And, for Pete's sake, keep your bloody trap shut!'

'Point taken.'

'Good,' says Lebonneur, looking hard at Terry.

'And, er, what are you going to do?' Terry asks.

'Me? I'm going to book a trip to Alderney.'

*　*　*

The guard saluted von Luck as he walked up to the front door of the headquarters.

'Good evening, Corporal,' said von Luck. 'Is Inspector Bouhler in?'

'Yes, sir,' the young NCO replied. His tone was nervous.

'Is anything the matter, Corporal?'

'No . . . no, sir.'

Von Luck eyed him carefully. There was clearly something the matter, as there was fear drawn all over his face: his eyes were bulging and he was swallowing repeatedly. Presumably he had heard the screams as von Luck had.

The guard opened the door and von Luck stepped into a small vestibule, to be confronted by an inner glass door. A sign on the wall indicated that he should ring the bell 'outside office hours'. Von Luck did so, hearing the ring deep inside the building. While he waited, he strained his ears for more screams, but none came. Thank God Pippa had not been there to hear them, he thought.

After a minute the door was opened by a small man wearing a brown suit. He bore a moustache clearly modelled on Hitler's, which told von Luck all he needed to know about the man's sympathies.

'Good evening. I am Lieutenant Colonel von Luck of the Field Command. I need to speak to Inspector Bouhler.'

The man's eyes narrowed. He was a revolting specimen, thought von Luck, the type of man who revelled in *schadenfreude*, a glee especially felt when he had inflicted the misfortunes himself.

'Inspector Bouhler is busy,' the man snapped.

Busy torturing, thought von Luck. 'I don't care if he's busy,' said von Luck. 'This is an urgent matter and I demand to speak to him.'

The man did not move, but continued to survey von Luck as though he was about to interrogate him. If the effect was to disturb, it failed. Von Luck leant down and put his face right up against the man's.

'I don't care who the fuck you are, but if you don't let me see Inspector Bouhler right now, I will have you shot for insubordination. Is that clear?'

The man nodded. 'I apologise, Colonel,' he said, 'but Inspector Bouhler told me that he was not to be disturbed. He is working on an extremely important state matter—'

'Rubbish! Are you going to let me in? Yes or no?'

Before the man could answer, the building rang with a scream, which caused the little man to smile. 'As you can hear,' he said, 'Inspector Bouhler is busy.'

This was too much for von Luck, who found himself automatically forming his right hand into a fist, then bringing it up rapidly and connecting it with the man's right eye and nose. The force of the blow sent him reeling back into the hall and on to the floor. Von Luck looked down with satisfaction. Nasty little worm, he thought.

The door behind him was suddenly pushed open. Von Luck whipped round.

It was the guard. 'I heard a noise . . .'

Von Luck put a finger to his lips. 'Not a sound, Corporal! Be quiet, do you hear?'

The corporal looked into the hall. 'But—'

'I said quiet!'

What should he tell him? The truth? Well, why not? He had seen the corporal's face – the man was as revolted by the screams as he was.

'Now, listen,' von Luck whispered, 'you are to tell nobody

about this. This little prick disobeyed me so I had to deal with him appropriately. You are to go back outside and to stay there. You heard nothing, I repeat, *nothing*. Is that understood?'

'Yes, sir.'

'If you do as I say, I shall reward you. What is your name, Corporal?'

'Ulrich Müller, sir.'

'All right, Müller, if you keep this quiet, then I shall get you two hundred cigarettes. How does that sound, eh?'

'Thank you, sir,' Müller replied. 'My lips are sealed. Anyway, sir, good for you – knocking that scum out.'

Von Luck grinned. 'That'll do, Müller. Now get back outside and stay there.'

'Sir!'

Müller did as he was told.

Where the hell was he going to get two hundred cigarettes? The thought disappeared as quickly as it had come. Von Luck turned and walked briskly into the hall, stepping over the unconscious form of the Gestapo functionary. He was tempted to wipe his feet on the man but decided against it.

He made for the staircase – the screams had clearly come from upstairs. What the hell were they doing to her? Just keep yourself under control, von Luck told himself. Don't end up doing something rash. Punching a petty Gestapo official was one thing, but shooting one was quite another.

Another scream, louder than the previous one. Jesus Christ!

Von Luck sprinted up the stairs, nearly tripping on the loose burgundy carpet. He reached the top and found himself on a dim landing. He stayed still, waiting for a sound.

He did not have to wait long. A scream, weaker than the previous one, but this time preceded by the swish of a cane. It had come from the room at the end of the landing, towards which von Luck ran. He kicked open the door with his foot, and was greeted by a scene that would remain, like an indelible stain, on his memory.

Half naked, tied to a table, was the form of a middle-aged woman – Mrs Campbell. She was lying on her front, her back exposed. Across it were several red welts, some of which were bleeding profusely. Standing over her was Bouhler, a leather cane poised in the air, ready for its umpteenth downward blow. Von Luck barely managed to contain himself: every muscle in his body wanted to do to Bouhler what he was doing to Mrs Campbell.

'Lieutenant Colonel!' said Bouhler, doing his best to sound calm. 'This is a surprise. You have caught me doing a little . . . overtime, shall we say?'

'What do you think you're doing, Bouhler?'

'It's a question I might ask you, von Luck. Did my assistant Bürkel not tell you that I was busy?'

'He did, but I didn't take no for answer.'

Throughout the exchange, Violet was sobbing. Unable to turn round, it was impossible for her to see that the visitor was not another torturer.

'Mrs Campbell,' said von Luck. 'This is von Luck here.' He had spoken in English.

'*Aah*,' said Bouhler. 'I see why you're here now. This is another of your tarts, isn't it? I must say, I didn't know you went for them quite this old, but she has a certain something, I admit.'

'You bastard, Bouhler,' von Luck replied, walking round to the other end of the table so that Violet could see him. 'Don't you understand that you're going to kill her if you carry on?'

Bouhler shrugged. 'It's what she deserves,' he said.

Von Luck bent down and gave Violet a reassuring squeeze on her left shoulder. 'You'll be all right now,' he whispered.

'How gallant of you,' said Bouhler. 'Anyway, how did you know she was here?'

'The Field Command,' said von Luck.

'But I haven't told anybody there.'

'What of it? Someone did, or I wouldn't be here, would I?'

Bouhler eyed von Luck with some squinted suspicion. 'It's funny, isn't it,' he began, 'how Mrs Campbell's daughter was last seen in the vicinity of Linden Court?'

'Is it?'

'One could almost assume that you are sheltering the girl yourself,' said Bouhler, 'and that you have come here at her behest to save her mother. If that is the case, von Luck, then you are even more of a romantic than I had heard. A mother and daughter, eh? You are a dirty sod!'

Bouhler may be a bastard, thought von Luck, but he's a clever one.

'The reason I'm here,' said von Luck, 'is not because Mrs Campbell is one my "tarts", as you put it, but because, unlike you, Bouhler, I am a human being. I object to your methods, no matter what "crime" Mrs Campbell is guilty of.'

'My methods, as you well know, Lieutenant Colonel, are perfectly legal.'

'It's not a law I subscribe to,' said von Luck.

'That is immaterial,' said Bouhler, 'although if you do not subscribe to your country's laws, you are little better than a traitor.'

Von Luck was fed up with this. 'I am here, Bouhler, not to argue the legitimacy of your odious organisation, but to take Mrs Campbell and place her in the custody of the army.'

'Really? On whose authority?'

'My own,' said von Luck, starting to untie the cord from around Violet's left wrist.

'Stop that at once!'

Von Luck did not deign to look up. His eyes were fixated on Violet's wounds, of which he estimated there were at least twenty. It was astonishing that the woman had not passed out.

'I'm warning you, von Luck!'

Von Luck freed Violet's other wrist. 'Warning me, Bouhler? Warning me about what?'

'If you do not leave immediately, I will have no option but to arrest you for obstructing a Gestapo inquiry.'

'Is that right?' said von Luck. 'Come on, Mrs Campbell, let's get you up.'

Von Luck put his hands under Violet's armpits and started to lift her. She cried out – the movement was clearly agonising, although not quite as painful as a further blow from Bouhler's cane, which made her shriek so loudly that von Luck thought his hearing might be damaged.

'Stop this!' Bouhler shouted, once more beating her back.

Von Luck let her down. He had hoped that Bouhler might take the easy option and let her go, but this was not going to happen. Bouhler raised his cane once more, but this time von Luck was ready for it, and caught it as it swung down. The blow stung badly, but von Luck maintained his grip, looking into Bouhler's face as the Gestapo man attempted to wrestle away the cane.

'This is your last chance, Bouhler! If you do not allow me to take Mrs Campbell with me, I shall have to force you to.' Von Luck had no desire to end up in a fight, but he also knew that he would not allow her to stay any longer in the arms of this maniac. Even now, as his body was tensing itself for action, a part of him was insisting that he shouldn't be here, that it was rash of him to risk any chance he might have in stopping the deportation.

Bouhler pulled at the cane hard, almost releasing it from von Luck's grip. Von Luck yanked it back, forcing Bouhler to fall on top of a still-screaming Violet. The poor woman, thought von Luck. Seizing the opportunity, he snatched the cane away from Bouhler, and brought it down hard on the back of his head. Bouhler yelled, but before he had time to get up, von Luck grabbed him by his shirt collar and threw him on to the floor. Instinctively Bouhler curled himself up, but it was not enough to stop von Luck meting out a savage battery of blows that connected with Bouhler's hands, arms, stomach and legs.

'Have that!' von Luck found himself shouting. 'You bastard! Fucking bastard!'

'Please!' shrieked Bouhler. 'Please stop! I beg you!'

But von Luck was not listening. He was in a rage, a rage out of which he could not snap. He found himself hitting Bouhler with increasing ferocity, not only with the cane but kicking him as well, driving the caps of his boots hard into the man's midriff and, when he could, into his face. It was, thought von Luck – echoing Bouhler – what he deserved. The bastard had spent years doing this to people, and now he was getting some of it back.

Stop this. Stop it immediately. What are you trying to do? Kill the man? That will ruin everything: you'll get yourself put in front of a firing squad. Von Luck looked down at Bouhler – he was moaning gently. Blood was oozing from cuts and bruises all over his swollen face; his mouth was a scarlet mess. It was too late, von Luck thought. He had gone too far. He cursed himself for losing his temper – it did not happen very often, but the stress of the day capped by the sight of Violet Campbell had pushed him to this.

How should he kill him? The simplest method was to shoot him, but that would make too much noise. Carry on beating him? That was unreliable and messy. Suffocate him? Yes – that was it. Von Luck looked around the room, his eyes momentarily drawn, as Violet's had been a few hours earlier, to the watercolour of the kittens. What was that foul thing doing here? After a few seconds, he found what he was looking for: a cushion. He snatched it from its chair, came back and sat down on Bouhler's twitching body. His breathing was erratic, coming as it did through ever-increasing amounts of blood and bile.

Von Luck placed the cushion firmly over Bouhler's face, which had the immediate effect of causing the Gestapo man to struggle. Enfeebled by the beating, Bouhler's efforts were not enough to stop von Luck pressing down as hard as he could. Bouhler thrashed and kicked, but it was hopeless. After half a minute, the struggling diminished, but von Luck resolutely held the cushion in place. Bouhler would have only just passed out – it would take at least another minute, perhaps two, to ensure his death.

While he waited, von Luck looked over at the table, at the form of Violet Campbell. She was motionless. Dead? Oh, God, please not. 'Mrs Campbell, I must get you out of here.'

He removed the cushion and looked down at Bouhler. He was quite still. Von Luck pressed his head to the man's chest, and heard nothing. He was dead, there was no doubt about it. He stood up and gave Bouhler's body a confirmatory kick. No sound, no moan.

Von Luck bent over Violet. Unlike Bouhler, she was breathing. Thank God, thought von Luck, she had only passed out. With some difficulty, he lifted her from the table. He did his best not to make contact with her wounds, but it was impossible. She needed a stretcher and an ambulance, von Luck thought, but such luxuries were out of the question. He carried her over his shoulder, and walked out of the room, stepping over Bouhler's body.

Shit, thought von Luck, as he looked down the stairs, shit. The other Gestapo man, Bürkel, what should he do with him? Kill him as well? Or take him back to Linden Court and hold him there? The latter – it had to be the latter. Von Luck had had enough of killing for one night. Killing Bouhler had been cold-blooded enough, but to kill Bürkel as he lay unconscious on the hall floor? He didn't have it in him.

When he reached the bottom of the stairs, von Luck laid Violet down. He checked her breathing and pulse – both seemed regular.

He then checked Bürkel.

Nothing. Not a sound. Was he dead? No – he couldn't be. Surely that was impossible. He pressed his head against Bürkel's chest. No movement. He slapped his face, attempting to revive him, but he didn't flinch or stir. He must have killed him with one punch.

Von Luck walked through to the vestibule and quietly eased the door ajar. He peered through the opening. 'Corporal!' he hissed.

Müller turned round. 'Yes?'

'Come here!'

Müller walked over briskly. 'Yes, sir?'

'I need your help,' said von Luck.

'Yes, sir!'

'I warn you, though – this will be worth a lot of cigarettes.'

*   *   *

Admiral Huffmeier was a light sleeper, but that night he slept worse than usual. His sailor's sense told him a storm was brewing, and a big one at that. If it was very bad, it might delay the deportation, something he most emphatically did not want.

His musings were interrupted by a firm knocking on his bedroom door. 'Yes?' he shouted, irritated by the disturbance.

The door opened and Huffmeier's orderly, Gebhardt, walked in, carrying a telephone.

Huffmeier looked at his watch. It was five o'clock, a good hour before he normally got up. 'Who is it?'

'It's Major Hempel, sir, he says it's very urgent.'

Huffmeier gestured to Gebhardt that he should bring the phone over. 'Hempel? What in God's name is this about?'

'I'm sorry to disturb you, sir, but I have bad news.'

An invasion, thought Huffmeier. It had to be an invasion. 'Where have they landed?'

'I'm sorry, sir?'

'The Americans! The British! Where are they?'

'No, sir, it's not that. It's about Inspectors Bouhler and Bürkel, sir. They've both been found dead at Gestapo headquarters.'

Huffmeier sat up. 'Dead? How?'

'Bürkel had a broken neck, and it looks as though Bouhler was beaten, then suffocated.'

Huffmeier breathed out slowly. 'Carry on, Hempel.'

'The sentry assigned to the building – a Corporal Müller – has disappeared, as has a prisoner, a Mrs Violet Campbell, who was being questioned about the two British escaped prisoners-of—'

'Yes, yes, I know about them,' Huffmeier snapped. 'Suspects, Hempel, are there any suspects?'

'No, sir, not yet. All we have to go on is the fact that a neighbour heard a car last night.'

'A car? Is that it?'

'Yes, sir.'

Huffmeier pinched the bridge of his nose and shut his eyes. This was appalling news, perhaps even worse than an invasion. At least then he could have proved his heroism by defending the islands to the last drop. There was nothing heroic in having to deal with a double murder.

The presence of a car suggested that the murderer – or murderers – was either a German officer or an islander such as Marais or Dr Aubin. Von Luck? No – that was surely impossible. Not even he would be so bold as to murder two Gestapo men. Besides, what motive would he have? Even if he had slept with Mrs Campbell, he was unlikely to kill for her – he was not that type of man. Could an islander have done it? Surely not. Men like Marais and Aubin were not killers. Perhaps it had been this corporal, Müller. But that seemed unlikely as well. The two

POWs, perhaps? It was conceivable, but only just. They had no car, no weapons, no means at all.

'What else do we know about the car, Hempel?'

'Very little, sir. One of the nearby residents, a Mrs Samantha de Mello, said she heard a car arrive at about nine o'clock, then drive off about fifteen minutes later.'

'So she didn't actually see it?'

'No. She told me she was not in the habit of looking at what went on at the Gestapo headquarters. Said it was none of her business.'

She was right, no doubt, thought Huffmeier, although he wished that this de Mello woman had been a curtain-twitching busybody.

'Have you told Inspector Fügen yet?' Huffmeier asked, referring to the now sole member of the Gestapo on the island.

'Not yet, sir,' said Hempel. 'I thought it best to call you first.'

'You did the right thing, Hempel. Don't call him yet. He'll only radio Berlin and I want to keep this under wraps for the time being.'

Huffmeier guessed that Hempel would know his reasons for keeping the matter quiet. One murdered sentry, two escaped POWs, two murdered Gestapo men, one missing sentry and a missing prisoner – all in the space of a fortnight. Huffmeier cursed his lack of luck. Nothing that had happened was directly his fault, but Berlin would think he was losing control. They might replace him, a notion that Huffmeier found unbearable, not least because he would be loath to receive no credit for the project on Alderney.

'What shall I do, sir?'

Huffmeier paused.

'Sir?'

'Yes, yes, Hempel! Hang on a second.'

The fact that Mrs Campbell was missing disturbed Huffmeier even more than the murders. He cared little for either of the dead men, but at least they had done their jobs well. It looked to Huffmeier that Mrs Campbell had been rescued, but who had had the ability to pull off such an audacious mission? If it was the islanders, he would need to carry out reprisals – perhaps execute a dozen every day until the culprits turned up – but for the moment he needed their co-operation for the deportation. Nothing was more important than that. Far better, then, to keep the investigation within the occupying forces, even if they were looking in the wrong place. Who cared about the truth anyway? All he had to do was ensure that Alderney went well. Everything else could be put to one side.

'All right, Hempel. This is what we will do.'

'Sir.'

'You're to put out an alert for Corporal Müller, stating that he is wanted for the murder of Bürkel and Bouhler.'

There was a gasp. 'But, sir—'

'Just do as I say,' said Huffmeier, calmly. He had expected Hempel to make some sort of protest. 'Give out no more information than that, and certainly do not mention that Mrs Campbell has disappeared. Is that understood?'

'Yes, sir.'

'Good.'

'And, Hempel.'

'Yes, sir?'

'Make sure that you're in church this morning. I don't want people to think we're panicking just because a couple of policemen have been killed. Now get off the line. There's someone I need to speak to.'

'Sir.'

Huffmeier handed the receiver back to Gebhardt. 'It should go without saying that you didn't hear that conversation.'

'Of course, Admiral.'

'Good. Now get me Mollett on the phone.'

* * *

Huffmeier's prediction about the storm had been correct, for by half past nine the rain was torrential, made worse by an accompanying near-gale. Those attending St Helier parish church were drenched as they made their way across Royal Square for the Sunday-morning service.

As usual, the congregation was made up of German officers and senior NCOs, with a handful of islanders – Jerrybags eager to catch a glimpse of last night's boyfriend among the pews; reluctant members of the States, including Marais himself; and the trenchant, who had maintained for five long years that, Germans or no, nothing would stop them worshipping in their local church.

The church was unusually dark that morning. A combination of the storm and an ensuing power-cut meant that the interior was candlelit, although the candles were few in number. Manufactured from some foul composite of wax and tallow, they smelt deeply unwholesome. Coupled with the odour emanating from damp uniforms, many of which had been unwashed for several weeks, the church that morning was no place for someone with a delicate nose.

Even if he had noticed the smell, von Luck would not have been troubled by it. Besides, his mind was focused not on any physical sensation but on the events of the previous day. As he walked into the church, he tried to maintain a phlegmatic expression, keen not to reveal either his anxiety or his exhaustion from a sleepless night. He had decided that to miss the service would look suspicious – far better to maintain a routine of normality.

Desperate to find a friendly face as he walked down the nave, his eyes alighted on Hempel, who was sitting two rows from the front. 'Good morning, Hempel,' said von Luck, as he sat down next to him.

'Good morning, sir,' said Hempel, quietly. 'Have you heard the news?'

'No,' said von Luck, his heart starting to thud.

'Bouhler and Bürkel of the Gestapo were found dead this morning.'

'Christ,' said von Luck, softly, forgetting where he was. 'Who did it?'

'We don't know – the admiral thinks it was the corporal who was guarding them. He's disappeared, along with Mrs Campbell, the woman who was arrested for hiding those two British officers.'

Part of von Luck wanted to tell Hempel the truth, if only to lighten the burden. He would dearly have loved to reveal how Mrs Campbell was presently hiding at Linden Court, and Müller was with the farmer who looked after his horse. The man had charged von Luck an atrocious amount, but he had had little choice. And, most of all, he longed to tell Hempel that it was he who had killed the two men.

'A corporal?' asked von Luck.

'That's right. God knows why he thinks it's the corporal, but what I do know is that Huffmeier wants to keep the whole thing quiet.'

Von Luck felt a mild surge of relief. 'Oh?'

'Yes – and he doesn't even want to let on that this Mrs Campbell has got away.'

'I expect he's worried that we'll be a laughing-stock if the islanders find out,' said von Luck.

'Probably,' said Hempel. 'Still, the whole thing is bizarre.'

'It's certainly that,' said von Luck. 'What would a corporal be doing rescuing a middle-aged Jerseywoman?'

'I agree – it clearly can't be him, but Huffmeier was insistent that that was the line of inquiry we were going to follow. You know what my hunch is?'

'What?'

187

'It's Petersen, the one over at communications.'

'*Petersen?* Why him?'

'He's disappeared, and he was always a little unhinged. It's not much of a case, but it's more convincing than some bloody corporal.'

'Did Petersen know Mrs Campbell?'

'That's what I'm going to look into.'

'So you're in charge, then, are you?'

'I am indeed,' said Hempel, laughing.

Von Luck was immediately struck by the irony of the situation. 'So how come you're in church?' von Luck asked. 'I thought you'd be running around the island doing detective work.'

'The admiral was keen that we should keep everything looking as normal.'

Von Luck couldn't resist a smile. Me too, he thought, me too. With the break in conversation, he took the opportunity to look at the congregation. There, two pews in front of them, was the admiral, surrounded by a retinue of toadies, most of whom wore naval uniforms. On the other side of the church sat some members of the States, among them Marais and Portelet. Peter Mollett was not there, von Luck noticed, but thought little of it.

As if guided by a sixth sense, Marais turned round as von Luck's eyes settled on the back of his head. He made eye-contact, and von Luck raised his brows in acknowledgement. Marais returned the gesture, and with a sideways nod towards the back of the church, indicated to von Luck that they should talk afterwards. Von Luck nodded in reply, then returned his gaze to the pew, from which he lifted the hymn book, emblazoned with a swastika and bearing a picture of the Führer on the flyleaf. He had a lot to tell Marais and, by the look if it, Marais had a lot to tell him.

'Good morning, Colonel von Luck,' said Richard Marais, sheltering under a rather battered umbrella. The two men were speaking an hour later outside the church. Surrounded by his fellow Germans, von Luck knew that it would be impossible for them to have an open conversation. 'Herr Marais,' he said, touching his cap with his index finger.

'I thought you should know that we held a meeting of the States last night.'

'Oh, yes?'

'And we agreed that we would oppose the planned deportation . . .'

'I thought you said—'

'. . . only if you were not able to stop it yourself.'

Von Luck nodded. 'Good for you,' he said. 'And was the vote unanimous?'

Marais paused. 'I'm afraid not,' he said, his expression almost sheepish. 'I regret to say that I had to use my casting vote as Bailiff.'

'I see,' said von Luck. 'Does this create a problem for you?'

'I hope not and, indeed, I hope the vote will prove academic.'

Such a politician, von Luck thought, a master of the indirect phrase loaded with meaning. 'I'm afraid I cannot give you any news regarding that at the moment,' von Luck replied.

Marais lowered his umbrella, creating a mildly conspiratorial air. 'I'm sorry to hear that,' he said, 'because there is something else I need to talk to you about. It concerns what's happening on Alderney. Some news has reached me that I need urgently to convey to you. Perhaps we could meet at noon at the dolmen at Faldouet. Do you know it?'

'I do,' said von Luck. 'I shall see you there.'

* * *

Von Luck arrived back at Linden Court ten minutes after his conversation with Marais. The first person who greeted him was Mrs May. 'Colonel von Luck,' she said, 'I really must protest!'

Von Luck sighed. His state of mind was very removed from dealing with domestic issues. 'Yes, Mrs May?' he asked, wearily looking over the sixty-year-old woman's shoulder.

'How am I going to feed all these people you've brought here? Another mouth, fine, hardly any problem at all, but another two? How are we going to manage? I shall need the miracle of the fishes and the loaves to feed all of us. I know you said that I had to keep my trap shut—'

'*Trap* shut?'

'My *mouth* shut, Colonel, my mouth.'

'Sorry, Mrs May. My command of English idiom is not quite as perfect as it should be after all these years.'

Now it was Mrs May's turn to look confused, although it was an expression that passed over her features rapidly. 'You must understand, Colonel, that we have hardly any food – it really is most serious.'

'Then, Mrs May, I shall get you some. Please, do not worry. All I ask is that you look after the Campbells to the best of your ability and, I cannot stress this enough, with your utmost discretion. Both of them are in great danger and any loose words will see them – and certainly me – lined up against a wall.'

Mrs May swallowed hard.

'I shall get you some food this morning, I promise. In the meantime, I'm sure my guests will survive.'

'That Mrs Campbell looks in a bad state. The poor woman! Whatever did they do to her?'

'They flogged her, Mrs May, almost to her death.'

Mrs May put a hand to her mouth.

'Now I must go and see how she is,' said von Luck.

Von Luck found Pippa and Violet in one of the bedrooms. The room smelt strongly of iodine.

'How is she?' von Luck asked.

'Not good,' said Pippa. 'But she's asleep at least.'

Von Luck noticed that she looked extremely tired. Her eyes were sunk into dark pools, but happiness seemed to be shining through them.

'Does she need a doctor?' von Luck asked quietly.

Pippa sighed. 'I don't know. The wounds still look pretty raw, but the iodine should help.'

'Let me know. Perhaps Aubin should have a look at her.'

'Aubin?'

'Yes – why? Is there anything the matter with him? I can't, after all, go to a German doctor.'

'Er, no, of course,' said Pippa. 'It's just that . . . oh, it's not important.'

'What?'

'Nothing. Honestly. I'll tell you when it's more appropriate.'

Von Luck could guess what Pippa was referring to. She was correct – the moment was not right. 'I think I understand,' said von Luck.

'You do?'

'Yes. Aubin spoke to me. I'm afraid I was not receptive to his comments.'

Pippa looked up from her mother. 'He *spoke* to you? About me? How dare he? It's none of his—'

'Pippa! *Please*. As you said, let's talk about this some other time. There are some other matters I need to talk to you about, matters that are far bigger than you or me.'

'What?'

Von Luck looked at his watch. He didn't have to leave for another half an hour.

*   *   *

The Occupation

The phone call comes late that afternoon, a couple of hours after Terry has left.

'Is that Mr Lebonneur?'

'It is.'

'Forgive me for calling you out of the blue, Mr Lebonneur, but I've heard on the, ah, grapevine, that you're in possession of a diary written by a German army officer stationed here during the war.'

The ash from Lebonneur's cigarette drops unnoticed on to the carpet. 'Who is this?' he asks.

'Um, you'll have to forgive me if I don't tell you my name.'

Lebonneur doesn't recognise the voice. It is well spoken, which could make it one of thousands of people on Jersey. 'I don't like it when people won't give their names,' says Lebonneur. 'They're usually trying to sell me something.'

'Well, what I have in mind is the opposite.'

'Oh, yes?'

'I'd like to buy something. The diary. You see, I, ah, collect memorabilia from the occupation, and von Luck's diary would make an excellent addition to my collection. I gather there is much interesting material in it, material that would be of much interest to an amateur historian like myself.'

Amateur historian. Bollocks, thinks Lebonneur. 'That still doesn't tell me why you're not revealing your name.'

There is a pause.

'I'm a very private man, Mr Lebonneur, and I like to keep myself and my collection a private matter. Normally I deal through my solicitors, but I thought in this instance I should strike quickly, as it were.'

'How did you hear about the diary?'

'Well, you know how it is on these islands – word tends to travel quickly.'

'Don't I just.'

'I'm willing to make you a generous offer.'

'Go on, then.'

'I'd be willing to give you two thousand pounds for it.'

Two grand – about the market rate, thinks Lebonneur. He's not offering silly money, because he obviously wants to keep this 'collection' charade going.

'Well, that's a very generous offer, Mr Whoever-you-are, but I'm afraid the diary is an heirloom and I'm reluctant to part with it.'

He hears a sharp intake of breath down the line.

'All right. I'm willing to offer up to three thousand pounds, but no more.'

'That's still very kind, but I'm afraid the diary is not for sale.'

'Are you telling me you don't have a price?'

'I'm afraid so, even an unemployed hack like me.'

'Three thousand pounds is a lot of money, Mr Lebonneur. I urge you to reconsider.'

'No,' says Lebonneur. 'No way.'

He's enjoying this, wants to see how high the figure will go.

'Three and a half, then. That's nearly twice my initial offer.'

'Which makes me think your initial offer was derisory.'

Silence.

'Hello?' asks Lebonneur.

'I think you're being very foolish, Mr Lebonneur.'

The tone of the man's voice had changed: more threatening, chilling, even.

'Foolish?'

'I think you know what I'm talking about.'

'Er . . . I don't think so.'

'Yes, you do, Mr Lebonneur.'

'I'm afraid you must have the wrong end of the stick. There's obviously—'

'Come come! I'm offering you a good amount of money, money that I'm sure will be very useful now that you're unemployed. Listen, Mr Lebonneur, I could make things difficult for you.'

'Is that a threat?'

'You can take it as you wish.'

'All right. It was a threat, then. How do you propose to make my life so "difficult", as you put it?'

'All I'm saying is that the best option for you is to take the money.'

'And if I don't?'

'Then, as I said, your life starts to get a little more difficult.'

'Bricks through windows, eh?'

'I'm not a child, Mr Lebonneur.'

'Neither am I. If either of us is foolish, I'd say it was you. After this phone call, I'm going to ring the police, and tell them that you have just threatened me. I'd expect a knock on your door later, if I were you.'

Laughter, condescending laughter. 'Despite your journalistic talents, Mr Lebonneur, there are still many things that you do not know about the Channel Islands.'

'What? That the police are corrupt?'

'No, not corrupt – just sensible.'

Lebonneur chews over the words. The man may well be bluffing, but Lebonneur has done enough stories on bent policemen to give him the benefit of the doubt.

'Four thousand pounds, Mr Lebonneur. Very generous indeed. I strongly encourage you to accept it.'

A small part of Lebonneur tells him to take the money, turn his back on all this. Four grand would come in useful, keep the family running for a couple of months, perhaps three. 'My answer is no,' he says.

'In that case, I wish you a good night.'

And then the dialling tone. A cigarette, Lebonneur thinks, that's what he needs.

* * *

Richard Marais's car was parked on the road just before the path that led to the dolmen. A few minutes after noon, Von Luck drew up behind it and switched off his engine. The rain beat down on the windscreen, and the wind rocked the car. He wanted desperately to sleep, but he knew there was no time for such a luxury. It had been the most dramatic forty-eight hours of his life, and he knew that it was only a prelude. He was failing, he thought. Last night's events had been a spectacular foul-up, and he knew that it was only a matter of time before the murders and Petersen's disappearance were linked to him. It was tempting to give up, to regard himself as the desk soldier that Petersen had described, a tag that von Luck found deeply insulting.

No. He was not going to do that. That was exhaustion talking, not the real him. He had done the decent thing, had rescued a woman from the Gestapo – there was enough to be proud of in that alone. To have saved her was an achievement in itself, but it was nothing compared to the many who were still at risk.

He opened the car door and stepped out into the rain, wrapped his greatcoat tightly around himself and looked around. He could see the roof of a farmhouse a few hedgerows away, but other than that he was not overlooked. Marais had chosen their meeting-place wisely, he thought.

The thirty-foot path down to the dolmen was sheltered by some bushes, which had been trained to form a tunnel. Without any leaves, the tunnel offered only partial respite from the wind and the rain, but von Luck was grateful for the protection. Under different circumstances it might even comprise a somewhat romantic spot, he mused.

He stepped out of the tunnel to be presented with a hedged-in area measuring around forty feet square. The dolmen – a huge slab of stone perched on top of a series of vertical slabs arranged in a semicircle – lay in the middle, with a passageway of four-foot-high stones leading to it. The site of a Neolithic burial ground, it had only been discovered a hundred years ago, and three skeletons had been unearthed, along with a collection of axes and pots. In the wet greyness of the day, the site instantly lost any of the romantic appeal that von Luck had just attributed to it.

'Marais?' von Luck called out.

There was no reply.

'Marais!'

Nothing.

Von Luck walked forward, sensing instantly that something was wrong. He edged towards the dolmen, his pistol at the ready. 'Marais! Are you there?'

Still nothing. What was going on?

Von Luck approached slowly. Because the rocks were imperfectly shaped, he would be able to see into the chamber formed by the dolmen. The rain hitting the brim of his cap seemed to grow heavier as well as the sound of his breathing, which was getting louder and faster.

He peered through a fissure in the rocks. His eyes took a few seconds to adjust to the dimness of the chamber, but as soon as they had, the object of their attention caused von Luck's breathing and heart-rate almost to double. He looked around, doing his best to stop himself panicking. On top of the exhaustion, what he had just seen was causing his brain to become overloaded almost to the point of helplessness and confusion. Get a grip on yourself. He felt terribly, crushingly sick. You've got to look, he told himself, you've got to go in there and look.

He stood up erect and then, with the pistol still in his hand, walked round to the end of the passageway. He went down the passage, looking from left to right over the tops of the rocks on either side of him. He held his pistol in both hands, the safety catch off, ready to fire at the slightest noise.

None came. Apart from the wind, and the sound of his boots squelching into the mud, there was nothing. Von Luck was looking ahead now, towards the dolmen itself. He felt the nausea return as he drew nearer, but he could control it now.

Crouching down, he walked into the small chamber. There, in the half-light, lay the body of Richard Marais. Next to it lay Marais's head, eyes wide open, staring up at von Luck with a look of terror.

Von Luck reached down and felt Marais's chest. It was still very warm. Marais must have met his end only a few minutes ago. Gingerly, he felt inside his jacket, searching for something, anything.

He was not disappointed. There, sticking out of Marais's inside pocket, was the edge of a white envelope. Von Luck took it out carefully and looked at it. Although the rain was starting to smudge it, the envelope clearly read 'Lt-Col von Luck' in black ink.

Chapter Six

'So MARAIS WAS meant to have had a heart attack, was he?'

'According to the paper,' says Terry, 'a constable found him lying underneath the Faldouet dolmen.'

'And presumably no mention in the illustrious German-controlled *Record* that the poor bugger, as we know from von Luck, was missing his head?'

'None whatsoever.'

'Surprise, bloody surprise,' says Lebonneur, holding the phone with his shoulder as he lights a cigarette. 'So presumably he had the full funeral – coffin draped with the flag, all that sort of stuff?'

'He did indeed,' says Terry, 'with Huffmeier even making a speech about what a great man Marais was, and, quote, "Even though I had my differences with the Bailiff, he was still a man whom I greatly respected," et cetera et cetera.'

'The normal bullshit. It never changes.'

'Indeed.'

'And we all know who succeeded him, don't we?'

'Peter Mollett.'

'Anything about him?'

'Oh, yes, there's plenty,' Terry says. 'I'll bring it all round when you're back from Alderney, but the gist of it, especially in a proclamation published by Mollett in the *Record* on the day after Marais's death, is for the population to stay calm and to co-operate with the Germans in the weeks ahead.'

'What a shit,' says Lebonneur.

'That's one way of putting it.'

'It's the *only* way of putting it. The man *was* an out-and-out shit, Terry. There's no other way to describe him.'

Terry laughs a little uneasily down the phone. He's not used to such language, unless, of course, he's talking to Lebonneur. There is a brief silence, broken by Terry. 'So, then,' he says, 'what are you going to do over on Alderney?'

'What I like doing best,' Lebonneur replies. 'Snooping around. Asking awkward questions. Annoying people.'

'When are you off?'

' 'Bout an hour. I don't know when I'll be back, but I expect I'll be there for a couple of days.'

'You flying?'

'Yup – with Le Maître's. Do you know them? They're this great little airline who fly Islanders around the islands. Not cheap, mind, but a hell of a lot quicker than the boat.'

'Well, good luck.'

'Listen, Terry.'

'What?'

'Just take care, that's all.'

'How do you mean?'

'Look after yourself. Keep an eye open, watch yourself. If you see anything out of the ordinary, just stay put. Stay at home, lock the doors.'

'Jesus, Bob, you're sounding paranoid.'

'Well, I've got every right to.'

'Why?'

Lebonneur looks at his watch. 'Look,' he says, 'I don't have time, but just take my word for it, all right? I'm not being paranoid, just cautious.'

'All right, then,' says Terry, with a note of reluctance, 'I'll do as you say.'

'Good. 'Bye, then.'

' 'Bye.'

Lebonneur puts down the phone and takes a final drag on his cigarette. He'd better get going, he thinks. He scribbles a quick note to Rachel and the kids, picks up his heavy overnight bag, which contains a small metal case borrowed from Dr Hent, the school's physics teacher, and leaves the house. Normally he would have left the front door unlocked, but today he thinks he should lock it.

'Hi, folks. My name's Ian Proffitt, and I'm going to be flying you over to Alderney today.'

The eight or so passengers in the departure lounge acknowledge the pilot's greeting with a mixture of grunts and smiles.

Lebonneur notices that the man is absurdly young, perhaps no more than twenty-five. He also sounds Australian, or perhaps Kiwi, and he wears the cliché Aviator sunglasses that are so *de rigueur* with pilots.

Lebonneur looks at his fellow passengers: a couple of men who look like workmen – he'll try to talk to them later – a middle-aged woman, a family of four, of whom two are teenage boys, and a businessman wearing a cheap suit. He would have expected more passengers, but it's only a Wednesday.

'As we're a fairly quiet flight today,' the pilot continues, 'I was wondering whether anybody would like to join me in the co-pilot's seat up front?'

'I'd love to,' says Lebonneur, and adds, as an afterthought, 'that's if nobody else wants to. Sorry, I'd forgotten my manners.'

The others sit in silence, a few shaking their heads. Lebonneur notices that the elder of the two boys looks narked, and it crosses his mind that he should have allowed him the first chance. 'I'm sorry,' he says to the boy, 'would you like to go instead?'

Before the boy can open his mouth, his mother butts in. '*Him?*' she says. 'Up in the front seat? You've got to be joking! He'll only press the wrong button or something.'

'You're sure?' says Lebonneur.

'Oh, yes,' says the woman.

'It looks like it's you, then, sir,' says the pilot. 'It's always good to have someone so obviously appreciative alongside me. What's your name, please?'

'Robert Lebonneur.'

The pilot jots it down on a black clipboard. 'Great. Nice to have some company. All right, folks, I'm just going to make a few checks on the old plane, and I'd estimate we'll be boarding in about ten minutes. Hope that's all OK with you guys?'

There is a collectively murmured, 'Fine.'

The Islander is far narrower than the average car although, with sixteen seats, there is more than enough room for the passengers. Lebonneur is the last to board, and sits to the right of the pilot. He feels an embarrassing surge of boyish excitement as he puts on his seatbelt and looks at the array of instruments. God knows what any of them are for, he thinks. These bloody pilots must be bloody geniuses.

The pilot gets on board and goes through his pre-flight routine, noting a bewildering selection of figures on his clipboard.

'That looks like a secret code,' says Lebonneur.

The pilot lets out an insipid chuckle – he's probably heard that line hundreds of times before, Lebonneur thinks.

The pilot turns round and addresses the cabin. 'All right, folks? Great. We're just about to depart, so I'd recommend that you put in some earplugs if you don't want to be deafened. It shouldn't take us much more than twenty minutes to get to Alderney, so I'm afraid there won't be time for a three-course meal.'

The joke is met with polite laughter. Good, thinks Lebonneur. At least the pilot's sense of humour is worse than his own.

'If you'd like, Mr Lebonneur, you could wear those headphones. It'll mean you'll hear me chattering away to air traffic control, but they're a bit better than the earplugs.'

Lebonneur puts on the headphones, and although they initially deaden any ambient sounds, they seem to do little to stop the surprisingly loud noise caused by the Islander's two engines bursting into life. Lebonneur lifts away the headphones from his ears, and realises that in fact they are doing a lot.

With some fascination, he watches the pilot manipulate the controls as he taxis the plane. There is almost too much to look at, he thinks – two sliding red knobs that read 'mixture', two sliding blue knobs whose purpose is unclear, a large selection of orange digits that Lebonneur supposes are radio frequencies, no fewer than twenty dials that indicate arcana such as 'manifold pressure', two linked black levers that the pilot is pressing backwards and forwards with his right hand, the control column, and countless other switches and knobs marked with acronyms. They may as well be hieroglyphics, Lebonneur thinks.

The pilot pauses the plane at the start of the runway. Lebonneur can hear some conversation through the headphones, but can barely understand it. However, its purpose is clear, as the pilot pushes the black knob forward – the throttle, thinks Lebonneur, it must be the throttle – and with it the plane. The acceleration is not outstanding, but it is enough to push

Lebonneur back into his seat. By the time they have covered just under half the runway, the pilot pulls back on the column, there is a feeling of weightlessness, and they are airborne. This is fun, thinks Lebonneur – much more like flying than sitting in an air-conditioned jet.

Fifteen minutes into the flight, with Alderney approximately five miles ahead of them, Lebonneur notices that the pilot is looking agitated. He is rubbing his left shoulder with his right hand, and twitching in his seat, as though he has a bad back. He grimaces, too, as though he is in pain. 'Are you all right?' Lebonneur asks, over the headphones.

'Yeah, mate, thanks – I'm fine. Just a little twinge in my shoulder. I must have slept badly on it last night.' His tone suggests that he is anything but fine.

'You're sure? Is there anything you want me—'

Lebonneur's question is interrupted by the pilot's sudden loud moan. He slumps to his left, the sound of his attempted breathing horribly loud in Lebonneur's ears. Simultaneously, the plane banks in the same direction as the pilot's hands drag the control column with him.

It takes Lebonneur less than a second to grasp what has happened, and what is going to happen. The pilot is having a heart attack, and they are now going to die. In less than thirty seconds they will hit the water and be fucking killed. Oh, please, no, God, please, no. Frozen, Lebonneur looks at the pilot, watching his torment as the tight vice of a stopped heart

207

tightens round his chest. He is aware of some movement and sounds from the seats behind him, but he is transfixed by the man's agony and his own sheer terror. Death. He'd known it would happen one day, but not today, not a nice day in August when he's only forty-five. There's so much to do, and too much to miss – Rachel, the kids. Lebonneur is screaming, although he doesn't know it, screaming, 'No.'

Fucking do something. The voice is quiet at first, but it gets louder. Who's saying that? DO SOMETHING. Anything. It's him saying it, not out loud, but inside his head. Listen to that voice. Do as it says. ANYTHING. Just grab anything. The plane is heading down now, heading down and to the left quite rapidly. There is a whining noise of airflow, which reminds Lebonneur of watching *Battle of Britain*. It's the same sound! How about that?

DO SOMETHING. Just grab the column in front of you and yank it back, come on, you've seen enough films. The screaming is getting louder now, really fucking loud.

'Stop fucking screaming!' Lebonneur finds himself shouting. 'Fucking stop it!'

Lebonneur is wrestling with the column, but it won't move. Why the fuck not? Has it been disabled? No, it can't be. Come on, you fucker, move, damn you, move!

Unseen by Lebonneur, the hands of the businessman in the bad suit pull the pilot back off the control column. With the plane plummeting, it's not a task that's easily achieved, but the man manages. Lebonneur immediately feels some movement in the column on his side of the aircraft. Of course! They're linked! He pulls back, pulls back hard. Nothing! Fucking nothing!

Keep pulling, you bastard, keep doing it. It's your only chance. Come on, pull man, PULL. Something's happening! The plane's not going down so quickly. Is he imagining it? He can see some sky in front of him, not just the water. And then a crushing feeling, as though they're being forced down into their seats, like drawing-pins under thumbs. He's pulling hard still, and now they're going up. Sky. All he can see now is sky – a few clouds, perhaps, but not much else. Push, the voice tells him, push the control column.

Lebonneur pushes, but he pushes too hard, causing the plane to start to descend. The suddenness of the motion causes him to lift briefly off his seat. Pull back again, pull *back*, for Christ's sake, but more gently this time. Lebonneur draws the control column towards him and stops when the plane is in more or less level flight. He is breathing heavily, sweating profusely.

A moment of euphoria. They're not dead! They're actually fucking alive and he's actually flying this fucking plane. The realisation makes him feel faint. Oh, God, what now? He looks at the instrument panel. 'Smoking is strictly forbidden.' The chipped plastic sign makes him want a cigarette. God, he'd *love* a cigarette. If he gets out of this, he thinks, he's *never* going to give up smoking.

Come on, man, think, think. The radio. He remembers how

the pilot pressed the red button on the yoke with his thumb when he wanted to speak. Lebonneur does the same.

'Er . . . Mayday! Mayday! Mayday! Fucking mayday! Can anyone hear me?'

He releases his finger from the button.

Nothing.

'Mayday! Mayday!'

A voice crackles in his ear. 'Alderney control tower receiving you. Please state your problem, over.'

'We've lost our pilot!' Lebonneur shouts. 'He seems to have had a heart attack! Over.'

No reply. What's happened to them? Where have they gone? The red button! He's forgotten to release it.

'. . . over.'

'Sorry, please say that again,' Lebonneur says.

'Are you in control of the aircraft? Over.'

'Sort of,' Lebonneur replies.

'Are you a pilot?'

'Fuck, no! Listen! I need some help. Someone's got to tell me what to do. I haven't the first fucking idea. I can hold it steady, but that's about it.'

'You're doing well. What's your name?'

'Bob Lebonneur.'

'All right, Bob, my name is Andy Hill. I'm the air traffic controller here on Alderney and I'm also a pilot. I'm going to tell you exactly what to do and you're going to land that plane as though you were parking your car.'

'I'm hopeless at parking.'

Laughter. Much-needed laughter.

'Now, then, Bob, tell me what you can see. Can you see any land?'

Lebonneur looks around. Ahead, nothing. To his left, nothing. To his right, something. Is that Alderney?

'I think I can see land to my right.'

'That'll be us,' says Andy. 'Hang on a second, Bob. I'll be right back. Just keep it steady.'

'All right,' says Lebonneur. It is not all right, but he has no choice. Please let this man Andy know what he's doing.

He's feeling more confident now, sure enough to glance behind. The passengers look as terrified as he feels. Must calm them down. Tell them something, preferably a lie.

'Don't worry!' he shouts. 'I've had a few flying lessons, so we'll be fine.'

He watches a modicum of relief enter their expressions.

'I'm not making any promises,' he continues, 'but I have landed a plane before. I've got someone on the end of the line who's going to help me, tells me it's like parking a car.'

The odd smile. Good. At least he's made some impact. The last thing he wants is a plane full of panicky passengers.

'Bob?'

'Hello?'

'It's Andy here. Listen, we can see you and you're looking great.'

'You've got to be joking!'

'I'm not. You're about three miles to our west and you're heading roughly due north. What I'd like you to do is to turn right, then head towards us.'

'How do I do that?'

'Tell me, Bob, can you see the altimeter? It should be straight in front of you.'

Lebonneur looks around the instrument panel until his eyes alight on what looks like a clock.

'Er . . . yes, I can . . . It looks as though we're at, um, one and a half thousand feet. Does that sound right?'

'That's great. You've got enough height in which to turn.'

'All right. I'll take your word for it.'

More laughter.

'I'll think you'll find that I'm your new best friend, Bob.'

'Best friend? I'll *marry* you if you get us out of this.'

'You've yet to see how ugly I am! All right, what I'd like you to do now is begin the turn. All you do is just turn that thing you're holding to your right. Gently, mind, very gently. As you do so, you'll lose a bit of height, but don't worry, you've got enough to spare. After you're heading towards us, pull the plane back up – you know how to do that?'

'Yeah,' says Lebonneur, 'I can do that.'

'Great, let's give it a go.'

'All right.' Lebonneur is so nervous that he can feel his bowels loosening. Oh, God, please don't let me crap myself. That would be just too awful. He clenches his buttocks tightly, which seems to help.

212

'And just remember, Bob, I'm watching you.'

'Thanks, Andy. OK, here goes.'

* * *

Cold, damp, hungry, both feeling bad-tempered, Captain Fellowes and Pilot Officer Smith left their woodland hideout at around six o'clock that Sunday morning. Even though they lacked a mirror, Fellowes knew that their ragged condition would indicate to even the greatest dullard in the German garrison that they were fugitives.

Instinctively, Fellowes wanted to head north, into the countryside, but in order to find a telephone he knew they would have to head south-east towards St Helier. That meant avoiding roadblocks, patrols, even the attention of the islanders, few of whom Fellowes regarded as trustworthy.

Using every ditch, hedge, tree and wall as cover, the two men made their way towards the island's capital. At one point, they stopped at a small stream, from which they drank copiously, the water temporarily filling their stomachs. Fellowes knew that they would have to get some food soon, but finding Dr Aubin was a priority.

They reached the outskirts of St Helier a little after nine o'clock. Up to that point, they had seen only a German lorry heading down a single-track road, and a farmer out with a skeletal sheepdog.

'All right,' said Fellowes, as they crouched behind a wall.

'This is where it gets difficult. Keep your eyes peeled for a phone box. There must be one somewhere.'

Smith nodded. On the other side of the wall was one of the main roads that led into St Helier from the north. They could see some houses a couple of hundred feet away that represented the beginning of the town.

'And should we be looking for cover?' Smith asked. 'Or do we just walk nonchalantly down the road?'

'We walk nonchalantly down the road,' said Fellowes. 'The rules have changed. Darting around between buildings in broad daylight looks too suspicious. Come on, smarten yourself up a bit – tidy your hair, tuck in your shirt. It is Sunday, after all.'

Smith licked his hands and smoothed down his hair. It made little difference, Fellowes thought, but now was not the time for a discussion. 'That's a bit better,' he said. 'Come on, let's go.'

He stood up, looked from side to side, then vaulted over the wall. Was this madness, he thought, walking straight into St Helier? Perhaps it was, but they had little choice other than to starve. Had he been sure he could have trusted the population, he would have knocked on the first door they had come across, but he suspected that people like Mrs Campbell and her daughter were all too rare. In Fellowes's eyes, such lack of bravery was inexcusable. He had risked his life countless times for their freedom, so why the hell shouldn't they risk theirs for him?

They were walking past the houses now. Fellowes expected to be followed down the street by a mass twitching of net curtains and old women staring out of windows, but it did not happen. There were a few people around, but not many – a middle-aged couple in their Sunday best, a couple of young boys and a woman furtively walking towards them with a bundle of sticks. Well, thought Fellowes, at least she's someone we won't have to fear, a lawbreaker herself with her contraband fuel.

As the woman passed them, both Smith and Fellowes touched the brims of their caps. The woman smiled anxiously and scuttled away. Evidently she did not care for the greetings of two rather unwholesome-looking labourers, thought Fellowes.

The two men continued walking for another couple of minutes, their eyes searching desperately for a telephone box.

The streets were busier now, which made them less conspicuous. Fellowes was glad to see that they weren't the only scruffy people around. Many of the inhabitants were in clothes whose state their wearers would have considered disgraceful in peacetime. They looked painfully thin, thought Fellowes, far thinner than those in England. Although the rationing at home was severe, most were eating a healthy diet, which could hardly be considered the case here. Faces were drawn, haggard, almost lifeless in some cases.

Another difference that was immediately apparent to the two men was the plethora of German street signs and road markings. 'Verboten' was painted on the entrance to one road they passed. *Verboten*. Even that one word was an infringement, thought

Fellowes. Imagine that being painted on the bloody Mall. It was inconceivable, and yet here they were, in a part of Britain that had been invaded. Would the people back home have behaved like the islanders? Fellowes hoped not. He did not wish to acknowledge the small part of his mind that told him perhaps they would have done.

A far larger cultural shock lay in store for the two men as they passed some shop windows. Photographs of Hitler, swastika flags, German–English dictionaries – all were for sale in Burton's, no less.

'Look at that!' Smith whispered.

'Sssh!' said Fellowes. 'We're meant to be used to all this.'

Nevertheless he could not help but share Smith's outrage. It was the little things that revealed how complete the occupation was. Would all this be remembered after the war, Fellowes wondered, or would it be forgotten, swept under the carpet as something shameful? Was he being too harsh? Perhaps. The islands could hardly have fought off the Nazis on their own, and they were too claustrophobic to mount a decent resistance movement, the type Fellowes had heard they had in France. His and Smith's present difficulties were testament to that. But, thought Fellowes, *but*. Surely the islanders could be doing more to express their displeasure? According to Miss Campbell, there had been a campaign of daubing V-signs on walls a while back, but that had quickly petered out after the Germans had cracked down.

And then there were the informers the Campbells had

mentioned. According to them, no one would ever directly name an informer, but everyone had a good idea who was writing anonymous postcards to the Gestapo, telling them how their neighbour kept an illegal radio, or how they'd heard that someone had been hoarding coal under their floorboards. That was how the Nazis kept control, Fellowes thought. They just used the worst side of human nature and twisted it to suit their purposes.

Fellowes's musing was interrupted by a twenty-strong group of German soldiers marching towards them.

'Just keep walking,' he said to Smith, 'and keep talking. I think there's a storm brewing, don't you?'

Smith looked up. 'You're not wrong there. There's quite a wind getting up. I reckon it's going to chuck it down.'

The Germans were a mere twenty feet away, marching down the middle of the road. So far they were showing little interest in those around them. Fellowes found himself torn between wanting to look at them, and wanting to turn away – which might look suspicious. He compromised, and made himself look at their feet, which, he noticed, were hardly shod in the finest quality boots. 'Still, not unusual for this time of the year,' he said, struggling to maintain his nerve.

'That's right,' said Smith, his voice jumping almost an octave.

The boots were right in front of him now, which caused Fellowes to look up and straight down the pavement. To continue looking down would be as guilty as hell, he thought. He fixed his attention on a distant Boots shop sign, whose ordinary, everyday nature seemed so discordant with his present situation. Come on, he thought, just walk past, you bloody goons, just walk past.

Neither Fellowes nor Smith noticed the first of the German heads to turn, but they did notice the second, which had been prompted by the first to look at the two scruffy islanders walking down the pavement.

Run, or keep walking? Fellowes quickly decided on the latter. To run would seal their fate, but to keep walking would maintain an air of innocence and, with it, a fraction of a chance. Maybe the two Germans in the middle of the group were looking at something else, perhaps someone just behind them – maybe a pretty girl he had not noticed.

Although it took less than two seconds for the soldiers to pass, it was more than long enough for Fellowes and Smith. But pass they did, the sound of their boots ringing menacingly off the walls of the buildings. Fellowes knew there was at least another few seconds before they were in the clear, a few excruciating seconds that might decide whether he and Smith would be shot tomorrow or die in their beds as old men.

Suddenly there was a hubbub among the soldiers, a few sentences of urgent German, and a stop to the sound of the boots.

'You there! Halt!'

Fellowes didn't believe he had heard it. He was so expecting the words that when they came he believed them to be the product of his imagination. Fellowes looked at Smith, who looked back, his face disfigured with terror.

'I said halt!'

Fellowes turned to see the Germans were looking back at them. The sergeant who led them was walking rapidly towards them, his finger pointing in their direction. 'Er, yes, Sergeant?' he said.

The sergeant looked at them. 'No! Not you, you fucking peasant! *Him!*'

The sergeant was pointing at a man who had been walking a few steps behind them, a rather fat man who was wearing a Sunday suit.

'Yes, Sergeant?' asked the man.

'You promised us that you would get us some Red Cross parcels,' said the sergeant, who had now drawn up by the man and was prodding his chest, 'so where the fuck are they?'

'I – I don't know what you're—'

'Of course you do, Mr Tyler! If you don't get them to me by noon, I shall have no option but to arrest you for corruption. Or, even worse, I could simply tell your fellow Jerseymen how you are cutting deals—'

'Please!' said Tyler. 'I shall do as you ask. But by noon will be very—'

'I don't care!' the sergeant shouted, spit flying out of his mouth and showering Tyler's face. 'None of us has had a fucking cigarette in days. And as for chocolate – years!'

The sergeant turned to face Fellowes and Smith. 'What the

fuck are you two looking at? Come on, *schnell!* Get out of here!'

The two men needed no further prompting. Only too happy to obey the order, they broke into a half-trot down the road.

After another minute, their sense of elation was heightened by the object of their quest: a phone. There, outside the post office, a red box that signified hope and safety.

* * *

Von Luck drove back to Linden Court as fast as he dared on the wet roads. He knew that the image of the beheaded Marais would stay with him for ever. Who had done this? Who had known that Marais would be there? Why the particularly gruesome method of killing? Had Marais known his killer? Why had he, von Luck, been allowed to live? Why had it been done?

Of all the questions that von Luck posed to himself, he suspected that the latter would be answered by what lay inside the envelope. As soon as he had turned off the engine, he reached inside his pocket and took it out. His hands trembled with anticipation, causing him to open it clumsily, almost tearing the single sheet of foolscap that lay inside. It was a handwritten letter, headed with Marais's crest and his address, and dated that same morning.

Dear Lieutenant Colonel,

I write to you on a matter of grave importance, a matter that may be more important than the deportation itself. It concerns the events on Alderney, the ramifications of which are threatening not just to the stability of our dear islands but to the course of the Allied war effort itself.

It has come to my knowledge that something terrible is being built there under the aegis of one Professor Karl Fellner. I am informed that it is a weapon that may result in carnage on an incomprehensible scale, perhaps with the ability to destroy London. If what I am told is true, then the nature of this device is more than a matter of Germany versus Britain, but one that threatens vast numbers of our innocent fellow human beings.

I write to you, von Luck, because I know that I can trust you. You are one of the few Germans who knows that the war is lost for you, and I believe that you are possessed of enough humanity to see the evil folly in your fellow countrymen in unleashing a weapon whose only purpose is to kill on a vast scale. I believe that you, of all the people on the islands, have the wherewithal to stop it, and I beg your assistance.

By the time you have read these words, I shall already have told you more about what I have learned, but for the sake of posterity, I want this simple fact to be known. Guard this letter well, von Luck – it may prove to be your saviour in the event of a tribunal.

Yours ever,

Richard Marais, Bailiff

Von Luck read the letter again, then put it back into its envelope. He stared through the rain-obscured windscreen, watching thin rivulets of water twist their way to the bonnet.

Deep down, he had suspected something like this, but not something so monumental. In a way, Marais was right: the deportation was now of secondary importance, but without the extra labour, presumably the work on this weapon would be severely hampered. Would stopping the deportation be enough? It might be, but could he risk it? If what Marais said was true, this was not a matter for a gamble. He needed to go to Alderney and deal with the problem there. How, in God's name, was he going to do that?

Von Luck stepped out of the car. As he hurried towards the front door, he felt a needling sense of guilt. Perhaps he should not try to stop it – perhaps to do so was treachery of the vilest kind. Despite Marais's trust, von Luck was still a German, and he was still, in his own eyes, a patriot. He *should* want Germany to win the war, because Germany was his *Heimat*, the representation of everything that was dear to him.

However, this was no longer a war, he thought, but the opportunity for the madmen among them – and there were many – to indulge in their favourite activity: killing. He was going to have no part in that. His country was wrong – or, rather, it had been wronged by some of its own men. They were like a cancer, and if you are trying to excise a cancer, you helped the surgeon as much as you could, even as he was cutting pieces of you away. If you stopped him, the cancer spread. Not one cell could be left, because just one cell had the opportunity to threaten the whole body.

Von Luck stepped inside to be greeted by Mrs May. 'Colonel! Have you got any food?'

Food. It seemed so trivial.

'No, Mrs May,' he replied, struggling to maintain his temper, 'I do not have any food. I have been rather detained by other matters.'

'But, Colonel, all we have to eat is a few tins of beans . . .'

'Then we shall eat those!' von Luck snapped, heading up the stairs. He knew it was unfair of him to take it out on her but, well, too bad. He would apologise, but there was no time to do so now. He walked along the corridor and opened the door to Pippa and Violet Campbell's room.

'Max! I mean, Colonel,' said Pippa.

Von Luck saw that Violet was awake. Her expression was groggy, but her eyes were most definitely open. No wonder Pippa had corrected her intimate appellation so swiftly. Von Luck knelt down next to her. 'Mrs Campbell,' he said softly. 'How are you?'

There were tears in her eyes. 'How can I begin to thank you?' she asked. 'You have done . . .'

Von Luck reached out a hand and touched her shoulder gently. 'Please, Mrs Campbell,' he said, 'there is no need. I did what anybody would have done.'

'You know that's—'

She coughed, which evidently caused her pain as it caused her involuntarily to move her back. 'You know that's not true,' she finished.

She was right, but modesty forbade von Luck to acknowledge such a high compliment. 'How are you feeling, Mrs Campbell? Do you require a doctor?'

'I'm feeling wretched,' she said. 'Wretched for you. Wretched for my daughter. Wretched for Fellowes and Smith . . .'

Von Luck looked up at Pippa quizzically.

'The POWs,' Pippa explained.

Von Luck nodded.

'There is no reason for you to feel like that,' he said. 'You are a very brave woman, Mrs Campbell. There are not many who have the courage to serve their country in the way you have. However, I have to say that I am more concerned with your physical well-being than your state of mind. I can summon Dr Aubin here if you wish.'

'I don't know . . . I don't want to make him take a risk . . .'

'From what I know of Dr Aubin he'd be more than happy to come here,' said von Luck.

'He's right, Mummy,' said Pippa. 'And your back does need looking at. You know I'm no nurse.'

Violet sighed. 'Perhaps you're right,' she said, 'but I'd feel so guilty if . . .'

'Nonsense!' said von Luck. 'I shall call him immediately!'

He stood up and looked at Pippa. Without her mother noticing, he gesticulated with his right thumb that she should join him outside in the corridor. She nodded.

She joined him a minute later. 'How are you?' she asked. 'You look as though you've seen a ghost.'

Von Luck would have smiled if any semblance of a sense of humour had remained with him. 'I've seen something far worse than a ghost,' he replied.

'What?'

'I . . . I can't tell you,' said von Luck.

He could see that Pippa found his reply far from acceptable.

'Is it Fellowes and Smith?' she asked. 'Have they been captured? Shot?'

Von Luck shook his head. 'No, it wasn't them. It was someone else.'

'Who?'

Should he tell her? What was the reason for not doing so? There wasn't one, at least not a good one. He could certainly trust her – he had told her everything so far – so why not this? Old-fashioned chivalry, that was what it was, a misplaced sense that women should not be informed of the true horror of war and violence. Well, that was *Quatsch*, rubbish.

'It was the Bailiff,' he said. 'I found him at the dolmen. He had been killed.'

Pippa gasped, simultaneously bringing her hand to her mouth. 'Oh, my God! Richard Marais? Are you . . . are you sure? I mean, sure that he was killed?'

'He had been beheaded.'

Pippa opened her mouth but evidently her brain could not find any words that might do justice to the magnitude of her shock. It stayed open, then closed, and opened again. 'But . . . but . . . why?'

'Because he knew something about Alderney that he shouldn't have.'

'Alderney?'

'Yes. He knew the real reason for the deportation. It's not to build some bloody gun control tower or a fort, but a new weapon.'

Pippa stepped forward and touched von Luck's forearm, which he did not discourage. He could do with some physical contact, he thought, yearned for some comfort.

'What sort of weapon?' she asked.

'I wish I knew. But what I do know is that whoever killed Marais is probably now wanting to kill me.'

'What are you going to do?'

Pippa was clutching him even tighter now.

'I'm going to go to Alderney,' he said. 'I know there's a transport of Todt workers – Russians and Poles mostly – going there first thing tomorrow. I'll be on that boat.'

'What? Disguised as one of them?'

'Precisely.'

'But even if you get there, how will you destroy the weapon?'

'Special weapons need scientists,' he said, 'and scientists can be killed. Without the scientists, there is no weapon. The scientist I need to kill is one Professor Karl Fellner.'

'Surely there must be a better way?'

'Well, let me know if you think of one. In the meantime, I need to speak to Peter Mollett not only to tell him about Marais but also that the islanders must resist the deportation, not just for the sake of themselves but also for their fellow countrymen. Oh, yes, and I must ring Aubin about your mother as well.'

He hadn't expected it, but he had been wanting it for a long time. It came in a sudden serpentine darting movement, reaching up to him in the way a snake might strike. The rapidity came because Pippa was unsure whether she was doing the right thing, and she felt that if the kiss was quick, then it would be easier to excuse it as a mistake, a mere spur-of-the-moment *amuse-bouche*. Nevertheless, it was a kiss, and despite the quickness, it was a firm kiss on von Luck's mouth.

His head filled with matters entirely unromantic, the kiss came as a shock to him. He knew this wasn't the right time, but it did feel right, much more so than with any other woman he had kissed over the past few years. There was something deeply heartfelt in the way that she had done it – a sudden expression of emotion and tenderness rather than a leaden gesture designed as a mere prelude for hasty lovemaking.

He seized her by the arms, more firmly than he realised, and pulled her to him. This time it was his turn to kiss her, and he did so passionately but quietly. She murmured, and stopped. He looked into her eyes, searching for a clue as to her feelings, and saw that she was doing the same. 'Thank you,' he said.

Pippa smiled, her mouth closed. 'You deserved it,' she said. 'And you deserve much more.'

Von Luck frowned. 'I don't want you to think . . .'

'I'm not,' she said. 'I would have done that anyway.'

Von Luck bent forward and kissed her again. For a few seconds, he was somewhere else, a long way from reality. Her lips felt soft and for the first time he could smell her – it was not perfume but her natural smell. With some women, it could be unpleasant, but with Pippa it was the opposite.

'Are you really going to go to Alderney?' she asked.

'I must,' he said.

'In that case, I would like to stay with you tonight.'

Von Luck recoiled.

'What?' asked Pippa. 'Is that not . . .'

'Not at all, I just wasn't expecting . . .'

Pippa brought her head forward and kissed him again.

* * *

Von Luck arrived at Peter Mollett's house just after half past one. An eighteenth-century farmhouse, in the parish of St Lawrence in the centre of the island, it was an unusual choice for many members of the States, thought von Luck, many of whom lived in St Helier. He had tried to call Mollett in advance, but the storm had done what storms always had for the past five years and crippled the telephone service. He had got through to Aubin, but St Helier was usually less badly affected than more rural areas. All it seemed to take these days was one drop of rain, thought von Luck, and the whole system went down.

Von Luck knocked firmly on the door. He had not prepared his words: he would just be truthful and direct. Mollett was now the *de facto* Bailiff, and it was essential for von Luck to ensure that Mollett maintained the States' position against the deportation.

The door opened fractionally. 'Yes?' came a male voice.

'Herr Mollett, it's Lieutenant Colonel von Luck. I need to speak to you.'

'Von Luck!' The door opened fully to reveal the large frame of Mollett. At six foot four, he was the same height as von Luck, but he was built like a wrestler. 'Please come in,' he said, wiping his mouth with a napkin. 'You'll have to forgive me, my wife and I were in the middle of lunch.'

'I apologise,' said von Luck stepping inside.

'Not at all,' he said. 'I would, ah, offer you some, but you know . . .'

Von Luck held up his hand. 'That's quite all right, Herr Mollett. I've already eaten.' He looked around. They were standing in a large hall festooned with family portraits. One was a photograph, showing a young boy aged about ten. 'Your son, Herr Mollett?'

'My nephew,' said Mollett. 'I'm afraid Rose and I never had any children. It means that we dote on my sister-in-law's boy. I'm sad to say that his parents died during the Blitz, so he's being held in an orphanage until the end of the war.'

'I'm very sorry,' said von Luck. 'There are many stories like that.'

'On both sides.'

'Indeed.'

Children. He had never given the idea of fatherhood much thought, but to be the father of a boy like that, well, it would give him much pride.

'Herr Mollett, is it possible that we might sit down? I'm afraid I have some very bad . . . no, appalling news to tell you.'

'Yes, of course,' said Mollett, then turned his head towards the corridor that led to the back of the house. 'Darling, you carry on! I need to speak to Colonel von Luck.'

Von Luck heard a sigh, which caused Mollett to smile uneasily and raise his eyebrows, as if to say 'women'.

'What is it?' Mollett asked.

'Perhaps if we sat down?'

Mollett's eyebrows knitted together. 'Yes – all right. If you think it's necessary.'

Von Luck nodded, whereupon Mollett led him through to a drawing room that smelt faintly of damp. The walls were hung with equine portraits, a couple of which von Luck identified as having been painted by George Stubbs. Mollett sat in an evidently well-loved oxblood leather armchair next to the fireplace, and indicated to von Luck that he should take the green sofa opposite.

'Herr Mollett, I have to tell you that the Bailiff is dead.'

Mollett sat up. '*Dead?* Dick? How?'

'I found at him at the dolmen at Faldouet just after midday. He had been murdered just before I found him.'

'*Murdered?* By whom?'

230

'I don't know, Herr Mollett. Do you have any ideas?'

'Good God, no! Dick was well liked – no one would have wanted to murder him.'

'Excuse my flippancy, Herr Mollett, but it seems as though they did.'

At first, Mollett appeared too shocked to speak. 'How . . . how was he . . . how was he killed?'

'His head was chopped off.'

Mollett shut his eyes. 'Oh, my God.'

'Someone must have hated him,' said von Luck.

Mollett didn't reply.

'I gather you had a rather acrimonious meeting of the States last night.'

Mollett looked hard at von Luck. 'Who told you?'

'Marais did. This morning, outside the church.'

'I see. And what did he tell you?'

'He told me that the vote on whether to oppose the deportation was split. Apparently it was only decided by his casting vote.'

'That's all true,' said Mollett, 'but why're you mentioning this now? Surely that can't be a reason for someone to want Dick dead.'

Von Luck reached into his pocket for a packet of his filthy cigarettes. 'Would you like one?' he asked Mollett.

'No, thank you, but please do. There's an ashtray.'

'Thank you,' said von Luck, lighting the cigarette. He took a long drag, coughed it out, then another. Fucking things. Should he mention Alderney? Something told him not to. No, he wouldn't. At least, not yet.

'Well,' said von Luck, 'it might be a reason. There are plenty of reasons why people are murdered.'

'Yes, but not over last night's meeting. I mean, it got pretty heated, but it wasn't a matter of life or death, for Christ's sake. *Beheaded*? I still can't believe that. It's too . . . it's too horrible.'

'Yes,' said von Luck, slowly.

'Does anyone else know about this?'

Von Luck shook his head. 'I thought you should be the first. His death means that you are now acting Bailiff, and therefore I thought it only right.'

'So you haven't told Huffmeier?'

The admiral was the last person von Luck wanted to talk to. He could hear the awkward questions: what were you doing meeting him at the dolmen? What did he want to tell you? How do I know you didn't do it?

'No,' said von Luck, 'I haven't – he will know soon enough. Before that, I want to talk to you about the deportation.'

'What about it?'

'It's essential that the States maintains its line against it. I want you to use your new position to ensure that that happens.'

Mollett stood up and walked over to the fireplace. He leant proprietorially against it with his left elbow.

'Is there a problem?' von Luck asked.

Mollett took a deep breath. 'There may be. Look, I'm sorry, but I just don't think I can keep the States on our side. The meeting was split as it was, and despite my and Dick's efforts, there was a lot of pressure to let the deportation go unopposed. Of course, this is all academic if you manage to stop it, von Luck.'

Von Luck let his cigarette smoulder between his fingers, the smoke being drawn towards the fireplace. 'So what are you saying, Herr Mollett?'

'All I'm saying is that I can't promise anything. Dick's death will probably change everything.'

Von Luck wanted to stand up and shake the man until he spoke sense, but he kept calm. 'I'm doing my best to stop it,' he said, 'and it would make me a lot happier to know that the States were doing their best as well. You must realise that you'd be sending a thousand of your fellow citizens to their deaths if you let it go ahead.'

'I know that, von Luck. But now he's gone, the pressure from the others will become so much greater. I'm not sure that I can . . .'

Alderney. Should he mention Alderney? It looked as though he would have to. 'There is lot more to this than the deportation, Herr Mollett.'

'Oh?'

'Yes!' von Luck snapped. 'This is about what is actually going on over on Alderney. We are not simply constructing another anti-aircraft battery or a new range-finder, but a new weapon that will kill many thousands. That is why Major Schwalm requires all this new labour. You do realise, don't you, that if the States does not oppose the deportation, they will be actively assisting in the mass murder of many of their fellow countrymen?'

'Who told you about this – this weapon?'

'Marais did,' said von Luck. 'He wrote me a letter.'

'Well, he never told me about it.'

'He was a very discreet man, the Bailiff.'

'More so than I could have imagined,' said Mollett.

'You seem angry,' said von Luck.

'I am angry, von Luck, very angry. I wish Dick had told us about this – it would have made a huge difference at last night's meeting. What else do you know about this weapon?'

Von Luck shrugged his shoulders. 'Nothing,' he said.

'Nothing? You're quite sure? I mean, the more I know, the easier it will be for me to persuade the States to oppose the deportation.'

'As I said, Herr Mollett, I know nothing more.'

'What are you going to do about it?'

'I'm going to Alderney.'

'To do what? To try to stop it?'

Von Luck nodded. 'That's right,' he said. 'Which means that it's unlikely I will be able to do more about the deportation. It's more important that I get to the root of the problem, don't you think?'

'Er, yes, quite.'

'Which means that it's up to you and the States to assist me by not assisting my fellow countrymen.'

'I see,' said Mollett, mollified. 'And what if I can't?'

'Then you will have history to answer to.'

Mollett folded his arms. 'It will be difficult, though.'

This was too much for von Luck. 'Difficult, Herr Mollett? *Difficult?* I've spent four fucking years on this island doing my utmost best for your people, and you tell me that this is *difficult?* The easiest thing in the world for me would have been to let you all starve. Who helped get the Red Cross here? Me. Who turns a blind eye to the black market? Me. And who the hell do you think is risking his neck to stop you all being slaughtered? Me, that's who! I demand your help, Mollett, I absolutely insist on it. If you refuse, then everybody on this bloody island can be sent to Alderney as far as I damn well care!' Von Luck did not mean his words, but he was enraged. How else was he going to get through to this damn fool?

'All right, von Luck, you've got a point. I apologise. It's just a lot to take in, that's all. It's not every day that one of your oldest friends is murdered. Of course I'll do my best, you have my word.'

'Good,' said von Luck. '*Good.* I, too, apologise, but I must stress the severity of the situation.'

'Don't worry, von Luck, you have.'

Condescending shit, thought von Luck. He looked at his watch. It was coming up to two – time he headed back to see if Aubin had arrived.

*   *   *

Lebonneur struggles to keep his hands steady as he turns the Islander to the right. The plane responds, and he experiences a brief moment of acrophobia as he looks down at the water over a thousand feet below him. Jesus Christ, he thinks, don't let me cock this up. That's enough turning now, let's get that nose back up. He pulls back, and there they are, heading in a straight line towards Alderney.

He puffs his breath out. That wasn't too bad, not exactly professional, but not too bad.

'Hey, Bob! That was great!'

Andy's voice crackling through his headphones gives Lebonneur a brief start, causing him to jog the control column enough to make the plane wobble.

'Thanks, Andy,' Lebonneur replies, 'but please don't shout like that next time. I'm jittery enough as it is.'

'Apologies. All you've got to do now is head in a straight line, make one big turn, then land.'

'That simple, huh?'

'Piece of the proverbial.'

'Just like parking a car?'

'Exactly so. All right, listen to this. You're heading in from the west, and the runway runs east-west. Now I don't give a monkey's which way you land, but so long as you don't try to land *across* the runway I'm happy. Got that?'

'Got it.'

'Good. Otherwise you'll be crashing into our old SS concentration camp, and we can't have that.'

For a moment, and it is by no means a long one, Lebonneur is reminded of why he is travelling to Alderney in the first place. He knows all about Lager Sylt, knows all about SS Hauptsturmführer List and Major Schwalm. He knows exactly why it was built and what was done there. He has read all about the executions, the tortures, the mass graves. Furthermore, he knows that it was there to help construct a project whose existence remains largely unknown, which he is going to uncover.

'Bob? Are you still there?'

Lebonneur doesn't reply. It crosses his mind that the pilot's heart attack was no accident. Someone wants to stop him, and they will do anything, even if it involves killing a planeload of innocent people. It's history repeating itself, he thinks. What's happening to him happened to von Luck. It's just the same.

'*Bob!*'

'Yes, Andy, I'm still here. Sorry, I was just – just thinking.'

'Meditating, were we?'

Lebonneur laughs. 'That's right!'

'You're doing fine without it. Just keep on that course, and when I say when, I want you to circle the airfield, all right? You can't miss it – it takes up about half the island.'

'All right,' says Lebonneur. 'Although I bet you I can miss it.'

It takes less than a minute for Lebonneur to reach the island. The plane judders as they start to fly over land, enough to give him a scare. Just down to the left he can see the unmistakable form of the runway. All he has to do, he thinks, is get this hunk of metal down there on to that strip of concrete. How hard can it be? He must be cleverer than most pilots, so surely he should be able to do it. Who was that bloke at school? Charlie Bell, that was him, didn't he get his pilot's licence? He did, too, and he was as thick as pigshit in a fridge.

One look at the instrument panel is enough to dispel Lebonneur's bravado. He feels a panicky surge coming on. Don't let it win, he tells himself, don't let it beat you. You're not going to die because you cock up the landing: you'll die because you gave up, because you were weak. Well, you're not going to do that, you arsehole, because Rachel and the kids want a husband and a father, even if you're not a very good one. And Mannez Heights? Forget that for the time being: it can wait.

'OK, Bob, it'll be time to start turning soon.'

'Which way?'

'Fly over the island, and keep the runway to your left. When you've got about three-quarters of the way along it, and it's slightly behind you, I want you to make a big turning to the left so that you land in a westerly direction. And remember to keep your height up – above a thousand feet if possible.'

'Understood.'

Lebonneur looks down. Once again, there is water below them. He looks ahead and sees the runway. He keeps heading straight, and soon the runway is down to the left. It's hard to keep an eye on it, especially as the body of the pilot is obstructing his view. Fuck it, he'll just have to guess when to turn. Now feels about right, he thinks. How about now?

With a little more confidence than with the previous turn, he moves the control column to the left and the plane banks. It's too early to say that he's getting the hang of this, but he is becoming accustomed to the feel of the aircraft. It is far more sensitive than he could have imagined.

'Bob! There are some of us down here who say you're a natural. That looked great.'

'Thanks, Andy.'

Lebonneur feels his throat dry. He is looking straight down the runway. He knows this is it, the moment when he has to land. The chances are he'll fuck it up, and they'll dive nose first into the ground.

'All right, Bob, this is what you're going to do next. Listen carefully. First, you need to descend. You're going to do that by controlling the throttle. Can you see it? Those black handles to the left of the blue and red handles.'

'I see it.'

'That's your accelerator, all right? Push it forward to go faster, pull it back to go slower. Do you want to give it a go?'

'What? Pull it back?'

'That's right.'

Lebonneur reaches down for the handle and pulls it gently. Instantly the pitch of the engine noise lowers. Some of the dials start moving – the airspeed going from 120 knots to 100, the altimeter showing that the plane is slowly descending.

'That looks good from here, Bob, keep it going. What I want you to do is to try to make it so that you're going about seventy knots when you're a hundred feet off the runway. You got that?'

'How the fuck do I do that?'

'Just pull that throttle back gently, that's all.'

'All right.'

He wants to shut his eyes now, wants to be somewhere else. He breathes deeply – he doesn't want to show the passengers how much he's shitting himself. If they lose it, he'll lose it, and then they'll definitely be dead.

'And keep that nose so it's no lower than six inches below the horizon.'

'Huh?'

'You don't want to descend too quickly, Bob, so make sure that your nose is only six inches below the horizon, OK?'

Lebonneur sits up in his seat. Six inches? How, in God's name, is he going to judge that? Just take a punt. This feels good as it is, let's stay like this.

'What's your height Bob?'

'I'm at seven hundred . . . no just under seven hundred feet.'

'Still going down nice and steadily. Let's ease back on that throttle a bit more now.'

Lebonneur obeys Andy's voice. Andy was right – he is his new best friend, the best friend he's ever bloody had.

The engine goes down in pitch again.

'Nice, Bob, nice. What's your airspeed?'

'Er . . . about eighty, just over.'

'Perfect. You're a natural! I told you! All right, Bob, we're getting close now. Here's what you have to do. When you get to a hundred feet, I want your speed to stay at about eighty knots. Got that?'

'Eighty knots.'

'Good. Then I want you to ease off the throttle very, very gently. Just as you're about to touch the ground, pull back on the throttle the whole way. Got that?'

Lebonneur repeats the instruction.

'Excellent, Bob, excellent. Now, just before your wheels touch the ground, pull back gently on the column, OK?'

'OK.'

'When you touch down, you're going to use those pedals on the floor. There are two sets, and you're going to use the bottom ones, which control the direction of the nose wheel. Right means right, left means left. After you've done that for a bit, try the brakes, which are the ones above.'

'Why can't I use them first?'

'You'll be going too fast. You should normally use them with the flaps, but for our lesson today, we're not going to bother with them.'

'I'm glad to hear it.'

'Altitude now, Bob?'

'Two hundred.'

'You look good, I think I can even see your face from the control tower. All right, let's ease off the throttle a bit more.'

Lebonneur does so.

'Altitude?' asks Andy.

'Just above one fifty.'

'Good. OK, let's try and keep those wings steady, you're fluttering a bit.'

There is too much to think about. Lebonneur feels overwhelmed, flooded by information. He'd heard about those who could do equations in their head while having a dogfight, but he's certainly not one of them. His talents lie elsewhere.

'Steady, Bob, steady. Tell the plane who's boss, although not too hard, mind.'

'For fuck's sake, Andy! I'm doing my fucking best!'

'You're doing more than that. That's nice, easy now. Altitude?'

'A hundred.'

'Good! All right, let it come in now – you've got plenty of space. You know something, Bob, you're going to make it, you're going to bloody make it!'

A white lie to encourage him? Or genuine? Who the fuck cared?

Their speed feels so slow that Lebonneur swears he could just get out and walk. A look at the airspeed indicator tells him that they're doing seventy-five knots. What's that? A bit more than sixty miles an hour? No way.

'And remember, Bob, just before you touch the ground, bring the control column back a bit.'

Lebonneur hears but he is no longer listening. He is sure that he is going to crap himself, he really is. This is the fucking end, oh, my God, oh, my God. Fifty feet ... forty ... thirty ... twenty. Things are looking a lot faster now, a lot bloody faster.

And now there is a shudder. A loud banging. A big, deep thud and then shuddering, a huge shuddering. Noise, a loud screeching noise. What the hell was that? Tyres? Have they landed? Andy is saying something in his ears but he can't bloody hear. This is too fast, this is way too fast. Press the pedals, do anything, do fucking anything. Who's screaming? Lebonneur doesn't know it, but he's panicking, hyperventilating, but he has just enough presence of mind to try to sort it out. Come on, slow down, you're actually bloody slowing down!

The sky is the right way up. It's still the right way up. This is good, Bob, this is tip-bloody-top. Oh, shit. Oh, Jesus Christ, no, please, God, no.

And then there is darkness.

Chapter Seven

'YOUR MOTHER IS a very strong woman, Miss Campbell,' said Dr Aubin.

Pippa looked down at the sleeping form of her mother, to whom a sedative had recently been administered. She looked so peaceful, she thought, so like a child. 'And how are the - the wounds?' she asked.

'They'll heal, but they're going to take a lot of time. It's essential that you see they don't get infected. Keep applying the iodine as often as I told you, but try not to use too much, eh? Not only for her sake, but for mine - I've hardly any left.'

'All right,' she said.

'And how are you, Miss Campbell?'

'As well as can be expected. It's obviously not easy living like this, but we shall manage. Max - Colonel von Luck is a good man, you know, despite what you told me.'

Aubin eyed her suspiciously. 'It can't be denied,' he said. 'Saving you and your mother was . . . well, it was heroic.'

Heroic. The word sounded melodramatic, almost excessive,

but there was no denying that what von Luck had done was heroic. There was, however, a note of reluctance in Aubin's voice, a sense that he would rather not have to compliment one of the enemy.

'It was certainly that,' Pippa replied.

'However, I think it's important to remember the conversation I had with you the other day,' said Aubin, peering over his pince-nez and snapping shut his Gladstone bag. 'It's at times like these when . . . let me see . . . certain *events* can occur because of the stresses people are under.'

The weapon on Alderney, the deportation, Marais's beheading – these were the things to think about, thought Pippa. She had neither the energy nor the will to argue with Aubin – that he was going on about sexual mores at a time like this was, frankly, berserk, but there it was. She wanted to shock him, to tell him that she had kissed von Luck earlier, and that she had asked to stay with him. She could imagine Aubin's face if she told him that. He would probably try to give her a sedative as well.

'I understand you, Dr Aubin,' Pippa replied, restraining herself. 'In fact, such matters were completely out of my head until you brought them up.'

Aubin stuck a finger under his collar. A gesture of unease if ever there was one, Pippa thought. Good, the bugger deserved it.

'On a different matter, Miss Campbell, some good news. I thought I should tell you that both Fellowes and Smith are safe.'

'They are? Why didn't you tell me so before? How are they? Where are they?'

'They're currently with me and they're fine, perhaps a little exhausted and filthy. However, I don't know how much longer my wife and I can look after them without them starving.'

'But what happened to them?'

'It seems they overheard a patrol being briefed about your mother's capture and their forged identity cards so they lay low in a wood overnight. They made their way into St Helier this morning to find a telephone, whereupon they called me.'

'But it's amazing that they didn't get—'

'Get caught? Exactly. They said they had a close shave near Boots, but the Germans were haranguing some bloody black-marketeer for not giving them some Red Cross parcels.'

Pippa didn't comment on that – such goings-on were far from noteworthy. 'What are you going to do with them?'

'I'm not sure,' said Aubin. 'As I said, I can't keep them indefinitely.'

'Well, Doctor, it looks as though you may have to,' said Pippa, folding her arms. 'Obviously the Campbell "hostelry" is out of action, so we're of no use to you. Perhaps you'll now realise what a strain it is . . .'

'What're you trying to tell me, young lady?'

'That it's bloody hard looking after them, and I don't—'

'Miss Campbell! I have done more than my share! I have forged identity cards, treated escapees, and carried out many tasks that have involved much personal risk! How dare you suggest that I've not been under any strain? Not only that, but have you *any* idea what pressures we few doctors are under? Well, have you?'

Pippa held up her hands. 'I'm sorry,' she said. 'It was foolish of me. I suppose my real target was not you, Dr Aubin, but all those who have done nothing. I find it shameful, despicable, even.'

'Apology accepted, Miss Campbell, and for once I agree with you. There are going to be some tough questions to ask ourselves after the war.'

'Oh, I doubt anybody will ask them. They will simply be swept under the carpet, and the islands will carry on as before.'

Aubin pursed his lips in contemplation. 'I hope you're wrong, Miss Campbell, I really do.'

'I think people have got too much to lose if they ask themselves questions that have awkward answers. No, I think the occupation will probably be celebrated in a way – made into something that bound us all together, made us stronger. Well, it'll all be rubbish, and everybody, deep down, will know it. The mainland will want us to be heroic as well because, let's face it, we'll be seen as an example of how the country would have behaved if the Germans had invaded in 'forty. Within six months of the war being over, you won't hear about informers, the black market, the labour camps, the Russian workers, none of it. It'll all be gone, and instead we'll all be reminiscing about how clever we were in making bramble-leaf tea and rose-petal ciggies.'

'That's quite a speech, Miss Campbell.'

'I happen to believe it, Doctor.'

'And so do I.'

Both Pippa and Aubin turned towards the bedroom door. Von Luck had entered and, judging by the wry smile on his face, had overheard some of the conversation.

'Good – good afternoon, von Luck,' said Aubin uneasily.

'Good afternoon, Dr Aubin,' von Luck replied, icily polite. 'And how is Mrs Campbell?'

'She's doing well. I was just telling Miss Campbell here that she is a very strong woman – she has taken a beating that many half her age would not have survived.'

'And how long will her back take to heal?'

'A few weeks at least. Is it possible for her to stay here?'

Von Luck shrugged his shoulders. 'Of course,' he said. 'Although I shall have that dragon Mrs May to answer to. Linden Court suddenly has a lot of mouths to feed because of me.'

Pippa noticed that as von Luck was talking, his eyes kept darting to her.

'The only problem, though, is that I may not be here much longer,' he went on.

'Are you being posted back to Germany?' Aubin asked. 'I'd have thought getting there was almost impossible.'

'Far from it. No, I am going over to Alderney tomorrow where I have some urgent business to attend to. The only problem is that I may be there for quite some time.'

'But you cannot leave—'

'I'm sorry, Dr Aubin, but I have no choice. What I have to do there is essential, of the utmost importance.'

'But this is—'

'I have asked Miss Campbell to stay here and look after her mother. If I do not return from Alderney after four days, then it will be necessary for them to seek accommodation elsewhere. Naturally I expect you will be only too willing to help.'

'But I cannot look after them!'

'And why's that?'

Pippa felt Aubin's eyes settling on her now.

'I'm . . . er, far too busy with my patients, Colonel. I would not be able—'

'You have a wife, Aubin. Surely she can help?'

'She would find it very difficult.'

Pippa watched von Luck's features blacken. '*Difficult*, Doctor? Why do I keep hearing that bloody word?'

'Max!' said Pippa.

Von Luck did not hear. 'Every time I do something for you people—'

'Max!' Pippa almost had to shout to be heard.

'Yes?'

'You're not being fair,' she said. 'Look, I might as well tell you. The doctor already has a full house, if you get my meaning.'

Von Luck tilted his head back and looked down his nose at Aubin. 'Has he now?'

Aubin's face was visibly reddening. 'Miss Campbell!' he stormed. 'You are out of line!'

'How can I be out of line? The Colonel is our *friend*, can't you see that? We can trust him utterly, not just because of what he has already done but for what he's going to do. He is no longer our enemy, Dr Aubin, but our ally.'

Aubin slapped his thighs in resignation. Von Luck looked at Pippa. 'Fellowes and Smith?' he asked.

Pippa nodded. She could see a twinkle in von Luck's eye. 'What are you thinking?'

'I'm thinking that I could do with some help,' he replied. 'Doctor!'

'What?'

'Are your two houseguests, as it were, in good shape?'

'Smith has a cold, and they're both famished, but otherwise they're pretty healthy.'

'Excellent! And I assume, since they escaped, that they are resourceful men?'

Aubin nodded.

'They're both very capable,' said Pippa. 'Very brave.'

'Anyway, why do you ask?' said Aubin.

'Because I need two men like that to help me on Alderney.'

'Help you do what exactly?'

'To help me fight for *their* country,' said von Luck.

'I'm sorry, von Luck, I'm not following you.'

Von Luck looked at Pippa. 'Can he be trusted do you think?'

Pippa paused before replying. 'Yes,' she said, albeit with reluctance.

* * *

As a result of an anonymous phone call from von Luck, Richard Marais's body was discovered later that Sunday afternoon. One of the first to be informed was Major Hempel, who was summoned from his investigations at Gestapo HQ by an urgent telephone call from Heidi von Aufsess, the admiral's secretary. She informed him that it was a matter of even greater importance than his current task and that he should waste no time in getting to the Field Command.

There, Hempel found the admiral in a solemn, yet not altogether depressed, mood.

'The Bailiff has just been found dead,' said Huffmeier. 'Someone chopped his head off some time this morning at some sort of standing stone at Faldouet, wherever that is.'

Hempel did not know whether to be more surprised by the statement or by the baldness of its delivery. 'This – this is quite extraordinary, sir. Do we have any idea . . ?'

'None whatsoever. As you can imagine, this is going to kick up a fucking stir, and I want you, Hempel, to deal personally with the investigation.'

'And how about my investigation into the—'

'That can run in tandem, Hempel. It wouldn't surprise me if they both led in the same direction.'

Hempel frowned. 'Is there any reason why you say that, sir?'

'Just common sense, Hempel, pure common sense. We have had a spate of murders now, and this is not a large island. It is unlikely that there is more than one murderer on the loose at any one time. We have here a maniac, Hempel, and it is up to you to stop him.'

'And what about Fügen, sir? Is he to be involved?'

'Who?'

'Fügen, sir, the remaining Gestapo member.'

'Oh, him. No, the man's an idiot. I'm not going to have him involved. Besides, he'll only tell Berlin, and I've told you before, I don't want Berlin to have the slightest whiff of all this.'

This was highly irregular, Hempel thought. It seemed spurious to establish whether the Field Police or the Jersey Constabulary would be involved. There was no doubt that Huffmeier was doing his best to maintain his reputation, but surely even he knew that all these murders – and especially that of Marais – would be common knowledge soon enough and, one way or another, Berlin would find out. Berlin always found out, Hempel thought.

'All right, Hempel, what are you waiting for? You should be going up to Faldouet, or is it down?'

'Up, sir. From here, most things are up.'

Huffmeier allowed himself a smile. 'I'll let that one go, Hempel, because it was clever.'

'Yes, sir,' said Hempel.

The man was like the worst kind of schoolmaster – sarcastic, and just a little too smug.

Fifteen minutes later Hempel arrived at the dolmen. It was still raining, although not so hard that he noticed. Two guards were standing next to the entrance to the dolmen, both of whom saluted as he walked past. They looked grim – as they no doubt would, having seen a beheaded body. Accompanied by the garrison's senior doctor, Oberstabsarzt Siegfried Thomas, Hempel walked down the same covered path that von Luck had trodden a few hours before.

'You ever been here?' Hempel asked Thomas.

'No,' Thomas replied. 'Is there anything we should know about it?'

'I don't suppose so – these places were old burial grounds. It might suggest that the murderer has some sense of history, or perhaps it's just coincidence.'

'I expect it's the latter,' said Thomas, 'although the place does have a certain *atmosphere*.'

'I know what you mean – you think that someone is looking at you through the bushes.'

Thomas looked around. 'Yes. Perhaps the odd ghost. Perhaps even of Marais himself.'

Hempel thought that a little close to the bone, but put it down to the typical black humour of the medical man. Thomas had been invalided off the Russian front after two years of surgery in the most atrocious conditions imaginable, so it was hardly surprising that he made light of death.

'So the body is under that whatever-it-is, then, is it?'

'Apparently,' said Hempel.

'Are you going to look as well?'

'I suppose I should.'

'I'd have a handkerchief ready if I were you.'

Hempel felt in his pockets – he didn't have one. 'Don't worry, I'll be all right.'

'Just don't say I didn't warn you, Major,' said Thomas, with a gap-toothed smile.

Within the space of the next thirty seconds, Hempel had seen Marais's body and detached head, and had vomited copiously, the sound of Thomas's laughter in his ears. 'I told you, Major!' Thomas shouted, from within the dolmen.

Hempel didn't reply. How could the man sound so bloody cheerful? Surgeons constituted a strange breed – they seemed to revel in gore.

'Can you see anything – anything noteworthy?' Hempel asked, from outside the dolmen.

'Well,' said Thomas, 'whoever did this had to be very strong. It's a clean wound – done with an axe, I'd say. Pretty barbaric stuff!'

'An axe? Are you sure?'

'I can't see what else could have done it.'

There was a silence for a few minutes while Thomas went about his business.

'There are some bruises on the upper torso and the upper arms, which suggests that there was a struggle or a fight. Let's just have a quick look at the head now . . . Ah, yes, just as I thought – the poor man's got a black eye and a cut lip, although that's the least of his problems.'

Would the man ever stop being so flippant, Hempel wondered.

'By the way,' asked Thomas, 'what did you want doing with the body?'

'We had better keep it,' said Hempel. 'The admiral wants this to remain an army affair for the time being.'

Thomas walked round to join him. 'No Gestapo, eh?'

'Exactly,' said Hempel. 'Besides, two-thirds of them are dead. Huffmeier is convinced whoever killed them killed poor Marais here.'

'An elegant and neat theory,' said Thomas.

'A little too elegant, a little too neat.'

'I agree. Elegant and neat theories tend to be incorrect. The world is a little bit more complicated than our black-and-white admiral would believe.'

Hempel paused. He would keep his opinion concerning the intellectual qualities of the admiral to himself. 'Right,' he said, clapping his gloved hands. 'I had better do some detective work.'

'I shall leave you to it,' said Thomas. 'I shall see you by the car.'

'You're not going to do anything else, Oberstabsarzt?'

Thomas shook his head. 'The man's dead, Major. I could perform an autopsy on him, if you like, but I think the cause of death is clear. All I need to do is to supervise the ambulance when it arrives.'

That flippancy again, thought Hempel. If Thomas was his junior, he would have rebuked him. Instead, he just had to take it.

'Many thanks, Oberstabsarzt. You have been most helpful.'

The doctor saluted and walked off, his air as carefree as that of a young boy going for a summer's day walk.

What to look for? Hempel was no detective, and neither did he profess to be one, no matter how amateur. He had a great deal of common sense, which was useful, but he found it puzzling that the admiral should have chosen him to investigate a matter of such importance. Was he merely a useful idiot for Huffmeier, a delaying tactic? It was an uncomfortable thought, which he tried to dismiss.

Hempel began by walking slowly round the dolmen, delaying the moment when he knew he would have to look at the body and the head again. He tried looking for clues such as suspiciously flattened grass and footprints, but there were none to be found. Certainly there were some dents in the mud, but you would need to be a Red Indian tracker to decipher them, he thought.

He took a deep breath and glanced up the small path that led to the dolmen. He had to have a proper look: that was his duty. He had already seen it once – come on, it couldn't get any worse.

He walked up the path slowly, blaming himself for being a coward, and at the same time telling himself that it was only natural to feel this revulsion: it was only old dogs like Thomas who were immune to it.

After he had gone no more than five or six steps, his eye was caught by a small piece of white paper. He bent down to study it, and realised that it was a cigarette end. A clue? He took off his thick gloves and picked it up gingerly – it was damp and liable to fall apart. It was not so damp, however, that the cigarette's brand had been removed. It was a brand that Hempel knew well, although it was not well known. He had encountered it many times before, and had once commented to the man who had supplied him with them how smart it was to have one's own coat of arms emblazoned on one's cigarettes. That man was Max von Luck.

* * *

Lebonneur lifts his eyelids slowly. Looking down at him is a face he has never seen before. It is a large face, adorned with a sumptuous grey beard, above which peers a pair of narrow, but friendly, eyes. 'If you're God,' Lebonneur croaks, 'then you're just as you're meant to be.'

The face smiles. 'I've heard that before,' the man says. 'Although I'm pleased to tell you that I am, in fact, Dr Ben Thomas and you're currently in our small hospital here on Alderney.'

'So if I'm not dead,' says Lebonneur, 'what *has* happened to me?'

'You're a very lucky man, Mr Lebonneur. The plane ran off on to the grass and came to a pretty violent stop as its nose pitched forward. You were knocked unconscious. A few cracked ribs, and an ugly cut on your forehead, but you're in one piece. You'll be getting some plastic surgery a few months down the line, I'll warrant.'

Lebonneur feels a smile creep across his face. 'And the others?'

'Head injuries – a couple of fractured skulls – but they'll be all right. The pilot, I'm afraid, did die.'

'A heart attack?'

'I'm afraid we won't know that until we carry out on an autopsy. He was a young, fit man, so a cardiac arrest would seem unlikely, especially as the airline's pilots are screened regularly for heart conditions.'

Murdered, that's what Lebonneur thinks, he was murdered. For the time being, he will keep his suspicions to himself. 'The poor bugger,' he says quietly.

'Indeed.'

A small silence.

'You do have another problem, Mr Lebonneur.'

'Yes?'

'I fear you will shortly be experiencing Andy Warhol's fifteen minutes of fame.'

'Oh, Christ. Have they called already?'

'They most certainly have. Even from London. The *Daily Mail*, I believe, was first off the mark.'

'Oh, fuck.'

Dr Thomas smiles. 'You have little time for journalists, then?'

'Littler than you could imagine, Doctor. The person I would most like to speak to is my wife.'

'I think it's best you get some rest first. But don't worry, she's been told you're OK and she's on her way over.'

'Thanks,' says Lebonneur.

'Don't mention it – you're a bloody hero doing what you did.'

Hero. A bit melodramatic, thinks Lebonneur, a bit, well, excessive.

Lebonneur knows that it's pointless to refuse the attentions of the press, but he decides to allow only one journalist into the room: Glen Owen from the Channel Islands Press Bureau, which Lebonneur knows is simply a grand title for one man and his camera. Glen's a good bloke, has done Lebonneur a few favours in the past, so he reckons the man deserves a nice exclusive. The one person he takes the most delight in refusing to talk to is that little twerp Henderson from the *Record*; Lebonneur tells him to piss off back to St Helier.

'All right, Bob,' says Owen, as he comes into the room, a wide smile on his face. 'You're going to be all over the nationals, do you know that? You're a star for giving me the exclusive on this, you bloody are.'

'Not at all,' Lebonneur replies. 'Just you make sure you buy me a nice drink.'

'Oh, I will, don't you worry about that.'

'Some Jack Daniel's would be nice.'

'What, now?'

'Perhaps after we've done this. You wouldn't mind smuggling some in, would you? And a packet of fags. I could murder a bloody Raffles.'

'No problem. Anyway, I wouldn't have thought it'd be a problem. You appear to have saved eight bloody lives, as well as your own. Jesus, Bob, who would have thought you had it in you to fly a fucking plane? It's a bloody miracle, it really is.'

'I still don't believe it myself.'

'Shall we get down to business, then?'

'Fine.'

'And afterwards some snaps, if you don't mind.'

'Did you bring any makeup with you?'

Owen chuckles. 'Oh, yes,' he says, 'and I'll want to get one of you and this bloke Andy Hill from the air traffic control tower.'

'He's the real bloody hero,' says Lebonneur. 'We would have been dead without him. Where is he, by the way?'

'I'm afraid he's being crawled over by everyone else.'

'Poor bugger.'

'And then there's someone else who wants to be photographed with you.'

'Oh, yeah? Who's this, then?'

'The Judge of Alderney. Bloke called Ian Mollett.'

Lebonneur tries sitting up, but the movement causes a bolt of pain to shoot through him. Fucking ribs, he thinks. 'Did you say "Mollett"?'

'Yeah – what of it?'

'Is he related to Peter Mollett, the Jersey Bailiff from the 1940s?'

' 'Sright. He's his son – or, rather, nephew. Mollett senior adopted him after the war. Mollett's real parents died in England during the Blitz. Why do you ask?'

'Nothing. Er, no reason.' Jesus Christ, thinks Lebonneur,

why hadn't he put two and two together before? It had been Mollett – Mollett who had phoned him, Mollett who had warned him that life would get 'difficult'. Well, that was an understatement. And now he was going to come here, was he? Wants to have his pretty picture in the papers shaking the hand of the hero of the hour? It is the last thing Lebonneur wants, but he cannot refuse the request because what reason can he give? That he thinks the Judge of Alderney is a murderer? He can't say that – at least, not yet. Well, let the bastard come here and smile and lie, if that's what he wants. He'll get what's coming to him soon enough.

'When does he want to come?' Lebonneur asks.

'In about half an hour, I think.'

'All right, then. I suppose so. Always happy to press the flesh, us celebrities, you know. Do our bit.'

Owen laughs. 'I can see your sense of humour is unfortunately still intact.'

'Piss off, you hack,' says Lebonneur, with a broad grin. 'Journo scum. Now, start asking me some questions.'

Despite the bravado, Lebonneur's brain is in a spin. He is glad to be alive, so very, very glad, but deep down, he is scared, absolutely fucking petrified.

He is shorter than Lebonneur expects. The pictures he's seen of his uncle Peter show a huge man, but Ian Mollett's not a blood relative, is he? He looks distinguished all right, typically so. Tall and slim, grey-black hair neatly swept back, a dark blue suit complete with waistcoat, even a bloody watch-chain. He's like something out of the sodding 1930s, thinks Lebonneur.

'Mr Lebonneur!'

That voice. It is the same as the one on the phone a few days ago – patrician, upmarket. Lebonneur nods in acknowledgement. He's feeling tired, drained, and he'd rather get some sleep. If he's going to see anyone he would rather it was Rachel and the kids, but his curiosity has got the better of doctor's orders.

'Allow me to introduce myself. My name is Ian Mollett – I am what we call the Judge here on Alderney. May I take this opportunity to thank you on behalf of the whole island for the splendid job you did today?'

Splendid job. The man makes it sound as though he'd just built him a nice shed. Lebonneur studies his face, looking for signs of guilt, mendacity. There are none, or at least none that Lebonneur can detect. He is looking for a warning, some sign that Mollett knows that Lebonneur knows, but the man is too good an actor.

'Thank you, Mr Mollett.'

'I've also had the pleasure to thank Mr Hill at the airport for the first-rate job he did talking you down like that.'

'Mr Hill is my new best friend,' says Lebonneur. 'Most of the credit must go to him. I was simply following his commands.'

'Poppycock! I won't hear it! You're a hero, an absolute hero. Even Mr Hill tells me that not many a man could have done what you did.'

'You're too kind, Mr Mollett.'

'Not at all.'

Glen Owen clears his throat at the other end of the bed. 'I was wondering, Judge Mollett, if I could take a few pictures of you and Mr Lebonneur?'

'Of course, young man. I don't see why not.'

Lebonneur manages a smile as Mollett poses next to him. This will make a great picture, especially when the truth is out. He is envisaging the headline even as Owen sets to work with his ridiculously large Nikon. 'THE SMILE OF THE KILLER'. Or how about 'MEETING YOUR MURDERER'? He likes that one, even if it's not true, strictly speaking.

'Come on, Bob, let's look a little happier.'

'Sorry,' says Lebonneur. 'I'm doing my best.'

Mollett, on the other hand, is smiling like the Cheshire bloody Cat, putting on his best local-newspaper-photograph face as Owen snaps away.

'All right, I think I've got enough,' says Owen.

'Excellent,' says Mollett, getting up from a crouch. 'Excellent. I think I should leave you in peace now, Mr Lebonneur, although I suspect our paths will cross again.'

'Oh, I don't doubt it,' says Lebonneur. 'I'm sure we'll, uh, run into each other.'

'It's not a large island, so that's an inevitability. Anyway – I quite forgot to ask – what were you here for?'

As if you didn't bloody know.

'The birds, Mr Mollett. I gather there are some very rare birds here on Alderney.'

'Well, there are indeed, Mr Lebonneur. Did you know we even had a Slavonian grebe here the other day?'

'No,' says Lebonneur.

'Oh, yes, it caused quite a stir.'

'Where's the best place to go?'

'Well, the Garden Rocks are great if you like gannets. And then there's Bibette Head, as well as near the lighthouse.'

'How about Mannez Hill?' Lebonneur watches Mollett carefully.

'Mannez Hill? *Really?* Oh, no. I'm afraid you won't have much luck bird-watching up there, Mr Lebonneur. You see, we're building a hotel on Mannez Hill, and it's impossible to get up there at the moment. No, I think it's better to stick to the coast. Much better.'

Although Mollett does not look agitated, his manner has certainly changed. He is speaking much more quickly, far less fluently.

'Well, if it's a building site, I'll steer well clear,' says Lebonneur.

'Well, quite. They're not very attractive places at the best of times.'

'Nor very safe,' says Lebonneur.

Lebonneur expects Mollett's reply to be full of bluster. It's anything but: he speaks slowly, his tone lacking the superficial bonhomie of before. 'You're quite right, Mr Lebonneur. They're not very safe. I'm sure you've had enough danger for one lifetime, eh? Best to stick away, if I were you. Don't want to make life too difficult, eh?'

Difficult.

'That sounds like good advice, Mr Mollett. Many thanks for visiting me and, as I said, I'm sure we'll run into each other soon.'

'Once again, many congratulations. You will be an inspiration to many, I'm sure of it.'

With that, and a cursory nod to Owen, Mollett leaves the room.

'Blimey,' says Owen. 'What was all that about?'

'Search me,' says Lebonneur. 'Anyway, what a wanker.'

'You're not wrong. He's well known for it.'

'What? Being a wanker?'

'Yup. And for being greedy. People think he uses his position to line his pockets, but it's never been proven.'

'Oh, they all do that, Glen.'

'Fair enough, but Mollett's meant to be one of the worst.'

'Obviously learnt a trick or two from his adoptive father.'

'Why? Was he a crook?'

'Like you wouldn't believe,' says Lebonneur. 'I'll tell you all about it one day, but will you do me a favour?'

'Cigarettes? More whisky? Class A drugs? You name it.'

'No, nothing like that. I want you to find out about Mollett's family, do some spadework in the records. Can you do that for me?'

'What do you want to know?'

'Anything you can find, but specifically I want to know everything about Mollett's real parents. Spend as much as you have to – I'll refund it. There's a bloke I know in London called Figg, he's pretty good at sniffing through Kew and places like that. Give him a call and as much cash as he wants.'

Lebonneur is asleep when Rachel arrives. She sits next to his bed and cries, holding his hand so tightly that Lebonneur's fingertips go red. She is overjoyed that her husband is alive and, even better, that he is a hero. But what tears her apart, what she struggles to come to terms with, is the news she has to give him when he wakes up. She will have to tell him his friend Terry is dead, killed in a car crash that morning.

* * *

Aubin brought Fellowes and Smith round to Linden Court within forty-five minutes. Crammed into the footwell and on the back seat, with a couple of blankets and a plethora of medical equipment scattered over the top of them, a cursory inspection by any sentry would have told him that the good doctor was simply moving half the contents of his surgery. However, Aubin suffered no such inspections and arrived at Linden Court unmolested, although his nerves were such that if he had had any suitable medication he would gladly have taken it.

Pippa's first action upon seeing the two men was to run up and hug them, which caused an unexpected pang of jealousy to shoot through von Luck. Control yourself, he thought, you are not normally like this – she is merely expressing herself.

'I can't tell you how glad I am that you're both alive,' said Pippa.

'Neither can we,' said Fellowes, keeping one eye on von Luck. 'And how is your mother? Dr Aubin told us she took one hell of a beating.'

'She's on the mend,' Pippa replied. 'The doctor says she's very strong.'

'She's most certainly that, Miss Campbell. Strong in more ways than one.'

'Thank you, Captain. She feels wretched that she forgot to burn those scraps of paper with your signatures on.'

'Tell her she mustn't worry. *Please*, you must tell her that. You've both done so much for us. We'll never be able to repay you.'

'Just think of it as us doing our bit.'

'I wish there were more like you,' said Smith.

'So do I,' said Pippa, looking at Aubin.

'Have you any idea who betrayed us?' asked Fellowes.

'Well, I suppose I shouldn't mention any names if I'm not sure,' said Pippa, 'but, oh, God, what the hell? My money's on that old bitch Mrs Miere who lives next door.'

'Just give me one minute with her,' said Fellowes, 'one minute, and she'll get what's coming to her.'

'As I said, Captain, I really can't be certain. An interfering bag does not an informer make.'

Von Luck coughed. 'In my experience, Miss Campbell, some of the best informers are indeed "old bags", as you call them.

The Occupation

The Gestapo informer in my village was the laundrywoman, a real "old bag" if there was one.'

'What did you do to her?' asked Pippa.

'There was very little we could do. Her family had been working for mine for five generations, so we could not dismiss her. And even if we tried, that would only have aroused the suspicion of our local Gestapo, who well knew that the von Lucks were not the most enthusiastic supporters of the regime. Anyway, let's forget about all that.'

He turned to Fellowes and Smith. 'Captain Fellowes . . . and Pilot Officer Smith, I am Lieutenant Colonel von Luck. Thank you for coming here.' He saluted the two men, a sign of respect that they found difficult not to acknowledge. They saluted back, albeit with less formality than von Luck's parade-ground exactness.

'Please, I urge you to relax,' said von Luck. 'You're quite safe here for the time being.'

There was no visible sign of the men easing in their manner. Standing in front of a man wearing the uniform of a country they had been at war with for nearly six years was clearly not something they would become accustomed to within minutes.

'We, um, appreciate it,' said Fellowes. 'Although we're a little mystified as to why you want us here. We know that you saved Mrs Campbell and, of course, Miss Campbell, so we know you're on the right side, Colonel. However, we cannot see why you should want to put up with us. We're rather a liability to you, I would have thought.'

'Quite the opposite,' said von Luck, with a smile. 'But perhaps it's best if we discuss this over a cigarette and a glass of something in the living room?'

The men's eyes lit up as von Luck had been sure they would. He did not expect to buy them with such luxuries, but the tobacco and alcohol might make his proposition easier for them to swallow.

Hempel's car drew up at Linden Court, just as von Luck had concluded a most fruitful discussion with Fellowes and Smith, both of whom had agreed to accompany him to Alderney the next morning. Von Luck recognised the car immediately, and its presence produced mixed feelings. What was he here for? A social call? It was the time of day when Hempel liked to have a drink, certainly, but somehow he doubted that was the reason for the visit. Perhaps he was simply here to tell him the news about Marais, because Hempel would, no doubt, have been informed. There was, of course, the possibility that he was here to arrest him for the murder of Bürkel and Bouhler, and it was this that made von Luck uneasy.

'You'd better go upstairs,' he said to Fellowes and Smith.

They did as he asked them. Mrs May would be infuriated that there were now five 'guests' in the house, but as none would be here by this time tomorrow, von Luck had no time for her inevitable complaints.

Von Luck walked to the front door and opened it before Hempel had a chance to knock. 'Good afternoon, Hempel.'

The expression on Hempel's face was the opposite in mood to von Luck's cheery greeting. Standing behind him were two dull-faced NCOs.

'Are you all right, Hempel? You look as though you have the world on your shoulders.'

'Can we go inside, please, sir?' The request was formal, stiff.

'Of course. Is something the matter?'

Von Luck led Hempel into the hall. He was about to close the door when Hempel stopped him. 'I'd appreciate it if you kept it open, please, sir,' said Hempel, pointing at the two soldiers, who remained outside.

'What the hell is this, Hempel?'

The two men looked at each other. Von Luck knew that something was badly wrong.

Hempel cleared his throat before speaking. 'There's no . . .' he began, then cleared his throat again.

'A glass of water?'

'No,' said Hempel, emphatically. 'I'm quite all right. Look, there's no easy way to say this, Colonel, but I'm arresting you for the murder of Richard Marais.'

'What?'

'You heard me, Colonel. I'd appreciate it if you handed me your pistol and came with me down to the Field Command.'

'This is monstrous, Hempel! What the hell are you talking about? Who's put you up to this? And who says Marais is dead anyway?'

'Don't tell me you don't know, Colonel.'

'Of course I don't know!'

'Please be very careful, sir. Any lie now is going to look very bad.'

'Lie, Hempel? *Lie?* For heaven's sake, Hempel, this is me, von Luck. I'm not some murderer! This is the first I've heard of this.'

'I'm afraid that is a lie, sir, which only convinces me of your guilt.'

'Hempel, you are a decent man, and you know that I, too, am a decent man. I'm not in the habit of murdering people, for heaven's sake.'

Hempel reached into his pocket and produced a small bag.

'What's this?' asked von Luck. 'The answer to all our prayers?'

'No,' said Hempel, his tone utterly phlegmatic. 'It's one of your cigarette ends.'

Von Luck studied it. It was one of his cigarettes. Had he had a smoke when he was at the dolmen? No, he most certainly hadn't, he was sure of it. 'How charming, Hempel. And I suppose you're going to say that you found it next to the body or some such nonsense.'

'That's exactly where I found it, Colonel. Now, your firearm, please. There's no point in making this difficult. I only have to call for the two guards, don't I?'

Von Luck was not listening. How the fuck had that cigarette end got there? Someone had planted it – there was no doubt about that. Who, though? Mollett. It had to be. Peter Mollett, the Bailiff's loyal deputy, the man von Luck had dealt with countless times over the years – could it really have been him?

Why would he want to kill Marais, and why so gruesomely? There was something sacrificial about the method of execution and the location, something that stank of clandestine societies, secret orders. There was a whiff of Freemasonry about it, thought von Luck, but his ignorance of that society was too great to know whether murdering each other with axes was a Masonic practice.

'Colonel,' said Hempel, 'your firearm. Before I have to have you overpowered.'

Von Luck opened his holster and slowly removed his pistol. There was no way he could fight his way out of this situation. Hempel was younger than Petersen, and the guards were expecting trouble. He would be killed if he tried anything. All he could do was appeal to Hempel's better nature and sense of reason. 'You can have my weapon,' he said, 'but you must understand that I did not murder Richard Marais.'

Hempel took the pistol. 'We can discuss it down at the Field Command,' he said.

'Hempel, before we go there, I need five minutes with you. We can talk in front of the guards if you wish, but I'd prefer not to. They will only gossip. Will you accept my word that I will do you no harm and that I will not try to escape?'

'Colonel, you must see that this is impossible. I'm here to arrest you, not to join you for a drink.'

'I do not wish to beg, Hempel, to plead. You know that I am not that type of man. But I must assure you of two things. First, that I did not murder Marais, but, yes, I did know about it. It was I who discovered his body. Second, his murder is part of a much larger conspiracy than the Bailiff was aware of before he was killed. It is a conspiracy whose ramifications are far bigger than any one of us, Hempel, but in arresting me you will be doing the work of the conspirators.'

'Come on, von Luck! This is madness!'

'Is it? Is it any more mad than the notion that I beheaded Marais?'

'So you know how he died!' said Hempel, triumphantly.

'Of course I bloody well did! I've just told you I discovered his body. The reason why I did so was because I was due to meet Marais at the dolmen at midday. He came up to me after church this morning to request a rendezvous. When I got there, I found the poor man dead. For heaven's sake, Hempel, this is the bloody truth.'

'So why didn't you contact the Field Command straight away?'

'Because I needed to talk to the man who planted my cigarette end at the dolmen.'

Hempel's brow furrowed. Good, thought von Luck. It meant that he was listening.

'Hempel – there is a lot more to this than one murdered Jerseyman. Will you please let me explain?'

Hempel turned to the guards. 'Come in here and wait in the hall,' he ordered.

The men obeyed him and entered the house – one even wiped his feet and saluted von Luck, who saluted him back.

'Let's talk in your drawing room,' said Hempel. 'This had better be good, von Luck.'

Von Luck pulled a relieved smile. 'The one thing this is not, Hempel, is good.'

* * *

'You shall shortly be a very rich man, Herr Mollett.'

Mollett merely nodded at the admiral's prophecy. He was already a rich man, but the extra money would not be unwelcome. Anyway, he would do well to be polite to his benefactor. 'Thank you, Admiral. Of course, let me assure you that I'm not really in this for the money.'

'I hope not, Mollett, I hope not. Otherwise I would regard you as nothing more than one of those Algerian whores they have in the camps.'

'Well, quite.'

'And now that Marais is out of the way, you can promise me that the deportation will go ahead unopposed on Wednesday morning?'

'Yes. Yes, I can.'

'I'm glad to hear it. The last thing the project on Alderney needs is a delay, especially one caused by lack of manpower.'

'And may I ask how the project is going?'

'It's going well. It's now being run by Hauptsturmführer Max List of the SS, who is a vast improvement on that idiot Schwalm.'

'I hear the SS are effective in getting people to work.'

'They are indeed. Of course, List will doubtless require more

275

manpower over the next few weeks, which I'm sure you'll be happy to provide.'

Mollett shrugged his shoulders as if to suggest the request was a mere bagatelle. 'Naturally,' he said. 'How many did you have in mind?'

'Another two, perhaps three thousand.'

'Well, I see no difficulties there.'

'Really?'

'I'm sure there'll be the odd scuffle – I can't guarantee complete compliance, of course – but I really don't see those sort of figures presenting a huge problem.'

Admiral Huffmeier stood up from behind his desk and walked to the window. The light was fading, the evening sky having something of the disturbed quality that he remembered from his days at sea. 'I like working with you, Herr Mollett. You have the necessary ruthlessness and good sense that we like in Germany. When the war is over, I'm sure you'll be welcome in Berlin.'

'You are kind to say so, Admiral. For what it's worth, I like working with you too. Now that that idiot Schmettow has gone, one can finally get on with some decent work.'

'Schmettow was a fool, a bumbling old Junker whom Berlin should have got rid of years ago. He should have hanged after July 'forty-four, even if he wasn't a conspirator. They did so with plenty of others, so why not him?'

'And von Luck too – why wasn't he strung up?'

'Von Luck was lucky. He is a snake, that man, a real snake. He's no fool, even if he is soft on the islanders. Not that it matters, anyway.' Huffmeier turned from the window and smiled. He looked at his watch. 'By my reckoning, Hempel will be bringing him back here in about ten minutes. Have you spoken to the newspaper to tell them to get their pages ready?'

'I have,' said Mollett. 'Not only will they be publishing my proclamation, but they will also be carrying a full report of how Marais suffered a heart attack while out on a walk.'

Huffmeier all but rubbed his hands in glee.

*　*　*

'This is an incredible story, von Luck.' Hempel was holding the letter from Marais, which his eyes were repeatedly running over. 'What sort of weapon is he talking about?' he asked.

'I don't know,' said von Luck, 'which is why I'm planning to go to Alderney to find out.'

'You? Going to Alderney? When? How?'

'Tomorrow morning, if you'll let me. I'm planning on inveigling myself into a group of Russian workers who are sailing there tomorrow.'

'All on your own?'

'No – I shall have some help.'

'Who?'

'I can't tell you that, Hempel.'

'Why not?'

'Because, quite frankly, the less you know the better.'

At first Hempel looked offended, but his expression soon relaxed. 'All right,' he said. 'I understand.'

'Thanks, Hempel. So, then, are you still going to arrest me?'

Hempel took one of the cigarettes von Luck was proffering. 'Now you've explained things, no, of course I shan't. But it does leave me returning to the Field Command empty-handed. The admiral already knows that I was on my way to arrest you – I shall have some explaining to do.'

'You could just say I wasn't here.'

'He's under the impression that you were.'

Von Luck frowned. 'What do you mean?'

'Well, when I came back to the Field Command, I told Huffmeier about the cigarette end and how I suspected you might have been responsible.'

Von Luck pinched his nose. He wanted to curse Hempel, to tell him that he had been a fucking idiot, but he knew it would do no good. Besides, it had not been unreasonable of Hempel to suspect him. 'Carry on,' he said.

'Huffmeier clapped his hands, and said words to the effect of "Got him!" He then said, "He's at Linden Court – go and arrest him immediately." He shooed me out of his office, giving me the impression that I should have been here before he had finished speaking.'

'You're quite sure he said, "He's at Linden Court"?'

'Positive.'

Von Luck stood up.

'Where are you going?' asked Hempel.

'I have to leave immediately,' said von Luck.

'But where are you going?'

'I need to get some people to safety as quickly as possible. Listen, Hempel, I have no intention of risking your life. Do what you have to do, say to Huffmeier what you have to say, but stay away from me! Just go – go and spin them some yarn that they'll half believe. Say anything! But please buy me some time, that's all I ask.'

'But who are these people?'

Von Luck made for the drawing-room door.

'Von Luck!'

Von Luck's hand rested on the door handle. 'Again, I think it's best if I don't tell you.'

'Listen, von Luck, I'll help you.'

Von Luck turned. 'You would?'

Hempel nodded. 'It's time I did something decent with my life.'

* * *

At fifty-five, Nancy Lemprière was young for a widow of fifteen years. Her husband, David, had been pulled away to his death by a particularly strong current in Bouley Bay, leaving her to look after two teenage boys and one of the finest houses on Jersey – Rozel Manor.

The boys had quickly become men and, at the outbreak of war, despite their mother's pleading, had travelled to London to enlist in their father's regiment. Within two years James, the elder boy, had been killed in North Africa, and Edward, now a major, had survived Normandy and was now advancing into Germany.

During the occupation, Nancy had maintained cordial, although not overly friendly, relations with the German officers who had called upon her. Although she had little time for many of them, there were a few who made her regret the circumstances of their having met during wartime, and of these the handsome young Count von Luck was her favourite. He reminded Nancy of her boys, especially James, and although she was never to tell him so, she knew that he had the sophistication to realise it.

She therefore indulged him and the officers to whom he was closest. Cakes were miraculously brought out when he called at weekends, the run of the estate was given to him on which to go shooting (although she recognised that, as an invader, von Luck effectively had the run of the island), vintage port was produced from the cellars and the contents of David's humidor were offered.

The relationship worked well for both parties. For von Luck and his friends, Rozel Manor was a haven of gentility and civility, and Nancy liked the company of elegant young men. Even though she had her patriotic misgivings about entertaining the enemy, she thought it more practical to offer rather than wait for it to be taken.

At half past six that Sunday evening, Nancy was doing what she always did at that time, which was to go through the household and estate accounts. Her work was interrupted by the sound of a car – or was it two? – coming up the drive. She put down her pen. They were going terribly quickly, she thought. Whatever was the matter? She left her desk, wrapping her cardigan round herself as a gesture against the cold. 'Thelma!' she shouted, as she hurried through to the hall. 'Who is it?'

'I don't know, Mrs Lemprière,' said Thelma Ferbrache, the housekeeper. 'I've been in the kitchen.'

'Well, you'd better get back there,' said Nancy, an order made not because she felt that the kitchen was Thelma's natural home but because if there was going to be trouble she did not wish Thelma to be part of it.

Nancy walked to the front door, hearing the sound of urgent footsteps on the gravel outside. Normally she would have waited for a knock on the door, but she was too curious to obey protocol. Instead, she pulled open the vast oak door, and was presented with the sight of Lieutenant Colonel von Luck and Major Hempel hurrying up the steps.

'Mrs Lemprière!' said von Luck, as he bounded up. 'I am so sorry to disturb your Sunday evening, but I urgently need your help.'

'Of course,' said Nancy, clutching her necklace. 'Whatever can I do?'

Von Luck reached the top of the steps and smiled down at her. 'Good evening,' he said, a little breathless. 'I'm afraid that this is a rather large favour.'

'Anything, my dear Colonel,' she replied.

She had never seen von Luck like this. Normally he looked so calm, so on top of the world, but this evening he seemed haunted and tired – exhausted, even. There were huge bags under his eyes, and his shaving that morning had clearly been a rushed affair.

'I was wondering whether you could accommodate me and a few friends?'

Nancy did her best not to show any surprise, but that was her overriding emotion. 'Of course. Who are these people?'

'Can they come in first? I'd rather not leave them outside in the cars.'

Nancy tried looking past von Luck to the drive. She thought she could see a woman's face in one of the car windows. Oh, no, she thought, he hadn't got a girl into trouble, had he? Not her dear von Luck, not *him*.

* * *

He was just about to fall asleep when he heard the handle to his bedroom door turning. The sound caused him to sit upright and reach for his pistol from the bedside cabinet. He released the safety catch as the door edged open. The only light was provided by the full moon, which somehow managed to infiltrate the room through the thick curtains.

'Stop right there!'

Whoever was trying to get into the room did so.

'I have a gun pointed towards you. If you move, I'll kill you.'

'Max! It's me! Pippa!'

Thank God for that, thought von Luck, and indeed, for different reasons, thank God again. He found himself smiling in the darkness. 'Come in,' he whispered.

'I can't see a thing.'

'Hold on.' Von Luck put down his pistol next to the short stub of candle that Nancy Lemprière had provided. He lit it, and the room was suffused with a tender yellow glow.

'That's better,' said Pippa.

She remained standing in the doorway. Von Luck had never seen her look more attractive. Her feet were bare, but otherwise she was fully dressed. The expression on her face suggested that this was a temporary state of affairs.

'Aren't you going to come in?' von Luck asked.

'It's possible,' she said, with a smirk.

'Or do I have to come and drag you?'

'You'd better not do that – the floorboards creak rather too much.'

Pippa crept across the room and slid swiftly under the blankets. Von Luck opened his mouth to speak, but she put a finger over it, which he kissed. She then removed her finger and touched her lips to his.

As they began to make love, von Luck thought how confident she was, how sure of herself. The Jerseywomen he had slept with before had never been so sophisticated. 'The English girl', he had once written in his diary, 'will surrender to her partner readily enough, provided this can be effected in proper privacy.

The Englishwoman is astoundingly simple, effortless and swift in her lovemaking.' Frenchwomen, thought von Luck, were far more involved, far more intellectual in matters of the flesh. Pippa, he surmised, was much more like a Frenchwoman.

After they had finished, von Luck thought that maybe he had been wrong: Pippa was better than any Frenchwoman he had slept with. This time had felt different, utterly fulfilling. He knew why. He had fallen in love – with a woman he was probably never going to see again.

As they lay in silence, the last flickers of the dying candle dancing around the ceiling, von Luck decided he had to tell her. It was so unlike him, so out of character. 'Pippa,' he whispered.

'Yes?'

'*Ich liebe dich.*'

'I love you too,' she said. 'But couldn't you have bloody said it in English?'

For fear of waking Pippa's mother in the room next door, they had to stifle their laughter under the covers.

* * *

'Has anyone slept with her before?' asked List.

'No, Hauptsturmführer,' a young private replied. 'She is quite fresh.'

'Fresh, eh? Like an egg?'

The private laughed sycophantically. 'Very much so, sir.'

'Good. In that case I shall have her now. All right, you can wait outside. You'll need to take her back after I've finished.'

The conversation was conducted over the head of the seventeen-year-old French girl in question. Although she did not understand German, she could guess what they were saying. She fought back the tears, realising that she was about to have her virginity raped out of her.

The only consolation she had was that the act was brief. However, there was little time to draw any comfort from that, no matter how small, because List shot her through the back of her neck a few seconds after he had withdrawn from her.

'Private!' he shouted.

The man ran in to find List doing up his breeches over the corpse.

'I've finished with her. You can take her back now.'

Chapter Eight

When Lebonneur hears that Terry is dead, he starts screaming, and goes on for so long that the doctor is forced to sedate him. When he wakes up a few hours later, he starts screaming again. After he has calmed down, he lies in bed staring at the ceiling, not listening to Rachel, who is imploring him to tell her what he has been up to, begging to know what all this is about. He doesn't want to tell her, because she will hate him for risking his life. 'I'm so sorry,' he says. 'I'm just so sorry.'

'But what for, Bob?'

'For being the wrong type of man. I'm sorry I'm so fucking unreliable. I'm sorry I chucked my job in. I'm sorry I swear so bloody much. I'm just sorry for everything, that's all.'

Rachel starts to cry, although not copiously. 'You're being silly,' she says. 'I love you so much. You must see that. I love you in spite of all your weaknesses and bad habits, because we all have those.'

'*You* don't.'

Rachel smiles through her tears.

There is a brief silence.

'How're the kids?' Lebonneur asks.

'They're great,' says Rachel. 'Katherine and Ian are looking after them. They think you're a hero, which you are, Bob, you truly are. I suspect they'll be filling several scrapbooks with all the press cuttings there are going to be about you.'

'The only time I've been proud to appear in the papers,' says Lebonneur.

'Oh, don't be like that! You've been proud of countless stories you've done. Remember the one on the pollution at St Ouen's? You were terribly excited about that one.'

'I suppose so,' he says. 'It just all seems so insignificant now that this has happened. Terry, poor bloody Terry. The bastards! And it's my fucking fault.'

'I still don't understand what really has happened.'

Lebonneur shifts painfully so that he can face her better. 'Listen, Rachel, it's my fault that Terry's dead. We were working on something together that some people – some very powerful people – didn't like. And the same people who killed Terry are the same people who killed the poor pilot on my plane.'

Rachel holds her hand to her mouth. The action is almost demonstratively comic-book. 'You're not serious! Don't tell me someone's trying to get you – to get you *killed?*'

Lebonneur nods. 'Yes.'

'No – it's not possible.'

'Of course it is. Look what happened to Terry, for Christ's sake!'

Rachel stays silent. She knows there is no point in saying anything.

'Anyway, I can prove it,' says Lebonneur.

'How?'

'I'm going to need your help.'

'Sure. What do you want me to do?'

'I need you to get my bag from the plane. I'm praying it's still in one piece. Can you do that for me?'

Lebonneur has a long, frustrating hour to wait. It occurs to him that his bag, even if it has survived the crash, may have been stolen by *them*.

'What the hell's in this, Bob? It weighs a ton.'

Lebonneur grins. Rachel is struggling into his room with his large brown overnight bag. 'Thanks, darling,' he says. 'Plonk it on the bed, would you?'

Rachel does so and rummages through an ill-packed assortment of clothes before she produces a metal briefcase. 'Is this what you want?'

'Yeah – open it up.'

She fiddles with the catches before the lid pop opens with a satisfying click. The contents cause her brow to furrow. Packed neatly into thick grey foam are three items, all of which are equally mysterious. The first is a plain white plastic rectangle, the second a larger rectangle, which features a couple of knobs and a display, and the third what Rachel can only think to be a handheld grille.

'What on earth is this?' she asks.

'That,' says Lebonneur, a note of triumphalism in his voice, 'is an RM6 with scintillation alpha probe type AP3.'

'A what?'

'I don't know what that means either, but if I said "Geiger counter" you might have a better idea.'

'And what are you intending to do with it?'

'I'm going to take it for a walk.'

'When?'

'As soon as I get out of this blasted place.'

'I'm more confused than I was before now.'

'All right – have another look in the bag. You should find a small book in it.'

'This one?'

'That's it. Have a look through.'

'But it's all in German.'

'Maybe, but it'll tell you all you need to know.'

*   *   *

Von Luck got out of bed just after four o'clock. Pippa was fast asleep, the only sign of life a gentle rising and falling of the blankets. He knew this would be the last time he saw her and, for a few seconds, he allowed himself to look at her in the moonlight. He tried to work out what he would sacrifice to be able to stay in bed with her, to make love all morning, then go outside for a walk in the sunshine in a land that was at peace. It was an impossibly romantic dream, and he felt a surge of resentment that it should be so. To lie in bed with a woman you loved, and to go for a walk – these were simple human pleasures that had been denied to many millions over the past six years, all because of a collective madness that said your country was more important than the people in it, the people you loved.

He got dressed quickly, not in his uniform but a collection of clothes that had once belonged to the gardener at Linden Court. His intention was to look as scruffy as Fellowes and Smith. Together the three men hoped to blend in with the ragtag assembly of Todt workers who would be making their way to the quay at St Helier. Hopefully, the only difference between them and the workers would be the weapons they carried – an assortment of pistols, knives and even a couple of hand grenades that von Luck had kept in his study at Linden Court. He knew their arsenal was nowhere near large enough to damage any installations, but it would be sufficient to kill plenty of key personnel.

His diary. What was he going to do with that? If he took it and he was killed, it would be lost for ever. That must not happen, he told himself. Its contents were too important to be thrown with their owner into a mass grave on Alderney. Pippa – she was the obvious choice to keep it.

Von Luck walked over to the window and opened the thick curtains a fraction. A suggestion of dawn crept coldly into the room, providing enough light for him to write. He flicked through the pages of the diary, reminding himself of some of the happier times he had had on Jersey – the long summers, the flirtations and subsequent conquests, the dinners at Rozel Manor, the robust discussions on philosophy with Hempel and Cleve, the shooting, riding Satan along the beach at St Ouen's Bay. As wars went, thought von Luck, he had had it easy. It was time he proved himself, time he acquitted himself with the same sort of valour that had been shown by his father and grandfather, even if he was going to fight against Germany.

Von Luck turned to the last entry in the diary, which he had completed last night. He started a new page with today's date, and wrote a letter to Pippa.

My dear Pippa,
Last night I loved you more than I have ever loved before. I can confidently write that I will never love a woman as much again, because soon I will be dead. That we had our short time together has made my life fulfilled in a way that I never thought possible. My only regret is that my life will not have been complete, because for that to be so, we might be looking forward to the things that others in our position could reasonably expect – a marriage, children, a home. We shall never have those things, and it pains me to think it. All that I can leave you with is this, my diary. Please guard it well – it is yours now, as am I.

Yours always,

Max

Von Luck reread his words, inserted Marais's letter between the diary's pages, then closed it. He shut the curtains, and stole across the room to leave it on the table next to Pippa's side of the bed. He looked down at her for a few seconds, and then he was gone, out into the corridor, leaving behind that world for good.

Along with Fellowes and Smith, von Luck left Rozel Manor just before half past four. They had eaten, and stuffed their pockets with, as much food as they could find in Nancy Lemprière's kitchen, knowing that their diet from now on would consist of little more than watery soup. They drove in silence, each man reflecting on what the next few days would bring, or whether they would even be alive to see them. They might be dead in a few hours, rumbled by some observant guard on the quayside, then processed by a rapid judicial system that would see each of them at the end of a rope by nightfall.

They hid the car in some bushes just outside St Helier.

'Where next?' asked Fellowes.

'We wait by those trees over there,' said von Luck.

'Wait?'

'That's right.'

Von Luck looked at his watch. Reflecting that he should keep it well hidden, for it was Swiss and expensive, he saw that it was approaching five o'clock. 'In a few minutes, a column of a thousand Todt workers will come marching past on their way to the ship. I thought it best that we try to join them here, where there is more cover and a bend in the road.'

'Good thinking,' said Fellowes.

'Suits me,' said Smith.

Although he had misgivings about working with von Luck, Fellowes found that he had warmed to him swiftly. The man was clearly capable, and he had a quick, easy manner that made it natural to slip into his way of operating. Perhaps it was because he was a bloody aristocrat, Fellowes thought, and had spent his whole life giving orders. Instead of telling people what to do, Fellowes noticed, they just seemed to follow him – it was a rare quality. The German army had wasted him here in this backwater.

Von Luck's persuasiveness had convinced the two Englishmen that it was essential they went to Alderney. Smith had initially been reluctant, saying that there was no hope of doing anything effective, but a two-pronged verbal assault from von Luck and Fellowes had made him see the error of his position. Von Luck had complimented him on his realism, but reminded him that war was not a time in which decisions could be made on the balance of probabilities. If that was the case, said von Luck, the Luftwaffe should have annihilated the Royal Air Force in the summer of 'forty, a well-placed reminder that touched a nerve in Smith. For his part, Fellowes stated that Smith had little option, as he, Fellowes, was going, and what was Smith going to do? Fend for himself?

The three men ran across the road to the trees, many of whose lower branches had been cut away by a fuel-hungry populace. They crouched low, listening for the approach of the column. All that was audible was birdsong, accompanied by the occasional drip of dew falling from the branches on to their clothes.

'Where the fuck are these workers?' asked Smith.

'Patience!' von Luck muttered. 'You should know by now that not everything we Germans do runs like clockwork.'

The light-hearted remark was made more for his own benefit, for he shared Smith's anxiety. Where the fuck were they, indeed? He looked at his watch again – it was five past five. They were certainly late, but not appallingly so.

They had another five minutes to wait before Fellowes said he could hear something. 'There!' he whispered. 'What's that?'

Von Luck smiled. The slowly increasing sound of footsteps and hoofs was coming from somewhere round the bend in the road.

'That's it,' he said. 'Now, listen. We wait until about a third of the column has passed us and, depending on the positions of the guards, we dash in and join the workers. It doesn't matter if we're not all together, just so long as we're close.'

'And what if any of the workers makes a fuss?'

'Bribe them with some food. That, I guarantee you, will do the trick. Those poor bastards will be nearly starving. Mind you, only do it as a last resort. The presence of food might cause a riot.'

Fellowes and Smith patted their pockets. Both men were reluctant to give up the bread and cheese they had taken from Rozel Manor.

The first sign of the column was a horse, on top of which sat a rather old sergeant. Neither the animal nor its mount looked particularly alert, thought von Luck, an attitude he hoped would be shared by the rest of the column. 'Keep still,' he whispered, to Fellowes and Smith.

The rest of the column was appearing now. Shuffling – rather than marching – six abreast, the men were a pitiful sight. Their faces were sallow, their posture bent and twisted, their loose-fitting clothes black with dirt, far dirtier than von Luck had accounted for.

'Quick!' said von Luck. 'Before they get here, make yourselves more dirty.'

Thankfully the dampness of the ground made such an operation relatively simple. Within a few seconds, the three men had smeared mud over their clothes and faces. Their efforts certainly did not make them look as filthy as the real prisoners, but there was an improvement.

The guards were walking alongside the column at haphazard intervals. As von Luck had hoped, they looked as alert as anybody would be on an empty stomach at five o'clock on a cold, damp morning.

'You see the first guard on our side of the column?'

Fellowes and Smith nodded.

'As soon as he's gone past us, that's our moment.'

As von Luck finished his sentence, the sergeant rode by. Von Luck winced at the state of the poor horse. It looked painfully thin, and it had cuts and sores on its legs. However, it did not look as bad as the first of the workers who were now walking past them: their skin, von Luck noticed, was yellow and translucent. They were walking corpses, he thought.

He felt Fellowes and Smith tense. The column was no more than fifteen feet away, close enough to smell the workers' collective stench, an indescribably foul mixture of stale urine and shit, coupled with the reek of old sweat impregnated in clothes that had not been washed for several weeks. Not one of the workers was looking ahead or up; they stared vacantly at the ground, their destination of no interest to them.

The first guard walked past. His expression was not much different from that on the faces of those he was escorting, although he looked a little better fed. His rifle was dirty and slung over his shoulder, and von Luck also noticed that a sole was loose on his right boot, which caused him to lift his right leg high so as not to let it catch on the ground as he walked.

Von Luck looked up the road towards the bend. There were no other guards in sight. He glanced at Fellowes and Smith. Without a pause, the three men broke cover and rushed forward.

At first von Luck thought that the workers' senses were so dimmed they simply would not see them, but the chattering started as the three men tried to shove their way into the ranks.

'Quiet!' von Luck hissed, holding a finger to his lips.

A couple of workers obeyed him, but a few more were complaining in a language von Luck could not understand. He looked up ahead to see if the guard had noticed the hubbub, but he hadn't, or at least not so far.

'Shut up!' von Luck whispered again.

He glowered at the complainers, who looked back at him resentfully. Who are these tall strangers? their eyes were asking. What are they doing? Whose food do they think they will get? Von Luck felt for a piece of bread in his pocket and allowed it to peep out so that the men could see it. They instantly started for it, but von Luck pushed them away. 'Later!' he said, pointing at his wrist. 'Later!'

The men backed off. They seemed to understand. Clearly they were in no mood to pick a fight, at least not now. Perhaps they were waiting for the hold of the ship. That, thought von Luck, would be a hellhole.

* * *

As von Luck was walking down to St Helier, a few of the town's residents who had risen early were discovering the fate of their much-respected Bailiff from the *Jersey Times*. They learnt that Marais had suffered a heart attack while out on a walk, his body discovered by an alert German soldier. Sipping their bramble-leaf tea and chewing stale slices of bread spread with a foul confection that passed for jam, they read that Peter Mollett was to become Acting Bailiff, a position that would be ratified in the near future by a meeting of the States. They also read a proclamation by their new Bailiff, which called for calm and a mood of sobriety in which the islanders could reflect on the life of the man who had led them so capably throughout these difficult years. Furthermore, he added, the Germans were requesting some volunteers to go over to Alderney to work on a non-military building site; there was a promise of good food and conditions for those who went. The project had the full backing of the States, and volunteers could be assured that they would not be inadvertently helping the German war effort.

* * *

Von Luck was right – the ship was a hellhole. However, there was one difference between what he had imagined and the actuality. The latter was far worse. A thousand men were crammed into a hold that was clearly only designed to hold cargo. There were no portholes, no bunks, no lavatories – nothing that could conceivably be used by a human being to gain any form of comfort. Each man had to make his way to the hold down one of four steep ladders, and in the scramble engendered by the guards, several lost their grip and fell twenty-five feet. Von Luck was unable to see how badly they were injured, and he assumed that the chances of their receiving any treatment other than a few kind words from their fellow workers were non-existent.

The three men did their best to ensure that they were not separated, but in the confusion it was difficult. By the time the hold was full, there was little room to move, and von Luck found himself standing beside a man who was about half his height. Several workers away to his left were Fellowes and Smith, both of whom looked perturbed by the claustrophobic nature of their surroundings. Von Luck gave them a wink, partly because he could think of no other gesture that might encourage them.

After the workers had been loaded, the guards shut the doors to the hold, plunging them into darkness. There was some shouting, but not as much as von Luck had expected – obviously the men were used to being treated in this way. However, the heat soon built up, and he was uncomfortable in his heavy coat. He wanted to take it off, but he could not risk losing the pistol and grenades it contained. Too bad, he thought, he would just have to endure it.

After what might have been ten minutes – or perhaps an hour, it was impossible to tell – von Luck felt a stream of warm liquid against the back of his legs. Someone was pissing on him. He stopped himself turning round to remonstrate – where else was the man going to piss? Also he did not wish to attract attention to himself. The last thing he wanted was to be noticed, to be someone who stood out. Von Luck knew enough about what happened to men in captivity to know that the sore thumb often got hammered down. If there was a third reason, it was guilt. His fellow countrymen were doing this to them, and they had been doing it to people all over Europe for the past six years. The least he could do was endure just a fraction of what the countless victims of the Reich had been through.

He hoped that Fellowes and Smith were also keeping cool. Fellowes would probably be fine – he was a tough one – but he was less confident about Smith. He was just a boy, thought von Luck, so very young. Still, he was an extra pair of hands, a commodity that von Luck did not have in large supply.

Eventually the boat's engines throbbed into life, sending a shudder down the entire vessel. A cheer came up from the men with the realisation that their entombment down here was not to be infinite, that they were indeed going *somewhere*. If only they knew, thought von Luck. The regime under the SS was going to be far tougher than anything they had experienced under the Todt Organisation on Jersey. A few had died on Jersey but now within a few days of their arrival on Alderney, many would have been worked to death.

About an hour later von Luck heard a commotion.

'Get off me!'

It was Smith, shouting in English. Von Luck tried muscling his way through to where the shout had come from, but the going was slow.

'Get the fuck off me!'

There was some laughter, followed by taunting in yet another language von Luck couldn't understand. He could hear a fight now, blows being exchanged, grunts. Hopefully Fellowes would be wading in – far fitter and stronger, he should make easy work of whoever was having a go at them.

And then there came a scream, clearly from the young pilot officer.

Von Luck felt enraged, impotent.

'Over here!' Fellowes shouted to him. 'I think he's been stabbed.'

Von Luck pushed harder now, using his height and strength to fling the workers out of the way. It was like swimming through a soup of limbs, and as soon as one was wrenched away, another filled its place.

Smith's screaming was getting worse. 'Help me! Someone help me! I don't want to die! Please! I don't want to die!'

Von Luck shoved forward with all his might, withstanding the odd punch and kick. He barely noticed, partly because the blows were ineffective, and partly because he was focused on what was happening.

'Oh, God!'

He could hear Fellowes speaking now, calmly. 'Come on, lad,' he was saying. 'You'll be all right. We'll sort you out.'

Von Luck followed the voices, and in the dim light could just about discern Fellowes kneeling next to Smith. He came and knelt next to him, looking down at Smith, who was clutching his stomach and whimpering loudly. 'What happened?'

'One of these bastards tried to pinch something off him,' said Fellowes, 'and when Smith tried to stop him he got stabbed for his pains.'

Von Luck leant down to examine Smith. He could see the fear in his eyes, and he smiled at him. 'Smith, can you hear me? You're going to live, do you hear? You are going to *live*. When we arrive, we'll make sure you see a medic.' He knew they were hollow words, and he supposed Smith knew it as well. Judging by the amount of blood, the wound was deep.

'Can't you . . . can't you get one n-now?' asked Smith. He

spoke with great difficulty, his chest heaving dramatically as each bolt of pain shot through him.

'We'll get one soon,' said von Luck. 'I promise.'

This was a disaster, thought von Luck, a fucking disaster. One of these idiots skulking in the darkness had just stabbed a man who was trying to save all of them.

'I need a doctor,' Smith was saying. 'Please don't let me die. Please!'

Smith's hand shot up and grabbed von Luck by the lapel of his coat. 'Don't let me fucking die! Do you hear? I'm – not – going to die.'

Von Luck didn't attempt to release himself. The poor boy was doing what anybody would in his circumstances. 'I'm not going to let you die, Smith. Just . . . just keep still. Your wound probably feels worse than it is. Lie still, that's right.'

Smith was releasing his grip now. 'Oh, God,' he was saying. 'Just stop the pain. Please, please, stop the pain.'

His voice was feebler. Von Luck felt Fellowes nudge him. He knew what that meant: he's dying.

Von Luck found himself stroking Smith's forehead. There was nothing else he could do, apart from let the boy feel a little tenderness before he slipped away. For the next half-hour, von Luck did just that while Fellowes pressed his hands on Smith's wound. Smith's cries became weaker, until he suddenly found the strength to shout, 'My mother! I want my mother! Oh, Mum, please, Mum!'

Von Luck held Smith tightly. He had gone.

* * *

Pippa awoke as von Luck left the room. She was tempted to get up and run after him, but she stopped herself. There was no point in a long goodbye, and if he had wanted one, he would have woken her. She knew she should go back to her mother's room, but she wanted to stay in this bed for as long as possible, shrouding herself in last night. She could smell him still, just a trace. She buried her face in his pillow, breathing in the remnants of his presence. She knew she would never see him again, she could feel it. She should have been crying, but for some reason she couldn't. She was smiling, happy in the knowledge that at least they had shared a night together.

She only noticed the diary when she lifted her head from the pillow. She picked it up and flicked through it. She was disappointed to find that it was all in German – well, why wouldn't it be? She turned the pages once more, noticing the elegance of his handwriting, until she came to the letter from Marais, which she had read before. She removed it and, upon doing so, noticed von Luck's words to her.

She only cried after she had read them. It was a crime, she thought, that they could not be together. He was a decent man, a good man, and now he was going to die. Pippa did her best not to imagine how he might meet his end – such scenes were too horrific.

The sound of a car starting made her leap out of bed. Naked, she ran to the window and peered through the crack between the curtains. Down on the drive she could see von Luck's car reversing. The light was still dim, and there was a reflection on the windscreen, but she could see his hands on the steering-wheel. His face was not visible, which made her wish that she had never run to the window at all.

The car slowly headed up the drive, then turned left on to the road and disappeared behind a wall. Pippa walked back into the room. She sat on the side of the bed and picked up the diary, holding it on her lap. So this was all she had – not even a photograph. It would have to do.

* * *

They found Petersen's body later that morning. As soon as Major Hempel had reported back to Huffmeier that von Luck was not to be found at Linden Court, the admiral had ordered a search of the house, with the coda to 'raze it to the fucking ground if necessary'. It was a task to which Hempel had set with reluctance, but he knew there was no way he could avoid it.

The discovery of Petersen greatly unsettled him. Von Luck had not told him anything about his secret in the cellar, an omission that made Hempel begin to doubt the colonel's story. Could he have made it all up, he wondered. No – the presence of the letter from Marais suggested he had not. Such thoughts were coursing through Hempel's mind as he stood in the admiral's office at around nine o'clock that morning.

'So it looks like he's killed no fewer than five people,' said the admiral. 'The two Gestapo officers, Marais, and now Petersen. And, for all we know, the guard at the Gestapo HQ – what was his name?'

'Müller, sir,' Hempel replied.

'Müller has also been killed. The man is even more of a maniac than I could possibly have thought.'

Hempel could do nothing but nod.

Huffmeier turned to Mollett, who was sitting quietly in a chair next to the admiral's desk. He looked very relaxed, thought Hempel, very comfortable.

'The population must not hear of this,' said Huffmeier.

'I quite agree,' said Mollett. 'It would only cause a panic if they knew a madman was on the loose.'

'So where is he, then?' snapped Huffmeier at Hempel. 'And where are those bitches, the Campbell women? They'll all be hiding in the same place, you mark my words.'

Hempel shrugged his shoulders. 'He could be in any number of places, sir.'

'You can do a hell of a lot better than that, Hempel! Come on, he must have some friends on Jersey, some fancy women who would be willing to put them up.'

'Not that I know of, sir.'

Huffmeier snorted. Hempel knew he would have to give him something, some titbit, or the admiral would suspect him of stonewalling. 'Come on, Hempel! I thought you were close to von Luck.'

'I am, sir, but his reputation for befriending islanders is not as deserved as you might think.'

'That's a little rich,' said Mollett, casually examining his fingernails. 'Von Luck has carved his way through scores of women since he's been here. The first I heard of was Mrs—'

'With all due respect, Bailiff,' said Huffmeier, 'this is hardly the time to outline the extent of the man's conquests.'

'You're quite right,' said Mollett. 'I apologise.'

There was something a little forced between the two men, thought Hempel. They were behaving as secret lovers might in public, as if there was a lack of intimacy between them, but acting so hard that the pretence spilled over into a sham, exaggerated indifference.

'How about Mrs Lemprière?' asked Mollett.

'Mrs Lemprière?' said Hempel. 'At Rozel Manor?'

'Yes,' said Mollett. 'I thought von Luck was friendly with her.'

'Not in the way you are insinuating, I don't think.'

Mollett raised an eyebrow. 'You're quite sure of that, are you?'

'Quite sure,' said Hempel, resentful at being questioned by an islander. What right had he to do this? Or did he in fact know where von Luck was, and the line of questioning was a test?

'Who is this woman?' asked Huffmeier.

'She's a widow,' said Mollett. 'A very rich one.'

'And do you think von Luck could be with her?'

'It's unlikely, sir,' said Hempel. 'Knowing von Luck as I do, I do not think he's the type of man who would put anybody else unnecessarily in danger. And he has too much respect for Mrs Lemprière to force himself on her.'

Mollett laughed a little at the *double entendre*. 'That would be a first,' he said.

'All right, all right,' said Huffmeier. 'Well, Hempel, I want you to follow the Bailiff's hunch and go round to this woman straight away. You'd better take a whole company with you. Surround the grounds. Comb the house. That sort of thing. Who knows? You might find another dead body.'

Shit, thought Hempel.

* * *

'Right, I've had enough of this.'

'But what are you doing? Surely you're not trying to get up?'

'I bloody well am,' says Lebonneur.

'But your injuries,' says Rachel. 'You're not fit.'

'What would you rather? That I lay around here all day, waiting to be killed?'

Rachel stands up from her perch on the edge of the bed. She waves her arms in frustration. 'I don't know. If what you say is true, you should go to the police.'

'The *police?* The Jersey police are in the States' fucking pockets, and they always have been. Come on, Rach, you know that as well as I do. No, the only thing that's going to stop people dying is if I find the evidence. Without any evidence, no one's going to do a thing, especially the bloody police.'

Lebonneur heaves himself up. The movement is painful, but not as bad as it was yesterday.

'Are you really getting up?'

'What does it look like?'

'I wish you wouldn't.'

'Well, wish away, sweetheart. This is my fucking Lazarus moment.'

Lebonneur throws off the sheet and swings his legs out of bed. Slowly, he places his feet on the cold hospital floor. He feels light-headed, but he's not going to let Rachel know that.

'Bob! This is madness!'

'I'm sorry, darling,' he says. 'I'm sorry – I really am – but I have to.'

There is a knock on the door.

'Who is it?'

'It's me, Glen.'

'Hold on a sec!' Lebonneur looks at Rachel, who is wiping away a tear. 'Do you mind?' he asks. 'Do you mind if I let him in?'

Rachel sniffs. 'No.'

Lebonneur kisses her forehead. 'Come in.'

Glen enters the room, his face alight, an expression that changes when he sees Rachel. 'Oh, look, I'm sorry – I can come back later.'

'It's all right,' says Lebonneur. 'What is it anyway?'

'I've heard back from Figg. There's something about Mollett's parents that you should know.'

*

Despite Dr Thomas's protestations, Lebonneur and Rachel walk out of the hospital just before six o'clock that evening. Lebonneur tells the doctor that he's coming back, a lie. Rachel is keen to find a bed for the night, but Lebonneur is insistent that, first, they walk up to Mannez Hill. He cannot wait any longer, he says, and besides, the place will be crawling with workmen during the day.

Arm in arm, like any other holidaying couple, they make their way round the sweep of Braye Bay. It has hardly changed since they were last here, he thinks, except that it doesn't feel quite so busy. Children dart past on bicycles, other couples stroll along, occasional mêlées of young men swagger in the direction of St Anne. Under normal circumstances, Lebonneur would have suggested a drink, but he wants to get on.

Twenty minutes later Mannez Hill comes into view. Although the entire hill is not immediately visible, Lebonneur can see the cranes and scaffolding scattered around it. He shudders, as if he is suddenly cold. Why isn't someone stopping them? They've already tried killing him once, and they've killed Terry, so why are they being allowed to walk right up to it? 'Can you see anything?' Lebonneur asks.

'See what?'

'Anything out of the ordinary.'

'I wouldn't know what was out of the ordinary,' says Rachel.

'Just keep your eyes peeled.'

They walk in silence for a few minutes. To their left is the sea, which looks calm and idyllically deep-evening blue. The hill is to the right – Lebonneur can see why they'd want to build a hotel there. It must offer a sensational view all the way to France.

'We can go right a little further along,' says Lebonneur. 'There's a railway line that leads to the old quarry at the foot of the hill.'

'You're very well informed.'

'Well, I like to think I retain some journalistic talents.'

'Ha!'

A seagull hovers above, riding the breeze. It looks down at them contemptuously, then soars away. Lebonneur doesn't like seagulls, and he especially doesn't like seagulls that act as though they're winged spies. Christ, he thinks, he really is getting paranoid now. They walk on another two hundred yards, Lebonneur all the while expecting a car to come shooting down the road, a man with a machine gun leaning out of the passenger window.

'Shit,' he says.

They have come across their first obstacle – an eight-foot-high wooden wall. Further ahead, there are some large aluminium gates, which comprise the site entrance; they look as impenetrable as the wall. It bears the occasional poster, showing a computerised mock-up of the hotel, complete with shots of well-groomed middle-aged couples laughing over blackjack tables and expensive-looking food. Wankers, thinks Lebonneur. Why do the men in these photographs always have to wear their jerseys tied over their shoulders?

'What are we going to do?' asks Rachel.

'We'll find a way in, don't worry.'

'But what about that?'

'What about what?'

'That sign.'

'Warning,' it reads. 'This site is private property. Area is patrolled by guard dogs 24 hours a day. Trespassers will be prosecuted.'

'What a load of rubbish,' says Lebonneur. 'And I love the picture of the cuddly Alsatian! Come on, Rachel, since when did you ever see a building site that had a guard dog? Those signs are just lies, they always were.'

'All this feels wrong.'

'I know, I know. Neither of us was brought up to break into building sites, but then neither was I brought up to be able to fly a bloody plane. Sometimes it's good to do things that go against your nature.'

'Look, you can break in here if you want to, but I'm going to head back. All this is nonsense, it really is.'

'But, Rachel, I've told you what's in von Luck's diary. You know what's in this place. The truth has got to come out.'

'I haven't read it for myself,' says Rachel. 'I've just got to take your word for it.'

'That sounds perilously close to accusing me of lying.'

Rachel sighs. 'I'm not accusing you of lying, I'm simply—'

Lebonneur is not listening. Instead he is opening the box to the Geiger counter. How the hell do you put this thing together? What did Hent say again? Battery first, into the back of the main bit with the dial. All right, that seems fairly straightforward. Now for the wand – where does it plug in? There it is – that hole at the bottom there. Good, all set.

Lebonneur flips the little black switch underneath the display. The instant he does so, the needle jumps a little way along its dial. An occasional clicking sound comes from a small speaker. 'Right,' says Lebonneur. 'Do you hear that?'

'Yes,' says Rachel, visibly unimpressed.

'As far as I can remember, from what Hent told me, these things work by detecting the ionisation produced by radioactive particles. Each time a particle of radiation is detected, the counter clicks away. The more clicking, the more radiation, and the higher this needle should go.'

Rachel shrugs her shoulders.

'Now,' says Lebonneur, 'if I point the counter towards the hill, we should hear a few more clicks. Correct?'

Slowly Lebonneur angles the wand so that it faces the building site. The counter clicks violently, like rapid staccato static. With a smile, he watches the needle climb about a quarter of the way along the dial. Good old von Luck, he thinks. 'Do you hear that?' he asks.

Rachel nods.

'That sound means I'm right,' he says.

'You always bloody are.'

After fifteen minutes of searching, Lebonneur and Rachel find a gap in the wall they can squeeze through. The building site is a mess of concrete mixers, diggers, lorries, cranes and scaffolding. There are a couple of Portakabins, as well as a few portable lavatories, with a door swaying in the breeze, exposing an interior that looks particularly unwholesome. Much of the work is sited on top of the hill, which is a shallow climb up a muddy road.

'Come on,' says Lebonneur. 'Let's get up there. Do it quickly.'

Hand in hand, the two walk up the hill. With the extra breathing required, Lebonneur finds it a strain on his ribs, but he is not going to allow a bit of pain to stop him, no way.

'Aren't we going to get irradiated or something?' Rachel asks.

'Not at this level. Hent says you've only got to worry when it gets to this point on the dial. Besides, I don't reckon on spending much time up here.'

'That's the first thing you've said that I actually agree with,' says Rachel.

After a couple of minutes, they reach the top of the hill. Some vast concrete foundations have already been laid, out of which stick hundreds of small iron posts.

'It's going to be quite a place,' says Rachel, her hands on her hips.

'It would have been quite a place,' says Lebonneur. 'There's no way that they can finish it – look at the reading.' He shows her the Geiger counter. 'That's approaching the danger zone,' he says. 'How would you like to spend a couple of weeks here? It's no wonder those builders are falling sick, especially the ones that have been working deep in the hill.'

'So, what now?'

'We go back to St Anne.'

'I didn't mean right now, I meant—'

Rachel's words are interrupted: the Geiger counter has been invisibly punched out of Lebonneur's hand. It lands about ten feet away, a mangled wreck of plastic and wiring. For a moment, they stand there, bewildered, stunned.

'What the fuck was—'

Before Lebonneur can finish, he realises what has happened. Ignoring the pain in his sides, he grabs Rachel by her front and pulls her down, falling on to the rough ground beside her. Just as he does so, a large piece of concrete about ten feet behind them chips into the air.

'Someone's trying to shoot us!' he shouts in Rachel's ear. She is too shocked to reply. All Lebonneur can hear is the sound of her hyperventilating. 'Keep calm!' he shouts, more for his benefit than for hers.

What the fuck now? They can't stay here – they'll be hit for sure. 'Rachel! We've got to move, do you hear me? We've got to fucking move!'

Two yards away from Lebonneur's feet, the ground kicks up in a flurry of earth and stones. Jesus Christ – to have survived that fucking plane and now this! He feels himself starting to panic again, the same feeling as he had when he was up there. Stop this, *stop* this. He is clutching Rachel tightly – just don't let him hit her, no, please, not her.

More concrete shatters behind them. How many shots was that? Three? Seven? Did it matter? Where were they coming from? They had to be from somewhere near the coast, the lighthouse. The lighthouse! That was it – the perfect place for a sniper. He lifts his head and looks towards it – is anybody there? He can't tell – it's at least three hundred yards away and he's not going to take a nice long look.

'Bob!'

It's Rachel. She's starting to scream. You've got to stop her, he thinks, you've got to calm her down.

'Listen, Rach, the shots are coming from the lighthouse. We've got to run that way, do you understand? That way!' Lebonneur is indicating down the hill with his hand, but Rachel doesn't look up. They've got to move now, he thinks, there's no time to wait. Rachel's screaming is getting louder. What should they do? Wait for the next shot and then run? Or run now? Lebonneur stands up and pulls Rachel by the hand. 'Run!' he shouts. 'Fucking run! Follow me!'

His sides are hurting badly. He just wants to lie down and rest, but they must keep moving, keep running.

'Just over there!' he shouts, pointing to a little mound.

Another shot, this time flying past his head. Jesus! He could hear it go through the air – a funny high-pitched wheezing whine. Just don't let Rachel be hit, he pleads again, that wouldn't be right – it wouldn't be fair.

They reach the mound a few seconds later, crash to the ground and roll behind it, another shot narrowly missing them. They lie still, panting furiously, trying to come to terms with what is happening to them.

'Are you all right?'

Rachel doesn't reply, just nods furiously, her face covered in dirt and cuts. A dull thud comes from the mound – their would-be killer is obviously firing at it in frustration. Lebonneur looks around. The ground slopes away down to the perimeter wall about a hundred feet away. 'Down there, and then over the wall. Do you see?'

Rachel looks back at him, wide-eyed. 'We're going to die, aren't we? We're going to bloody die and it's all your fault! What's going to happen to the boys – our poor boys?'

'Rachel!'

She is starting to cry. He's got to stop this, because he knows that in a few seconds she will refuse to move, and will remain petrified and weeping. He grabs her by the shoulders and shakes her hard. 'Listen to me! We're *not* going to die! We – are – not – going – to – die. We are going to get out of this. We're going to get on to the other side of that wall and we're going to run and run.'

Rachel continues sobbing.

'Come on, Rachel! Let's go – come on!'

Rachel gets to her feet. She stares at Lebonneur wildly, her expression a mixture of fear and hate.

'Run!' he shouts. 'Run!'

This time his words get through, and Rachel starts to run.

'Come on! In front of me!'

She overtakes him, and within a few more seconds they have reached the wall. Thank God they're still safe from fire, he thinks, at least for the time being.

'How the hell are we going to get over this?' Rachel asks.

'I'll sit on the top and pull you up,' says Lebonneur. 'Come on – give me a leg up.'

'How do I do that?'

'Cup your hands together like this and let me stand on them.'

'But I might not be able to hold–'

'Of course you will, it's only for a second. Come on – lean against the wall. That's it.'

Rachel does as she's told. This is going to be hard, he thinks. He's no bloody gymnast, and his ribs hurt so much. He steps on Rachel's hands as carefully as possible.

'Bob!'

'You can do it.'

'I can't hold you!'

'Of course you can!'

His hands reach the top of the wall. Normally, he would never have been able to pull himself up, but fear and the desire to escape has given him a strength he didn't know he had. He can feel the muscles in his arms screaming, but he yanks himself up, Rachel doing her best with her hands.

The top of the wall is only six inches wide, but it is just enough for Lebonneur to sit astride. He worries that the extra elevation has exposed him to the lighthouse, but they are in luck. He reaches down with his right hand. 'Come on, Rach, take my hand!'

She does so. This is going to hurt, he thinks, really fucking hurt. With his left hand holding on to the top of the wall in

318

front of him, he pulls Rachel as hard as he can. Pain, such tormenting pain, pain that just isn't possible. Shot. He thinks he's been fucking shot, and now he's going to die.

'Bob!'

Somewhere he can hear Rachel. Where is she?

'*Bob!*'

She sounds near, very near.

'Come on, Bob! Let's get down!'

Rachel. Her face right in front of him. She is sitting on the wall. She got up here. How did that happen? He doesn't remember it at all.

'Jump, Bob!'

He watches Rachel jump down. She lands heavily, but falls to her side like a parachutist. He's got to follow her, he thinks, he must jump too. Seconds later he is on the ground, being helped up by Rachel. Their roles are reversed – she is the one doing the coaxing, forcing him to act. 'Come on, Bob, let's go!'

Lebonneur gets to his feet. Every step is agony, but he knows he must keep moving. He doesn't know where they're going and, what's more, he doesn't care. Just to get as far away as possible, that's all he wants. His sides are hurting more now, and the more he pants, the worse they feel.

They run for a further ten minutes, but to Lebonneur it feels like days. He is flagging now, running almost at walking pace. They need to hide somewhere, he thinks, they can't keep running. 'Rachel!' he pants.

She doesn't respond, just keeps running.

'Rachel!'

She stops and turns. 'What?'

'We've got to hide, I can't keep going.'

'A little further, Bob, come on.'

He shakes his head. His hands are resting on his knees, and he is about to be sick. 'I think I'm going to be—'

And then he is sick, puking up the foul hospital lunch of mince and overboiled potatoes. He feels Rachel's hand on his back, stroking it. The heaving motion plays havoc with his ribs – how much longer can he keep this up?

'All right, Bob,' she's saying, 'better out than in.'

This hasn't happened for a long time, he thinks. The last time he was drunk, really drunk. She helped him then. That felt pathetic, but this is different. There's no condescension in her, no opprobrium, no 'you stupid drunk'.

The puking finishes, thank God. He feels cold and trembles. 'I've got to stop, Rach, I can't go on. I really can't. Let's just hide somewhere.' He looks around. To their left is a short valley that leads down to the sea. Ahead is the dirt track up which they have been running, and to their right is a path that goes into some undergrowth. 'There,' he says. 'Nobody will find us there.'

Rachel nods. 'All right,' she says.

The undergrowth is a thick, waist-high mixture of ferns and brambles, which tears at their clothes. Neither Lebonneur nor Rachel feels the assault on their legs by the thorns, but are grateful for the cover.

'What's this?' asks Rachel, after they have walked for a minute.

'What's what?'

'There's a little opening – just over there.'

Lebonneur looks to where she is pointing. Sure enough, partly obscured by vegetation, a low stone arch is set into the side of a large bank.

'Let's try it,' he says. 'It looks like a tunnel.' He peers in, trying to adjust to the gloom. 'Must be an old mine shaft or something,' he says, fishing around in his pocket for his lighter. He finds it, then holds it above his head. The small flame casts little light, but it is enough for Lebonneur to make out that the arch is indeed the opening for a small tunnel that extends horizontally into the bank.

Lebonneur edges ahead, taking tentative steps. The tunnel is low enough for his head to skim the ceiling, which he notices is damp. His nostrils are assaulted by a musty smell, of damp and decay.

'It's cold,' says Rachel.

'You're not wrong.'

Lebonneur extinguishes the lighter flame – his eyes have adjusted now. 'Can you see all right?' he asks.

'Yes, not bad.'

About fifteen feet ahead, Lebonneur can make out that the tunnel opens into a room. He walks more quickly now, because he thinks he knows where he is.

'Careful, Bob.'

'I am, don't worry.'

The room is very dark, the only light coming from a couple of small apertures about twenty feet above them. Some steps lead up to one, thickly festooned with brambles.

Lebonneur almost trips over a lump of concrete, but retains his balance. 'I think I know where we are,' he says.

'Where?'

'In the heating block and bathroom for Sylt concentration camp.'

'Where?'

'Sylt camp is – or was – the SS concentration camp here on Alderney.'

'I didn't know there was one.'

'Well, you're in it now. That tunnel led from the commandant's house out there to this room here. No doubt SS Captain List didn't want to have to walk all the way round to the front of the camp to have a bath. Those steps lead up to the main camp, which is just next to the airport.'

'Where is his house?'

'It got rebuilt somewhere else on the island, over on Longis Common, I think.'

'What a charming thing to do.'

'Quite,' says Lebonneur. 'Anyway, we're safe here.'

Within seconds, Lebonneur's confidence is obliterated by the slow crunch of footsteps echoing down the tunnel.

Chapter Nine

THE ABSENCE OF birdsong wasn't immediately apparent, but as she sat with Mrs Lemprière in the breakfast room of Rozel Manor, the windows fully open, it was not long before Pippa grasped that something was missing.

'Have you noticed?' asked Pippa.

'Noticed what, dear?' said Mrs Lemprière.

'The birds have stopped singing.'

Mrs Lemprière paused, her head turned towards the windows. 'So they have. Normally they're quite noisy at this hour.'

The two women looked nervously at each other. Pippa stood up, rushed to the windows and looked out on to the vast lawn. Was anything there? She stared hard at the bushes a good fifty yards away, trying to detect movement, but there was nothing. 'Round to the front!' she said.

Without waiting for Mrs Lemprière to reply, she raced out and through the sitting room into the hall. She ran up to the windows and looked up the drive. Again, nothing. Upstairs, she thought. She'd have a better view from there.

Taking the steps three at a time, Pippa sprinted up to the second floor and looked out of a landing window. From there, she could see the length of the drive, and over the wall that ran along the road. Still nothing. Perhaps the birds had stopped singing for some other reason. Was she being paranoid? Well, it was hardly surprising, and forgivable in the circumstances. She looked again, to some trees that were planted on her side of the wall. What was that under their branches? It looked like the roof of a lorry.

A hollowed-out feeling of dread. They were here. How had they known? Had someone betrayed them? Hempel? He didn't seem the sort, but it must have been him. Bastard! Bloody Nazi bastard!

Pippa shot down the stairs. 'They're here!' she shouted. 'They're here!'

She saw Mrs Lemprière and the housekeeper at the foot of the stairs.

'The Germans!' Pippa shouted. 'They're here.'

'Where?'

'There's a lorry on the road!'

'Are you sure?'

'Absolutely! I'm going to get my mother.'

She ran down the corridor to Violet's room and burst in, waking her. 'Mummy! The Germans are here! We've got to hide.'

Violet looked at her drowsily. 'Germans?'

'Yes, Mummy. We've got to go.'

'Go where?'

324

'Anywhere but here. The grounds of this place are massive – we could hide in some bushes.'

'I'm not sure I can move.'

'Nonsense! If we stay, we're dead. Come on, Mummy, we've got to go right now.'

The scars on her back were still far from healed so every movement caused Violet extreme pain. Pippa did her best to lift her gently from the bed, but her mother cried out in agony. 'It's no use,' she said. 'I really can't get up, darling, it's just too painful.'

'But you must,' Pippa urged, 'or we'll be caught. Everything that von Luck did for us will be wasted.' She pulled her mother up by the arms. Violet cried out again, but this time Pippa ignored her. She would have to be tough with her, bully her along.

'Shoes,' said Violet. 'I need shoes.'

'There's no time! Come on!'

Pippa led her mother out of the room and into the corridor. There she found Mrs Lemprière, face pale, eyes wide. 'They're coming down the drive.'

'The back door,' said Pippa. 'Take us to the back door.'

Mrs Lemprière froze.

'For heaven's sake!' Pippa cried. 'The back door!'

'Yes, yes, of course. Follow me.'

She led Pippa and Violet down the corridor to the back stairs, which consisted of narrow, winding stone steps. It was impossible to go quickly down them, but they soon came out into the pantry, which had clearly been neglected for the last few years. 'This way,' said Mrs Lemprière. 'Through here.'

They went into a boot-room, at the end of which was a large oak door.

'This is the tradesmen's entrance,' said Mrs Lemprière. 'When you go out of here, turn left. That will lead you round the house to the back terrace. Just down to the right there are some rhododendron bushes, which you should be able to hide in.'

She gave them both a peck on the cheek, and opened the back door. Pippa half expected to be presented with a huge German soldier, but there was nothing visible except the brick wall of an outhouse.

'The diary!' said Pippa.

'What diary?' asked Mrs Lemprière.

'In my room, on the bedside table, is Colonel von Luck's diary. He entrusted it to me, and it's vital it isn't lost. Could you hide it for me?'

'Of course. It will be quite safe here. Even if they search the house from top to bottom they'll never find it.'

'You're quite sure?'

'Absolutely.'

The distant sound of the front-door bell reached their ears.

'You'd better go – quick!'

'Thank you,' said Pippa.

Pippa led her mother outside. They ran down the narrow passage that led to the terrace, pausing before they broke cover. 'All right, Mummy?' Pippa whispered.

Her mother's eyes looked red and wet, but she nodded.

'Let's go, then.'

They ran out on to the terrace and, for a couple of seconds, Pippa expected a volley of bullets to slam into them. The lawn seemed to stretch out for hundreds of yards, and as they ran along she felt exposed and vulnerable. She glanced around for the rhododendrons and spotted them.

Without saying anything, she dragged her mother across the lawn, the occasional whimper breaking from Violet's mouth. The bushes seemed so far away, so distant. Wouldn't it be better just to give themselves up rather than go through all this? No, she told herself. You've got away with it once, you can do it again.

The rhododendrons were huge and ancient and, as a result, almost impenetrable. Pippa broke, twisted and snapped a way into them, taking care not to let the branches whip back into her mother's face.

'Here we go, Mummy, this should do.'

They stopped in a hollow, catching their breath.

'How are you?' Pippa whispered.

Once again, Violet did little more than nod. Pippa hugged her, and as she removed her hands, she saw that they were covered with blood.

'Oh, Mummy!'

It was obvious what had happened: some of her wounds had broken open, and were bleeding profusely, soaking through the white nightshirt Mrs Lemprière had lent her.

'Mummy,' said Pippa, 'tell me the truth, how bad does it feel?'

'Awful.'

'Here, let's try and make some space for you to lie down.'

Violet held up her hand. 'Don't do that,' she said. 'It will make too much noise.'

For the next minute, the two women were silent, straining to hear any sounds coming from the house. They heard none, not even a door slamming or a guttural German shout. She felt her mother's hand clutching hers, squeezing it tight.

Then a dog barking told them they were done for. Pippa and her mother looked at each other.

'I just wish . . .' Violet started.

'Wish what, Mummy?'

'I wish I could see your father just once more.'

Pippa kissed her mother's cheek.

'He'll be proud of us, Mummy. Very proud.'

'I don't know – I think he would have been happier to have a living family than a dead one.'

'Don't say that.'

More barking. Pippa struggled to see through the vegetation, but it was impossible.

'What should we do?' asked Violet.

'We should stay here,' said Pippa. 'If we try to run, they're bound to see us.'

They fell silent again, listening to the sounds of the search party. There was a lot of shouting, and Pippa estimated that there must be at least three dogs. She'd thought the occupiers had eaten them all. The barking was getting nearer now, making its way down the lawn. Come on, she urged, go past us, you bastards, just keep going. She felt her mother stroking her hair, as she had done when Pippa was small. It felt comforting, but at the same time it made her feel weak, made her want to curl up into her mother's bosom and escape from reality.

They must have been no more than twenty feet away. This is it, thought Pippa. In a few moments one of the dogs would smell them, and it would all be over. Her mind turned to last night, to Max. She had lost him, she knew that, but she still couldn't accept it.

Pippa felt her mother stop stroking her hair. They could hear a dog and its handler approaching the bush.

'*Sachte*, Heidi! *Sachte!*'

They could hear the dog's panting. It was fast, excited.

'*Ist jemand in der Nähe*, Heidi?'

Pippa had picked up enough German over the past five years to answer the question. 'Yes, there is someone here,' she might have said. But she kept quiet, hoping that the dog would be distracted, that the handler would be ordered to search somewhere else.

Her hopes were in vain. The dog was trying to get into the bush now, its nose telling it that the bush smelt of more than rhododendron.

'If there is people in there,' said the handler, 'it is advisable to remove yourselves!'

Pippa heard the sound of a machine pistol being cocked. She looked at her mother, who was near to tears. She kissed her again. She wanted to say something, but words would be meaningless, empty.

'Come on! Out!'

A loud whistle.

'Over here!' the handler shouted. 'Over here!'

Pippa and her mother got slowly to their feet. 'We're coming out,' Pippa said. 'Please don't shoot. We are unarmed.'

They stumbled out of the bush, their hands in the air. The face of their captor was not unfriendly, Pippa thought, but as it represented everything she hated, it was the ugliest face imaginable.

'Get on the ground.'

Pippa did so. It was damp, and she felt the dog sniffing around her.

'Get on the ground.'

I am on the ground, thought Pippa. Oh, God – Mummy! She turned her head to see her mother still standing, her back covered with blood. She was facing the soldier, whose hands were clearly shaking.

'Mummy!'

'Get down or I'll shoot!'

But Violet was frozen, either through fear or pain or both. Pippa was never to know which, because at that moment the guard opened fire. The bullets tore through the already weakened body, ripping off pieces of flesh covered in white nightdress, which splattered over Pippa and the dog.

'*Mummy!*' Pippa shrieked. '*Mummy!*'

Violet's body was thrown to the ground with terrible force, landing a few feet to Pippa's right. Pippa crawled to where she lay, all the time letting out a silent cry. There was no sound she could have made that would express what she was feeling. Her mother lay quite still, the front of her body oozing large patches of blood. Her eyes were half closed, as if she was very tired.

Major Hempel arrived half a minute later, breathless after the run from the house. Pippa never heard him when he yelled at the guard, never heard him when he shouted for a medic, never heard him when he repeatedly expressed his sorrow and regret.

However, she did feel his hands on her shoulders, his strong hands, which were trying to pull her up, to wrench her free of her mother's warm body. She shook violently, trying to break free not only of his grip, but also from what she could see in front of her.

Her yelling was audible now: there was actually a sound coming from her mouth. She was brought to her feet, but she struggled still, trying to get back to her mother, to hold her, to hug her, to touch the hands that had been stroking her just a few moments ago.

Hempel turned her round. 'Miss Campbell!' he was shouting, but his voice sounded as though it was underwater.

'Miss Campbell! Listen to me!'

She looked at him, her eyes rolling in her head as if she was drunk or demented.

'Miss Campbell!'

He was shaking her now. How dare he do that? There were others around him, plenty more of these murderers who had killed her mother.

Hempel. Major Hempel. But he had *helped* them. He had brought them here. He was supposed to be a friend, a decent man. Pippa spat at him as hard as she could. She then tried to hit him, but he was too strong for her.

'Do not say anything!' he shouted. 'Say nothing!'

Why was he saying that? Why the hell shouldn't she say something?

'You're a bastard!' she screamed.

He was shaking his head, his eyes wide open. They were imploring her, begging her. There was something desperate about them, she thought, like the eyes of a small child. What did he want from her?

And out of her mouth came the words that threatened Hempel's existence: 'You betrayed us! You're a traitor!'

'No!' he replied. 'You are mistaken.'

'But you brought—'

Pippa could not finish her sentence, because Hempel, in an act of self-preservation, had slapped her so hard round the face that she was knocked out.

*　*　*

It was raining when they arrived in Alderney, as von Luck had thought it would be. The journey had taken six hours, in which the hold had accumulated a thin layer of every variety of human effluence. Von Luck and Fellowes had done their best to keep Smith's body from being trampled on, but with the pitching of the boat, and the crowding in the hold, it was impossible. The other workers had little respect for the dead, and as Smith was not the only one of their number to have died during the crossing, an individual human corpse was as unremarkable as that of a rat.

The rain cooled and cleaned the workers, although only partially. Nearly every worker had been sick, von Luck and Fellowes included, and the rain helped to wash away the vomit that was stuck to their clothes. Slowly, their legs still wobbly, they climbed the ladders out of the hold, at the top of which stood around twenty SS NCOs. Their faces looked brutal, thought von Luck, barbaric. He knew there was no point in trying to ensure that Smith got a decent burial – no doubt his body would be thrown into the sea along with all the others. At the top of the ladder, von Luck looked down into the hold, and said goodbye to Smith, wishing him a silent prayer.

'What the fuck are you doing? Come on! Hurry up, you great peasant!'

Von Luck felt the blow of a wooden truncheon across his shoulders, delivered with such ferocity that it almost knocked him down the ladder. He wanted to strike back, but he checked himself and turned to face his tormentor.

'Come on, scum!' shouted the SS private. 'What do you want to do? Stay in the boat?'

Von Luck avoided eye-contact and simply stepped up the

333

ladder on to the deck. His back was smarting, but he could take it. For the moment, all he had to console himself was that he could easily have beaten the man in a straight fight, and that the man probably knew it. It required all of his will, which was strained by the voyage, not to reply but walk on. In a grim way, perhaps it was better that Smith had already died – his quick temper might have proved a liability. Fellowes was calm, solid, reliable – he could trust him to keep a cool head.

Von Luck drew up alongside him in the gaggle of prisoners waiting on the quayside.

'You all right?' asked Fellowes quietly.

'Not bad,' said von Luck. 'It hurts a little.'

'You did well not to deck him.'

'Deck him?'

'Punch him. Knock him out. Knock him on to the deck.'

'I see,' said von Luck, almost allowing himself to smile.

They watched a couple of workers bring up a dead body from the hold. Smith's? No, it was too small. Another came up a few minutes later, followed by seven more. Of those, Smith's body was the last, almost unrecognisable beneath its film of blood, vomit and mucus.

'I'm sorry,' he whispered to Fellowes. 'I'm very sorry.'

'It's not your fault.'

'In a way it is. When the war is over, everybody in Germany will be saying all this was not his or her fault. The Nazis will always live next door or in the next village. Well, I may not be a Nazi, but in my own way I have helped to make this happen.'

'But you're different from these—'

'I know. But I've helped them, haven't I? I've done my duty as a German officer, and that has helped the regime. All of us Germans are aware of what we're doing.'

At first Fellowes didn't reply. There was nothing he could say, thought von Luck, because he probably agreed. 'It doesn't matter,' said Fellowes. 'Not now, anyway. Not now you're here.'

Von Luck stared at the pile of corpses. Smith's head was tilted back, its face staring emptily at them. Von Luck had to look away. He wanted to look anywhere but at that heap of death. He looked out to sea, looked along the breakwater, looked up at the wet sky, looked over to the houses along the beachfront, but there was nothing that provided a respite from grimness, that provided any hope. This was a grey, desolate place, the 'arsehole of the world' indeed.

'Get in line!'

Von Luck had heard the shout before, many times, when he had had to visit the labour camps on Jersey. It was high-pitched, desperate, almost insane in its willingness to command. It was not the voice of a natural leader, he thought, but that of exactly who it was – a prisoner acting as a helper for the guards to curry favour: a *kapo*.

Slowly, the men shuffled into some semblance of ranks and files. Von Luck found himself next to a heavily bearded man who was carrying a broken pickaxe – he had to be in his sixties at least. It was a miracle he had survived so long. No doubt he would not see out the week. But, then, neither will I, thought von Luck, as they started to move.

It took forty minutes to march to Sylt camp. By the time they had arrived, the light was fading, and the temperature was dropping rapidly. The prisoners shuffled under the gates, above which von Luck noticed there was no sign or inscription. As soon as the men entered, the collective mood, although it had been far from light-hearted, turned to one of fear.

'Line up here.'

The men did as they were told, assembling into neat rows in the middle of the camp. Von Luck looked around: it was surprisingly small, a little larger than a football pitch. There were no more than seven or eight wooden huts, and about the same number of more permanent structures. Von Luck assumed the former were for the prisoners. If the camp was already occupied, it was going to be almost as claustrophobic as the boat.

'How the hell are we going to fit in here?' asked Fellowes.

'I was wondering the same thing,' said von Luck.

Suddenly a hush fell over the guards. Along with all the other prisoners, Fellowes and von Luck craned their necks to see what was happening. A party of four men was approaching from the other end of the camp, at their centre a figure dressed in the uniform of an SS captain.

'Maximillian List,' whispered von Luck. 'He's in charge. He's also a maniac.'

List stood up on a wooden chest. He was shorter than von

Luck had imagined, and his face was softer, more feminine. 'Workers!' List shouted, his voice notably hoarse. 'Welcome to Sylt camp here on Alderney. You are privileged to be here.'

Nobody dared laugh.

'You will find the conditions excellent. You will be well provided for, but only if you work hard. I am a tough man, but I reward those I see fit.'

The workers stayed silent, each man knowing he was being lied to.

'I should tell you that you are working on a project that is of immense importance to the Reich. What you are helping to build will go down in history. You are lucky to be a part of it, very lucky.'

Von Luck and Fellowes exchanged a brief look, but kept quiet.

'Are there any questions?'

The workers looked down at the ground, at each other, anywhere but at List. And then, amazingly, a man near the front put up his hand. Even List looked surprised. 'Yes?'

'I was wondering if we were going to get any food and water, Herr Commandant. It has been a long day, and so far we have not been fed—'

'Step forward!' snapped List.

The man did so. Von Luck could just about see him through the mass of workers. He was short, and his voice had sounded young.

'What is your name?' asked List.

'Andrezj Lewinsky.'

'And you are a Pole?'

'Yes, Herr Commandant.'

'I hate fucking Poles.'

The man stayed silent.

'Poles are no better than Jews,' List shouted. 'They steal and they lie. They are fundamentally dishonest, which makes them subhuman. And here is one demanding to be fed! Great big fat Pole! Who do you think you are?'

List turned to his left and said something to the SS sergeant next to him. The man nodded and hurried off.

'Well, then, Lewinsky,' said List, 'are you thirsty?'

Lewinsky did not move.

'Speak up!'

'Yes, Herr Commandant.'

'Good. In that case, I shall get you something to drink.'

For a minute, the entire camp waited in silence. The sergeant came back, trailing a hose behind him. Before Lewinsky could move, two privates rushed forward and grabbed him, holding him on the ground. Von Luck noticed that the men had not been ordered to do this – plainly it was a well-practised drill, one of List's favourites, no doubt.

The sergeant brought the hose round to Lewinsky and shoved it brutally into his mouth. Lewinsky was struggling, but it was of no use. The sergeant turned to List, who nodded, his lips forming into a smile. The hose was turned on, instantly causing Lewinsky to redouble his efforts to break free. A hideous choking, gurgling sound came from him. Von Luck found his fists clenching. Your time will come, he told himself. Your time will come.

Many of the prisoners seemed unimpressed by the spectacle. Perhaps they had seen it many times before, played out at hundreds of camps across the Reich. Lewinsky had stopped struggling now, his body bloated by the volume of water that had been pumped into it, and was now pouring out of his mouth – there was no room for any more. The sergeant looked at List once again, who gestured that his underling should move on to the next part of the ceremony. The sergeant jumped on to Lewinsky's stomach. A squelching sound came from the body, a burbled croak from the mouth, and then there was stillness. The man was dead.

'Would anyone else like a drink?' List shouted.

As von Luck had predicted, there was no room in the wooden huts. By the time he and Fellowes had entered theirs, the bunks were full. The hut's existing incumbents were aghast at the new arrivals, and made it clear that they should go somewhere else.

Von Luck and Fellowes, along with a couple of hundred others, tried to settle down for the night in the narrow corridor that ran down the middle. They were packed tightly, the only benefit of which was an accumulation of body heat that kept the cold at bay.

They slept badly. Although there was no lavatory in the hut, it quickly became apparent that one of the corners had become an improvised latrine, and every ten minutes or so, von Luck was awoken by a clumsily placed foot. At one point, he nearly got up to hit the offender but, once again, managed to check himself.

In the brief moments that he lay awake undisturbed, his mind turned to Pippa and the night before. His situation was now so different from what it had been that the events of last night seemed otherworldly, fantastical. The notion that Pippa even existed seemed impossible. He knew that he would never see her again, so perhaps it was best to keep her as a memory, as something that had happened to him in another life.

* * *

Beset by grief, Pippa's interrogation seemed to her like some narcotic-inspired dream. Voices came at her out of the dark, voices that taunted her, voices that caressed her. She felt hands over her too, touching her hair, her breasts, and even exploring under her skirt. She didn't care. Nothing could be more horrific than watching her mother shot dead, nothing more painful. Let them do what they wanted to her because she no longer cared. She had given up, yes, she had surrendered. There was no Max to save her, because Max was in Alderney. Max was doing something far more important than rescuing her or her mother.

'So, where is von Luck, eh?'

A slap in the face. It had not been the first.

'I bet he enjoyed fucking you, didn't he?'

A pinch of her breasts. Pippa had expected that.

'Quite a catch for von Luck, you little whore! You know you must be the four-hundredth slut he's had since he's been here. You're nothing special, Miss Campbell. Don't you see that? You're just another of his loose Jersey cows.'

Laughter. Such wit, Pippa thought.

'Come on, Miss Campbell! There's no point in protecting him. He's not loyal to you, so I see no reason why you should be loyal in return.'

Pippa thought of the diary, of von Luck's message to her. Could it have been insincere? It was possible. No, it was sincere – don't doubt him. Don't let these people win. They have killed your mother right in front of you. Don't let them take any more.

'You should be grateful that you're not in the hands of the Gestapo, Miss Campbell.'

Pippa knew why she wasn't – it was because Max had killed most of them. Pippa kept her mouth shut. There was no point in reminding the man how Max had run rings around them, and was still continuing to do so.

'I'd also like to ask you some questions about Major Hempel.'

Pippa shifted in her chair. She couldn't see her questioner, because he was now sitting behind a bright lamp. 'Major Hempel?'

'Yes. When you were captured earlier, you told him he had betrayed you. I find this very interesting, Miss Campbell, very interesting indeed.'

'Do you now?'

'Oh, yes. Would you like to tell me more?'

Pippa strained to remember Hempel's face from a few hours ago. It seemed like months, perhaps longer. She remembered that he had been pleading with her. Was that cowardice, simply to save his neck? But hadn't von Luck called him a 'decent man', said that he was 'one of them'? Stall, she thought, stall. 'What do you want to know?'

'I want to know how long he has been colluding with von Luck. We are holding Major Hempel in the cell next door, where one of my fellow officers is, ah, having a chat with him.'

'As far as I am aware,' she said slowly, 'Major Hempel has not been colluding with Colonel von Luck.'

'Really? So why did you call him a "traitor"?'

'Did I?'

'Yes, you did.'

'Well, I don't remember. And if I did, then I don't know why.'

'That's not very convincing, Miss Campbell.'

The man was right, but Pippa was not about to take his condescension. 'My mother had just been killed.' She shouted, so loudly that the man went silent. Perhaps there was some humanity in him after all. 'I take it you have a mother?' she said.

Silence.

'How would you like to see her machine-gunned in front of you?'

Still silence.

'You're all bastards. Fucking animals. Savages. Why don't you just get this over with and kill me now? What's the point of all this? You're never going to get anything from me, so why don't you just kill me? Go on! Do it now! I really want to die. I just want to join my mother.'

Pippa broke down. It was impossible to carry on speaking.

'Forgive me, Miss Campbell, but I think you may be in shock.'

There were a lot of ways to reply to that, but Pippa said nothing. It just wasn't worth it. Nothing was worth it any more.

* * *

There were those who were bleeding from their noses and some, judging by the stains, from their anuses. Hands were swollen, as were feet, and many were coughing violently.

'What is wrong with them?' von Luck asked a worker with a comparatively approachable face.

'The sickness,' came the reply. 'They have the sickness.'

'The "sickness"?'

The man looked at him warily. 'Who are you anyway?' he asked.

'My name is Max,' said von Luck. 'I'm from Bavaria.'

'So you're German, huh? Why're you here?'

'Political.'

'I see. What did you do? Say something nasty about Adolf?'

'Something like that. How about you?'

'I'm Artur. Austrian. I'm here because I'm a pacifist. They chucked me in prison, and I'm here, but God knows for how much longer.'

'What do you mean?'

'Well, you see that lot over there? The ones with the sickness? They've got another three, four days to go. I'll get like that soon, and so will you, and then we'll be here no longer. Simple, huh?'

'And where do we end up? Over the cliff?'

'Nothing so poetic. There's a mass grave on the common up near the hill. It's constantly having to be dug deeper.'

Von Luck exhaled. 'And what is this sickness? What are they dying of?'

'We don't know, but someone told me it's your kidneys. There's something in the hill that eats them up, and when they've packed up, so have you. If you're lucky, it's a bullet in the back of the head.'

'What causes it?'

Artur shrugged. 'The rockets, I've heard.'

'Rockets?'

'That's right. It's something that goes into the top of the rockets that seems to cause the sickness.'

'How big are the rockets?'

'You seem very interested.'

'Of course I am. Aren't you?'

'Not particularly. I'll be dead soon, so I'm afraid I've lost my curiosity.'

'I've yet to get to that stage.'

'Don't worry. You will.'

Von Luck smiled. 'And the rockets?' he asked.

'Oh, they're only about two metres long.'

'Is that all?'

'Yes. But there are thousands of them.'

'*Thousands?* Are you sure?'

Artur nodded. 'Oh, yes. Why do you think you lot are here? You're going to be making them.'

Von Luck was about to speak, but he was interrupted by the snarling command of the hut's *kapo*.

'Out! Everybody out!'

Von Luck and Fellowes needed no further prompting, and moved towards the door, accompanied by Artur. However, many were proving more reluctant – those who were incapable of getting off their bunks.

'Come on, you lazy cunts! Up! I said up!'

There was a suggestion of movement from a bunk near von Luck's head. A man, who must have been no more than thirty, tried to lift his head. His clothes were covered with blood, and his skin was almost translucent. There was nothing von Luck could do – the man was going to die in the next few hours, even if he had the most advanced medical attention.

'*Up!*'

The shout filled the hut, causing the sick man to redouble his efforts.

'Just stay there,' von Luck murmured.

Quizzical, the man turned his head. Von Luck smiled at him, glanced back to see if the *kapo* was visible, then swiped a blanket off the bunk below. He laid it over the man, and indicated that he was going to put it over his face. The man closed his eyes in seeming agreement. Von Luck pulled up the blanket, knowing that by the time it was removed, the man would be dead. At least he would have some dignity in his departure, and would not be bawled at or publicly executed for being 'work-shy'.

'Come on, out! Move!'

Von Luck and Fellowes stepped out of the hut. It was still dark. It was going to be a long day.

* * *

Professor Karl Fellner lit his eighth cigarette of the day. This morning he was expecting an influx of new workers who had been shipped over from Jersey. The poor bastards, he thought. Most would be dead within a few weeks, and they would die horribly. He had seen it too many times, yet he was too much of a coward to protest. He knew that if he did, List would either kill him or ship him back to Berlin, where he would be killed.

'You're smoking for Germany.'

'I wish that was all I was doing for Germany,' said Fellner.

The comment had been made by his colleague, Dr Heinz Pleiger, a good enough man, thought Fellner, although he did not seem to share Fellner's troubled conscience. Sure, he hated the way the workers were treated, but what could they do about it?

Pleiger tutted playfully at Fellner's response. 'Careful, Professor,' he said. 'Talk like that will only see you swelling the ranks up on the common.'

'I know, I know,' said Fellner wearily. If he was being honest with himself, and such moments were rare, he would say that he was too much of a coward to shoot himself. However, the greater part of him tried to convince himself that what he was doing was right, that it was for the greater good of mankind that Germany should win the war.

'Mind you,' said Pleiger, 'if you ended up there we could all go home.'

That the project would fail without him had preyed on Fellner's mind for months. But there was another conflict too: a fight between the scientist and the man of morals. He wanted to see the V3 work because it was something he had been striving for all his life. Ever since he was a young student, he had dreamt of heading such a project, which would never have happened without his expertise. Had Karl Fellner never lived, neither would the V3. But his sense of morality told him that had Karl Fellner and the V3 never existed, many thousands, perhaps hundreds of thousands, might not have died. That was the choice he was staring at, and it was partly the reason for his chain-smoking. I am a weak man, he told himself, because I cannot make a moral judgement.

Fellner's internal deliberations were interrupted by the arrival of Professor Kramer. He looked excited, unusually so.

'Herr Professor!' he said, removing his glasses with some panache.

'Yes, Albert, what is it?' asked Fellner.

'I think we might be ready.'

'Ready for what?'

'A test firing.'

Fellner dropped his cigarette. 'So soon?'

'Yes, Professor, perhaps by Wednesday we should be able to use barrels two and four.'

'At full operational capacity?'

Kramer nodded. 'At full capacity, Professor.'

There was a silence in the room as Fellner and Pleiger weighed up the gravity of Kramer's words. Soon they would be starting to murder people on a repulsive scale.

'You do not look very happy, Professor,' said Kramer.

Fellner lit another cigarette. 'Ah . . . no . . . I'm, ah, quite delighted.'

Kramer put his glasses back on. 'Good,' he said. 'Good. Now, then, I shall go and tell List the good news.'

Fellner made as if to stop him, but before he could open his mouth, Kramer was already out of the door. His hands slumped to his sides. He turned to Pleiger. 'I am just about to achieve my lifetime's ambition,' he said, 'and yet as a man I am a complete failure. Oh, Pleiger, what have I done?'

* * *

The walk to the hill was not a long one – some three miles – but it claimed at least four workers *en route*. Unable to stand the pace, they dropped to the ground and were too weak to get up, despite being threatened at rifle-point. Each man was shot for 'disobedience', and although von Luck did not witness the killings, he could guess what had happened.

'It's worse than I could ever have imagined,' said Fellowes, as they marched.

'I agree,' said von Luck, still ravaged by guilt that the murderers were his fellow countrymen.

'Didn't you know about all this?'

'I'm ashamed to say that I did. Although, like you, I didn't think it was so bad. We don't have the SS in Jersey, and the workers there are treated comparatively well.'

They fell silent as the two-hundred-strong column overtook a cartload of corpses. There must have been at least twenty, some wearing the striped uniforms of concentration-camp prisoners, a few naked.

'Jesus,' said Fellowes, under his breath.

Von Luck said nothing. This was medieval, he thought, like a painting by Bosch. Who would have thought it could be happening now? As the column climbed a slight incline, von Luck's rage increased. The mass grave that Artur had spoken about was in view: a hundred feet up to the left, with a well-worn track leading to it, was a pit measuring about forty yards by ten. At its edge prisoners were throwing bodies into their final resting-place; some were so light they went in with ease.

A gentle warm wind blew down from the pit, carrying with it the smell of putrefaction. Many members of the column coughed; a few vomited. The stench assaulted von Luck's nostrils, instantly causing his stomach to churn the little amount of food it contained.

'I expect we'll be in there before long,' said Fellowes.

'I'm going to jump off a cliff as soon I get sick,' said von Luck.

'Do you think we'll definitely get it, then?'

'What does it look like?' said von Luck, gesturing with his head back to the pit. 'There must thousands of bodies in that.'

The entrance was surprisingly nondescript, merely a twenty-foot hole cut into the hill. A narrow-gauge railway ran into it, along which chuffed a small locomotive pulling at least thirty covered wagons. There were workers everywhere, digging, hauling, lifting, all being shouted at by teams of SS guards and *kapos*. Much of the site resembled a quarry, as indeed it must once have been, von Luck thought.

As yet, he had no inkling what their work was to consist of. He didn't mind what it was, as long as it got him and Fellowes close enough to the heart of the project to kill the scientists. If that meant incurring the sickness, they were resigned to it. The chances of being able to escape alive were non-existent and, as von Luck had said, they would probably be dead before the sickness could claim them.

'Halt here!' shouted the *kapo* at the head of their column.

An SS sergeant stepped up on to a box and addressed them. 'From now on, you men will be working inside the hill. The work does not require great skill, but it does require diligence. Any worker who does not meet the required level of productivity will have me to answer to.' As he said that, he patted the holster on his left hip, leaving the workers in no doubt as to the nature of any punishment. 'The time is now six o'clock. You will work until twelve, when you will have a twenty-minute break for lunch. You will then continue to work until eight o'clock, at which point you will return to the camp. I'm sure you'll agree that these are reasonable hours.'

The sergeant wore an ironic smile, indicating that he knew the hours were anything but. A murmur of complaint came up from the column.

'Silence!' he shouted. 'Silence at all times! If there is any talking, the whole detachment will work until midnight.' He stepped down from his box. 'March!' he shouted.

The column moved forward, and von Luck's heart quickened. They were going to enter the hill, the site of the weapon that had already caused so many deaths. He looked at Fellowes and raised his eyebrows. Fellowes's face was set firm, expressionless. A decent man, thought von Luck. Fellowes was certainly that.

The installation was vast. Dimly lit, a huge concrete corridor had been bored into the hill. The railway line ran along it, and the smell of smoke hung heavily in the air. Von Luck coughed as he entered, reckoning that there was almost more smoke than oxygen in the place. The end of the corridor was not visible, but he estimated that he could see at least four hundred yards along it. No wonder the project had required so many workers, he thought.

The column walked along quickly, passing entrances to smaller corridors on the left. After they had advanced fifty yards, a huge passage opened up to the right, above which was the sign *Rakete Kanone 1* – Rocket Gun One. Von Luck nudged Fellowes, who nodded at him – evidently he had guessed what the sign meant. Von Luck looked up another corridor as they passed, and saw what appeared to be a series of large black pipes. They were elevated at an angle of seventy to eighty degrees, and he assumed that they ran all the way up through the hill to exit at the top. Clever, he thought. No wonder the Allies had not bombed this place: all that could be seen from the air were a few slits at the top of the hill, nothing to catch the eye of any photo interpreter. The visible work, with its railway line, would look like a quarry.

They passed another corridor – *Rakete Kanone 2*. Von Luck snatched another peep, and saw that several men in white coats were standing next to the foot of the cannon. They had to be scientists. Was one of them Fellner? They were walking too quickly for him to see. Patience, he urged himself. Patience.

The column turned left and entered a narrow corridor. A sign on the wall above an arrow read *Sprengkopf Montagewerk* – Warhead Assembly. So that was where they were going, thought von Luck, to the place where you would get the sickness. Walking down here meant that you were definitely going to die, and soon.

More men in white coats and suits passed them. Von Luck's eye was briefly caught by one who wore glasses and a broad smile. There was something about the smile that von Luck didn't like, something that suggested things were going too well.

'Halt!'

The column did so.

'You are now about to enter your place of work,' shouted the sergeant. 'Do a good job, men, and remember, work brings freedom.'

With that preposterous phrase, the sergeant, accompanied by three NCOs, marched past them towards the main corridor. Judging by the expressions on their faces, they were only too happy to leave the area.

'This way!' shouted a *kapo*.

The column moved forward once more, and came into a large workshop that contained scores of workbenches and pieces of machinery.

'Everyone stand at a workbench!'

Two hours later von Luck picked up his first warhead. It seemed innocuous enough – just a grey canister about the size of his fist – but it weighed a few kilos. So this was it, he thought. This was what would kill him. To hold one's nemesis in one's hand felt bizarre. The moment should have been more dramatic, but instead it was matter-of-fact. Here was a piece of metal. Insert it into the rocket here. Seal up the rocket as instructed. Wait for the next rocket and the next warhead.

At midday, the *kapo* called a halt. The workers were escorted down the concrete corridors and back into the daylight; the brightness caused von Luck to squint. Standing next to Fellowes, he waited in line while a couple of workers doled out a watery-looking substance.

'How are you feeling?' von Luck asked.

'Not bad,' said Fellowes. 'Starving, but other than that, fine.'

'Perhaps those were a different type of warhead.'

'Let's hope so,' said Fellowes.

'Or maybe the reaction is not immediate.'

'That's probably more likely.'

Von Luck looked at his fellow workers in the queue. Many looked relaxed, happy, even.

'Shit!' said von Luck.

'What?' said Fellowes.

'We don't have bowls.'

Fellowes turned round. Sure enough, every man was brandishing some sort of container – a bowl, a mug, even a helmet.

'We're going to bloody starve,' said von Luck.

'We could ask someone,' said Fellowes.

'Not a chance. It's every man for himself. We'll just have to see if they'll let us use our hands.'

They were nearly at the front of the queue. Von Luck cursed. How could he have been so foolish? He had known that the workers on Jersey had to provide their own bowls and utensils, so why hadn't he thought of it before?

'Where is your bowl?' asked the prisoner at the soup drum.

'I don't have one,' said von Luck.

'Well, then, no bowl, no food.'

'But can't you put some in my hands?'

'No. That's against the regulations.'

'Come on,' said von Luck. 'Have a heart. We're new here.'

The prisoner looked at his comrade, who shrugged his shoulders as if to say, 'Well, why not?'

Von Luck held out his hands, whereupon the ladler crudely dumped a portion of grey watery broth into them. Von Luck tried drinking it, but much of it seeped through his fingers on to the mud. It tasted foul, as though it had been made from rotten meat. He held out his hands again.

'Not a chance! Get out of it.'

Von Luck walked off – he was not going to plead a second time. If only he could find a damn bowl. He searched the site, looking in vain for anything that might be suitable. There was nothing, not even a piece of metal that could be twisted into shape.

'There's nothing, is there?' said Fellowes.

'No,' said von Luck. 'Did the same thing happen to you?'

Fellowes nodded.

'Still, it was probably just as well. Whatever it was looked abominable.'

'We must find *something*,' said von Luck. 'Otherwise we're going to starve.'

'We'll find something back at the camp,' said Fellowes, 'from one of the dead men.'

It was incredible how quickly one started adapting to a new reality, von Luck thought. Within a short space of time, he and Fellowes had been reduced to contemplating the removal of bowls from corpses. Nothing else seemed more important.

Important. Of course it bloody was! This was what the hunger was doing to them, thought von Luck. It was distracting them from their mission. He had never been so hungry before, and he had underrated hunger's power to control one's life. 'We have to forget about food,' he said. 'We must concentrate on why we're here.'

'I agree,' said Fellowes, 'but if only we could—'

'I know, I know. But I don't want us to be distracted by having to find a damn bowl!'

Fellowes snapped his fingers. 'There! Look!'

Von Luck's eyes followed to where he was pointing. About seventy yards away, driving through the gates to the site, was a *Kubelwagen* – a small, open armoured car – in the back of which sat two men. The first von Luck recognised as List. The second had grey hair and a round face, out of which stuck a cigarette. Fellner.

The driver of the car was pressing the horn agitatedly, insisting that the workers should get out of the way.

'This is our chance,' said von Luck.

'Let's do it, then,' said Fellowes.

Von Luck felt for the reassuring weight of the grenade in his coat pocket. His pistol was in his other pocket, but he might not need it. With a well-aimed throw of the grenade into the car, he would kill both Fellner and List, thereby removing the project's two most important elements.

The driver was angry now: the workers, docile from long hours and lack of food, moved slowly out of the way. It could not have been better planned for von Luck and Fellowes, who were striding towards the car.

'You've got your gun?' said von Luck.

'I have,' said Fellowes.

'As soon as I've thrown the grenade, start firing at anyone wearing a uniform. Got it?'

'Got it,' said Fellowes.

Suddenly von Luck felt intensely exhilarated. He was not looking forward to killing, but the thought that he might achieve his goal was making him feel almost ecstatic. A few curious workers were watching him and Fellowes stride purposefully towards the car, but von Luck did not notice them. All he was looking at was Fellner, his chubby face expressionless, puffing at the cigarette. Not only was it shortly going to be the end of Fellner's life, it was also going to be the end of von Luck's. He was certain of it. In ten minutes he would no longer be alive.

It was time to get the grenade out, prime it. After that, there was no going back.

'You ready?' von Luck asked.

'Yup,' said Fellowes.

They were twenty yards away, nearly close enough for von Luck to throw the grenade, but too far to guarantee its accuracy. In his limited experience, he knew that stick grenades were notoriously difficult to throw straight. Just another five yards, just another few seconds.

The car edged forward. Von Luck saw that its way was now clear – any second now it would accelerate away. Damn! A moment's indecision. Continue, and hope to get there in time? Or wait, and hope for another chance?

'Hey! You!'

Von Luck heard the voice immediately. He recognised it, although he was not sure whose it was.

'Yes, you, the tall one!'

Von Luck stopped. There was no way he could get a grenade out of his pocket now, not when someone was addressing him. Fellowes stopped too, and briefly met von Luck's eye. He looked wound up, frustrated.

Von Luck turned to see one of the prisoners running towards him. What the hell did he want? And then it became clear. It was one of the two men who had been manning the soup drum.

'Look what I've found!' he shouted.

'What?'

'A bowl!' With some pride, the worker held it up. 'You can have it for five cigarettes! It's your lucky day!'

Von Luck turned back briefly to see Fellner and List's car heading towards the mouth of the tunnel. Lucky day indeed.

Chapter Ten

LEBONNEUR FEELS RACHEL grab his arm in the darkness. The footsteps are getting louder now, closer. Oh, fuck, he thinks. This isn't happening, please tell me this isn't happening.

'I'd stop if I were you!'

The voice is Lebonneur's. It quavers, but he can't help it.

The footsteps do not stop.

'I'm warning you, I'm armed!'

Rachel stares at Lebonneur, her eyes asking him whether what he has just said can possibly be true. It's a lie, of course it is, but it might buy them some time.

The footsteps stop.

'So, too, am I.'

Lebonneur recognises the voice. It is commanding, well spoken: it is that of Ian Mollett.

'No further,' says Lebonneur. 'You stay right there, Mollett.' He points to the steps. That's their only way out, although getting through the brambles and the vegetation at the top will be tough.

Another footstep.

'I said stop!'

A snort-cum-laugh echoes down the corridor. Lebonneur pushes Rachel in the direction of the steps. He can't tell her what to do because Mollett will hear him. She looks back at him in the dim light, confused, terrified. He points once again at the steps. Just go – just bloody go!

The silent command seems to get through, and Rachel stumbles to the steps. There are concrete blocks scattered everywhere, and it's hard to move without tripping. They might work to their advantage, thinks Lebonneur.

Rachel is running up the steps now. God knows if she'll get through the brambles, but even if she cuts herself to pieces it'll be better than staying down here.

More footsteps. What now? Wait here and be slaughtered? Or go on the offensive, seize the initiative? Lebonneur is tempted to pick up some rocks and throw them down the corridor, but that's far too risky. He puts himself in Mollett's shoes. He'll be nervous too, and he won't be able to see well. Neither will he know where Lebonneur is hiding so he can't exactly walk in and open fire.

Lebonneur creeps over to the corridor entrance. He'll wait here, just next to the opening, ready to leap at the bastard as soon as he shows his nose – or muzzle. That would be best, wouldn't it? Grab the gun, wrestle with it. It's going to be hell on his ribs, but that's too bad.

He can hear Rachel struggling. She's whimpering and Lebonneur wishes she wouldn't. He knows she can't help it, but it's going to tell Mollett that she's trying to get away. There must be a way through the brambles, thinks Lebonneur, they're only bloody plants, for Christ's sake!

A final footstep, just outside the room. The bastard's right there. Should he charge him now? Or wait for him to come in? Perhaps he'll do what they always do on films and burst in, gun pointing at the corners of the room. Let him try, thinks Lebonneur, let him bloody try – besides, if he does that, he'll probably trip over.

Rachel's making a hell of a racket. Perhaps those brambles are impenetrable, in which case she's in a very bad place. At the top of the steps, with no way out, she'll make an easy target. She sounds angry that she can't get through, occasionally swearing under her breath.

'Don't try to escape, or I'll have to shoot you.'

He hears Rachel gasp, and then a flurry of activity as she tries desperately to get through the brambles.

'If you come out with your hands up, I shall spare your lives.'

Crap, thinks Lebonneur. He's stalling: he doesn't want to come in because he knows he might get a nasty surprise.

'This is your last chance!'

He can hear Rachel struggling harder now. It must be agony, the poor woman.

Suddenly a bright flash illuminates the room, followed immediately by a loud crack. Lebonneur is momentarily stunned, long enough for Mollett to run into the room, reloading his rifle as he does so.

Before Lebonneur can react, he finds the muzzle pointing straight at his chest.

'Now, stay quite still.'

Lebonneur has no intention of disagreeing.

'Come down, Mrs Lebonneur. That is an order.'

Silence.

'I said, come down!'

Nothing. Thank heaven for that, thinks Lebonneur, she's free. Good for her! She'll be able to get help, he thinks, but he knows it will be too late. He looks at Mollett, who is just a shadow pointing the gun at him. He's wearing what looks like a boiler suit. Dressed for work, thinks Lebonneur.

I'm going to die, he thinks. This is it. The moment of my death, here in an old SS concentration camp. I'll be joining lots of other dead people – I shall be in good company, shan't be lonely. The boys. Rachel. He'll miss them so badly. They'll be all right, though. They hadn't had a perfect husband and father, but at least they'd had one who was fun. Oh, well, he'd done his best to be a family man, and it had nearly worked. He'd never cheated on anyone, not once. And this, all this. This was decent as well – trying to find out about this was a good thing to do surely. It will make up for all the drinking, swearing, badmouthing and irresponsibility.

'You're a very lucky man, Mr Lebonneur.'

'You'll forgive me if I disagree.'

Mollett chuckles. 'Good point,' he says. 'But you're lucky. I fired at you on numerous occasions, and you always moved just in time.'

Lebonneur is tempted to tell Mollett that he's a bad shot, but decides against it. 'Before I . . . before I . . .'

'Get killed?' asks Mollett

'Yes, before I get killed, I'd appreciate it if you told me why you're allowing a hotel to be built on a hillside full of uranium.'

Mollett waves away the comment with an arrogant flick of his left hand, causing it to leave the rifle, but not long enough for Lebonneur to do anything about it. 'Underneath all that concrete, Mr Lebonneur, the uranium's radioactivity will barely register.'

'Even if that's so, Mollett, what about all those workers you're allowing to die?'

Mollett shrugs. 'Well, too bad. Workers are always dying. They lead unhealthy lives, eat chips, drink too much beer, that sort of thing. Most of them would have had heart attacks by the time they're fifty anyway.'

Lebonneur cannot believe this: the man sounds like a Nazi eugenicist. 'That's if they're not pushed off some scaffolding in the meantime.'

'An unfortunate accident.'

'I'll bet. No more accidental than this, I imagine.'

'Quite, Mr Lebonneur. You have a good brain.'

'Not that good,' says Lebonneur. 'If I were a cleverer man, I'd be the one pointing the gun, wouldn't I?'

'Well, I agree with you, Mr Lebonneur.'

At any second, Lebonneur expects to feel that final pain. 'So this is just about money, then, is it, Mollett?'

'I don't deny that I have certain tastes, Mr Lebonneur.'

'Is that a yes?'

'No.'

'So it's not just about money?'

'No.'

'Forgive me for asking, but what else is it about?'

'I think you know that, Mr Lebonneur.'

'I don't think I do, Mr Mollett.'

'Oh, come, come – don't play the innocent with me.'

'All right. I'll hazard a guess that this is about your adoptive father.'

'Go on.'

'He was a collaborator, wasn't he?'

'An interesting suggestion.'

'One that's been made before, hasn't it? But the accusation has never stuck.'

'That's because it's not true.'

He's getting a little worked up now, Lebonneur notices. The rifle is twitching in his hands. Please don't fire – please, God, don't let him fire.

'Why do you think he was anyway?' asks Mollett.

'That's quite simple, Mr Mollett. I have a diary that says he is.'

'Aah, yes. The *diary*. I was hoping you were going to mention that. Colonel von Luck's diary, no less, which has mysteriously turned up in your possession. I, of course, telephoned you about that, made you an exceptionally generous offer, but you were rather obstinate. Life would have been simpler for you, had you just accepted the money.'

Poor bloody Terry. If only Terry had kept his mouth shut he wouldn't be dead, and Mollett would have been none the wiser.

'So you decided to kill me instead. And my friend Terry. And, of course, you nearly killed all of us on the plane. I did enjoy that photo-opportunity in hospital by the way. You're quite an actor, Mr Mollett.'

'That comes with my job. And you're a very bad one, Mr Lebonneur.'

All this formality is more than absurd, thinks Lebonneur. They're talking as if they're having some polite committee meeting at the States. Perhaps it's just as well, he thinks. All these 'misters' keep the heat down.

'I would, of course, like to see the diary,' says Mollett. 'My father once told me about it, said he'd heard rumours of its existence. I'd love to see these fantastic claims made by a German Lothario against a knight of the realm.'

A knight of the realm. Big deal. As if that meant anything, these days. Pompous prick.

'I'd love to show it to you, of course, but I'm afraid it's not on me.'

'Where is it, then?'

Mollett thrusts the rifle into Lebonneur's stomach. Despite the threat, Lebonneur is starting to feel that his hand, although not the upper one, is stronger than he had thought. 'If you shoot me, Mr Mollett, you will never find out. And if I die, the person who has it will be sure to publicise its contents.'

'Who is it?'

Another jab to the stomach.

'Fuck!' says Lebonneur – the pain in his ribs seems to shoot all round his body.

'Who?'

'I'm not going to tell you,' says Lebonneur, the pain crying out for him to tell Mollett that Glen Owen has it.

'If you don't, I shall kill you.'

'But if you ... kill me, then you're effectively dead as well.'

'Your wife! She has it!'

Lebonneur shakes his head. 'Perhaps we could make some sort of deal, Mr Mollett.'

'Oh, yes?'

'My life in exchange for the diary.'

Mollett relaxes the pressure of the rifle. 'An interesting suggestion, Mr Lebonneur. A little dearer than four thousand pounds, wouldn't you say?'

*   *   *

The sickness started later that day. On the walk back to Sylt, von Luck was suddenly overcome by a wave of nausea, and had to stop to vomit.

'Keep walking!' shouted a *kapo*, but it was impossible to obey the order.

He was going to die, he knew it now for certain. Before, it had been a rational hypothesis, a question of evaluating probabilities.

Now it was assured. He felt Fellowes's hand on his back. 'How are you feeling?'

'Pretty bad,' said von Luck, standing up. 'How about you?'

'I don't know yet. I keep waiting for something to happen.'

'Maybe you're immune.'

Fellowes smiled. 'We'd better keep walking.'

Von Luck nodded, wiping his mouth on the back of his sleeve.

The steps were getting harder now, and he knew they would get harder still. The one thing he had to keep whole was his resolve – it was essential that that should stay intact. They had missed their chance today, but there would be other chances. He had to stay alive, had to finish what he was here to do. The sickness would take over in time, there was no doubt about that, but he had to take advantage of that time.

* * *

The next morning Hempel cracked.

He did his best, but it was not enough. The questioning was most thorough, and no matter how much he protested his innocence, they always came back at him with Miss Campbell's words: *You betrayed us. You're a traitor.* What did that mean, Major? Tell us, and we won't hurt you.

Hempel did his best to explain away the words. Yes, Miss Campbell was a friend of von Luck's, and yes, so was he. That was not a crime, was it? He had met Miss Campbell on numerous

occasions through von Luck, and it might have been that she
supposed Hempel was on her side in some way. She was mistaken,
of course, but there it was. Her mother had just been shot –
clearly she was not in a lucid frame of mind.

'That's not what she told us.'

'Well,' said Hempel, 'whatever she told you was fantasy,
because that's the truth.'

'Miss Campbell has told us that you were helping her and her
mother and, what's more, that you are also helping von Luck.'

'That's untrue!'

'Is it?'

'Then why didn't you arrest him as you were ordered to on
Sunday night?'

'Because he wasn't there, dammit! How many times do I have
to tell you that?'

His interrogator held up a few sheets of paper. 'These,' he
said, waving them demonstratively, 'are statements by the
NCOs assigned to help you that evening. They state quite
clearly that von Luck was there. I think it is unlikely that these
two men are lying, don't you?'

Those bastards, thought Hempel. They had sworn to keep
quiet, but presumably the prospect of increased rations and a
few packets of cigarettes had seen to that. Hempel was stymied,
he knew it. His interrogator knew it too, because he was smiling.

'Come on, Major, let's be reasonable. We all know that
loyalties exist between men that are greater than those that exist
between men and organisations, or even men and the Führer for

that matter. We know that you and von Luck are good friends, but can't you see that he is a murderer? There has to be a point when those bonds of loyalty snap, don't you think?'

Hempel didn't reply.

'In a way, helping a friend is an admirable thing to do, but perhaps in this instance you have been a little . . . misguided, shall we say? Von Luck has abused your friendship, he has made you risk your life in going along with him.'

Hempel was tempted to agree. Perhaps the man was right: perhaps what he was saying could be taken at face value, not regarded as another interrogation tactic.

'The best way you can repay him, and the best way you can help yourself, Major, is to tell us where he has gone. If you co-operate, it will be taken into account. Perhaps you will only be court-martialled on the grounds of refusing to obey an order. You'll be demoted, certainly, spend some time behind bars, but you'll live! That's the important thing, Major. Let me spell this out for you – you are not going to die. I can guarantee that.'

Hempel believed him – there was an honesty about him that he found appealing. Hempel had never met this man before: his uniform said that he was a captain in the navy. Perhaps he was one of Huffmeier's new appointments, brought over to do dirty little jobs like this. Whoever he was, he was good at his job. He appealed to Hempel as a fellow officer, as his peer. 'Can you really guarantee that I won't be killed?'

The interrogator nodded. 'You have my word as an officer.'

Hempel thought of von Luck, thought of him on Alderney.

Perhaps the man had gone mad, chasing his personal demons all over the islands. And maybe he was in love as well – perhaps that had affected his judgement. This captain was right: he didn't owe von Luck anything. The letter? Well, that was all conjecture by Marais, and it might be nonsense. Was he really going to stake his life against that and von Luck's word? Of course not.

'You look as though you are chewing it over, Major Hempel.'

'I am. Although I need some reassurance that you can guarantee my life.'

'You can have it in writing, if you like. Or, even better, I could get Admiral Huffmeier to give you his word. Like us, Major, he is a pragmatist, a man of the world. He tells me he is happy to make a deal. All he is concerned about is the whereabouts of von Luck.'

Hempel took a deep breath. This felt wretched, but what choice did he have? He certainly did not want to die. Von Luck would just have to keep his 'decent men'.

'All right,' he said. 'He's on Alderney.'

*　*　*

That night Fellowes fell sick. He was sharing a single bunk with von Luck when it struck, and he only just managed to avoid vomiting over both of them. He retched on to the floor, the sound accompanying that produced by at least another ten prisoners who were doing the same.

'I'm sorry,' said von Luck. 'This is all my fault.'

'Don't be,' said Fellowes. 'I knew what I was letting myself in for.'

'I don't think either of us did.'

'Well, I still would have come.'

Thank God for Fellowes, thought von Luck. He was perhaps the most decent man he had met during the whole war, and it was ironic that he was an enemy. He felt helpless, though, impotent. There was nothing he could do for Fellowes, and there was nothing he could for himself.

The walk to the hill was harder that morning, and von Luck wondered whether he would make it. He knew that he was weakened not only by the sickness but by a lack of sleep and nourishment. His tall frame needed more than the slop they were served up, and he felt permanently close to fainting. Fellowes was in a similar state, and von Luck wondered whether they would have the strength to get through the day, let alone attempt to kill Fellner. 'I said it yesterday, and I'll say it today,' he whispered, as they passed the mass grave, 'I am *never* going to end up there.'

'Neither am I,' said Fellowes. 'No bloody way. I'm with you over the cliff.'

Von Luck wondered how many more had chosen the cliff as their preferred means of death. There was more dignity that way, he thought, more control.

'I don't think we're going to have very long,' said von Luck. 'This feels bad, very bad.'

'We should try today, then,' said Fellowes. 'At lunchtime?'

'Yes. We'll break off and look for him. You do know that we'll probably be dead by this afternoon?'

Fellowes walked on in silence for a few moments. 'I do,' he said. 'And in a way I'm glad, because I know we're doing the right thing. I've seen too many people die over the past few years for the wrong reasons – botched attacks, incompetent leadership, you know what I mean. I always thought I'd be killed in this war, although not like this.'

That morning von Luck almost collapsed. Fellowes had to prop him up against the workbench as they assembled the warheads, encouraging him to tighten the odd screw here, a bolt there, to give the impression to the *kapo* that he was working.

One of their fellow workers did collapse, and he was quickly removed, no doubt taken outside and executed for being work-shy, his body to be thrown into the burial pit with the next delivery of corpses. Von Luck noticed a couple more vomiting although, like him, they did their best to give an impression of industry.

'Are you sure you're going to be all right?' asked Fellowes.

'Definitely,' said von Luck, willing the word to be true.

He was feeling worse than ever. His insides felt as if they were turning inside out, the back of his throat permanently in a state of convulsion. If these warheads were doing this to workers, God knows what they would do to the poor people they landed on.

'It's nearly twelve,' said Fellowes. 'Time for lunch.'

'Stop working!' the *kapo* shouted.

'You ready?' asked von Luck.

'I'm ready,' said Fellowes, patting his pocket.

They stood quietly in line, waiting for the order to march. When it arrived, von Luck struggled to keep up with the pace, but somehow he managed it. Just before they reached the main corridor that led outside, he nudged Fellowes. 'Now!' he hissed.

Together the two men broke off from the group and pressed themselves up against an ill-lit part of the corridor. A couple of workers looked at them suspiciously, but von Luck crouched over, pretending to be sick, which he was now able to perform with ease.

They waited for a minute, listening to the diminishing echo of the group's footsteps.

'If we're stopped,' said von Luck, 'we'll say we've been ordered to collect some samples to deliver to our workshop.'

'Fine.'

'And I've always got my watch as a bribe. Have you got one?'

Fellowes shook his head. 'It was, ah, "borrowed" from me by one of your fellow countrymen when I was captured.'

'On behalf of the German people, I apologise to you, Captain Fellowes.'

'You've got your sense of humour back.'

'It's a struggle,' said von Luck. 'Come on, let's go and do this.'

* * *

'Alderney!'

'That's right, sir. Hempel says he's over there in an attempt to damage the new weapon project.'

Admiral Huffmeier had gone puce.

'But this is a disaster! How the hell did he get there?'

'Hempel told me he went over with a group of Todt workers on Monday morning.'

'God in heaven! Hempel should be shot!'

'I'm afraid I promised him his life, sir, in return for his co-operation.'

'You did? Well, too bad. Hempel *will* be shot, no matter what you told him. This is a monstrous crime!'

'I agree, sir.'

Huffmeier picked up the phone.

'Heidi! Get me List on Alderney. And if you can't get him, get that fat idiot Schwalm.'

Huffmeier slammed the phone down before Heidi had even said, 'Yes, sir.'

'And did Hempel tell us *how* he was going to destroy the V3?'

'I'm afraid not, sir. Hempel told me that von Luck would not tell him. All I do know is that he appeared to join forces with the two escaped prisoners-of-war, Smith and Fellowes.'

Huffmeier shook his head. If von Luck sabotaged the V3, he knew his own head would roll. Well, he thought, that was not going to happen. He had survived this war for too long, and he was not going to die now, not when the end was in sight, when the final victory was theirs for the taking.

The telephone rang. Huffmeier snatched it up. 'Yes!'

'It's Captain List for you,' said Heidi.

'List! Huffmeier here! I have bad news for you. Listen, that renegade officer I was telling you about, von Luck, appears to be on Alderney with the expressed intention of destroying the V3.'

'You're being serious, Admiral?'

'Of course I bloody am! He came over on Monday on a ship full of Todt workers, so he should still be with them. He's with a couple of British prisoners called Fellowes and Smith.'

'In that case they'll be in Sylt, under my nose. All right, Admiral, I'll find them, don't worry.'

'You sound confident, List.'

'Well, I am in complete control of this place. They won't get far, I assure you. Anyway, how are these idiots going to destroy the place?'

'We don't know.'

There was brief lull in the conversation.

'Hello?' said Huffmeier. 'List? Are you there?'

'I am here, Admiral. I've just had a thought.'

'Yes?'

'If I were in von Luck's shoes I'd go after the scientists, Professor Fellner in particular.'

'What would happen if Fellner was killed?'

'Put simply, Admiral, we would have no V3. London would be spared, and we'd be sitting on a toxic shithole full of uranium and concrete, twiddling our thumbs, waiting to be sent back to

Berlin. You see, the weapon is Fellner's brainchild – no Fellner, no weapon.'

'All right, all right! You've made your point. You'd better make sure Fellner is safe.'

'Don't worry, Admiral – I shall. I will put a special guard on him immediately.'

'You do that, List.'

'To the admiral's irritation, List put the phone down. Typical SS – no bloody manners.

* * *

The main corridor was eerily quiet. In the distance they could hear occasional voices, doors slamming, a shout, but for the most part it was almost silent.

'Which way?' asked Fellowes.

Von Luck looked up and down the corridor. 'Straight down,' he said. 'My guess is that the laboratories are at the end.'

'They would be.'

Suddenly von Luck felt faint, once more about to collapse. Fellowes gripped his right elbow. 'Listen,' he said. 'Give me the grenade. I can go it alone.'

'No!' von Luck snapped, startling Fellowes by the severity of his tone. He stood up straight. He was not going to give up, would not surrender to this damn sickness. Let it do its worst, he thought, but not yet. It could claim him any time after he had killed Fellner, but not before. 'No,' he said. 'I'm fine.

Just a hunger pang, that's all.' He started walking down the corridor, anxious to show Fellowes that he was capable. Even now, he wanted to retch, but he refused to allow himself to do so.

Rakete Kanone 3. They had another two corridors to pass, and then they would have reached the laboratory. Von Luck looked behind him. The tunnel exit looked distant, the sunlight struggling to reach deep into the hill. Would that be the last daylight he ever saw?

Rakete Kanone 4. Some voices were coming from that corridor. Fellner's? No, ignore it. He's most likely to be in the laboratory, that's the place to start. A whistle interrupted his thinking, giving him a start. Where was it coming from? Another whistle. It was a train whistle, thank God for that. Coming towards them, out of the dimness, came the locomotive, hauling a series of empty wagons. Workers wearing concentration-camp uniforms were perched on the sides of some of the wagons, their faces emaciated and grey. They looked hollow, thought von Luck, their eyes vacant and staring.

Rakete Kanone 5. Very close now. Would there be any guards? If so, they would just have to seize the initiative and shoot them. For the first time in hours, von Luck was not feeling weak. Adrenaline was combating the sickness, providing him with an extra cell of energy. 'You'd better get your pistol ready,' said von Luck. 'We're nearly there.'

The two men stopped and looked around. There was a gaggle of workers some fifty yards away – not close enough to concern them. The two men turned back, removed the pistols from their pockets and checked them over.

'Your weapon all right?'

'Looks good,' said Fellowes. 'Yours?'

'Fine. I'm going to keep mine in my right pocket.'

'And the grenade?' asked Fellowes.

'In my left. I'll use it to damage the laboratory after we've got Fellner.'

Von Luck held out his hand. 'Good luck, Fellowes,' he said.

'Good luck, von Luck.'

*   *   *

The laboratory was quiet that lunchtime, and Professor Fellner was taking the opportunity to read an ancient copy of the magazine *Signal*. A cigarette hung out of his mouth, and he took occasional gulps from a flask of cold ersatz coffee. A sandwich lay untouched on his table, its corners curling up. He had no appetite, relying instead on what he termed a 'fumatory lunch', an all-too-common occurrence, these days. A couple of technicians busied themselves around the laboratory. They made as little noise as possible, knowing how much Professor Fellner liked his peace and quiet.

Fellner looked at his watch – five past twelve. The meeting to discuss the test firing was not due until half past, so he had a while in which to relax. He was not looking forward to it, especially as one of the attendees would be List, who was making Fellner feel more uneasy every day.

Somewhere at the back of the laboratory, the telephone rang. Fellner ignored it. It was always bloody ringing, disturbing his concentration. No doubt this call would be the same as any other – some moronic enquiry from some damn fool who hadn't listened to what he had been told.

'It's Captain List, Professor.'

Shit. Fellner put down the copy of *Signal*. The man's name was enough to set his heart racing. What did he want? Please let him say he couldn't make the meeting. That was unlikely, he knew, but there was always hope. Fellner walked slowly round the laboratory and picked up the phone. 'Fellner speaking.'

'Professor,' said List, 'is there a guard stationed outside your laboratory?'

Fellner peered past a column and looked through the laboratory's semi-glazed door. 'No, it doesn't look like it.'

'In that case I insist you lock the laboratory door.'

'Why?'

'Just do it, Professor. Do it now! I shall have a detachment sent round immediately.'

The line went dead. Fellner looked at the phone quizzically, then handed it back to the technician.

'Everything all right, Professor?'

'I'm not sure. Willi – do you have the key to this place?'

'Yes. I have it on me.'

'That was Captain List. He wants us to lock the laboratory door.'

The technician frowned. 'Really? Why?'

'I've no idea. You'd better lock it, though.'

* * *

They could see the laboratory. It was quite clear. Not only was it painted with the word *Laboratorium*, but von Luck also noticed a man in a white coat at the door. What was he doing? He looked as though he was locking it.

'Quick!' said von Luck. 'They're locking the door!'

Von Luck and Fellowes ran forward, all the time keeping an eye on the scientist at the door. Von Luck pulled out his pistol, knowing that this was the point of no return. Until then, they could have walked away, rejoined the group, but for what? To sit around and wait for the sickness to win?

This, thought von Luck, was living. If there was purpose in life, it was this, to die for what was right.

'Don't touch the door!' von Luck shouted.

The technician disappeared from sight, ducking at the sight of von Luck's pistol. Von Luck reached it and turned the handle, finding it locked.

'Now what?' said Fellowes.

Von Luck reached for the grenade from his coat pocket. 'Stand back!'

Fellowes did as he was hold, while, with a single twist, von

Luck primed the grenade. He placed it by the door and ran to join Fellowes, his hands over his ears.

The explosion coincided with the ringing of the alarm. The force almost knocked the two men off their feet, but they stayed upright, albeit a little unsteadily. Simultaneously they turned and ran into the cloud of dust and debris, choking on it as they did so. Keep the advantage, von Luck told himself. Never mind the alarm, never mind that they're probably on to you, just keep going. They raced into the laboratory, stepping over the door and the body of the technician. The poor bastard, thought von Luck. He didn't look at him for long, but whatever had been his face was now a deformed mass of bone and blood.

The alarm seemed deafeningly loud in here. Von Luck could just about make out the sound of a telephone ringing. There were two men in the room – a younger one, and one he instantly recognised as Fellner.

'*Hande hoch!*' shouted Fellowes.

The two men swiftly obeyed. Von Luck noticed that Fellner was still holding a cigarette in his right hand.

'I think you can guess why I'm here, Professor,' he said.

Fellner didn't move. His expression indicated an awareness of his imminent death.

'I am a German, Professor. My name is Lieutenant Colonel Max von Luck of the Field Command in Jersey.'

Fellner's expression mutated from one of terror, to terror combined with confusion.

'I'm here because I don't like your weapon, and I don't like what it will achieve. I am now going to shoot you, because if you die, many more people will be saved. That is the reason why I am killing you. I thought you should know.'

'Thank you, Colonel,' said Fellner. 'I'm glad you have come. In a way, it was me who sent for you.'

'How?'

'I wrote to Mr Marais on Jersey, telling him about my weapon. I had expected him to contact the British, but the fact that my nemesis is German seems more fitting.'

This was hardly the response von Luck had expected. Nevertheless, the surprise was not enough to stop him squeezing the trigger.

'Wait!' shouted Fellner.

'What?'

'May I make a request?'

'It had better be quick, Professor.'

'I'd like to do it myself.'

'Why?'

'Because I've been wanting to for a long time. I've not found the courage, you see. But now that I know I am going to die, I would rather do it myself.'

Von Luck looked at Fellowes.

'I think it's a bad idea,' Fellowes said.

'I don't,' said von Luck. 'Keep your gun pointed at him.'

Von Luck paced over to the professor. 'Here is the gun, Professor. Do you know what to do with it?'

'Yes.'

'If you turn it on me or my comrade here, he shall shoot you immediately.'

'I understand, Colonel, but I assure you that won't happen.'

Fellner took the gun with a shaking hand. His eyes met von Luck's; the colonel saw that they were shining, the rest of the scientist's face almost elated. Von Luck stepped back. He knew nothing about Fellner except that he was a brave man.

'You see, Colonel,' said Fellner, 'I have done a terrible thing. This weapon is brilliant, yet it is evil. If it is used, it will kill many, all in the name of a regime that is morally bankrupt. I am responsible for it, and therefore it is right that you should have come here to kill me.'

'Forgive me, Professor,' said von Luck, 'but we have little time.'

The professor smiled, his top lip covered in beads of sweat. 'I understand.'

Fellner gripped the pistol with both hands, opened his mouth and placed the barrel on his bottom teeth. He closed his eyes. He paused. He's not going to do it, thought von Luck, I'm going to have to kill him.

The din in the laboratory was briefly augmented by a loud report. Fellner's head snapped back, his body quickly following the same trajectory against a workbench and then on to the floor, taking with it his flask of coffee. For a few seconds, the three men looked down at the body, the sound of the alarm and the ringing telephone still filling the air.

Von Luck stepped over and removed the pistol from Fellner's hands. A sticky pool of blood was seeping away from his head, mingling with the coffee, the only sign that the man was dead. His face was unblemished, still warm, the beads of sweat still there, the eyes still shining.

'What shall we do with him?' asked Fellowes, pointing his gun at the technician.

'Where are the papers?' asked von Luck.

'P-papers?' said the technician.

'Papers! Where are they? Blueprints! Designs! Your notes, man! Where are they?'

'We keep some in that – that – uh – safe over there.'

'Open it!'

The technician hurried across the room, followed by Fellowes and von Luck. The safe was already unlocked, and inside it were scores of box files.

'We need a grenade for this lot!' said von Luck.

'We can burn them,' said Fellowes.

'Do you have any petrol?' asked von Luck, pointing his pistol at the technician, who nodded nervously.

'Get it!'

Von Luck bent down into the safe and threw the box files on to the floor, emptying them as he did so. Fellowes started helping, and within less than a minute, a chaotic pyramid of paper and boxes had accumulated. The technician reappeared with a small canister of petrol. 'Come on! Pour it on!' von Luck barked.

The man did as he was ordered. It was clear that the destruction of the blueprints was going to cause him almost more anguish than witnessing the death of Professor Fellner.

'Right! Now light it!'

The technician scurried over to a workbench and fetched a book of matches. His hands shook so badly that von Luck was forced to snatch it and light a match himself.

'All right! Stand back!'

Von Luck threw down the match, instantly setting the papers ablaze. The whoosh of flame caused him to recoil, and he narrowly missed falling over.

It was time to go, he thought, the job had been done. He should have felt ecstatic, but instead he felt resentful. All this, this place, this bloody war, was such a waste of time, a waste of lives. He should be at home, looking after the estate, rearing cattle, raising a family, doing all the things that he should be doing, but not this. Not having to watch some professor blow his brains out. Not having to suffer the sickness that would shortly kill him. He thought of Pippa: her face was in his mind as he ran out of the laboratory. If only he could see her again, just for a minute, perhaps he wouldn't feel so cheated.

He knew it wasn't going to happen, but it kept him going as he ran down the corridor, following Fellowes and the technician. He was running fast, faster than he thought possible, almost as if he was flying. Was he dying? This didn't feel normal, this felt strange, light.

What was that ahead? It looked like scores of soldiers running towards him. Fellowes stopped in front of him. Bizarrely, he held out his hand.

'Goodbye, von Luck,' he was saying. 'It has been an honour serving with you.'

Von Luck heard the words, but they didn't enter his brain. He shook Fellowes's hand, then saluted him, a reflexive gesture. He watched Fellowes salute him in return, and then, without warning, Fellowes put his pistol to his temple and fired.

Fellowes's body seemed to fall slowly to the ground, a crimson jet spurting from the side of his head. Von Luck watched the body's progress in a daze, as though he was drugged. He should be doing the same, he thought, but he felt so weak. The alarm bells filled his ears, the noise almost rattling his brain inside his skull. You must do something. You're just standing here, looking down at this bleeding head, mesmerised by the rhythm of the blood as it leaves this broken skull.

A decent man. There was no doubt that the men who seized him were anything but that. They were shouting at him, punching him, kicking him. He was going to die now. Well, perhaps it was the right time.

* * *

'He got Fellner.'

Huffmeier couldn't speak. His heart palpitated.

'What – do you – mean? "Got him"?'

List's voice was uncharacteristically quiet. 'He killed him, Admiral, and then he burned all the technical drawings.'

'You fucking idiot! You fucking shit-headed idiot! This is your lax security that is to blame. You'll be at the end of a rope, just you wait.'

'As will you, I expect, Admiral. After all, you allowed von Luck to get here.'

Huffmeier knew that List was right. They were both dead, but he wasn't going to admit it. 'Can the project still go ahead?'

'We were due to have a test firing, but without Fellner it's difficult to know how we can proceed.'

'Well, you'll just have to. Put Kramer in charge.'

'I already have.'

'What does he say?'

'He doesn't know yet. He says it depends on how much damage von Luck has done to the files. He said he will let me know later today.'

Huffmeier wanted to scream, to punch something. That bastard von Luck, that treacherous bastard. Germany's last chance to turn the tide of the war, and he had destroyed it. He would have to contact Berlin, but he couldn't face it, not yet. Perhaps the test firing would go well, and he could paint Fellner's death as an unfortunate accident, as suicide, even. Yes, that might work – might save their skins. 'All right, List. Let me make one thing clear. None of this is to go back to Berlin, do you understand? That is in both our interests, I think.'

'I agree with you, Admiral.'

'For the meantime, we can treat Fellner's death as suicide. Say he had an attack of conscience or something.'

'All right.'

'And finally, von Luck. Where is he?'

'I'm holding him in Sylt. Don't worry – it's impossible to escape.'

'How is he?'

'He's alive. Just. He's got the sickness, I think. He's also been, uh, worked on.'

'Keep him alive. I'm going to send a plane over. I want him back here.'

'But he's my—'

'No, List. He is on my staff. He is therefore my prisoner. Got that?'

List went quiet. At long last, thought Huffmeier, the man was beginning to do as he was told. A bit late, though. A bit fucking late. He put down the phone, then picked it up again.

'Heidi?'

'Yes, sir?'

'Get me Mollett!'

*   *   *

He was in a plane – a Fieseler Storch, he thought. He was hurting all over, not just on the outside where he had been beaten but inside. He felt as if he was being consumed by an acid that burned away as it trickled round his organs.

Although he was in pain, von Luck was happy. He had succeeded, had done something worthwhile. He could have just sat it out on Jersey, let the islanders suffer, let the weapon go ahead, and stayed alive. That was what everyone else was doing, but it was not for him.

That he was going to die was now almost academic. The only question was when. Today? That was a possibility, but he guessed that Huffmeier would want to keep him alive for as long as possible, would want to question him, beat the facts out of him. Well, let him do that. It didn't matter any more.

Von Luck looked out of the window through the one eye that could open. It was a nice day, he thought, the sea a pleasing blue, the skies free from cloud. He hadn't been in a plane for a long time. He rather liked flying: it made him feel free.

Huffmeier was there to meet him. He felt like a visiting dignitary, swooping down from the sky to be met on the ground by the best the island could offer. His hands tied behind his back, his ankles in manacles, von Luck was bundled out of the plane by two of the largest soldiers on Jersey, both of whom were taller than him. He was dragged in front of the admiral, and held upright, his weakened body constantly wanting to lurch from side to side.

'You are a disgrace to our country, to your uniform, to your title, and to your family,' said Huffmeier, his attempt at self-control clearly a struggle.

Von Luck smiled. The man had obviously prepared his speech. 'I'm a disgrace to none of those things,' he slurred, owing to a heavily bruised lower lip. 'It is my country that I find disgraceful. It is men like you who are disgraceful.'

The comment earned him a slap in the face. 'Do not feel, von Luck, that just because you are going to die you can say whatever you like with impunity. We can make your last days here on earth very unpleasant for you.'

Von Luck didn't reply. There was no point. He was looking at the loser – he wasn't going to dignify him with any more remarks. Instead, he just smiled. After all, he had won.

* * *

She had no idea how long she had been in the cell. It might have been months, or it might have been minutes. She didn't care any more. All she could see, whether her eyes were open or not, was her mother being flung on to the ground. Its repetition had numbed her, gouged her out.

Footsteps. They were coming towards her cell. She knew what would happen next – the hatch on her door would shoot open and a pair of eyes would study her. The hatch would then snap shut, and she would be alone again.

Keys, the sound of keys. What was this? Food? Unlikely. They didn't seem to have food here, wherever she was. There was water, but it tasted foul and she left it untouched in the earthenware pitcher. Death, then, that was what it was.

The door was slammed open. A man wearing the uniform of a German naval officer was standing there.

'Good evening, Miss Campbell.'

Pippa tried to reply, but her throat was too sore.

'I've someone you might want to see.'

'Who?'

'I want to show you what happens to traitors,' said the man.

The man turned to his left and nodded. Two guards muscled a tall figure into the frame of the cell door. He looked familiar, but he was wearing the wrong clothes. They were workman's clothes, shabby, covered with dark stains. His face was familiar too, although it was heavily swollen and bleeding.

'Max!' she croaked.

'That's sweet,' said the naval officer.

Pippa got up and almost fell down immediately.

'Max!'

She noticed the noose round his neck, but tried to ignore it. Von Luck smiled at her, but she could see that it hurt. Some of his teeth were missing, and his mouth was filled with blood and saliva.

'Oh, my God – it's Max!' She stumbled up to him, all the time feeling the glare of the officer on her. 'Max! Can you hear me?'

Von Luck nodded.

She put her arms round him. There was so much to say to him, so many emotions she wanted to express, but all she could say was his name, over and over again.

A low moaning, hissing sound came from his mouth. He was trying to say something.

'What is it Max? What was that?'

Still the sound came out, but Pippa couldn't make out what it meant. 'Tell me, Max! Tell me!'

The only reply she got was another croak. Still, it was enough to hold him. He felt different somehow, thinner, weaker. What had they done to him?

Hands pulling her away once more from a person she loved. 'That's enough now, you tart!'

Hands that shoved her brutally back into the cell. Hands that pulled her Max away, pulled him down the corridor, pulled him out of sight. 'Max!' she screamed. 'I love you, Max!'

What had he wanted to tell her? He smiled, though, he had actually smiled. She didn't know what to feel. There was joy at seeing him, but horror at the state he was in. What were they going to do with him?

'Come back!' she screamed. 'Bring him back!'

Von Luck could hear Pippa's shouts as he was forced down the corridor. He had endured days of torture, days of beatings, days of humiliation, and now this, taunting him with the woman they knew he loved.

Love, thought von Luck. At least he had had love. Even when the noose was being tightened, that was a great consolation.

*   *   *

'It's an interesting proposition,' says Mollett.

'I thought you'd like it,' Lebonneur replies.

'The only problem, of course, is that if I let you live, you'll no doubt open your big fat mouth anyway.'

The man has a point, thinks Lebonneur.

'I suppose my word won't be good enough for you, will it?'

Mollett smiles and shakes his head. 'I'm afraid not. I don't really trust journalists, especially ex-journalists.'

A cheap dig, thinks Lebonneur, but right now his reputation is the least of his problems. 'And, of course,' he says, 'I just have to take it on trust that you won't shoot me anyway once I tell you where the diary is.'

'I'm afraid you do.'

'Sort of stalemate, then, isn't it?'

'It looks like it.'

They stand in silence. The situation has become almost comical, a real Mexican standoff.

'I suppose to show you my good will, I could tell you what was in the diary.'

'All right, why don't you?'

Lebonneur clears his throat. 'Well, von Luck writes that he suspects your father of killing Richard Marais. Apparently he went so far as to behead him, although the official records say that he died of a heart attack.'

Mollett gives another of his snorted laughs. 'Carry on, Mr Lebonneur.'

'He writes that your father was in cahoots with the Germans, and was helping them to prepare a mass deportation of Jersey citizens over here to Alderney. A thousand were going to be sent over apparently to help on constructing the weapon in Mannez Hill. If they'd come, von Luck says they'd all have died, as the death rate here was astonishing. My speculation is that many of the workers died through handling uranium.'

'As you say, Mr Lebonneur, speculation.'

'Quite, but not unreasonable. That Geiger counter you shot out of my hands was most persuasive. Anyway, Marais was opposed to the deportation, and wanted the islanders to oppose it, which at that stage in the war would have proved a real headache for the weakened and morale-free German garrison. The German commandant, Admiral Huffmeier, needed a man on the States he could . . . well, let's say, *work* with. Your father, Mollett, was his man. However, the deportation never happened, because the project here was abandoned, presumably because von Luck was successful in his mission to put the weapon out of action. He writes in his diary that he was going to come here and kill Professor Fellner, who was the chief scientist on the weapon.'

'Quite a fantasist, wasn't he, von Luck?'

'Well, maybe – and maybe not. I'm convinced, though, and the fact that you're pointing that gun at me means that what he wrote must also carry some weight with you.'

Mollett doesn't say anything. *Touché*, thinks Lebonneur.

'Anyway,' he says, 'nobody knows what happened to von Luck, so we do have to speculate.'

'Well, there you really are wrong,' says Mollett.

'Really?'

'I know what happened to von Luck.'

'What, then?'

'The Germans hanged him. My father told me. They hanged

him for murdering two Gestapo officers and a naval captain called Petersen.'

'That would tally, but odd, then, that there's no record of his execution.'

'Such documents went missing.'

'That's a possibility, but I'd suggest the Germans were not all that keen to publicise and record that one of their senior officers on Jersey had destroyed a weapon that might have significantly affected the war.'

'More speculation, Mr Lebonneur.'

'Well, at least we all know what happened to Peter Mollett, don't we? Knighted after the occupation, he lived to a good old age, didn't he?'

'He was eighty-four.'

'Better than three score and ten. What I found puzzling, Mollett, is why your adoptive father collaborated with the Germans to the extent that he did.'

'You're working on the assumption that he did, in fact, collaborate, Mr Lebonneur. Your logic is somewhat faulty but, then, journalists are not renowned for their exactitude, are they?'

'No, we're a pretty sloppy lot. Oh, well. Perhaps you're right, Mr Mollett. Perhaps von Luck was a fantasist. Perhaps there was no weapon. Perhaps there is no uranium. Perhaps those workers dying really was an accident. Perhaps Terry's car crash was accidental. Perhaps my pilot really did have a heart attack. Perhaps you weren't just trying to kill me, and I merely got in the way of you shooting a pheasant or whatever it is people like you enjoy killing. And, finally, perhaps you're not pointing that gun at me.'

'Your sarcasm is a little wearying, Mr Lebonneur.'

'I'm sorry. It must be another of those journalistic habits I've picked up. But you can see my point. There's no smoke without fire, if you'll excuse the journalistic cliché. However, I do have one theory about why your adoptive father collaborated.'

'I'm all ears.'

'Your real parents weren't killed in the Blitz, were they?'

Mollett doesn't speak.

'No, they were interned as enemy aliens under Defence Regulations 18B in 1940. Your mother was German, and your father half German, so they were prime candidates for being locked up. Unfortunately, they both died in the internment camps. I understand your father had a heart attack on the Isle of Man, and your grief-stricken mother, who was interned with you in Surrey, committed suicide as a result.'

'How do you—'

'It's all in the records, Mr Mollett. You were then installed in an orphanage until the end of the war, when you were adopted and brought to Jersey by your new parents. Like her sister, of course, your adoptive mother was German, wasn't she? She wasn't Rose, she was Rosa. I think your adoptive father never forgave the treatment your real parents suffered, which split his loyalties. Coupled with his greed and ambition, it was perhaps inevitable that he would collaborate, and even go so far as to murder.'

'Even if this is true,' says Mollett, 'it's all ancient history. People don't care about it any more. They don't want to know what happened in the war. They'd prefer to forget it.'

'They don't if it affects their lives in the present, Mr Mollett. It's all true, and you know it.'

A crunching sound in the corridor makes both men turn their heads. Rachel! thinks Lebonneur. It has to be Rachel! He doesn't pause, doesn't decide: he just acts. With his right hand, he knocks away the barrel of the rifle and rushes at Mollett. Both men fall over, with Lebonneur landing on top of Mollett, his hands gripping the rifle.

'Help!' shouts Lebonneur. 'Rachel! Help!'

Mollett is very strong. Together the two men roll from side to side, smashing each other into the concrete blocks strewn on the ground. Lebonneur's ribs feel so bloody painful, but he knows that to give in to the pain will see him killed.

He tries bashing Mollett in the face with his forehead, but he misses, hitting his head on a piece of concrete. A sudden daze, a sudden wooziness. He's under water, sinking. Keep hold of the rifle. That's all that counts. Lebonneur feels like a savage animal, his entire being dedicated to aggression.

He wants to shout, to swear, but he's panting. The struggle is exhausting, and Mollett is not only strong, but fit. He's getting the upper hand now – he's about to wrench away the rifle, about to wriggle it free. That's not going to happen, thinks Lebonneur, that's not going to fucking happen.

He tries another head-butt, but it doesn't connect. The pain is everywhere now, the pieces of concrete and stone digging into his sides, his legs, even his crotch. He's losing, there's no doubt about it, he's going to lose. Mollett is going to shoot him, the bastard. Why do these people always win?

Stillness. Mollett is no longer moving.

'Bob!'

It sounds like Rachel.

'Ra-Rach?'

'It's OK! It's all right, Bob! I've hit him!'

Lebonneur looks down at Mollett. His eyes are closed – unconscious.

'Oh, Rachel! You star! You fucking star!'

Rachel bends down and helps Lebonneur off Mollett. His hands are still clasped to the rifle, as are Mollett's, and it is with great difficulty that they unpick them.

They stand in silence, Lebonneur holding the rifle tightly, the barrel pointing shakily at Mollett's chest.

'What are you doing, Bob?'

'I'm going to kill him!'

'No! Don't do that!'

Lebonneur cannot control himself. He badly wants to pull the trigger, to empty the gun into Mollett's body, to watch him die. The desire is overwhelming, brutal.

'Bob, please don't do it.' Rachel is grabbing the rifle now.

'You'll be as bad as him!'

He knows that, but he wants to kill.

'Bob! No! For me, don't do it! Think of me!'

Rachel's face is imploring him. He's never seen her look quite like that. How strange.

'I love you,' she is saying. 'I love you. Please don't do it. Please.'

The words filter through. He doesn't want Rachel to look like this, to look scared of him.

'Give me the rifle. Come on, Bob, give me the rifle.'

Slowly, he moves the barrel away from Mollett's chest.

'Here,' he says. 'I never want to hold a gun again.'

Rachel takes it and Lebonneur holds her tightly. It's all over, except for the writing. Oh, this is going to make such a fucking good story, he thinks. Perhaps it might even make a book. He knows to whom he'll dedicate it as well: his father.

A very nice young man that gave her the attention that over
hours. Why was she like this? She had given everything for these
people. And had done a little. Would she think that she was
selling herself short but once because it was Christmas? Frankly

Epilogue

PIPPA LEFT JERSEY a week after liberation. At least fifty of them were taken to the mainland for their own safety – Jerrybags mostly, and the worst of the collaborators. It didn't matter that she had been incarcerated by the Germans – a Jerrybag she was and a Jerrybag she would remain.

Her mother's death and the experience in prison had sapped her, rendered her emotionally and physically fragile. When she had missed her first period, she had thought little of it, knowing it was common for women in her state of health. Over the next few weeks in the holding camp, she put on a little more weight and still her period didn't come. The pregnancy was finally confirmed by a doctor who told her openly that if it was a German baby she had every right to abort it.

It was this comment that gave her the strength to go back to Jersey. Why should they win? She had given everything for these people, who had done so little. Who did they think they were, telling her to abort her baby because it was German? There was nothing wrong with the Germans: it was their system that had failed them.

Pippa never told anybody what had happened. She knew that, as a Jerrybag, she would not be believed. Mannez Hill had been plugged up with ton upon ton of concrete by the Germans, and her prediction that people would want to claim the occupation as a positive experience for the islanders was correct. She knew that Mollett was a collaborator, but she feared him, knowing she could end up like Marais. It was better to keep quiet for the sake of the child.

Her father had been against her return, but Pippa had insisted, saying it was her child's birthright to be born on the island its father had loved and done so much for. It was he who suggested that she change her name to Lebonneur, saying that perhaps Campbell had become a dirty word on the island. Reluctantly Pippa agreed, the decision made easier because Lebonneur, according to her father, was a Norman pun on the name von Luck. The French for 'luck' was *bonheur*, he explained, and thus Lebonneur, which sounded suitably indigenous.

Pippa liked the idea. She knew Max would have too.

*   *   *

'It is, of course, in need of modernisation, Mr Lebonneur, although there are plenty of nice period features. I think, with the current market, we're talking a value in excess of . . .'

Lebonneur's ears shut out the rest of the man's spiel. It feels wrong and crude to have his mother and grandmother's house reduced to estate-agent spiel. He walks out of the room, leaving the man perplexed.

Here, then, is the living room, the place where his grandmother was arrested. Just a normal room, with a tiled fireplace and a good-sized sash window. It is bare now, with nobody alive to fill it with their memories. He tries to imagine the goings-on, his mother as a young woman, the grandmother he never met, going about their routine during the occupation. There must have been a lot of tension in here, especially when men like Fellowes and Smith were hiding in the attic.

Oh, Mum, he thinks, why didn't you tell me about all this? Was it really better to forget? That's what they all did – forget. Perhaps it was the only way to get on with one's life, just to get up and never look back, never to see who pushed you. You let them get away with it, Mum, men like Mollett and his son. Why did you do that?

Lebonneur walks out of the living room and finds himself confronted by the agent in the hall.

'Mr Lebonneur, as I was saying, the market is pretty buoyant at present . . .'

He still doesn't listen, but walks into the kitchen and towards the coal-burning stove at the end of the room, expecting it to radiate warmth – warmth that doesn't come.

You did it for me, didn't you? You let them win so I could be normal, could have a happy childhood. I was more important than anything else, and you never let me forget it. Well, I've repaid you now. Mollett's son is in prison, the hotel's being stopped, and the contents of the hill are being removed by all sorts of men in white coats from London. I've finished it, Mum, done what you and my father had started.

'Sir?'

'Just send it to me in the post, would you?'

'Certainly, sir.'

Lebonneur walks out of the front door and heads up the short path. He doesn't turn round, because there's nothing left to see. Goodbye, Mum, he thinks. And, of course, goodbye to you, Dad, or should I say *Auf Wiedersehen?*

HISTORICAL NOTE AND
ACKNOWLEDGEMENTS

THERE WAS INDEED a V3. Located at Mimoyecques in the Pas de Calais region of northern France, it was targeted at London, although its warheads were equipped with conventional explosive. It was never fired. The Allies captured it in late 1944, and demolished much of the site after the war. A portion remains intact, and is open to the public.

Sylt concentration camp on Alderney also existed. Parts of it are still visible today, including the tunnel and heating room in which Lebonneur finds himself. The camp gates still stand – testament to the presence of the SS on British soil. Visitors will find no signposts to Sylt, but it lies south-west of the island's runway. Those seeking more precise directions will find them on my website, www.guywalters.com.

The camp's commandant, SS Hauptsturmführer Maximillian List, existed. A war criminal, he evaded justice after the war, and lived near Hamburg until he died in the 1980s. He was responsible for the deaths of hundreds of prisoners. Admiral Huffmeier also existed, although he was not a war criminal.

The character of von Luck is based on Baron Max von Aufsess, who was the head of civil affairs on Jersey. Handsome, erudite, humane and with an eye for young women, von Aufsess is still regarded with some fondness on Jersey. His diary of the occupation, *The Von Aufsess Occupation Diary* (Phillimore, 1985), makes entertaining reading. Von Luck's relationship with Pippa and Violet Campbell is an extrapolation of von Aufsess's relationship with a Miss Elaine Fielding and her mother, who lived on Wellington Road near Linden Court, von Aufsess's home.

All other characters are fictional, and it should be stressed that, while there was a degree of collaboration and acquiescence towards their invaders, the islanders' complicity with the Germans in *The Occupation* is exaggerated for literary effect.

There have been countless books written about the occupation, but by far the most intelligent and even-handed is Madeleine Bunting's superb *The Model Occupation* (Pimlico, 2004).

I would like to thank James and Pippa Campbell, Adrian Weale, Andy Hill, Vanessa Andreae, Martin Fletcher, Tif Loehnis and the staff of the Société Jersiaise for their help with the writing of this book.

The Eagle and the Wolves

Simon Scarrow

As the Roman armies invading Britain face bitter resistance from unyielding natives, Macro and Cato find themselves standing between the destiny of Rome and bloody defeat.

In the summer of AD 44, tense undercurrents amongst the tribe of nominally friendly Atrebatans are ready to explode into open revolt. It falls to centurions Macro and Cato to provide aged ruler Verica with an army, training his tribal levies to protect their king and enforce his rule. With a scratch force of raw recruits, unversed in the techniques of war, they must find and destroy a resourceful and cunning opponent. But can they do this whilst surviving the deadly cross-currents of plotters threatening to destroy not only Macro and Cato, but all their comrades serving with the Eagles?

Praise for Simon Scarrow's previous tales of military adventure:

'A thoroughly enjoyable read . . . The engrossing storyline is full of teeth-clenching battles, political machinations, treachery, honour, love and death' Elizabeth Chadwick

'A good, uncomplicated, rip-roaring read' *Mail on Sunday*

'Scarrow . . . sweeps the reader into the past as if the fighting were happening today' *Oxford Times*

'When it comes to the battle scenes few can surely touch Scarrow in his vivid descriptions' *Eastern Daily Press*

0 7553 0114 5

headline

The Leader

Guy Walters

The Treaty of London had been signed, and the future sealed. Today was a good day for Britain, the Leader said, a good day for Germany, a good day for Fascist Europe. The Germans are our friends now, he said, Herr Hitler has brought miracles to his country, and I shall do the same for ours . . .

Great Britain, 1937. Edward VIII and his new bride, Wallis, are preparing for their coronation; Winston Churchill is a prisoner on the Isle of Man; and Prime Minister Oswald Mosley – the Leader, as he is known – consults Adolf Hitler on a 'more permanent' solution to the 'Jewish problem'. In exchange for full bellies, the British population has yielded to a regime of terror, enforced by Mosley's secret police.

James Armstrong, a hero of the Great War, is on the run, wanted by Mosley for organising a resistance movement to the government. The Leader is determined to see Armstrong hang. But Armstrong is every bit as clever as the evil men on his trail . . .

0 7553 0058 0

headline

The Traitor

Guy Walters

There was something powerful about it, something magnetic. He had witnessed the effect of such uniforms in the newsreels; now he was about to wear one. But this SS uniform – the uniform proudly worn by so many maniacs and murderers – bore a Union Jack and the three lions. It was an insult to King and Country.

In November 1943 British SOE agent Captain John Lockhart is in Crete, fighting with the partisans. Captured by the Germans, Lockhart faces a stark choice: betray his country, or die.

Lockhart strikes a bargain with his captors. In return for the life of his imprisoned wife, he will change sides. But he is stunned to learn of his mission: to lead the British Free Corps, a clandestine unit of the Waffen SS made up of British fascists and renegades culled from POW camps. Aware that he, like them, will be branded a traitor, Lockhart seeks to redeem himself by destroying a terrifying secret weapon that threatens to change the course of the war . . .

0 7553 0056 4

headline

Now you can buy any of these other bestselling Headline titles from your bookshop or *direct from the publisher*.

FREE P&P AND UK DELIVERY
(Overseas and Ireland £3.50 per book)

Mandrake	Paul Eddy	£6.99
The Leader	Guy Walters	£6.99
Street Dreams	Faye Kellerman	£5.99
The Conspiracy Club	Jonathan Kellerman	£6.99
The Dead	Ingrid Black	£6.99
The Arraignment	Steve Martini	£6.99
Long Lost	David Morrell	£6.99
Four Blind Mice	James Patterson	£6.99
The Jester	James Patterson with Andrew Gross	£6.99
The Devil's Banker	Christopher Reich	£5.99
No Good Deed	Manda Scott	£6.99

TO ORDER SIMPLY CALL THIS NUMBER

01235 400 414

or visit our website: www.madaboutbooks.com

Prices and availability subject to change without notice.